BIRCH LANE PRESS PRESENTS

American Fiction

BIRCH LANE PRESS PRESENTS

American Fiction

The Best Unpublished Short Stories
by Emerging Writers

Number 2

Introduction by GUEST JUDGE

Louise Erdrich

Edited by Michael C. White
and Alan R. Davis

A Birch Lane Press Book
Published by Carol Publishing Group

A Birch Lane Press Book
Published by Carol Publishing Group
Birch Lane Press is a registered trademark of
Carol Communications, Inc.

Editorial Offices
600 Madison Avenue
New York, NY 10022

Sales & Distribution Offices
120 Enterprise Avenue
Secaucus, NJ 07094

In Canada: Musson Book Company
A division of General Publishing Co. Limited
Don Mills, Ontario

Manufactured in the United States of America

10   9   8   7   6   5   4   3   2   1

Carol Publishing Group books are available at special discounts
for bulk purchases, for sales promotions, fund raising, or
educational purposes. Special editions can also be created to
specifications. For details contact: Special Sales Department,
Carol Publishing Group, 120 Enterprise Ave., Secaucus, NJ 07094

Library of Congress Cataloging-in-Publication Data

Birch Lane Press presents American fiction : the best unpublished
   short stories by emerging writers number 2 / introduction by guest judge
   Louis Erdrich : edited by Michael C. White and Alan Davis.
      p.   cm.
   ISBN 1-55972-074-3
   "A Birch Lane Press book."
      1. Short stories, American. 2. American fiction—20th century.
   I. White, Michael C. II. Davis, Alan. III. American fiction.
   PS648.S5B56   1991
   813'.0108054—dc20   91-659090 (ISSN 1056-1161)
                                              CIP

This book is dedicated
to Seymour Epstein, who taught that
stories may sometimes instruct,
often ennoble, but must
always humble

Contents

Editors' Note

This fourth edition of *American Fiction* marks our second year with Birch Lane Press. Each year, we choose some twenty finalists from among hundreds of manuscripts submitted through an open, national competition. A guest judge—Louise Erdrich this year, Anne Tyler, Ray Carver and Ann Beattie in past editions—then selects prizewinners and writes an introduction. From the beginning, the introductions, along with glowing critical praise, have consistently trumpeted *AF's* goal of publishing deserving new writers.

Writer's Digest recently chose *AF* as one of the nation's fifty best outlets for short fiction. Reviewers have called it "a must-read collection for all short-fiction enthusiasts" with "a wealth of imagination and talent" (*Booklist*), "a good, solid collection" (*Publishers Weekly*) which "holds its own" (*Kirkus Reviews*) while treating "traditional subject matters in startlingly fresh narratives" (*The Review of Contemporary Fiction*). The stories in *AF* give "good value" and eschew "ironic posturing and 'minimalist' aesthetics in favor of straightforward, unpretentious narratives about ordinary people coping with life's crises" (*Library Journal*). Likewise, Louise Erdrich, in the introduction which follows this note, has pointed out that "the stories in this collection attempt to clutch a slippery truth," and "succeed impressively."

As editors, we look forward with a great deal of pleasure to the batches of manuscripts which arrive each spring. As writers ourselves, we appreciate the chance to bring good fiction to the attention of a reading public increasingly drawn, as Anne Tyler pointed out last year, to "complete, fully rounded, beginning-

and-ending *stories* (in some cases life stories, whole histories) as opposed to brief episodes." As Ray Carver wrote two years ago in these pages, "It seems to me that there must be a healthy ambition afoot to extend the reach of stories past the ten to fifteen page manuscript, perhaps toward a scope which takes advantage of what have been more novelistic strategies."

We think that's true, by and large, though we read every submission on its own terms, and worthier shorter fictions consistently appear in these pages. What we look for simply are stories with something to say, stories, in brief, which *must* be written because the writer has no choice. If we have any bias at all, it's a belief that character can still be fate. Fictional strategies can weigh against character, taking catastrophe and holocaust (or merely the materialistic *Zeitgeist*) into account, or they can weigh against fate, insinuating moral or ethical culpability, but they ignore the scales of such justice (or injustice) at their peril.

We'd like to congratulate this year's prize-winners: the $1000 First Prize goes to Clint McCown for his story "Home Course Advantage"; the $500 Second Prize to Heather Baird Donovan for her story "Basin and Range"; and the $250 Third Prize to David Cole for his story "Being Here Is Good for the Children." And, of course, we'd like to congratulate the other seventeen finalists for their fine stories.

We'd also like to thank several people and places: first, Louise Erdrich, for graciously accepting and admirably fulfilling the role as this year's Guest Judge; Liza Wachter, our patient and watchful editor at Birch Lane Press; Moorhead State University and Springfield College for both financial and moral support; Deb Marquart, an editorial assistant in Moorhead, and Debby Hayward and Irene Graves in Springfield; the C.F. White Family Foundation for generous past support; and finally, the hundreds of writers who allowed us to read their work and by so doing gave us a great deal of pleasure as well as an education.

Michael C. White
Springfield College

Alan R. Davis
Moorhead State University

Introduction

BY LOUISE ERDRICH

All of the stories in this collection attempt to clutch a slippery truth. The writer plunges after it, or sits back hoping it will fall through the words like the most even grains of rice through a sieve. The stories I've chosen for the three prizes and honorable mention seem to most subtly contain an essential truth. My husband, Michael, once reminded me that you can hold more sand in an open palm than in a closed fist. I've often found this to be accurate in art as well as life, and these stories, open and unforced, seemed to simply hold more sand. They were good containers.

"Home Course Advantage" is that rare thing, a real story. Clint McCown's perfect pitch for detail, the weighted presence of a mistreated dog, the startling use a narrator makes of his golf clubs, is irresistible. McCown proved to me that any subject, taken on with wit and an eye for detail, can win over readers. Golf doesn't seem the most exciting game in the world, and life as a golf course manager would not suggest days filled with depth or complexity, but Clint McCown brings every small moment in the day of his narrator to life. Perhaps it is the matter-of-fact way an eight-foot cardboard alligator, a problem with partially melted ice cream bars, new grips on a finicky woman's irons, a dead dog, and an escalating and mysterious encounter with a golf cart thief blend together. It took skill to manage all of the elements here, and Clint McCown is a graceful storyteller.

Heather Baird Donovan's "Basin and Range" has an interesting after-effect. The characters reverberate in the mind along with certain details—a sunflower bedspread, suntan lotion, the sheer emptiness of Nevada. The close and yet skittish relationship between the two women is especially provocative, and well-thought out, as is the portrayal of a girl's curiosity about her parent's extra-marital relationships. There is a certain amount of fatalism in this story—curiosity kills, after all—but there is also an engaging affection for the people and the landscape.

Both of these stories are driven by narrative, as opposed to "Being Here Is Good for the Children," which proceeds in a meditative fashion, making crooked connections through the random logic of thought, and telling a story less definite though no less compelling than the others. Again and again one is arrested, in this piece, by the quality of the writing and the consideration that David Coles gives to each sentence. This is a cadenced and ruminative piece of work. "I am an English teacher at a public high school and before me, on the table, is a bottle of single malt whisky. . . ." From this situation, all things proceed. A box has been delivered to the teacher's house. "It felt like an intrusion," he says, "something quick and uninvited, but also something terribly enduring, like the arresting recognition that comes when a plate or coffee cup is knocked from a counter and all one can do is turn with enough time to wince before it breaks and scatters across the floor."

It was impossible not to single out Marvin Diogenes' "Forbrengen," a tightly written psychological drama. The narrative draws in the reader, but the suspense that Diogenes manufactures is not that of a typical thriller plot, but of an interesting moral question. Will or will not the protagonist accept the gender inequality built into the religion he has otherwise embraced? Will this marriage be saved? Will this man be saved?

Halfway across the world, in the beautifully rendered "Korean Lessons," a war is evoked from a stifling office, a desk, the lonely memorabilia of normal life. In another story, the disintegration of an ideal marriage is forecast by a videotape. Joann Kobin's fascinating and mournful "Wildlife" plays with the juxtaposition of emotion and surface, of life lived in a car lot, at a distance from wild and threatening dreams. In "Naked

Woman" a devastating, brutal relationship changes the future of peripheral characters, of a rescuer who becomes endangered along with the victim she saves.

Most of these stories represented voices from non-ethnic, mainstream America, exactly those quiet sufferers portrayed in Lewis Turco's spooky and surprising story "The Museum of Ordinary People." Few of the characters in the works were very rich or very poor. Most problems stemmed from drinking or infidelity, most settings were lower to middle class but often lifted clear of the concerns one might expect in a quiet life. For instance, Diane Stelzer Morrow's "Bird Watching," set in a calm St. Louis suburb, takes on the troubling questions of suicide, and salvation. "The Empire Beauty Salon" becomes, through the powers of Anne Whitney Pierce's descriptions, a place as real and convincing as any character, a beauty shop that forms the plot of the story itself; and Marilyn K. Krueger's "Rituals" contains a tough, evocative portrayal of place, seasonal change, and the cruelties and necessities of hunting. It was wonderful to discover people playing Acey-Deucey in Perry Glasser's "Recapitulation" and to become involved in a plot within that plot, to dwell in that longing of children for their parents which seemed, more than any other theme, to inform these particular stories.

Perhaps that is where all truths lie, at least in their genesis. Our first longings, the foundations of recast, destroyed, or reciprocated love seem to forecast the shape of one's lifelong bonds. We do the best we can in this imperfect world. Similarly, these stories strive for wholeness in a fractured country, and to portray something true in a consumer society, where truth is all too often relative. They succeed impressively and I am proud to introduce this collection and thank each of the writers who have clearly and beautifully committed themselves to the written word.

BIRCH LANE PRESS PRESENTS

American Fiction

Home Course Advantage

BY CLINT McCOWN

Even while he was gluing the new set of grips on Mrs. Davies' old Patty Berg irons, Rod couldn't stop thinking about the carcass of the dog. The dewfall would have settled over it by now, which he hoped might dampen the smell. In the three days since he'd cut too sharply into the parking lot and caught the mangy stray unawares, the temperature had seldom slipped below ninety. This morning a couple of the club members had complained. The odor, they said, had been sucked in through their car air-conditioners. They wanted it taken care of. The member-guest tournament was just a few days away, and a lot of out-of-towners would be coming in for practice rounds. It didn't speak well of the club to leave a dead dog at the entrance to the parking lot.

So Rod had called the highway department to see if they'd come out and get the thing. They said they would, but it might take a couple of weeks—most of their trucks were tied up in the Route 15 bypass project, and road-kills had become a low priority. He told them he'd take care of it himself, and as he hung up the phone he made a mental note to pass the chore on to the Wickerham kid, who was running the grounds crew this summer.

But then the special shipment of Izods arrived, the one he'd ordered to beef up his sweater stock before the member-guest weekend, and he had to check the merchandise for damage. When he'd finally logged in all the stock numbers, he set to work assembling the eight-foot cardboard alligator they'd sent

1

as a new promotional display. He was still trying to insert tab M into slot Q when Beverly Tomson came in from the snack shop to tell him the freezer unit was making clacking noises and defrosting itself again. It took him half the afternoon to track down Ed Betzger, who held the service contract on all the club's appliances, and by the time Ed had the unit working again, the ice cream bars were showing clear signs of strain. So Rod had to call Teddy Mumford, the club's insurance agent, to find out how far the melt-down had to go before the bars could be claimed as a loss. Here there was a point of contention. Teddy said that partial melting didn't constitute spoilage, and as long as the ice cream was uncontaminated it could still be sold. Rod explained that the bars didn't even look like bars anymore, but Teddy said the snack shop could feature them on the menu as a novelty item. Refrozen ice cream sounded exotic, Teddy told him, like refried beans. Rod said maybe it was time the club got a new insurance agent.

Of course, that would never happen. Rod ran the daily operations of the club, but the board of directors made all the financial decisions; and Teddy Mumford was a member of the board.

The injustice galled him, and as soon as he got off the phone with Mumford he stormed into the men's locker room to air a few complaints. But it was late in the day, and there was no one there but Glen L. Hanshaw, himself one of the oldest board members, sitting naked on the bench in front of his locker. It was a disconcerting sight, and Rod lost his momentum.

"Look at this crap!" Glen L. said, and he held up a pair of boxer shorts. "I haven't had these a goddam month and the elastic's all shot to hell." He threw them into the bottom of his locker and kicked the door closed with his foot. "I swear to Christ!"

Rod didn't know what to say, so he looked at his watch and hurried on down the row of lockers.

"Hey, wait a minute!" Glen L. pushed himself up from the bench and followed Rod to the side door. In the diffuse light of the windows, his skin took on a bluish pallor, like a body washed up from the sea. "I had a complaint about you today," he said.

"What's the problem?"

"Shirley Davies says you were supposed to get her clubs back to her two weeks ago."

"The new grips haven't come in yet," he lied.

"Well, she was all over my ass about it." He ran a bony hand over his scalp. "I hear she's having a little trouble at home. Probably just needs to take it out on somebody. Anyway, I told her you'd take care of it."

Rod shrugged. "I'll see what I can do."

"Good man." Glen L. slapped him on the shoulder and padded off toward the showers. He moved unnaturally, Rod thought, as if he were picking his way across hot gravel. Strange what nakedness could do to some people. In his loud shirts and double-knit pants, Glen L. was the tyrant of his Cadillac dealership; here at the club, all the kids who worked in the pro shop were afraid of him. But now he seemed just one more small animal caught outside its territory. Rod didn't know why, but the thought depressed him.

He climbed the stairs to his workroom and set about regripping Mrs. Davies' old irons. He got out the new grips and settled in on his bench by the window to start stripping the shafts. Only then did he remember that he'd never spoken to Jimmy Wickerham about getting rid of the dog. Now it was too late— the last few twilight stragglers were just coming in off the course. The grounds crew would have left hours ago. If Rod wanted the carcass disposed of before tomorrow, he'd have to do it himself.

It took him longer than usual to do the regripping. Somehow he mispositioned two of the new grips and had to strip both shafts and start again. The seven iron gave him particular trouble. The glue had hardened in a lump where the left thumb gripped the shaft, and though he knew Mrs. Davies would never know the difference, he couldn't let the imperfection pass. The seven iron was his favorite club, his luckiest club. He'd once holed out a hundred-and-seventy-yard approach shot with a seven iron on the final hole of the Doral Open. The eagle jumped him up to eighth place, his best professional finish.

By the time he was satisfied with the positioning of all ten grips, it was after ten o'clock. He turned out the workshop light and stood for a minute by the window facing the highway. It was a moonless night, but the mercury vapor lamp above the machine shed cast a yellow haze across the deserted parking lot. The dog lay just inside the edges of the light, and Rod could see clearly the dark lump waiting for him on the carpet of manicured grass.

But what exactly was he supposed to do with it?

He couldn't just sling it into the clubhouse dumpster. The container wouldn't be emptied until Tuesday, and five days of dumpster heat was the last thing this dog needed.

He couldn't dump it anywhere on the course because the grounds were kept so immaculately trimmed it was impossible to hide anything larger than a golf ball. The only exception was the bramble thicket that ran along the out-of-bounds to the left of the third hole, but that entire stretch was usually upwind from most of the course, and there was too much stink left in the animal to risk it.

He sure as hell wasn't about to load the remains into the back of his new Audi and go cruising around the countryside looking for a safe drop zone. He'd bought that car because he thought it might foster an image of stability and class, and he was certain that a lingering bad-meat smell would undercut his efforts.

Of course he could always take the Teddy Mumford approach of cheapskate practicality: run the carcass through the tree-mulcher and spray the remains along the fairways for fertilizer. Even as he laughed at the thought, he felt a twinge of guilt toward Teddy. Mumford wasn't such a bad guy, really; he was just trying to keep the club's premiums low. It had been a heavy year for claims against their current policy—there'd been some major plumbing and electrical problems, a fire in the women's locker room, vandalism on two of the greens, and a lot of theft. In the last two weeks alone they'd lost over eighteen-thousand-dollars' worth of equipment: three electric Cushman golf carts and a small tractor mower. The insurance rates were bound to go up. Teddy had even told the board that unless the club could find a way to hire a night watchman, the home office might not let him renew their policy at all.

Rod hoped they would hire a watchman. He also hoped they'd hire a club manager, an accountant, a full-time assistant for the pro shop, and a couple of bag boys to help clean the members' clubs. Then maybe he'd have some time to work on his game. The way things stood now, he almost never got out on the course, and in the four years he'd been club pro, he'd lost a lot of ground. His putting was pretty much the same as ever—it came in streaks, and he rarely missed anything under five feet. But he'd lost some of his touch on pitch-and-run shots, and even with his wedge he couldn't seem to make the ball bite the way it used to. His overall game was about four shots worse than when he'd started here. At that rate he'd be a duffer long before retirement age.

He knew it was his own fault. Nobody had forced him to take this job. In fact, he'd been happy to get it. The course had a good layout, and even though the club ran on a pretty tight budget, enough money went into maintenance to keep it one of the finest nine-hole operations in the state. He didn't have to be ashamed of working here. Besides, he'd gotten tired of running with the rabbits, of driving from tournament to tournament all season long, scrambling for some share in the winnings. In three years he only made the cut nine times, and his career earnings wouldn't even cover his gas money. He quit the tour the week after the Doral Open, when his visibility was high enough to land him this steadier job. He didn't regret it. Even rookies had been finishing higher than Rod in the tournament standings, and the truth that sank into him after Doral was that eighth place was as high as he would ever go.

It was just as well, he told himself. He loved the game, but he wasn't cut out for business, and success made a business out of any game. Suppose he'd won the U.S. Open, or the Masters, or the P.G.A.; corporations would've come beating down his door for product endorsements. They'd have turned him into a "personality" and designed some ridiculous logo for his autographed line of leisurewear.

He did wonder what the logo might have been. Some animal, certainly—they were all animals. Alligators were already spoken for. So were penguins, seagulls, bears, jaguars, sharks, pandas, bulls, mustangs, dolphins, zebras, kangaroos, and flamingos.

No dogs, though, or at least none that he'd ever noticed—certainly no dead stray dogs; no bloody, bashed-in half-breed German shepherds embroidered with infinite care into the tight weave of cotton-orlon-dacron-acrylic. If he ever did hit the big time maybe that could be his logo. He might even insist on it.

He picked up Mrs. Davies' seven iron to double check the feel of it, and made his way downstairs and out the rear of the clubhouse. The night air was cool, and from the way the wind was gusting through the trees, he guessed a storm front might be moving in. Long rolls of heat lightning shimmered across the southern sky.

The window of the machine shed was unlocked, as usual, and Rod had no trouble reaching in for the shovel he knew would be hanging on the inside wall. As he walked across the lot toward the dead dog, a feeling of lightness came over him. Once he got the creature in the ground, the whole affair would be over. He'd never have to think about it again.

The night, he soon discovered, was the best possible time for the work. He'd been right about the smell; without the constant prodding of the sun, the flesh had sunk back into a more passive state of decay, and the dew seemed to keep the odor from rising. Only occasionally did little stabs of corruption dart up on the breeze, and by keeping the wind at his back and breathing carefully, he was able to avoid most of the stench. The flies seemed to have settled down for the night—or maybe the wind was now keeping them at bay—and, while there were probably slugs and other night-workers swarming the rotten underside, they were all invisible, hidden by dog or by darkness, so Rod could work easily, with his eyes open, in a way that would have been difficult for him in the full light of day.

The one thing that did bother him was the collar.

From the moment the animal had sprawled with a single yelp under the front left tire, Rod had avoided looking at it closely. He'd glimpsed enough to know the dog was a mixed breed, and from its general scruffiness he'd assumed it to be a stray. Now a queasy fear came over him that he'd open the morning paper and find some pathetic plea for the return of a family pet: Lost, in the vicinity of Route 30 west of town, a brown and black dog, part shepherd, answers to the name of . . .

A silver tag gleamed in the pale light. On it, Rod knew, there would be some identification, but he couldn't bring himself to bend his face down close enough to read what the inscription might say. Instead, he carefully hooked the head of Mrs. Davies' seven iron underneath the collar and began to drag the dead dog toward the putting green. The body stayed perfectly curled, firm now as a piece of sculpture as it scraped along the gravel lot. The weight of the thing surprised him. Until now he'd thought of the carcass as just a husk, and it amazed him to realize that the dog was no less substantial for the fact of having died.

He circled below the putting green and drew the dog alongside the practice bunker. The raised lip between the bunker and the green spread a less diluted night across the sand so that at first the trap seemed bottomless, a sinkhole yawning in the grassy slope. But soon his eyes adjusted, and the shadow gave way to the dingy sparkle of the sand itself. It was a perfect spot. The digging would be easy here, and when he was through there would be no broken turf to give the grave away.

He stepped down into the bunker and began shoveling the whiter top sand into a far corner to keep it separate from the brown foundation grit and the reddish dirt that lay below. It took him only six or seven minutes to work his way through the natural layer of topsoil, and though his progress slowed from the increasing density and rockiness of the ground, he continued to make headway.

It felt good to work the shovel in the earth, so good he started humming as he dug, improvising variations on a single jazzy theme for nearly half an hour, until suddenly, as he strained to pry loose a stubborn, buried stone, it came to him what song it was, and with that thought the sound of it died in his throat. It was a song that had haunted him for weeks now.

He didn't even know its name, but he took it to be an old blues number, maybe from the Billie Holiday era. The lyrics were hazy to him—some usual fare about love gone wrong— but what still burned in his mind was the one time he'd heard it, sitting in Herr's Tavern drinking his fourth double scotch, alone at a corner table in the otherwise crowded bar. A woman, heavily made up but still somehow breathtaking, swayed on a

low platform by the far wall and sang, with her eyes closed, in
the voice of a grieving angel. Even through the smoke and the
room's dim amber glow, he could see that her hair was red,
deep red, and it clung in damp curls to her cheek and forehead.
Her pale skin seemed unearthly, perfect, fragile as glass. She
poured herself like whiskey through the song, and Rod could
have believed she was all the beauty left in the world; and that
she was dying, now, in front of him. He envied her the grandeur
of such public despair.

When her song was over, she opened her dry eyes and smiled
warmly at the crowd, nodding to specific groups for their
whistles and applause. Then her whole face brightened—she'd
spotted someone particular at Rod's end of the room—and
without hesitation she climbed awkwardly down from the
makeshift stage, a long leg showing through the slit in her
gown, and weaved her way between the tables toward him. He
watched her intently as she moved, fascinated by the ease with
which she'd left the song behind, like a snake shedding skin, or
a butterfly, maybe, abandoning an outworn cocoon. It wasn't
until she reached his chair that he realized he was the person she
was crossing to meet, and before he could offer up any question
she flung an arm around his neck and kissed him earnestly on
the mouth. He was as stunned as if he'd been hit by a truck.

As she drew her face away from his, he opened his mouth to
fumble toward some trite compliment about her singing, but
before he could manage even a syllable a dark change came into
her eyes, and she pulled herself up straight.

"My God," she said, her right hand fluttering to her cleavage. "You're not Randy!" A bubble of embarrassed laughter
broke from her throat, then she turned abruptly toward the
stage. "Hey, Marcie," she called, "Look at this guy!" Half the
heads in the room turned in Rod's direction. "Doesn't he look
just like Randy?"

A woman from a table near the bar seemed to struggle for a
moment with the task of bringing Rod into focus, then sank
back into a confused frown. "You mean that's not him?"

"Hell, no! Can you believe this? And Christ, I just gave him
a big wet one." Several people laughed, and she turned again to
Rod. "Sorry, Sugar. Thought you were somebody else." She

patted him on the cheek and threaded her way casually to the bar.

Rod felt like she took his whole identity with her. It was as if, for a few accidental seconds, he'd seen himself through her eyes and found that he was utterly invisible, a man so bland he could enter a look-alike contest for himself and still come away the loser. A shudder ran through him, and a spinning rose in his head that nearly tipped him over. He left the tavern without finishing his drink.

By now he'd achieved a pit nearly three feet deep, which he judged sufficient. He tossed the shovel into the hole and sat heavily on the upper rim of the trap. He was more than winded; the work had turned nasty toward the end and now ropes of undeveloped muscle began to knot along his back. He probably wouldn't be able to swing a club for a week. Still, he felt a sense of accomplishment, and in his sudden stupor of exhaustion he felt less finicky toward the condition of the dog—though he resisted the impulse to pat its mangled head.

The wind was stronger now and felt good against the side of his face, but the change in weather worried him. Clouds were swirling in thick and low, and if he didn't get the dog below ground in a hurry, he might end up soaked when the bottom dropped out. He pushed himself up from the bank and grabbed Mrs. Davies' seven iron, which was still hooked under the collar. The dog slid easily down the slope to the edge of the grave.

"Roll over!" Rod said, and with a twist of the iron the carcass disappeared into the hole. "Now, stay!" With some difficulty he retrieved the club, then tamped down the body with the shovel. The snug fit pleased him, though he felt somehow disconcerted that in the underground darkness he couldn't tell whether the dog had landed on its back or on its stomach. He even thought about getting a flashlight from the clubhouse to find out, but in the end fatigue convinced him to let it go. The dog wouldn't care, so why should he?

He was just pouring in the first shovelful of dirt when a pair of headlights swept across him from the highway. He froze like a startled animal and watched a large flatbed truck wheel into the lot. It pulled up by the machine shed fifty yards away, and a burly man in overalls climbed down from the cab. Rod saw at once that the man was ill-at-ease. Body movement, after all, was his specialty; he knew how to read imperfections in a stance, a turn, a swivel, a follow-through, and he watched this trespasser now with a coldly professional eye.

Whatever the guy was up to, it seemed to Rod that he needed lessons. There was a tightness in the man's shoulders, and he moved his head with a birdlike jerkiness as he scanned the dark outer reaches of the lot. Rod knew he was too far away to be seen, particularly by anyone standing so near the security light, so he kept still and let the blind stare pass through him. There was something appealing in this—in seeing without being seen, as if he were no more than a ghost—but the interest Rod had in that aspect of the situation was offset by the column of stench now rising from the pit at his feet. He set the shovel down gently in the sand and eased his way upwind to the cleaner, whiter corner of the trap. He was just crouching below the smooth cut of the lip when the man in the lot let out a loud, shrill whistle. Rod thought at first he'd been spotted, but then he realized that the man wasn't looking his way. He turned toward the machine shed with his head cocked to the side as if he were listening for something.

Rod listened, too. Except for the wind rustling the trees, everything was quiet. Even the crickets and frogs from the drainage ditch behind the first tee had grown still under the expectation of rain.

Then the man whistled again, but instead of waiting for a response he reached in through the window of the truck and took out what appeared to be a small tackle box. The next few steps were all-too-predictable. After so many years of golf, Rod knew how to trace a trajectory, and had only to watch the swing itself to know where the ball would land. When the man walked to the rear window of the machine shed and climbed inside, Rod could only shake his head. God, how he hated amateurs.

He climbed out of the trap and walked across the parking lot to the truck, Mrs. Davies' seven iron in hand. For a moment he considered bashing in the windshield, but gestures like that were more dramatic than effective, and anyway it might hurt the club. Instead, he just took the keys from the ignition and walked calmly back to his bunker. It was a good first move, he told himself. Every match hinged on psyching out the opponent.

A minute later the front door of the shed swung open and one of the new Cushman gas-powered carts came nosing silently out. Apparently the man had been unable to hotwire it, in spite of his tool kit, and he now trotted alongside the cart, pushing and steering at the same time. He maneuvered the Cushman into position behind the truck, then pulled out a pair of long planks from the flatbed and propped them in place as a ramp. After lining up the steering for a straight shot at the boards, he got behind the cart and heaved it forward. Rod thought this a foolish technique—the wheels could easily miss one of the rails or skid over the side halfway to the truck. But the man seemed unconcerned, and when the front left wheel did slip from its plank, he was able to hold the four-hundred-pound cart level as he walked it forward into the bed of the truck. Rod was glad he hadn't smashed this fellow's windshield.

As he watched the thief slide the planks back onto the truck, Rod wondered why he hadn't just slipped away to the clubhouse and called the police. What made him think he had to handle this himself? He'd always been a smart money player, always staying with the high-percentage shot, and he knew better than to try to clear a hazard when the odds told him to play up short. Still, it was too late to worry about it now. The time to think was before the shot, never in mid-swing.

He took a golf ball from his pocket and dropped it into the spongy grass just off the apron of the practice green. Then he took a narrow stance almost directly behind the ball and opened the face of the seven iron. It was a trick he'd learned for putting extra loft into a club, and though he'd never used the shot in competition because it was too difficult to control, he'd always known it was there if he needed it. He took a full swing across the ball, playing it more or less like an extreme bunker shot, and with a sharp *click* it vanished upward into the night.

The man across the lot was just lashing the cart to the flatbed when the clean sound of contact froze him in place, still as a photograph. For a full five seconds he held his pose, listening into the darkness. Then with a loud metallic thunk, the ball came down on the hood of the truck. It broke the stillness like a starter's gun, and the man bounded into the cab of the truck, slamming the door behind him.

Rod walked forward into the light and crossed the parking lot in long, brisk strides, like a tournament leader approaching the eighteenth green. He paused by the rear of the truck and for a long moment the two men stared at each other's reflections in the side-view mirror. At last the door swung open, and the cart thief climbed slowly out.

He was bigger than he'd seemed from across the lot—maybe six-foot-five—and old enough that middle age had parcelled his bulk evenly between muscle and flab. His face was round, almost childlike, with a dark, sparse beard that sprouted in random patches over his cheeks. As he faced Rod in the gravel, he tucked his hands in his overalls with an air of defiant calm. His mouth hung slightly open, and his dull eyes looked haggard even in the dim light. Rod felt certain the man was not a golfer.

"Evening," he said. The man nodded and coughed, but didn't speak. "I notice you've got one of our carts here."

The man glanced briefly to the cart, then took a studied look around him, as if he'd only that moment realized where he was. "Yeah, well, we got a call to pick it up for some repairs. The transmission's gone bad."

"You work odd hours."

The man shrugged. "Some days are like that."

Rod reached up and touched the fiberglass body of the new cart. "You know, I hate these bastards. They're an insult to the game."

"That so?" the man asked, nudging the gravel with the toe of his workboot.

"Yeah. They kill the grass. Most of the really good courses don't even allow them on the grounds." He shook his head at the cart, which gleamed in the glow of the vapor lamp. "But we're not exactly the Augusta National here, so I've got to put up with them. I even have to fix them when they break down. So I know you didn't get a call from anybody."

The man's slack-jawed pose fused into a more natural scowl. "Then you must have my keys," he said, and started toward Rod, who shifted into a bunker stance and drew the seven iron to the top of his backswing.

"Buddy, I know how to use a golf club," he said. It was one of the few positive statements he could make about his life, and he was amazed at how little impact it had. The man hesitated for a moment—only for a moment—then, with his eye fixed on the thin shaft of the iron, he gave a skeptical snort and lumbered into range.

The swing Rod used was smooth and relaxed—so much so that even the cart thief himself might have thought it a half-hearted effort. But the timing was there, and that's where the power lay in golf. There was a trick to it, like ringing the bell with a sledge hammer at the county fair. Rod rang the bell now. With a good body turn and a snap of his wrists, he transferred the entire momentum of his arc into the clubface. This was no stubby punch shot for getting out of tree trouble, but a full swing and follow-through, the kind that cuts down hard behind the ball and takes a deep, long divot. It did so now; the heavy blade caught the lower edge of the man's right kneecap and moved on through the shot for a clean, high finish.

With a startled gulp, the man tottered slowly sideways and crumpled to the rough pavement, too stunned at first to utter a sound. But that moment passed, and he launched into a shrill whine as he squirmed frantically on his crippled leg.

Rod stepped back to gauge the damage: the club was okay; the guy would be on crutches for awhile. "I'm really sorry about this," he said.

The man glared up at him and spoke through clenched teeth. "I oughtta kill you, you sonofabitch!" He looked as if he had more to say, but a fresh pain twisted through his leg and kept any words from forming. He turned his face away with a groan and began to rock back and forth in the gravel.

"I could call a doctor," Rod offered, but the man ignored him. He rolled onto his left side and whistled once more like he had when he'd first climbed down from the truck. The effort hurt him, and he groaned again. A queasiness rose up from the pit of Rod's stomach. "What are you whistling for?" he asked, though he thought he knew.

A strained smile broke across the man's face. "Somebody to tear your goddamn arm off," he said, and fell into a giddy laugh.

"It's a dog, isn't it?" Rod asked.

"It's a bitch," the man answered, and began to giggle uncontrollably. He leaned his weight back on his elbows and tried to straighten his leg in front of him, but the knee wouldn't unbend. "Christ," he said, still giggling. "What the hell have you done to me?"

"I think you've gone into shock," Rod told him.

The man lowered his head to the gravel and lay as still as he could through the small spasms of laughter, taking slow, deep breaths until he finally brought the pain under control. At last he raised himself up and leaned heavily against the grimy rear wheel.

"What about the dog?" Rod asked.

The man sighed and stared down at his crooked leg. "She got away from me last week," he said.

"What the hell do you mean, she got away from you?" The sharpness in Rod's tone surprised them both.

"I mean she jumped out of the truck to run down a rabbit," the man said, keeping a wary eye now on Rod's seven iron. "I couldn't wait around."

Rod hacked the club hard into the pavement, sending up sparks and a small spray of stones. The man flinched and huddled closer to the wheel.

"You asshole," Rod shouted. "Don't you know better than to leave a dog to run loose by a highway?"

The man shrugged. "I came back," he said.

Rod hated simple answers. They weren't enough. Besides, they always seemed to back him into corners. For as long as he'd been a part of the game, he could remember only two times when he'd given in to simple answers, and both times he felt cheated.

The first was when he was a boy, playing with his father's clubs. His father had been a left-hander, so for his first two years in the sport, Rod had been a left-hander, too. Then when he was twelve his father bought him a right-handed set. He was furious about having to start all over again, and he demanded a reason for his father's forcing him to give up so much ground. "You're not left-handed," his father told him.

The second time was when he decided to quit the tour.

He felt the same frustrations building up in him now, as if he were still somehow playing on the wrong side of the ball.

"You can keep the cart," he said.

The man narrowed his eyes. "What?"

"I said you can keep the cart. We've got insurance."

The man slowly pulled himself up on his good leg and steadied his weight against the side of the flatbed. "I don't know," he said, searching Rod's face for some sign of a trap. "That doesn't sound right. What's the catch?"

"I want you to give me your dog."

"What?"

"I want your dog."

The man looked around uneasily. "I told you, I already lost her."

"Then there shouldn't be any problem. From now on we can just say she belongs to me."

"And that's it?"

"That's all."

The man chewed the inside of his cheek for a moment, and nodded. "Yeah, okay. Sure." Then he frowned. "What about my keys?"

Rod pointed to the darkness at the lower end of the lot. "There's a sand bunker just below that ridge," he said. "You might start looking down there."

The man eyed him suspiciously. "How am I supposed to do that? I can't even walk."

Rod extended the clubhead toward him. "You can have this."

The man reached carefully forward and took the iron from Rod's hand. "Okay," he said, then shifted his weight onto the shaft of the club and limped away from the truck. He circled wide around Rod and made his way cautiously toward the edge of the dark. Rod watched him until he'd reached the bunker, then took the keys from his pocket and tossed them through the open window of the cab.

He'd have to order Mrs. Davies a new seven iron. She'd be mad as hell when he told her he'd lost this one. She'd probably try to get him fired. But that was okay. Sometimes you just had to give up what you were used to, or you might never get anything right.

For now, though, the only thing he wanted to think about was hitting a bucket of range balls. He'd lost a little control lately, he knew that; and if he didn't work on it, his problems would only multiply. Golf was an unforgiving game, with no use for shortcuts or excuses. A good swing was built on fundamentals. The grip, the stance, the take-away, the body turn, the follow-through—all had to be kept in balance. If one went wrong, the rest collapsed like a house of cards.

He would start with his wedge to see how his short game was holding up. Then he'd work his way right up through the driver.

But he'd have to hurry. The wind was rising stronger now, and it swept in from the course with the clean smell of the coming storm. To the south he could see the glow of the town lights against the low-hanging clouds. The rain hadn't hit quite yet, but it would before long.

He knew it was bound to.

Basin and Range

BY HEATHER BAIRD DONOVAN

My father leaned on the horn when he made the last turn into our drive with Sue McCollough in his truck. From my bedroom window I couldn't see them clearly in the cab, but from their silhouette against the dust cloud behind them I saw she wore his cowboy hat.

I had never met Sue before but I felt I knew at least half her life about her. She was my mother's best friend when they grew up in Fernley, and my mother talked about her like she was the one person she most wished would come and visit, other times like she never cared if she came at all. Now Sue had waited until my mother was dead four years. I was thirteen. Why now, I wondered; why not ever before?

When Sue called that morning she claimed some man had left her over at Twist Ranch, a dude ranch for Texans. She thought it was too good a coincidence that if she had to have the misfortune of getting left behind she got left so close to friends.

"Disaster?" I heard my father say. "No, this is a treat." I heard him tell her over the phone how he'd never expected to hear her voice anymore and there she was. He said it would take him fifteen minutes in the air to get there. We lived on a small ranch outside the town of Hawthorne, where my father had a short dirt airstrip across the back of our field where other families might have junked old cars. He made his living flying charters for rich people who wanted to play craps in Reno half the afternoon and catch a glitzy show in Las Vegas for cocktails. Sometimes he flew geologists looking for changes in sage

17

patterns that might lead to gold.

Now Sue stood just inside the screen door, wiping her finger across the dark green aviator glasses my father still wore, leaving a trail in the light dust on them. He smiled at her, took them off, and put them in his shirt pocket next to the clear plastic tube he used with his plane to siphon gas and check for water in the fuel lines.

"You two are definitely on your own around here, aren't you," she said, reaching to hug me. She carried five or six brightly colored silk dresses in a clear plastic bag folded over her arm—the plastic felt like water on the back of my knees.

She held me apart from her. "You don't look like your mother," she said. "Funny how you get an idea how you think someone will look."

I smiled and stood up taller, hoping in that way to look more like my mother, though I knew I didn't. "Dad says I look like the women on his side of the family," I said.

"And she does," he said behind me.

Sue handed me a brown paper bag with part of a tumbleweed sticking out. A few twigs caught in my sweater and I made a face at my father, as if to say, what's this for? but he ignored me.

She walked down the hallway like she knew where she was going. She stepped into the guest room and flopped the dresses onto the single bed with the sunflower bedspread my mother made. She took my father's hat off and placed it on top of the lamp. I worried it would burn if she left it there at night with the light on, but my father didn't seem to notice.

"What will you be wearing these for out here?" he laughed, standing in the doorway with several pairs of shiny high-heeled shoes dangling from their ankle straps. Sue turned around and flicked her middle finger against his stomach, like she was flicking off a mosquito, and she got up close to him.

"I never know when I might want to get dressed up," she said, smiling, with a tone of voice that made it sound private and tender. She turned away and pulled up the shade. Then she pulled the sheer curtains back off the window. "It smells like moth balls and old apple cores in here," she said.

My father slipped behind me, back into the living room to straighten things. "That isn't so, Sue," he called. I followed him. By the way nothing knocked to the floor I could tell he was trying to be quiet about what he was doing. He scooped my arrowheads into the basket where he kept matches, then he lined up all the magazines in a row on the coffee table and pushed a sock under the sofa with his foot. He looked at the magazines again and rearranged them to look a little messier. He ran his finger along the mantle, around the picture of my mother and him in front of his plane, both of them wearing white scarves, with me in front of them as big as a watermelon lying in a picnic basket lined with blankets. He used his handkerchief to wipe off the deer head's black glass eyes. He had his back turned to the doorway when Sue walked in and stood there, her hands pressed together like she was posing for a picture of a saint praying.

"You sure you don't mind if I stay?" she said.

My father looked at me. "All right with you, Nell?" The way he said it sounded like an afterthought, although I knew he meant it sincerely.

I shrugged. "Why not?"

My mother and Sue had known each other since they were six years old. They used to play blackjack, practicing shuffling and cutting and dealing double decks of cards, sitting on the floor of the cab of my grandfather's broken-down truck, where they wouldn't be seen. They were blood sisters, having pricked each other's calves where it wouldn't hurt with obsidian arrowheads from the petroglyph park. They spent hours, my mother said, planning for the day they'd run away to Reno together and get jobs at the Nugget. They'd get perms and have matching black skirts and tape their bosoms underneath their white scoop-neck blouses to give themselves cleavage. Cleavage, Sue told my mother, meant tips. She had a brother who told her so. When they were sixteen, Sue ran away to Reno, but my mother stayed. She said it was because my father had begun flying low by the trailer where she lived with her parents. He'd fly low enough to make the walls ripple, low enough to make their German shepherd howl and bark at the sky for an hour after. Her father, my grandpa, said it was my Dad that started his ears ringing non-stop, with his damn air-buzzing like he was some kind of stunt pilot. He could have gone and gotten a job being a Navy test pilot, my grandpa said, if he was serious about anything. But my father said he was most serious about my mother and he liked a plane you could park in your own backyard. That was the kind of thing my mother liked about my father, she said. He didn't need to puff himself up to be happy.

The first years after Sue left she sent postcards, and letters written on tiny cocktail napkins with jokes on one side. My mother kept them in a cigar box that she put in an apple crate as it began to overflow. I used to get that crate out of the back of the closet in the guest room, and have my mother tell me what the places were like. "Read for yourself," she'd say. "I'd only be making it up." Sue's handwriting was big and loopy. She always said the pay never went far, that she couldn't wait but didn't see when she would ever get a place of her own, with a real kitchen instead of a coffee pot and cooler. She said there were men enough to meet, and one had taken her to San Francisco for the weekend. She liked that city. She thought she'd learn Spanish from the maids in Reno and go there to work in the tourist industry. She knew she was good with the public, that's what she told her new bosses. I'd have to be able to buy a lot more dresses though, she wrote; San Francisco's just like Paris.

Several times my mother told me Sue missed her wedding. She hadn't been certain her letters even got to her until Sue sent a card from Chicago a year later. She wrote she hadn't meant to forget the wedding but there she had. She said she had the most miserable job ever, working a flagman's position in the snow while the road crews cleared one side of the roads and then the other. It's so cold here I must have freezed part of my brain off, Sue wrote. That'll teach me to follow some man who says he can get a job on the Stock Exchange.

Sue began to call when I was six and seven, always in the middle of the night. That was when she could think most clearly, she said. My father said it was when the man she was with was most likely sleeping. My mother would come in and wake me up and I would press my ear right up to hers on the phone. I liked to imagine the big oil derricks near Dallas that Sue described, or the fisherman standing over holes on the frozen lakes of Minnesota. She told us they used drills the size of pitchforks to get water that moved underneath, and that looking down those holes past the thick walls of ice scared her. One night the phone rang and I got up on my own, stood just inside my doorway waiting for my mother to call me in to listen. But she didn't.

"You know I'm always here, Sue," I heard her say into the dark. "There's not a lot of other places to be out here. We're all here, all the time. Especially now." I heard her put the receiver back into its cradle.

"She doesn't ask enough about Nellie," she said to my father. "She doesn't think I have any news worth telling."

"She calls you to feel like she has a home," he said. "Maybe she's jealous."

"Hah," my mother said. "She's the one who's seeing the world."

"Don't start this again," my father said. I wondered what he meant by this. My mother didn't say anything more. I heard her turn in her bed and then the radio came on to loud static. She softened it, then I heard the jump of pauses and chatter, of music and more static. If she was patient she could usually find a call-in radio show from somewhere far away: Los Angeles or Salt Lake.

"People are the same everywhere," my father said from his ·side of the bed. "Why can't you accept that?"

Every once in a while when my mother felt in a good mood towards Sue and wanted to reminisce about their times together, she'd have me help put together a care package; we baked cookies with M and M's, gathered up chewing tobacco, sour balls, a Buddy Holly deck of playing cards. I clipped news articles from the *Reese Reporter* about awards I had won in basketball and archery, or that the Eureka museum had borrowed one of my arrowhead displays. My mother would choose pictures of the three of us, and our house, with little lines pencilled in to show the new curtains and her new perm. We'd cut out paint chips and fabric swatches, so Sue could see the actual color of our house and everything in it. We sealed everything with many layers of tape in a box lined with foil and put it in our freezer until we got another card. Then Mom would wait until Saturday and we'd drive to Sparks and send it airmail, special delivery, put it in the hands of the postmaster ourselves to make sure it got to Sue absolutely as fast as it could, before she moved on.

My mother liked to drive and my father didn't. She bought herself a brand new Rambler convertible with money she got when grandpa died. She liked to see how far she could go in a day and still get home by dark. Many times she was home way after dark, and my father didn't like it.

"But it was so pretty," she'd say. "I stopped to watch the moon rise." Or, "I took that back road up to Ione, that one that cuts in toward Tonopah."

"You don't know who's out there," he said.

"They don't know who I am either," she said. "So don't worry about it."

When we got the highway patrol report my father stood in the living room and read it once out loud before he put it in his top dresser drawer. It said it was most likely my mother who caused the wreck. From what was scattered around, she might have been polishing her nails when she pulled out around a truck full of baled hay, and went head-on into a semi hauling quarter-inch gravel from Mason. She was coming home from Sparks again, where she'd taken a package I hadn't helped her prepare to send to Sue. I was nine then and spent all my extra time hunting for arrowheads. I still think about how I would have seen that truck coming and told her not to pass, would have sung out loud and clear and told her I'd hold the bottle of nail polish for her.

After a week Sue didn't get dressed in the mornings anymore, and just came into the kitchen with her robe drooping off one shoulder. She looked old to me; she had marks on whichever side of her face she'd been sleeping on. By the way my Dad watched her and began stirring his coffee, clinking his spoon against the porcelain cup in a way he never had before, I could see him warming up to her. It got to the point where he didn't get dressed in the mornings anymore either, just walked in like the old days with a towel around his waist. His time was his own, and as I made tomato and mayonnaise sandwiches for us I began to get the feeling that he wasn't going anywhere in a great hurry, that maybe neither one of them was planning on getting dressed in the near future.

One day I forgot my lunch and came home at noon, ran in the door to see Sue cut straight across the living room and up the hall, naked, her heavy legs jiggling. My dad picked magazines up off the floor and put them back on the coffee table. He had on her robe. He held up his hands and smiled, like, what could he say. I rode my bike back to school, hit dips and bumps hard rather than steering around them, and forgot my lunch. When I came home that night they were playing dominoes on the kitchen table, slamming them down hard and laughing, just like he and my mother used to do.

Maybe a month after, when my father started dressing for breakfast again and listening to the weather radio over his coffee to plan his day's charters, Sue came for me one day in the middle of school. I got a pink slip from the principal's office that called me out front.

"Miss McCollough says you've got a dentist appointment she forgot about," Mr. Morris said, looking at Sue's red shorts. She smelled like Sea and Ski. I could hear the radio from my dad's truck all the way out in the parking lot. Sue was all smiles and snap your fingers. She had chewing gum and she offered me and Mr. Morris each a piece.

"Might as well rot her teeth before we go as after," she said, smiling at him. She winked at me.

In the pick-up she said, "I got lonely. Let's go to the pool. I brought Cokes and sponge cake. You like sponge cake, right? Didn't your mom tell me that in a letter a long time ago?"

"I do," I said. "But we can't go to the pool. Someone will see us there."

She laughed. "We're not going to any pool around here," she said. She pulled out onto the highway and stepped hard on the accelerator. "What do you know about the pool at Yerington?"

"It's seventy miles from here," I said. "I don't know if they have a pool. Just a gold mine."

"I called," she said. "They do." She kept one hand on the steering wheel and with the other reached into a large paper bag on the seat between us. She rustled around in it, then looked inside, pushed things around. I reached for the wheel.

"Skittery, aren't you?" she said, and smiled at me. I could feel her breath across my arm. I let go of the steering wheel and she took it.

"Did your mother ever tell you about air sandwiches?" She laughed out loud. "Reach in there then and find the bread, will you?" I pulled out a loaf of sliced sour dough wrapped in clear plastic. The green and orange label said it came from San Francisco.

"Now tear off the crusts of four pieces," she said. I did. She took two pale pieces of bread from me and hung her arm far out her open window. "Do this," she said, and frowned at me in a mock stern look. I wanted her to watch the highway so I copied her. She began waving her bread around and I did too. I began to laugh though I wasn't sure why. There we were driving down the highway shaking pieces of white bread out our windows. She turned the air conditioning up full blast. Then she pulled her bread back in.

"Toast!" she announced. Mine was toasted too. Stale, dry, crisp on the outside. She stuck her gum on the steering wheel, pressed her pieces of bread together and took a bite.

"Air sandwiches," she said. She laughed and chewed at the same time. "Your mother and I used to do this all the time. Didn't she teach you?"

"No," I said.

"Well, we did," Sue laughed. "I can't believe she'd forget."

"We drove a lot," I said. "She wouldn't forget."

"Well." Then she tossed her bread out the window and put her gum back in her mouth. "Your father's getting too busy to notice the time of day. Or who's in his house, for that matter. He's getting too busy to notice the time of year. I'd forgotten how gorgeous it is here in the fall."

"It's nice," I said. I remembered the drives to Sparks with my mother. I remembered how good it felt to go fast and the hills didn't get closer for the longest time. Then all of a sudden you were up and over them.

"You probably think I'm crazy," she said.

"I don't know about that," I said.

She told the man who collected money at the gate and gave us our locker pins that I was her music pupil, that we were from San Francisco and headed to Nashville where they had Star Search. "She can play the steel guitar in such a way as to make you cry," she said, putting her arm around me.

The man shrugged and put two more dashes down in a tally on a piece of white paper. "Pool closes at five," he said.

"Why'd you lie?" I asked her when we were stretched out on our stomachs on the one big towel she brought. The pavement was too hot to sit on. "Why'd you tell him anything at all?"

Sue looked off through the chain link fence at the cloud of dust hovering above the Yerington mine. "It gets you places," she said. "I guess it's a habit. People like to be impressed. They like to root for you. It's not such a bad habit really."

"I can't see that he cares much."

"Oh, don't be such an old sourpuss like your Dad," she said. She punched me softly in the shoulder. "You're real tan, aren't you?"

Our Cokes were warm, so Sue got the man to get us some ice out of the snack bar. The pieces were too big to do any good but she said, "Here, I can do this." She took my Coke and then she took her time sucking on the pieces of ice like they were popsicles, shaping them into long cylinders and dropping them one at a time into each of our bottles. "There." She handed me mine and lay back on the towel, holding her arm over her eyes. Her upper arm was pale and flabby, but her stomach looked smooth under her black bathing suit.

"The sun sure can make you feel nice," she said. "All hot and liquid somehow."

I was lying on the very edge of my side of the towel. I didn't say anything.

"Your mother wrote me that nursing a baby made you feel something like this. She said it makes you feel filled up and hungry at the same time."

I noticed how the fullness of her breast flattened out when she lay on her back.

"I always wanted to know what she meant," she said. "I won't, but I always imagined it felt something like this."

"I don't know about that," I said. I wanted her to stop talking about my mother.

"Your father is a busy man," she said again.

"He likes to fly," I said. "He's always been crazy about it."

"I thought he and I might have something together," she said. She sat up and I looked straight ahead at the pool, not at her. "But I don't guess we will," she went on. "He's a hard one to pin down."

"I know that," I said. I thought of how when my mother died, after the funeral, he couldn't wait for everyone to leave the house. Then he left me, saying he'd be gone for a few hours. I lay down on the floor with my hands straight out, hoping to make myself as thin and flat as possible, trying to make the huge ball of grief I felt roll off me, trying to get it to roll just to my side where I could get up and walk away from it and then come back to it when I needed. But that didn't work and when my father came back I was curled up tight on my mother's side of the bed. He said he had flown himself to Arizona, to see the Grand Canyon from the air. He told me it was exactly the right thing to do, that seeing that slash in the earth was exactly the way his heart felt, a tear that went so deep and rippled off in every direction. That night he made a bed for me on the couch and he slept on the floor on blankets under the deer's head. We left the windows wide open for the noise of the wind, so we wouldn't feel closed in without her.

Sue pointed the nozzle of the bottle of Sea and Ski straight at me. "Turn around," she said. "Stick 'em up."

I felt the cool squirt on my back. She rubbed my shoulders and then my neck. She squeezed it hard and long, like she knew just how to make it feel good. I watched goose bumps raise the hairs on my legs and I sat up straighter. I felt taller, lighter. I wondered if she noticed how my waist was curving in.

"There!" She laughed and I turned around. She was rubbing her legs but she had so much lotion on them they stayed white.

"Help me out, will you?"

I wiped my hands and then the insides of my wrists along her legs. They felt prickly like my father's face in the evenings. I rubbed the extra lotion on my own legs. Then Sue turned her back to me, pulled her knees up to her chest to keep her feet off the hot pavement. She arched her shoulders back while I rubbed lotion on them. She pulled her suit straps down around her elbows. Her skin wasn't smooth like mine. She had moles on her back, and red marks from her suit straps. I tried to remember if my mother's back was marked like this, but I couldn't. In my mind her skin was always smooth as new soap.

"It's okay," she said. "Don't be shy. I could be your mother, you know." She twisted in such a way that my hand went near the crease where her breast hung down. I pulled it back.

"My mother told me about cleavage," I said. "She said you said it was important, that you still taped underneath your breasts."

"I'll bet she did," Sue laughed. "It's sad she won't be around to see any of yours." She hugged me to her.

I wished I hadn't brought up my mother. Sue pulled cards out of the paper bag and began shuffling them.

"I miss her too, you know," she said. She turned away from me then so that her back was in the sun.

I felt too hot and I didn't know what to do with my hands. Everything I touched, my Coke bottle or the Sea and Ski, felt greasy. I rubbed my calves for a while. "You barely ever wrote her," I said. "She thought you were too busy for her."

"That isn't true," Sue said. She looked over her shoulder at me. "I'm not getting any shadows from the fence, am I?" She adjusted herself so she didn't get any shadow from me either. "Your mother knew I cared about her. She used to gripe that I didn't but she knew better. I had a lot going on then. It was hard for me to keep everything together. But she knew. You want to know how I know that?"

I didn't but I said sure.

"We used to dream about each other whenever something went wrong. Didn't she tell you?" She began cutting the cards again and again, not looking at them. "I knew when she died. I shouldn't be telling you this cause you'll tell your father. Don't, okay?"

I shrugged and didn't say anything.

"It was one afternoon with a guy I knew, a sweet man who

was going to distribute French wine in Arizona and Colorado. We were in a motel, and usually, well, usually afterwards I'm wide awake. I like to talk after. You know?" She sat up and squinted at the pool. "I like to talk and throw open all the windows and see if the world has changed or if it is the same. But I didn't feel any energy. All I wanted to do was sleep. The man kept saying, 'Are you okay, honey? You want me to get you a cold drink or something?' I said no, it was okay. I just wanted to sleep. Right away, like someone turning up the lights everywhere, there was your mother standing at the end of a long tunnel of trees, with sunlight falling between them in patterns of shadow and light like railroad ties, like those pictures of country roads in Europe. She was tiny, and calling. I couldn't hear her at first. She had both hands up, like she was trying to stop something. Faintly, though all of her was straining to be heard, I heard your dad's name. Then yours. I knew it. And then that man woke me up rubbing ice on my neck. I forgot completely about it, until my mother sent me the news article."

I wanted to stop her and I felt like crying but I wanted to know more. How come you? I wanted to shout. How come she didn't come to me?

"I pieced it together," she went on. "That was the exact time she crashed. After that man and I broke up I found that one motel receipt in the bottom of my purse. What a way to remember him." She picked up her Coke and held it tilted in the air. "Well, cheers."

"Come on," she said. "I don't trust that old man to lifeguard. I'm not such an experienced swimmer."

She dove in gracefully anyway. I wondered if my mother would have grown into the same shape as she did: wide at the hips, thin in the arms. "I'm not bad, am I?" she called. She splashed me from the deep end. "Come in," she called, and I stood at the edge and dove. The cold water felt good the way a cold wind makes you feel alive after being inside too long. While I was underwater I felt I could think more clearly again, could find almost the exact feeling of pure emptiness that I found that night camped out with my father in the living room. I thought that I could come back up for air and tell Sue to stop talking about my mother. But then she was next to me, scissorkicking her legs against mine. I went to the side and hung on. She came over and hung on too, lifting one leg slowly up and down.

"Resistance repetitions are the best thigh toners," she said. "Have you got any boyfriends?"

I shook my hair out of my face. She thought that meant no and I didn't trouble to deny it.

"Your father," she said, "he was a looker." She cupped water in one hand, raised it to the cement and let it trickle out. Steam vapors rose and the dark wet splotches shrank at their edges until they disappeared entirely and were dry. "He's one of those men who gets better with time. Your mother and I both had crushes on him. But he wanted her. Anyone could see that. Have you ever been to Reno?"

I rolled my eyes, like, hasn't everybody?

"I ended up at Circus Circus dressed in a mini-clown suit serving cocktails. I even wore a rainbow-colored wig. Why I ever thought cleavage would get me anywhere I don't know." She laughed and started splashing me again. I swam for the ladder and pulled myself up. She followed me.

"Dive for me," she said. "I bet you're good." She walked back to our towel. I felt relieved she was leaving me alone. I walked to the short board and stood behind two little boys and a girl. They tiptoed out to the end of the board and crawled off, hung from the end and laughed hilariously before letting go. I worked for a while on my back flip, and then I tried my swan dive. Each time, I tried as hard as I could not to make any splash. Every time I hit the water I swam deep, and stayed under as long as I could, watched the little legs kicking and swirling above me against the white bubbling surface. I wanted to think down there, to get that really cold feeling that would make things new for me again, but I always had to come back up for air.

After a while Sue began clapping and whistling as I walked up to the edge of the board. I wanted her to leave me alone. I ran up to the edge and jumped in with a big cannonball. I wanted to see how big of a splash and how big a sound I could make to drown her noise.

"Watch the little ones," called the man who guarded the gate.

While she steered the truck Sue reached over and ran her finger behind my ear, as if she were pushing a piece of hair back, only my hair was shorter than that.

"You're not my mother," I said.

Sue brought her hand up to the rearview mirror. "You're right about that." She watched the road again and she pushed her own hair out of her eyes. She left her hand on her forehead to keep her bangs from blowing back in front of her face. "I used to come back to Nevada and not visit you," she said. "It was too hard. Your mother had everything: your dad, you, a nice house. She always looked so thrilled in those pictures she sent. I didn't want to see the real thing. I wanted to keep it just the way I had it pictured in my mind, as if I always had that to come home to." She pulled over to the right to let a big truck pass.

"Do you mind going slow?" she asked. "There's times I like to see things closer than if I whip right by them."

"OK by me," I said. We drove parallel to the flat-topped hill of mine tailings—it stretched alongside us as far as we could see. Sprinklers looped sprays of water on its surface.

"Now it smells like almonds," Sue said. "Like marzipan hearts."

"It's cyanide," I said. "They pour it over rocks. It takes whole truckloads of rocks to get an ounce of gold."

"That's a lot of smashed rocks. I suppose your dad explained it to you."

"He flies geologists sometimes."

"I know that."

We came to an open wedge in the hill where we could see across the hole. Red, yellow, and white flags jabbed veins of heap-rock, mill-rock, waste; it looked like a huge used car lot on sale day. Far away, toy-sized trucks moved slowly up ramps, carrying loads of boulders that looked like pebbles from where we were. High bells rang clearly across the wide space. On the far edge, fading in and out behind puffs of dust, white mobile homes were scattered like loose trash.

"This place looks so wrong," Sue said. "A mountain torn into a hole, nothing to stop it from going deeper and wider forever." She pulled over too fast on the shoulder, making gravel spray everywhere, not worrying about chipping the paint on my father's truck. "They just keep moving those old trailers farther and farther from the lip," she said. "Those people have to cling to the edge of that hole no matter how big it gets. It must be something to watch the earth being carved right out from under you and still call that home. That's one thing I don't even want to know about." She pulled back out behind a truck carrying red onions in two big bins. The oniony smell blowing into the cab reminded me of my dad cooking Denver omelettes, of the way the kitchen smelled when he diced green peppers, ham, and onion. Sometimes, in his sock feet, he danced with two knives like a crazy drummer. Chop chop. Hop hop. He still hadn't made breakfast since Sue's appearance.

I wanted to be home. I wasn't hot anymore and I didn't understand her. She made me angry, and she made me want her at the same time. A woman who could be my mother. I didn't want to hear about her feelings anymore. "Are we going home now?" I asked.

"Can I tell you a secret?" she said.

"No," I said. "I mean, no thank you. Maybe you should tell it to my dad."

"It involves you," she said. "I want to tell you."

For the first time I didn't like the way the hills spread out low ahead of us, the very ones I used to like to drive right up to and over, just like flying, my dad used to say, basin and range, basin and range. Nevada.

"Your mother, the day she died? She was coming back from Sparks, right? She mailed me a package. A care package like you and she used to put together. Only this one didn't have candy in it. It was full of letters from a man she never told me about. It wasn't your father. She'd been seeing him a long time, I think, though she said she didn't want to talk about it then. She used to get those letters sent to a post office box in Tonopah. He traveled for his business, I guess. She said he called it off when she wouldn't leave you and your dad. I tried to look him up when she died but I don't guess he's from around here. She wanted me to keep the letters for her until she got old and she could look at them again without feeling guilty. She didn't want them around your house for either of you to find."

I wanted to walk by myself. I didn't care how long it would take to get home. So my mother had a reason for being so restless. Not boredom like my father claimed. Not, like he said, wanting more of the world than any one person had a right to enjoy. Who was the man? What else wouldn't I know about her?

"Does my dad know?"

"I didn't think it my business to ask. I never did, anyway."

"You didn't come here by accident?"

"Not really. I didn't know how things would turn out. I think I wanted to see what your mom's life was like, finally. And I did, in a way. I can see why she was restless. I never thought I'd actually have a chance to live in her shoes, but there you have it. I did, at least for the last month or so."

She pulled out around the truck full of onions. The road ahead was nothing but a long straight line to hills with no buildings or trees, no place to stop for shade.

"You're awfully sweet, you know," she said. "There's something else. If you want to see those letters ever, I can't exactly put my finger on them. I mean, I know where they are, but it's a man I don't speak to anymore, a man in Denver. He had a house and a family and a place to put them. He said he'd keep them in his office safe. I never had a place like that. I'll give you his card when we get home. I'm sure he's still there. You could call him or something. Maybe he'd mail them to you."

"I want to go home now," I said. "Please take me home?"

For a surprise that night while my dad was making one-eyed jacks he told Sue to pull a rolled-up newspaper from his back pocket. "Lay it out," he said. "Look." It was an enlarged aerial photograph of our house that one of his passengers made. "Home sweet home," he said. "And look." He held the curling edges down on the table with his elbows, his spatula still in his left hand. He nudged his hip against hers. "There's Sue's red dress on the line, blowing straight out like a regular wind sock. Who'd have thought it?" He laughed.

"I think I'm going to be sick," I said. I pressed my back into the tile ledge of the counter.

He let the picture roll back up on itself and looked over at me. The whites of the eggs began to pop and smoke.

"I got too hot and didn't drink enough," I said. "That's all."

"Did you try salt water?" he asked. Sue reached for his arm and he turned to her. "Why didn't you look after her better?"

"It's not that," I said. I turned to face the sink to keep from crying.

"Honey," he said. "What is it? Run water on your wrists. It'll help."

I couldn't contain myself even without looking at him. I began to cry and I ran out of the kitchen and down the hall into his room. I flew face first on his plaid bedspread, searching deep in the pillow on my mother's side for the bitter smell of her hair just after a perm. I'd done that a lot after she died; it was the scent that had lingered longest. Now it smelled like Sea and Ski.

"She's at that age, isn't she?" I heard Sue say.

"She doesn't cry for no reason," I heard him say. I heard his footsteps walk into the living room. I knew exactly where he would stand, and how, with his back to the deer and the fireplace.

"You overprotect her," Sue said.

"You wouldn't know about that," he said, then, "I'm sorry. I wish I knew why she's upset."

"If you like, I'll check on her," Sue said.

"No," he said. "Maybe she's jealous you're here."

It isn't that, I wanted to yell, it isn't that at all. I heard him walk back into the kitchen, scrape the pan with a spatula.

"You should frame this," Sue said. "Can you get me a copy?"

In the morning there were twigs of tumbleweed down the hall.

"Sue said she had to get going," my father said. "Do you feel any better honey? She left you this envelope."

Inside was a picture of mountains with snow on them, and inside that the business card of a man in Denver.

"I gave her the picture," he said. "We can get another one."

"Sure," I said.

"Will you miss her?" he asked. "I could never quite tell."

I shrugged. "Sometimes she made me mad."

Four years later I saw Sue again. She was gluing new white

reflectors onto a highway guard rail on the road to Truckee just before winter. I was learning to be a court reporter, driving my boyfriend's truck to a deposition in Kingvale. She was the same pear shape in her bright orange jumpsuit and I pulled over and honked.

"Hey," she said. She put her hand on my door over the lip of the rolled-down window. With the other she held a bucket of reflectors. "I never left Nevada after I left you and your dad. Do you remember air sandwiches?"

"You mean you finally stayed somewhere?" I asked. She smiled proudly, almost the way a child does.

"Well, it wasn't like I planned it or anything," she said, "though I have had the same boyfriend for the last year. His name is Neal, Neal Truman. Have you heard of him? He owns Farley's restaurant in Reno."

I said no I hadn't heard of him but I hadn't been to Farley's either. Sue reached into her bucket and handed me a reflector. "Take it for good luck," she said. "God knows we can all of us still use some. How's your dad?"

In future nights the reflector would glare back at my head-lights from the dynamited rock slope I threw it on where the freeway slices hills outside Sparks. It caught the light where nothing grew, a misplaced landing beacon, a reminder I could not stop to bury or remove.

I told Sue my father was fine. I did not tell her how a man with gray hair came to our house two years after her visit and said he'd heard my mother died and where was she buried. I did not tell her how my father wanted to know who he was, standing on our porch, still on the other side of the screen door, and how the man, on finally seeing inside my mother's house, standing there seeing the deer's head and my arrowheads on the wall and all the things she described to him firsthand, broke down and cried. My father cried too. He held the latch tight and would not tell him where she was buried, although I think that wouldn't be so hard to find out in a place as empty as Nevada.

Sue stood there bent down to my window waiting for more news but I said I had to go and put my blinker on to pull out into traffic. I did not tell her that not long after that man's visit my father took his plane and flew to the Grand Canyon again. He said he followed the Colorado at a low altitude, trying to see more clearly the colors in the layers of rocks that press so many centuries together like paper. Maybe, I thought, studying the back of her jumpsuit as she stood up and watched the cars coming toward us, maybe he dropped close enough to see the people's faces above their thick orange life jackets as they waved up to him. At any rate, he did not follow the river to where it eases into Lake Mead, but instead caught a wing banking up to the south rim. Perhaps he had sun in his eyes. He doesn't remember. He was going slow, and he lived to tell about it, but after he mended he sold our land to a cactus enterprise from California. He had had enough of flying, he said. For the first time, he said, he was ready to leave Nevada.

I did not tell Sue that it was only me left here. I did not tell her that I was happiest thinking she was far away and difficult to locate. I did not tell her that after my father left I wrote the man in Denver, and that he wrote back saying he hadn't realized those letters didn't belong to Sue, and that he had thrown them out a long time ago. I wouldn't ever know who the man was who caused my mother to leave us, and my father to leave me.

I did not tell Sue that I no longer knew where my father was. But as I pulled out into traffic I told myself what I often do these days: I know where I started from; here, nearby, on an airstrip, with my mother and my father and a picnic basket, and no one else around.

Being Here
Is Good for the Children

BY DAVID COLE

In her old age my mother-in-law has developed a curious deathbed manner. Whenever she gets sick and my wife drives the six hours from our house in Vermont to the home where she grew up on Long Island, her mother blithely dismisses whatever accident or illness has befallen her (most recently a broken hip) and asks for two things: first, a drink of hot water, cayenne pepper and lemon juice, and second, that Isabelle read her the local newspaper until she falls asleep. Though I become despondent each time Isabelle leaves to attend to her supposedly dying mother, and though I inevitably end up sitting as I am now, at the kitchen table with the lights out, I am fond of the reversals: the daughter reading to the mother, the day's news replacing a bedtime story. It tells me there is some cyclic sense to our lives and even some gentleness routine does not allow for. Once my eighty-three-year-old mother-in-law has been rocked to sleep by the news of zoning board appeals and by tales of the most recent high school graduates who have left the southern tip of Long Island to seek their fortunes in small colleges and vocational schools, my wife calls me from the bedroom where she slept as a child. Last night she told me about the book she is reading, the diaries of Thomas Edison, and she talked about how she thinks the next time she comes down she'll be meeting her siblings at a funeral home. She talked about how unforgiving her bed is and I told her that I've changed the sheets on ours. When my wife is gone, I wake up stretched diagonally across the bed. I do not dream when she is away, though sometimes, in her absence, when I roll over I will hear a tiny voice muttering deep in my mind; it speaks with a gloomy wit the way Shaw's Captain Shotover does, saying things like, "Youth! Beauty! Novelty! They are badly wanted in this house."

I am an English teacher at a public high school and before me, on the table, is a bottle of single malt whiskey. I am not drunk and do not plan to be, but right now I am thinking about this bottle. Periodically students will give me a gift at the end of the year. Last June it was this bottle of whiskey, bought illegally and left at my door anonymously by members of my Shakespeare section who cut classes, drank beer on a beach on the Connecticut River, and then drove down my dirt road to leave the bottle at my door while I was in a faculty meeting called to resolve the problem of senior Skip Day. I remember that afternoon with a clarity the memory does not seem to ask for. The faculty meeting was, of course, of no consequence—a pointless debate on how best to punish adolescents whose biology requires them to break rules—but upon arriving home I found the bottle at our door with a note, "6/12/88 The readiness is all. Your Bloat Kings and Mobled Queens." As I stood on our warm step, digging for the "bloat king" reference in *Hamlet*, I felt my thinking slowly cease until I was aware only of the long June light lying across the dirt driveway and of the weight of the bottle hanging from my hand. I felt graceful standing in the doorway, a fifty-five-year-old man in a pair of thin trousers he has worn carefully for fifteen years, and, for a moment, I believed only the reckless affection of seventeen- and eighteen-year-olds could offer a luminous and gentle reprieve from things. Right now it makes perfect sense that I should listen to the noises of my house, have one drink from this deep green bottle, and wait for a phone call from my wife.

Solitude is not something I rely on for inspiration. It is the consolation that comes when I have felt myself at risk. Sometimes in July, after I've played tennis with the summer people on their rented court and am slouched in a director's chair, I will feel the sun finally losing its heat in the late afternoon, and

I will think of my father's heart, my doctor's warnings about angina, and feel as I do now. Sometimes this sensation will present itself suddenly, as in the sound of the phone ringing in the middle of the night. So far, my wife and I have never had one of these calls bring bad news (most of the time these calls have been wrong numbers; once, for example, an American serviceman in West Germany misdialed his sister's area code). Bad news, for some unknown reason, has always come during the day. Nevertheless, after hanging up the phone I will stand in the hallway outside our bedroom and feel invigorated, as though I've successfully deceived someone. Everything I think of seems fresh and splashed with cold water.

It is Friday, six days before Thanksgiving, and the wood in the stove is hissing loudly. The wood this year is wet, cut and split too late, so unless Isabelle and I begin to make a habit of bringing wood in to dry for several weeks by the stove before we use it, this will be a familiar sound this winter. And there is a dog at my feet. Her name is Emma. She is a Doberman pinscher, though she still has her tail and her ears were never pinned back. She arrived last year at the end of the summer, with a family from New York, who were renting the last house at the end of our road. A writer and his wife who had been renting it for years had given it to them for the last two weeks of August. Friends of friends, we were told. These people arrived with their two boys and Emma, and after a spree of cocktail parties, lost tennis balls and late-night swimming, drove away leaving the dog to fend for herself. We heard they sent a note to the postmaster suggesting they understood Emma would be cared for by the man in town who drives the plow after snowstorms, but he knew nothing of the dog and claimed only to have spoken with this couple once or twice at the meat counter in the Grand Union in Bellows Falls.

No one was surprised. They were loud people; self-concerned and obliquely pandering to us with their perceptions of living for short periods of time outside of "that crazy city," as they liked to say. Out of deference to their connection to Isabelle and myself, and an apparent interest in becoming as local as possible in a two-week period, they had us to dinner.

Isabelle and I nodded and laughed at all the right moments, as people will in August when the gin is excellent and the mint is fresh and the momentum of a three-month vacation feels like something that should never fade. The renting couple, quite enamored with their rented house, with the hillside, with the swimming hole, with themselves, with us, smiled and freshened drinks and filled a small dish with Greek olives steeped in garlic and oil. Isabelle and I were gracious as we listened to the younger couple recount the virtues of small, rural towns. The wife talked about a friend of theirs, a single woman, who was thinking of moving to Vermont or Maine to throw pots. A relationship had not worked out, her husband said. I nodded and thought to say something about a pilgrimage to the woods (because after all, this was what the two of us had done, but years earlier, of course, when JFK was launching the space program and the flight to the suburbs was fashionable), but I thought better of it because I knew I would end up telling these people whose Bombay gin I was enjoying that the world does not become kind and just or even patient simply because one wants to see it that way. I held my tongue, guessing that my words would fall on deaf ears or, at worst, be taken for indifferent sarcasm. The summer was not over; the world felt easeful and warm; I did not want to risk being misunderstood, so I drank my gin and bobbed my head to the pleasant lilt of the conversation and felt the breeze blowing in through the screens.

We talked until nine-thirty when the husband came from the kitchen with a steamed salmon on a silver tray; he set it down carefully—it was an enormous fish, much more than four of us could eat—saying, "It's so good for the children to be up here." Their children, as far as we could tell, did nothing but watch video cassettes rented at the gas station, though towards the end of their two weeks here, I remember, their small boys carried sticks and they walked up the riverbed that separates Dover from West Dover, where we live. Watching them from our kitchen as they disappeared into the lush summer trees at the end of the field beneath our house, I thought that perhaps the end-of-summer renters were right, that being here was good for their children. But still this was not something I wanted to give them credit for. It was the way the two of them would screech and howl each time they whacked a tennis ball over the backboard and chicken wire fence that was so irritating; it was as if their true nature had risen and they were shrieking peals of surprised laughter because that is what you do if you are from out of town and have two weeks in the country.

Needless to say, no one was surprised to see Emma loping from house to house looking for food after Labor Day weekend. Our neighbors, the people we buy our wood from, are dairy farmers and they feed Emma when she is willing to live like a barn cat. If she is feeling more domestic and is looking for some creature comforts, she comes to our house and waits on our step until Isabelle and I come home, which is where I found her today.

Though it could not have been much past four o'clock when I left school, by the time I turned down the last section of paved road that leads to our turnoff, the sun had fallen behind the hill so the stone walls were barely visible at the dark edges of the fields. Only the lights from the barn lent the landscape any sort of warmth, and as often happens at the end of a week when Isabelle has been away, I began to think of our youngest daughter, Erin, and realized it has been two and a half months since we last spoke with her. Twenty-three years old and convinced she will be a film actress, she left New York for London after a year of waitressing and fruitless auditions. I thought of her trip to England and was depressed to find my most vivid memory of her lay in a phone call where Isabelle held the receiver from her ear so Erin's deep, round voice could be heard across the kitchen table:

"He said he was going to kill himself if we broke up! I didn't know what to tell him. He said he was just going to go out and kill himself! Throw himself in front of a train or something."

Erin had been living with a man she'd met at work, someone who was making steady money in commercials.

"But he didn't kill himself, did he, dear?" said Isabelle.

"No, he just said he was going to become a priest, but now he says he wants to come with me to London."

"What are you going to tell him?"

There was silence on the other end of the phone. "I don't

know," she said finally. Erin was whining, and Isabelle looked at me and rolled her eyes slightly; I shrugged my shoulders and shook my head.

"Your father says that's what happens when you go out with an artist."

"Great, just great; tell him thanks a lot."

"What do you think you'll do, honey?"

There was another long pause, then a patented Erin sigh. "I don't know. . . . I'm just going to buy my ticket. He can do what he wants. . . . I'll figure it out."

She did go to England alone, where after eight months of illegal work serving pints of beer in a West End pub, she found intermittent work in a British soap as the young American doctor. We know from her letters that she is involved with a thirty-four-year-old violinist whose father is Dutch and mother West Indian. His name is Gert, and Erin tells us, "He is a man committed to his music; he listens carefully to only a few people." We try to understand this as a compliment. The two of them are in transit now, travelling by boat-train to Rotterdam, then on to Sweden, where his family has a small house on the ocean.

Erin has an instinct for creating opportunities for herself which seems to be part of the glorious character of youth. I hear it now in the unflappable resolution of her sighs, but I saw this quality for the first time when she was ten or eleven. After she learned to read bus schedules, she made a game of running away from home. Until she got her driver's license, Erin would lie about sleeping at friends' houses and instead would take an overnight bus to a large city somewhere on the Eastern seaboard. She would befriend older people, usually single grandparents, who would call us on Saturday or Sunday and relate the concocted story Erin had told them about how we were supposed to meet her in Baltimore or Newark, or wherever it was Erin had gotten herself to. At first we'd drive to pick her up, but after her third exodus, we began asking Erin's new guardians to put her back on a bus. We'd collect her, beg her in stern parental tones to keep us from feeling as though she'd been taken hostage, and she would listen with her head bent, kick at her toes, and tell us, yes, she'd not do this again. Eight or ten months later she would disappear. A note on the table would tell us about staying at somebody's house; we would call the police and bus companies, then sit at home and wait, too anxious to be angry. She was sending herself somewhere knowingly, I told myself. For the day or two it took to recover her, I could think of nothing but the randomness of things and an abduction that would qualify my daughter for the back of a milk carton. I'd convince myself that because she shipped herself off like a piece of freight with her address in her eyes, she would be returned to us safely and predictably, like a long-awaited letter.

So I suppose it was appropriate to arrive home to an unlit house with Erin on my mind, Emma on the front step, and a UPS slip stuck to the door. I let the dog into the house, put a wet log in the stove, then went to the old milking shed that we use as a garage for the package. The zip code on the slip was from Florida. My Aunt Rose in Orlando had written earlier this month to tell us she was starting to sort out her husband's possessions. She had mentioned his business records; she said she would send us some of his things. My uncle, my father's brother, died in January, and I cannot say I was struck with grief. Though he was seven years my father's senior, he lived fifteen years longer, a fact that suggests the universe is arranged for a profit motive. In the last twenty years of his life, he made a great deal of money erecting malls and industrial parks in and around Miami, but my uncle was not a generous man with his wallet or his heart. He shook hands with the vigor of someone who knows he is more tan and fit than his peers—a kind of happy, public gloating is what this looked like to me; he drank exotic fruit and vegetable juices, and for fun he and his friends took turns financing health clubs as personal investment ventures and would have tennis courts, weight rooms and saunas named after themselves. At the funeral Rose said, "It made him happy for people to be healthy."

His move from Boston to Florida and his venture into developing was supported initially by the sale of the trucking company he had bought from my father. It was not the fact that he bought my father's company and then sold it for a high return that was so damaging, but the small amount of time that passed between these events. Two years after Isabelle and I moved to Vermont, my father sold the company to his brother; two years later my uncle sold the fleet of trucks to a large New England distributor connected with the Pillsbury Gelatin Company. A quick and profitable turnover, it was as if he were practicing the speculation that would make him so much money in Florida. It was only a matter of months before he and Rose moved to Miami and began sending cards depicting palm trees, blue water and beach games with his development group's letterhead embossed on the inside. He would always mention a bungalow on Key Largo that a business partner maintained for his associates, and inevitably he would hint at an elliptical pool by the ocean and the fine deep-sea fishing afforded by a sunken battleship a mile offshore. "The fish," he would write, "they swim in all the crannies. You must come this winter." Though I'm certain he felt himself to be sincere in his offers of a Florida vacation, no one in our family ever went down.

I am an only child and it is fair to say my father's trucking company was like a second son. Like me, the business was his own, something he had brought to life, and though it was not explicitly stated, I believe he always assumed that after my tour in the Navy, I would return to Boston to work with him. For two years I did, and in that time I met Isabelle; we were married in July, I with my English degree and teaching certificate, she with her MSW, and we decided we would move to Vermont. I can say my father was gracefully reticent about our decision. I recall how he excused himself from the table and went to the kitchen to do the bills, something that never happened at home (the bills were my mother's territory) unless he was aggravated in a way he was unwilling—or unable—to articulate. My parents felt the news only as a rejection. There was, you could say, no joy in the house, no bright-eyed, chin-up cheering to send the boy on his way. I can still see my mother sitting back in her chair, wrapping her napkin in her hands, then winding her fists into her apron. In my innocent belligerence, I told her how we would only be two, maybe three hours away, how things would be no different than when I was in the Navy—we'd be closer, even, than when I was away, I suggested blindly—and my mother said that this was true and began clearing the table.

But, of course, it wasn't. In the six months immediately following our move to Vermont, my father's heart and blood pressure suddenly became a medical concern, though his workload had not changed, and a year and half later, when our first daughter, Elizabeth, was born, he sold his company to his brother. For my father a business couldn't be simply an organization that he presided over effectively, something that held its position in the marketplace through his smart choices and hard work. Longevity for him lived in things that could be passed from person to person, cared for like an old car, so when he saw his business stuck in his own generation, I think something inside him crumpled the way the roof of an old barn will cave in silently under a wet snow. In the shadow of his heart condition, I believe he sold the company to affirm the gesture of passing something on, never thinking it would be sold again so quickly or on the terms that it was. A giving away was what it became, a small but definite betrayal. He resigned himself to the sale in the same way he accepted the news from his doctors; he became a gray man with a broken heart.

At four-thirty the light beyond the kitchen was dim. There were no shadows, and the slight slope of hillside and the shapes of trees stood out in the cold, remaining light. I fed Emma the last of the lasagne Isabelle and I had shared the night before she left for Long Island and stood by the stove, thinking I ought to put my coat on again for the trip to the barn for the UPS package, but I decided not to. I thought the cold air on my shoulders would make me move more quickly. That was what I needed, to move more quickly and deliberately. It depressed me to think that some small piece of family history had come to our house while I was alone. It felt like an intrusion, something quick and uninvited, but also something terribly enduring, like the arresting recognition that comes when a plate or coffee cup is knocked from a counter and all one can do is turn with enough time to wince before it breaks and scatters across the floor. Sometimes I think this is the one sensation all families share, when the ache and routine of relations give way, revealing, for an instant, something resembling the brief sting of an incision.

I left my coat inside and went to the barn for the package. The box was not big. Rose's Cuban maid had packed it so the corners were neatly taped and our address was penned across one side in large, even script. Inside were many oranges and several grapefruit padded with plastic, green stuffing straw. I set the fruit in a large bowl on the table and could feel the wax on my fingers from the shiny yellow and orange skin. Beneath the fruit were my father's boxing gloves. My father was the better boxer, but both he and my uncle would spar with me in the kitchen when I was small. One of them would sit in a chair and toss me the gloves, then tell me to keep a thumb out when I jabbed to catch the bastard in the eye, while the other would start a ducking shuffle as I put the gloves on. After my father died, my uncle would remind me once or twice a year, along with his perpetual invitation to the bungalow on Key Largo, that I could have the gloves whenever I wanted them, so I was not surprised to find them finally arriving like this, buried beneath the fruit that had been coming every Christmas and Easter like a dividend he and Rose had reaped from their move south. Under the gloves was an old leather briefcase. The handles were barely attached and the initials on the lock were scratched and illegible. I thought perhaps this was my father's briefcase. I wanted to believe it was; it looked so venerable, a piece of an institution, a sign of a business that might have swung every day from his arm, but I had to admit that I could not remember seeing it anywhere before. I set it on the table and opened it, expecting, perhaps, the original ledgers my father had kept but found instead the transfer papers that he signed with my uncle. There were many old receipts and carbons of inventory slips from the Boston area, but primarily the briefcase was filled with thirty-year-old papers which detailed the sale and transfer of the trucking company from one brother to another.

I put on the boxing gloves and went to the window by the sink. Then I returned to the table and picked up a grapefruit in each glove and went back to the counter. Emma looked up at me with one ear lying inside out over her head. She cocked her head once, apparently puzzled—she seemed to have the quality of human patience—and I began rolling the fruit on the counter beneath my gloved palms, as if to make the slightly oblong grapefruit into perfect, softball-sized spheres. The motion was awkward because of the gloves, but I stood with my belt touching the counter and kept my hands rolling over the fruit so my arms moved in unison in a small sculling motion. I rolled the grapefruit and looked out the window and thought I ought to continue to roll the fruit until I noticed the light in the sky change somehow. That was what I needed: a waiting period of some kind. This occurred to me because when the days are short, the light in the sky decreases as if by notches, the way an aperture on a camera slowly clicks itself shut. This lessening of light seemed an interval I could watch for. I looked through the window at the field below our house and waited with my hands still moving in slow circles. When I was certain I had seen the sky lose a shade of light and the trees near the riverbed seemed noticeably darker, I took off the gloves, set them in the box on the floor and went for my coat. I returned to the kitchen counter for the grapefruit and dropped one in each pocket; then taking up the briefcase, holding it like a parcel, close to my side, so as not to tear off the handles, I went outside with Emma.

It seems strange to me now (and then, suddenly, it feels perfectly appropriate) that as I stepped out the door I was thinking about my mother and her weekly trips to church; for to think of her ritual Sunday car rides was, of course, to wonder about my belief in God, the thin notion that only when we act as if God is too busy to do anything for us do we ever experience what people like to call grace. It is a romantic idea, I admit, even a blasphemous and dishonest one, but it lets me wink at the ceiling occasionally and think something more than human voices keeps the sky in place. When I can believe God is simply busy, unavailable, like an overworked hardware store clerk, then, even in my fifth decade, the idea of omnipotence can become, for a breath or two, like a golden ladder I'll never know, but one I imagine climbing to see past things I do not understand. But truly there is no golden ladder. We do not see over anything; if we are lucky we see into things, but mostly we see nothing and move along slowly, taking whatever help appears as though it has arrived by accident. But what is wrong with a wink if it keeps the sky in place or makes a house seem less empty or the ground less frozen? Even a wink might be something divine, I told myself, as I walked towards the field, across the dry rubble of the driveway, over our fallow garden and through the open section of fence where, years earlier, after our neighbor told us he would not need the field for his cows, my daughters and I cut back the barbed wire. I walked quickly over the hard ground, with Emma following, until I came to the riverbed at the far edge of the field where I turned into the woods.

The riverbed was loose under my feet. Emma leaped ahead of me along the sandy strip that wound its way through the trees, but my shoes sank slightly with each stride and my gait shortened until I was moving as old people do, in short, calculated steps, almost as though my feet had become a pair of hands and were groping their way tentatively along the ground. I walked up the riverbed carefully and noticed how the sky that had seemed so dark from the kitchen appeared light and spacious when I looked up through the trees. When I came to the fallen oak that lay waist-high across the riverbed, I scrambled up the bank to where the large root system stood upended. This was the tree Erin and Elizabeth had discovered when they were old enough and brave enough to leave the house on their own. In the summers Isabelle or I would have to walk to this spot to retrieve them for dinner. Each side of the river would stand for a different country, and they would stay, each on her own prescribed territory, talking back and forth like small diplomats; before they left each night they would race over the log and leap off into the sand. They were flying, they'd say, as I'd walk up to call them home. They would sail off the log and roll to my feet like stuntmen.

I set the briefcase on the ground near the tangled root system. Though the tree was rotted, not at all the sturdy bridge my daughters had run across, the roots were still flexible. I pried some of the smaller tendrils apart and set the briefcase behind them so it was held in place snugly against the base of the trunk. When I stood up I could barely make out the briefcase, but standing next to the upended root system of the fallen tree I was certain—in a way I was not in the kitchen—that I had never seen the old, leather briefcase before. Remembering the grapefruit, my hands fell in unison to my pockets. I picked my way back down the shallow bank to the rotting tree trunk, bent over and placed them in a hollow in the log where a branch must have been. The woods were unspeakably quiet. The cold tree trunks seemed to have drawn themselves to attention for the ceremony of leaving the grapefruit and the briefcase. Emma had disappeared. Everything was still. The air smelled like dead leaves, and through the trees I could see our house backlit in a cold crescent of yellow light where the sun had fallen behind the hill.

I am hesitant to describe how I felt just then. I suppose I was struck by the indifferent silence of the place. I thought about the small voices of my daughters, of Isabelle swimming alone in the culvert below the house and of the luxurious weeds in the field that grow with a crazy lushness during summer. I tried to remember their names, the dandelions and bluets, the mustard and vetch, the buttercups that cows won't eat, the joe pye weed, black-eyed susans and goldenrod and salsifee. I thought of Erin and Elizabeth dropping their small bikes in the driveway and racing through the field towards the log, turning cartwheels in their sleeveless jerseys. I was lost in the sound of small voices. And then I was aware of dimming silhouettes of branches above me. The canopy of barren limbs was as motionless as latticework. I understood I was just an older man with his hands thrust deep in his pockets, standing where his daughters once had been, but this did not seem an unwelcome or unworthy thing to think. It seemed even hopeful, and again I saw pictures of their arms and legs spinning across the field, casting long shadows through the summer weeds.

I walked out of the woods feeling limber, though the front of my thighs had turned cold, and my breath, I could see, was swelling and pluming in front of me as I walked. The light was starting to leave the sky more quickly, but the darkness was not coming from above but from the sides—out of woods themselves, from the spaces between the trees. I was amazed at how quickly the light seemed to be vanishing, as though someone had begun to slash the air around me with a charcoal pencil; the lines and outlines of the tree trunks were no longer distinct but dim and grainy. Emma appeared from the woods with her thin dog tags chiming, and the two of us left the riverbed for the edge of the field where the stone wall was. I walked with one hand in my pocket and the other extended gently so my fingers and palm bumped occasionally on the top of the wall. Emma walked ahead of me, then circled back, her tail and shoulders swaying in unison. She bobbed in front of me again, following smells over the cold ground. I tried to picture the sounds and smells of my summer memory, but all of it was gone. It was totally unreachable. I know I must have been walking slowly because every twenty yards or so Emma would pause at the wall and turn around to make sure I was still with her. When we reached the corner of the field, we turned up towards the house, and I decided what I needed was a drink from the bottle of Scottish whiskey my students had given me in June. I thought I would walk the perimeter of the field, then go in to have my drink when I reached the driveway where the barbed wire fence meets the stone wall. But halfway to the corner I left the wall and headed more directly for the house, taking the hypotenuse of the triangle, you could say. I don't know why I did that. Maybe I knew in spite of my eyes, which had adjusted to the dark, that night had arrived. Or it could have been that I thought Isabelle might call earlier than she usually does; or perhaps part of me was saddened I could not call up pictures of youth and sunlight at will. I don't know. It was very cold, I remember, but even now I recall how warm I was inside my coat and how fiercely still the field was, how safe and dark it felt, as I turned from the stone wall and made my way with Emma back to the house.

Forbrengen

BY MARVIN DIOGENES

After six months in Montreal, David's French still wasn't very good, so Birnbaum only let David deal with customers after he, the owner and proprietor, first welcomed and spoke to them. If David heard French or Yiddish, he knew he would be allowed to continue with his paperwork. If the customer spoke English, Birnbaum waved David forward from his small desk at the rear of the bookshop, just to the side of the door to Birnbaum's office.

"My son-in-law will assist you, sir," Birnbaum would say, and then, turning to David, "Call me if there's a question you cannot answer."

Usually David could answer the questions of the customers, even if the inquiry concerned a very rare edition. The quiet of the shop gave him ample time to study the small inventory, which had been catalogued and annotated in Birnbaum's fine, cramped hand on specially-made, oversized sheets of paper, unlined and waxy to the touch. The inventory was made up mostly of religious tracts, the Talmudic commentaries of dead rabbis, and a few secular memoirs written by obscure Lithuanians and Poles about their shtetl upbringings. The aura of that lost time, musty, pictured in sepia tones through faded and brittle pages, attracted David, and he felt himself fortunate in his father-in-law's business. At night he pored over the bibliographies Birnbaum recommended, which listed all the manuscripts that had survived the holocaust, and also some that had probably been lost.

50

"It is the essence of our vocation to find what the customer seeks even when the customer does not know if such a text exists," was one of Birnbaum's maxims. David's goal was to become as knowledgeable as Birnbaum, and he had to remind himself, when his eyes felt like open wounds after hours of reading, that Birnbaum had acquired his expertise in the course of a lifetime, while he, at twenty-four, had only begun to learn.

During slow periods at work, when he daydreamed with his eyes on the scroll of Birnbaum's inventory before him, David couldn't picture himself in bed with Birnbaum's daughter, even though he slept with her each night. The image that first came to his mind materialized her securely in her father's house, helping her mother prepare the weekly Sabbath meal, which they all ate together after David and Birnbaum returned from the synagogue. He still saw himself as an outsider, not a husband, even when Birnbaum encouraged him to raise his voice to sing the psalm that welcomed the Sabbath, the bride of the pious Jew. His voice seemed thin, reedy, as if he had to force it up through the narrow tube of his windpipe. He knew part of what Birnbaum expected of him was earnest if not full-blooded singing, but he couldn't yet play the role of the God-driven hasid convincingly.

Though the singing embarrassed him, Lisa smiled, in her element only there. Without conscious effort he could picture her walking with her slight limp between the substantial pieces of furniture, the chairs that didn't give an inch when he sat down in them; or, imagining some intimacy between them, he saw her handing him a tea cup, the porcelain so thin he felt it would break off in his mouth when he sipped from it. In the apartment near her parents that they had moved to after the wedding, she seemed tentative rather than graceful, her limp more pronounced, a flaw rather than a compelling mystery. At night, when she came in her white nightgown to take him from his books, she floated, wraith-like, but still limped, as if the air of the apartment were an obstacle to her. He saw her mostly at her father's house or in the white nightgown, their shared, illicit secret illuminating the rapt darkness of his studies. Her being was split, and neither half seemed close to being a wife to him.

It had all happened at once, the betrothal and wedding; there had been no courtship in the modern sense, but instead the arrangements made by Reb Pinchas and Birnbaum after the union had been approved by the Rebbe. The two older men had been the lovers whispering of the future, slowly earning each other's trust with promises of the joys to come. David and Lisa had never been alone before the marriage ceremony. Reb Pinchas had told him when the matter was settled, and David had felt like a character from an earlier, simpler era, dutiful and unquestioning. It would be for a younger generation to undermine the reclaimed tradition. David remembered listening to the soundtrack album of *Fiddler on the Roof* in his parents' home when he was growing up. The show had been a smash hit in the conservative Jewish community, David now knew, because it presented the quaint, old world values as negotiable. It made his parents and their friends feel good about their comfortable lives, and so what if a child found love outside the faith. Now David remembered with shame how he had rooted for Tevye's daughters to free themselves from the customs of the town, and he felt himself the owner of an old soul, wise beyond his years. He thought of the boon he would have been to Tevye, a man with five daughters to marry off. He was studious, didn't eat much or require new clothes. All he wanted to do was seek spiritual peace and live quietly. In these areas, at least, David knew Birnbaum could have no complaints. His son-in-law was a bargain if not a steal.

David had still been living in New York at the time of his engagement, studying each day in the Brooklyn synagogue of the Lubavitcher hasidim. Pinchas had been his teacher and advisor since David had joined the sect two years before. They had only been separated during the summer David spent in Israel at Kfar Chabad, the Lubavitcher yeshivah outside of Tel Aviv. Now Pinchas had been chosen to work in the Montreal synagogue, to take charge of the effort to reclaim Jewish souls from McGill University, and he wanted David to accompany him. David himself wasn't a rabbi, so he needed a good reason for the move, and Pinchas decided that marriage, the beginning of a large hasidic family, would convince the Rebbe of the soundness of David's removal from Brooklyn.

"David, you'll soon be a groom," Pinchas had said one day,

closing the volume of mishnah they had been studying.

They were sitting at a bench in the study house, amidst the murmur of the other scholars. There was no air conditioning, but David liked to think of the constant hum as the whir of sacred machinery. Devotion to God was palpable in the room. All of the hasids worried the air with their hands and tongues, turned the pages of the heavy volumes with a slight electrical snap. David even forgave Pinchas for saving the news of the marriage until after they'd studied. Such details were incidental in the world of torah, David told himself, feeling a mystic thrill down his spine.

"Birnbaum takes my word that you are worthy of his daughter and his offer of a livelihood."

"What did you tell him about me?" David asked, not entirely trusting his mentor, who had a gift for hyperbole. He often told David that their studying would hasten the coming of the Messiah. By concentrating their souls they gathered the holy sparks scattered throughout God's universe. When all the sparks had been redeemed by honest men like themselves, the Messiah would come.

"I told him the truth," Pinchas said. "What else should I tell him? You're a good boy, a scholar, no bad habits, maybe a tzaddik in the making. I told him you'll make a good husband and a good son, since all he has now is a daughter."

"What about my background? I'm not exactly a thoroughbred, you know."

"Neither is Birnbaum. To tell you the truth, he isn't really a hasid at all. He's a businessman with a respect for learning. Your background, as you call it, impresses him. You know the world but choose to be a Jew. That's what he wants for his daughter. An example."

"What about Lisa?" David asked.

He had only seen the girl twice, on weekend visits to Montreal with Pinchas. He considered her beautiful, too beautiful to marry him, and he suspected her because of the circumstances. Why would she let her father arrange a marriage to a virtual stranger? The first time he sat in her father's house, Lisa spent the whole hour on the phone in the next room. He heard her giggling, silver splashing his ears, as he tried to concentrate

on her father's description of the book business. Birnbaum
went on about how he had assumed a responsibility to preserve
the written record of their race. He wanted an assistant not so
much to sell the books, his own least favorite aspect of his
business, but to *read* the books, to soak them up in the blood
and let them flow through his young veins. He, Birnbaum, was
in a position to support such an undertaking, just as secular Jews
had always kept a foot in God's presence by sponsoring young
scholars. David heard Birnbaum's words, but concentrated on
gathering clues of his betrothed's nature through her overheard
conversation.

Obviously she had girlfriends. Thus the giggling. Was she a
simpleton no man would approach, or was she perhaps too hard
to please? The girls he'd known before had managed to spurn
him on their own. Wouldn't Lisa spurn him, too, once she saw
how undistinguished he was? Neither Pinchas nor Birnbaum
found it strange that Lisa showed no interest in her future
husband. Later on Pinchas would not answer his questions
about the girl, preferring to expound on how David could
continue to study God's law even after assuming the responsi-
bilities Birnbaum had reserved for him.

"You've seen her," Pinchas had answered, leaning back,
"although I was against it." Pinchas paused a moment, raking
his beard with his fingers, a gesture usually reserved for considering unyielding Talmudic riddles. "She's young. She's sound.
The limp is not even to mention, thank the lord. It does not
affect her health. You know she hurt that leg horseback riding,
at some summer camp in the Holy Land." Pinchas paused
again, to let the absurdity of riding a horse in the Holy Land
sink in. Clearly, David was to consider the girl's views as
unimportant, for she could not think for herself. "She's a
chicken without salt, perhaps, but what do you want in a wife?
She will be the soul of your household, David, the mother of
your children. Think of that, nothing else."

But David could not help thinking about how she looked,
especially now that she was his wife. A slender girl with perfect
skin and finely chiselled features like Lisa's would have been
much sought after, a prize, where he had grown up, just outside
Chicago. He had been raised Jewish and attended public

schools, which he now looked back on as the breeding ground of his lust. He'd been miserable for most of his youth because girls like Lisa were out of his reach. His earliest memories were of the smiles of the little girls in his elementary school classes, and the emptiness he felt when they looked away. He couldn't believe that he had actually learned anything in high school, because by then his obsession had reached its height. He knew all the girls in his classes minutely, not through direct contact, conversation and dates, but rather through their habits, their favored articles of clothing, the easy way they chatted in the halls with their friends. He felt like a spy, or an alien sent by some unknown power to record everything observable about adolescent girls. The surveillance exhausted him. He'd chosen to attend Columbia, where his grades had earned him a scholarship, to escape the girls he knew so well but had hardly spoken to. They would be in Evanston, in Champaign, and he would be far away, where he could live in peace. Now Pinchas told him not to notice that he was married to a girl who bore no slight resemblance to his fondest, most long-lived dream.

David still met Pinchas for lunch several times a week. Pinchas insisted that David continue his studies despite the burden of his new career as Birnbaum's assistant. Their usual place was a kosher restaurant, not far from Birnbaum's shop, in the old Jewish section of Montreal. When David walked to the restaurant, the children of the neighborhood ran fearlessly past him in the cobbled streets, the ritual fringes of the boys' prayer shawls splayed against their churning thighs. David worried for them, because the spaces between the uneven stones appeared to him as ruts ready to trip the unwary who would dare to race through this world.

One day, David arrived at the restaurant a few minutes early. Without Pinchas, he felt out of place, surrounded by the Yiddish-speaking crowd. They all seemed to be fighting, in violent disagreement about the essential nature of existence. The old woman behind the counter, a fixture, a handkerchief flattening the top of her stiff wig, gestured with a plate full of knishes, causing them to roll around like soft, fleshy logs. A stooped man waved both arms at her, jerkily criss-crossing them at his waist, an infirm umpire signalling his argument safe. In the midst of the tumult, David considered himself a meek man. Some of his favorite passages of the Talmud concerned the value of holding one's tongue in public. It was better to walk barefoot on hot coals than to speak slanderously of another human being. He kept his eyes down to avoid the scene before him. He wanted no cause to think evil of the others in the restaurant, for an evil thought was as unconscionable as an evil word. With his finger, he started to connect the dots on the formica table top. He noticed that they followed no pattern, and he soon tired of tracing them. He pushed at the napkins in the squat tin dispenser on the table, letting them inch back, lazily, off the spring. The napkins, thin and white, reminded him of his wife's nightgown.

Sometimes when she called him from his studies late at night, they would make love. In their bed, she looked at him constantly. He'd always thought of sex, theoretically, as a fifty-fifty proposition, a borderless universe of possibility halved by consideration for the partner. He had been a virgin much beyond the age when virginity would have been fair or even useful, but as a result he'd had a lot of time to develop a philosophy about the meaning of sex. He had a theory about the intimacy of sexual partners. He asserted that sleeping together meant lowering all of one's defenses and accepting the other's needs as equivalent to one's own needs. He insisted that the closest thing to sex was the Vulcan mind meld performed by Mr. Spock on "Star Trek." He proved to his friends that such a state of abandon was threatening to a logical mind like Spock's, and that the Vulcan always looked exhausted afterwards because of the mind meld's primarily sexual nature. There had been fights about David's views among the other Trekkies of his acquaintance, the sons of members of his parents' congregation. They had met in the parking lot of the temple when they could escape the drone of the High Holy Days services to talk about important issues.

Later, at Columbia, he'd imagined himself approaching the girls milling past in the filthy hubbub of Broadway, at rest on the hard chairs of Butler Library, across the lecture hall intent on the words of the professor. They had to be intelligent to be at Barnard, the girls' school across the street. To be sure of seeing them he took many of his classes there. Often he was the only man in the classroom. These girls would see the logical imperative of his thinking: sexual love was to be shared like an intense form of knowledge; in its own way, the body was a sage. He believed that his dedication to his studies qualified him for sexual initiation. He felt his mind expanding daily with the great insights of philosophy and literature, and he wished with all his heart that his body would follow suit. He was afraid that his head would grow large and heavy, hydrocephalic, and tumble him into a book-lined trench from which he would never emerge. He disgusted his roommate, a Floridian with stringy blond hair and a genius for physics, by thinking out loud about his condition; his head was equivalent to a tumescent penis, and he had to find some release. He deserved it. In college, his plans had never worked out. Lisa was only the second girl he'd ever slept with.

Her total composure communicated itself to him. He considered the sex between them altruistic, not the cosmic release and commingling of essences he'd long expected. Although she assured him that her leg never hurt, he was careful not to put any of his weight on it when he got on top of her. Placing himself carefully, he thought of push-ups. When he settled on her he felt like a shroud of flesh, still draped in his black suit, even though he wore only his white prayer shawl to bed. She was so silent beneath him. She would make no move to take off her nightgown, so at first he bunched it at her breast. One night three months into their marriage, he mouthed her nipple through the fabric of the nightgown; she pushed him away and slid the nightgown off over her head, afterwards returning his head to her breast. He raised his head to look at her nakedness. He held his breath to hear her breathe, not believing she was real. From then on she removed her nightgown as soon as he touched her in bed. They never discussed the rituals governing the sexual union of a hasid and his wife. He didn't want to know if she knew that her nakedness was improper.

He did know that she watched a portable television in the spare room some evenings. He could hear it through the wall, the whispering spirit of his past life. The television was contraband; he knew Pinchas didn't know about it, and he wasn't sure if Birnbaum knew. Television distracted the soul from God, and even a woman should not watch it; there were simple books, in Yiddish, for women to occupy their time with, simple, homely tales of saints that illustrated piety. David remembered enough about the network dramas to know that piety was not a theme, and that no rituals restrained the sexuality of prime time. He could only guess what Lisa's fantasies might be, which star she imagined above her in their bed, whose tanned shoulders she kneaded when sex impassioned her hands.

"So why aren't you studying, David?" Pinchas asked, reaching down to cradle David's chin in his hand. "Does a Jew have time to waste with his eyes rolled up in his head?"

David, flustered, stood up and sneezed.

Pinchas slapped him on the shoulder. David knew his teacher was scattering the evil spirits, which, according to tradition, were always close by when one sneezed.

"Hold on to your soul, David," he said. "You have a cold?"

"It's the store," said David, pulling a napkin out of the dispenser and blowing his nose. "Birnbaum fiddles with the humidity to protect the books, so whenever I'm not there I sneeze."

"Every life offers its unique trials," Pinchas said, pushing David to sit and then settling himself. David was always sore for a day or two after seeing Pinchas because of his teacher's physicality. He punctuated every stage of their conversations with some sort of contact, prodding, poking, more like a wrestler than a scholar. Pinchas pulled a volume from the pocket of his coat.

David knew that they would have to study a chapter and a commentary before Pinchas would relax and eat. David was willing to appear purposeful this particular time, because he knew he couldn't expect to talk to Pinchas about Lisa if he didn't study well first. Gossip was appropriate for during the meal, but both food and idle talk had to be earned. David noticed the frayed threads sticking out along the entire length of the binding of Pinchas's book, and the way the paper was a deep butterscotch color where there was no print. David felt an aesthetic sense of revulsion, for Birnbaum would never allow a book in such a poor condition to be used and further diminished; such books needed to be catalogued and kept safe from moisture, from rough and careless hands. David reached out to pull a thread from the binding, but Pinchas pushed his hand away without stopping his elucidation of the tract. As he studied, Pinchas bent over and rocked back and forth, hard, so that the chair protested under him. His beard, sprinkled with red streaks like embers, brushed the table top when he rocked forward.

"So if a cow eats the grain of the farmer through no fault of the cow's owner, who shall pay for the damages to the field?" Pinchas asked, tapping the line of text to focus David's attention.

David furrowed his brow to encourage Pinchas to continue. It was a standard ploy, one he'd used all through high school and college to avoid being called on when he wasn't prepared. Usually his reputation as a brain had allowed him to get away with it. Today David cared nothing about the cow or the field, but the voice of his teacher was nonetheless comforting. Pinchas had always been the same, ever since David had left Columbia to study with the Lubavitchers in Brooklyn. Pinchas had quizzed him then, questioned his dissatisfactions with college, tried to convince him that quitting school was not the answer.

"This is a stage, maybe, David," Pinchas had said. "I have seen many boys the same as you, smart boys, but after a month of hasidic life they disappear like smoke into the blue sky."

"I know that I'm not satisfied with my life as it is," David said.

"Is that enough reason to change it in this way?" Pinchas asked. "A hasid enters into a contest with the Holy One, David. He tries to be the bigger mensch. Will you dare such a thing because you are not satisfied with your life?"

David had to persist for several months before Pinchas began to take him seriously. He never confessed that his original visit to the study house in Brooklyn had been prompted by an assignment for his Sociology of Deviant Behavior class. He had guessed that the professor, a sharp, thin woman named Rosegarden, would approve of an exposé of the hasids. When he proposed the field work in Brooklyn, she had nodded aggressively and told him to keep an eye open for the sexism that was still rampant in orthodox Judaism. At one point, however, long after the due date for the paper, which he never turned in, David felt that Pinchas had accepted him as an equal in spirit, if not in actual learning. And although his reb never ceased making caustic remarks about his secular background, David could always detect Pinchas's approval behind the words, no matter how mocking the tone.

He was so different in this way than Lisa, who seemed to become a different person with each language she spoke. On the phone, babbling in French with her childhood friends, she sounded so young and breathless that David felt like a father denied access to his daughter's life. She spoke in cascades, using so much slang that he hardly understood a word. At dinner, when he asked her to teach him the French word for some ordinary object, her earnest tone placed the word in quotation marks, set off from its everyday use. Repeatedly, he had to ask the word for "fork," for she said it in a way that made it impossible for him to remember. To her parents she spoke Yiddish, quietly, making the language a way of reaching out to them, to show respect. Even Birnbaum spoke softly to Lisa because of this, his own Yiddish losing its ironic edge, the jabbing elbow David felt whenever he overheard Birnbaum conducting business on the phone. David knew that Yiddish was a jumble, a hodgepodge, a language well-suited for the evasions of commerce, but in Lisa's mouth it lost its roughness and became as of a single cloth, like silk caressing his ears.

She spoke English only to him; she spoke it correctly, but tentatively. Her sentences had perfect posture, but they were stiff and unnatural. He found himself accenting the wrong syllables of words in his conversations with her, for she made English seem foreign on his tongue, too.

Whether she loved him, why she had consented to marry him, he had no way to ask her, and Pinchas would refuse to consider the questions.

He remembered Pinchas at the wedding the previous spring. The intensity of the celebration had frightened David. He'd been forced to dance endlessly in a wild circle of hasids, their arms flying like clubs, their legs kicking like the legs of mules. David had bruises like storm clouds on his shoulders and shins for days after the wedding. Pinchas had been the wildest dancer of all, his cheeks made round and red as apples from the vodka that he drank. He yelled the words of the hasidic songs so loudly that their sense was lost and only his boundless feelings remained. He pushed David into a wooden chair so brutally that David was sure the chair's back had cracked, or his own. Then the chair, with David in it, had been lifted off the floor by the other hasids. From his perch, both hands clamped on the edges of the seat, David saw Pinchas lope across the room with three others, past the divider that kept the women separated from the men. They put Lisa on a chair and lifted her, too. Husband and wife swayed and jolted in the air on opposite sides of the room. David could not catch Lisa's eye to see if she was outraged or afraid, or merely resigned, as he was. Below him the world was a churning black sea, the flushed faces of the hasids as evanescent as foam. He saw Pinchas's glittering, exultant eyes for an instant, but all fine perceptions were lost to riot and excess.

David remembered the wedding scene from *Goodbye, Columbus*, a scene that the rabbi of his parents' synagogue had attacked as slander. "One of our own," he had said from the pulpit, "portraying us as no better than animals." The scene had sickened David, too, because he recognized the truth in it. He had been to enough bar mitzvahs and Jewish weddings to know that little had been exaggerated: the rude appetite, the overloaded tables raked by the voracious fingers of a well-dressed, vulgar mob. He wondered how his wedding would appear to those specters from his youth; would they accept the fierce animal joy that was nonetheless spiritual? Was it slander for him to stand back and observe in this way? He had chosen a path, and he had to follow it, but his thoughts had lowered David into a morass of doubt. Perhaps he wasn't worthy of Pinchas's joy.

"Your mind is on lunch, maybe, David," said Pinchas. "Do you work so hard for the bookseller that all you can think about is your appetite?"

"I'm sorry," David said, realizing that he wasn't even looking down at the mishnah anymore. He leaned forward. "Where are we now?"

"That's enough for today. The words alone are meaningless

if the whole person is not involved. In my father's village, it was said that the righteous man studied even while he drove his ox through the fields, for the torah never left his thoughts." Pinchas shut the book and straightened up out of his learning posture. "But we don't live in a village, do we, David? Sometimes I find it silly to discuss some of these questions. We have no cows, we have no fields. Why do we study, then, David?"

David laughed at his teacher's ploy, relieved that he wasn't angry with him. "Because the moral sense is there. We must exercise the moral sense constantly. The Talmud directs us towards proper conduct in our everyday lives, so we offend neither the Holy One nor any of his creatures."

"You sound like a little parrot, David, but I think you understand. Now we will eat."

Pinchas went to the counter to order their food. Since David could not speak Yiddish to the old woman who ran the restaurant, he relied on Pinchas to choose something good. The only thing David couldn't eat was borscht, but Pinchas rarely ordered it. This day, he returned to the table with two bowls of barley soup and some brown bread. Murmuring in Hebrew, he gestured for David to follow him into the kitchen where they could wash their hands. When they returned, Pinchas didn't speak to David until he'd pronounced the blessing over the bread and swallowed the first bite.

"Besides the sneezing, how is your work, David?"

"Okay," said David, tearing the bread into small pieces.

"And how is your household. Did I find you a good wife?"

"I don't know her, Pinchas. I don't know if she's a good wife."

Pinchas stirred his soup, looking across the table at David. When Pinchas was thinking hard, David noticed how the blue of his eyes darkened, reflecting his soul's contact with the world of things and men. David shifted in his seat, scraping his spoon against the side of his bowl to offset the silence.

"She's not a wife to you? Do you mean she keeps herself from you?"

"She is a good wife in that way. Don't take me so literally."

In the next silence, as Pinchas stared at him again, David considered that he'd been more open in discussions of sex with his few high school friends, lonely, tortured boys like himself who battered themselves against the immutable fact of girls. They'd tried out and used up all the brazen, tingly words as they schemed and endlessly explained the alien gender to each other; now these were words that he could never use in front of Pinchas.

"You must start your family soon. Then you will know she's your wife, a gift from the Lord."

David was embarrassed by the dead end they had reached so quickly. He couldn't tell Pinchas that he was doing his best to guard against Lisa getting pregnant. He couldn't ask her to use birth control, for a hasid's family must be large to add to God's glory, so instead he used her sexual acquiescence to protect both of them. He kept a secret record of her menstrual cycle, pegging the date her periods began as best he could, and then he referred to an old college textbook on human sexuality he kept hidden in a closet to warn him of her most fertile days. During that time of the month he simply didn't reach for her, and she never asked why.

The only other girl he had ever slept with, a Barnard coed named Carmen Eisekovic, had refused to let him have anything to do with contraception. She had considered it her responsibility. "I've been in charge of my own body ever since I took the carnal plunge at fifteen, David. Don't trouble your little head about it. I'm a damn good caretaker," she'd said, flexing in his arms to tease him, for she knew how easily he was aroused. At first he had welcomed her self-sufficiency. It supported his theory about sex: all they had to do was give each other pleasure. He'd been devastated when he'd found out she was also giving pleasure to at least two other guys, one who lived in David's dorm.

"David, there's a forbrengen in New York next week. You should come with me to see the Rebbe."

"Are you afraid that I'm going over to the other side?"

"This is not a joking matter, David. Seeing the Rebbe can help settle your confusion."

"I'll talk to Lisa."

"She won't object."

"I'll ask her anyway. She's my wife."

"A wife has no say in this. For your own good, come with me. We will leave Thursday morning. Tell Birnbaum you won't be at your desk tomorrow."

Pinchas left, stopping as usual to pay the bill and exchange a few words with the old woman behind the counter. He was always restrained with her, and her agitated remarks and gestures disappeared into the expanse of his white shirtfront. He paused at the door, one hand on the glass, and said something in Yiddish. The woman laughed, poking tufts of her wig back under her kerchief and then dismissing Pinchas with a wave.

David left quietly a few minutes later to walk back to work. He took his time, puzzling out the French and Yiddish signs in the store windows between the restaurant and Birnbaum's shop. In New York, the signs in his neighborhood near Columbia had been in Spanish and Chinese. He'd felt like a stranger there, too.

He'd attended his first forbrengen while he was still a student at Columbia. Originally, it was to be the centerpiece of his field work on the hasidic sect. He'd introduced himself in Brooklyn as a young, perplexed Jew, and after he'd been directed to Pinchas, it was decided that he should return for the forbrengen. All of the Rebbe's followers would be there to see him, to wish him long life, to receive his blessing in return. The current Lubavitcher Rebbe had inherited the position from his father-in-law. Both were jewels in the dynastic line of tzaddiks, holy men, that had begun in the small Russian town of Lubavitch in the nineteenth century. It was said that the Rebbe had also inherited certain mystical powers due to his closeness to God. Just by looking at his followers, he could discern their thoughts, anticipate their futures, and sometimes even alter their fates.

This had piqued David's curiosity. He figured this would be a perfect opportunity to observe the hasidim in action. Their deviant behavior would certainly be most dramatic when they gathered in a large group. At the appointed time, he met Pinchas in the vestibule of the synagogue with a spiral notebook and a yellow felt tip pen in his pocket. The vestibule smelled like the subway stairwell that he had just exited. Looking around, he could briefly see a urinal through a closing door. Before he could start breathing through his mouth, like he did in the subway, Pinchas pulled him along towards what sounded like a windstorm.

Inside the main hall, all was bedlam. Hundreds of young men in black suits, with dark beards and thick, coiling sidelocks, stood in rows from floor almost to ceiling. They were singing ferociously, a raucous melody David didn't recognize from his own sedate upbringing. There were so many of them packed in so tightly that the steps they stood on could not be seen, and they seemed to hover in the air, bucked by the force of their frenzy. At ground level, in the valley of the quaking range of hasids, David noticed several tables. Older men with long white beards sat there, occasionally raising their heads to look around. Whenever the song threatened to subside, one of the older men would stand at the table and hold his arm up above his head. The young men then responded with renewed volume while the older men smiled.

David turned to Pinchas, who was looking not at the room, but back at him.

"The Rebbe will be out soon," Pinchas said. "Then you will see the hasidim celebrate."

Before David could answer, Pinchas took his arm and guided him into the throng. David tried to protest when he saw that Pinchas was leading him to the central tables, but his voice was lost in the crowd. As Pinchas elbowed his way forward, no one noticed him or David; all eyes were locked on the raised table at the far end of the room. David watched the path behind him disappearing as quickly as he progressed. He was lost in a riptide of black suits, the fabric scratching his face as the hasids leaped up to throw their voices into the room. He couldn't see Pinchas, but only felt his grip on his arm. Finally they emerged at the tables.

There was no room to sit, but Pinchas wedged him into a spot on a bench. The old men looked at him, their faces blank as parchment. He felt his corduroy sports coat and jeans marked him as a heretic. Pinchas stood behind him with a hand on his shoulder.

Hearing another roar rise above the steady clamor, David looked up to see the Rebbe coming out of a door to the side of the raised table. As he passed through the crowd, the men closest to him lunged forward to reach him, sometimes vaulting over the shoulders of those in the way, balancing themselves on the backs of their fellows just long enough to touch the Rebbe's arm.

"When he reaches his place, we will all toast his health." Pinchas was yelling into David's ear, but he could barely hear him. "You will hold up your glass until he looks at you. If he nods, your thoughts are pure, and you may toast him."

"You've got to be kidding," David said, but in a normal voice, which he knew wouldn't be heard. He hadn't really expected the mysticism of the Rebbe to have such a practical application. But the expression on Pinchas's face was solemn. And the hundreds of men around him were going berserk in a singleminded way that left no room for doubt. David concluded that they truly believed in the old man who had just reached his seat.

The followers began another song. This time it threatened to never abate, never end. The volume increased steadily each time the Rebbe so much as tapped the table in time to the melody. He seemed mildly amused by the havoc he created, his smile almost hidden by his gray-streaked beard. What David noticed most, however, was the weight of wisdom in the Rebbe's eyes, clear and shiny even from a distance, like water between the lands of the Rebbe's dark hat and gray beard. He felt that what the Rebbe understood would forever keep him from laughing, no matter how long the youths before him sang.

David reached down to touch the bench beneath him. The noise was making him dizzy. The men on all sides of him pushed frantically towards the Rebbe; the human waves rushed forward and back, battering against the set dimensions of the room, demanding that space itself become part of the unbridled dance.

Then, far back at the top of the room, David noticed the women's gallery. At first he didn't know what it was, but he focused his attention on the mesh screen that seemed to demarcate an island of calm until he could make out the people standing quietly behind it. They were all women, dressed in dark silk dresses. None of them danced. They were observers, and David couldn't tell if the screen was there to protect them from the savage joy in the room or to keep them from tainting something sacred.

Pinchas shook him and gestured towards the Rebbe. All around him, men were raising their glasses. The Rebbe looked at each man a long moment before he nodded. Then the recipient of the nod yelled *L'chaim*, embracing life, and emptied his glass in one motion.

David felt Pinchas press a squat glass of vodka into his hand. The glass was small enough that he could close his fingers around it and make it disappear. But it was too heavy to hide, too heavy to hold steady. David stood and held it out to the Rebbe. He stood for a long time. The Rebbe chose those he would see with care. David examined his thoughts, Would the Rebbe find him pure in spirit? Why should David care one way or the other?

When the Rebbe finally looked at him, David felt the noise and stale air fall away from him. He was for a moment separated from the rest of the world by the Rebbe's eyes upon him. He'd never felt such a profound isolation. Before, his frustrations and anxieties had seemed ordinary, run-of-the-mill, and his impurity meaningless because its cause was so common. It had always seemed to him shamefully normal to want from life nothing more than good grades and frequent unabashed sex. He was like everyone else, just more successful academically and less successful sexually, and no one, certainly not himself, had ever taken the time to assess the worthiness of his spirit before.

The Rebbe nodded, and David drank the vodka. He felt that he'd swallowed a burning bush.

David had long felt that he would never be personally responsible for any major change in his life. He had felt that perhaps another holocaust or a natural catastrophe, a mugger maybe, would change his circumstances. But he'd stayed that night with Pinchas after the forbrengen, talking about the Rebbe and the hasid's dogged pursuit of holiness, finally deciding to study there in Brooklyn. Now Pinchas thought that he needed another dose. David didn't know if it would do any good. If the Rebbe didn't nod, what would David do about his wife, his father-in-law, his teacher and friend Pinchas, all who'd accepted him on the condition that he be a good hasid. David was afraid for himself, too, for he had limited faith in his spirit's durability.

When Pinchas had seen the seriousness of David's desire to change, he'd arranged for him to go to Israel to study at Kfar Chabad. David had not seen himself in a mirror for the entire summer, for mirrors were not allowed in the yeshivah's dormitory. They would distract the students, who were supposed to direct their thoughts only to God and torah. One of the American students, Mark, a former secular Jew who continued to wear faded jeans and paisley shirts despite the jeers of the orthodox hasids, kept a mirror hidden in his room. David had once gone as far as to visit Mark in his room, hoping the mirror might pop up, but when Mark produced the small oval of glass in a blue plastic shell, David thought of Pinchas and didn't look into it.

He'd realized for certain that he was a changed man one mild night while he sat on the roof of the dormitory and watched the planes take off from the airport in Lod, twenty miles away across a bare stretch of land. The dormitory was squat and square, a tin housing hasids instead of sardines, and sitting on the roof, his legs dangling over the edge, David sometimes missed the person he used to be. When he was certain everyone else was asleep below him, he hummed songs from his youth, show tunes from his parents' collection, rock and roll from his stereo, or blues he'd heard in the night clubs on the upper west side of New York. That night he hummed "The House of the Rising Sun," and he realized that the melody had been transformed in his throat. He sung it like a *niggun* now, a hasidic tune embroidered with curling, melancholy grace notes. It was as if he were mourning the destruction of the temple in Jerusalem, a perennial chore of many saintly rabbis late at night. He knew he could sing as loud as he wanted and bring no censure from the hasids dozing below him. He was one of them, releasing the overflow of his lover's quarrel with God into the indifferent night. When he did see himself again, in a plate glass window at Kennedy Airport upon his return to New York, he was not surprised to see an ordinary hasid in a black suit, with dark sidelocks and a sparse beard.

He'd made one major decision in his life. He'd shed one skin

and emerged a hasid. Did he dare reincarnate himself again?
Even God had created man only once. A man was not a word to
be altered by the eraser on the end of a pencil, as if he were a
clerical error.

After an afternoon at work, during which he didn't mention
the forbrengen to Birnbaum, David went home and prepared
to eat dinner with his wife by washing his hands in the kitchen.
There were two square tables set side by side outside the kitchen
door, one a bit smaller and a bit shorter than the other. Each
was covered by a lace tablecloth with lace fringes. According to
Jewish law, a man and a woman could not eat at the same table,
and since Pinchas had helped Birnbaum order the furniture for
the apartment, the two tables had been there from the beginning.

He moved his chair to her table, the smaller one, and then his
plate, silverware, and glass. She looked at him but didn't speak.
They ate in silence for a long time, David full of questions that
only Lisa could answer. Her fingers, thin and lovely as the
tinkling shards of a chandelier, kept him from speaking. He
could not bring himself to efface her serenity with his awkward
words. He didn't know how to speak to her.

"Do you like my cooking, David?" she asked. "I have only
started to learn how to cook."

He realized that he had stopped eating.

"I'm sitting at this table tonight because I need to talk to you.
I don't want to sit apart from you." He looked down into his
plate, surprised by the bright color of the food, the carrots like
orange suns, the bread a deep flesh tone, the brown of the pot
roast assailing him, gleaming in its juices. He wanted to close
his eyes, to be walking down a surburban street through cool,
meaningless air. "I don't know what you think of me. I don't
know if you think I want to live this way. Do you think I'm a
hasid?"

"I think you are a good man, David," she said. She was
smiling at him, and he realized that he had pulled his arms in
close to his sides. He looked like a child awaiting a reprimand.
"I hope I say these things correctly, David. I am content to be
your wife."

"How can you be content? You're married to a stranger."

"You're not a stranger to me, David. I see you go to work.
My father tells me you work hard, so you make him happy in his
business. I see you come home. I see you eat and I see you study
until your head droops. I am with you when you sleep and when
you wake up. And sometimes in between those times." Lisa
smiled. "How can you be strange to me?"

"But we're not friends. We don't share anything." He
paused, feeling as awkward as a teenager. "I hear you talking to
other people on the phone. I don't know them. I don't know
what you tell them about me."

"I tell them what I feel. They want to meet you, but they are
not proper Jews." David wondered what kind of proper Jew
Lisa took him to be. Lisa continued. "You will tell me what you
want me to know. My father says I should not bother you. He
says you are quiet with me because you are young and filling
yourself up with things to say. That's why he needs you in his
shop, David. To read and fill yourself up with his books. He says
a young man like you talks mostly to himself or to God because
he trusts no one else to listen as seriously."

David did not know if he could speak to Lisa of his fears. Was
a good man permitted to doubt his way of life, the choices that
led to his job, his home, his marriage?

Lisa continued. "I used to hear my father and my mother
talking in their bed at night. It helped me to sleep it was so nice
to hear them. I know that some day we will talk to each other
like that. I know this because I know you. Don't you think that
will be nice, David?"

Had she married with such modest hopes for their future? To
wait for his consuming inner fire to gutter so they could finally
talk to each other as husband and wife? She deserved a better
fate, he thought, his eyes locked on hers. There was laughter
there, and affection, too, and he never wanted to blink again, or
ever look away, but Lisa began to clear the table when he didn't
speak.

Throughout the evening, David debated whether to ask Lisa
if he should go to New York to see the Rebbe. As usual, she kept
to the spare room, leaving him to his studies. He heard the
theme music of a new show every half-hour, and he wondered
what theme would play over the drama of his life: heavy pulsing

chords betokening despair, or a light melody, a counterpoint to let the viewer know that the somber mood would soon break.

Pinchas had said that he should do what was necessary to shore up his own faith. He should put Lisa behind the screen with the women he had seen at his first forbrengen. But then he would never know her. He remembered with startling clarity one of his first and only dates in high school. The girl's name had been Debbie, and they'd gone to a basketball game and then to an acquaintance's house, where all the couples had quickly found their own corners and started making out. David, not knowing how to touch the girl, had confessed a dream of his, which he usually advanced as a theory. He wanted to be like Mr. Spock on "Star Trek," who could perform the Vulcan mind meld, thereby bypassing the need for speech and assuring perfect union. Only Spock could really, truly understand how another person thought, he told his date, straining to deserve her. Debbie had agreed that it was a neat idea, but David could tell from the set of her jaw and the way her eyes wandered around the darkened room that she would have preferred some action over all his talk. He never had the nerve to ask her out again.

David took the French-English dictionary from the bookshelf, and he looked up the words and phrases he would need to discuss the trip to New York. He would ask Lisa to voice her feelings, approach her by speaking her language, however poorly. Before he had thought that he would be imposing on her, but now he would be her husband, or at least try to be. They would begin talking now, while they were still young, while it mattered and could shape their lives together. Perhaps Pinchas would not approve, but even Pinchas had admitted that he was only David's teacher. Lisa was his wife.

He went to check his secret calendar. Lisa wasn't in the midst of her fertile days, but she would be soon. He made a plan: that night, when she came to save him from her father's books, the life sentence that tapered off into a solitary void, he would speak to her in French. Then, taking her in his arms, hearing her little puff of surprise, he would begin his life as a married man.

Korean Lessons

BY ROGER SHEFFER

Specialist Kiesler exercised his territorial imperative by keeping three major items on an otherwise empty desktop: a gold-framed photo of a beautiful woman, a coffee mug that said DON'T BUG ME, and a calendar of the Rocky Mountains, on which he methodically crossed off the days as he approached the end of his tour in Korea. The two of us worked together in a locked vault inside a windowless building at Camp Humphreys. The base had a library, PX, service club, and movie theater, but seemed impossibly remote from civilization, like being stationed at some listening post in the Aleutians. I knew from the map that Camp Humphreys lay only five miles from the Yellow Sea, but two weeks before I would leave Korea, when I hiked east five miles from the main gate to look for open water, I would find nothing but a dried-up river estuary curving away into the hazy distance.

My first day at work, I asked Specialist Kiesler, "Why do you keep a picture of Judy Collins on your desk?"

"I don't think she looks like Judy Collins. That's my wife."

"Your wife looks a lot like Judy Collins."

"I never thought she did."

"Anybody coming in here would say that was Judy Collins."

"Luckily, not many people do."

It was a long time before he let her name slip out. He protected her that way: "My wife went shopping in Seoul yesterday. That's not as simple as it may sound." Or, "My wife saw a flamingo on our front lawn." Even, "My wife would like

72

to meet you sometime."

Saying "my wife" must have been his way of pointing out the difference between us. He was married and I was single. Or a way of evoking wonder—that an American soldier still had his wife with him in Korea. Six months earlier the village outside the main gate had been closed to Americans after a race riot— the locals had tried to keep the black soldiers out of the clubs— and all the soldiers who lived in An-Jong-Ri had to return to the barracks, and those with American wives shipped them back to the States. Except Specialist Kiesler, who lived with his Judy Collins look-alike fifteen miles beyond An-Jong-Ri, in P'yong-Taek, a regular Korean city and not off-limits. Mrs. Kiesler could catch a train from there to go shopping in Seoul, he would point out proudly.

He described how they lived, but never said her name. During the time that An-Jong-Ri was closed, Kiesler had to take cabs back and forth, because in order to get on a bus, he would have had to walk through the main gate. Certain cabs could come through the gate, and if you weren't black, they'd give you a ride. So Kiesler spent five dollars a day commuting back and forth from P'yong-Taek. "Chicken Feed," he told me. "My wife more than makes up for that when she goes food shopping. She speaks better Korean than I do. She knows how to drive a hard bargain on the local economy." Certainly better than I could do. When I tried to speak Korean with my houseboy, he came back with English.

I felt as if my Korean language training had gone to waste. To perform my job I needed to know a hundred words, eighty of them military jargon. Specialist Kiesler and I broke code for the Army Security Agency. We worked in a vault because we used unauthorized materials to break that code. I mean, these materials had been stripped from the dead bodies of North Korean agents, in violation of the Geneva Conventions, but Kiesler and I were cleared to a high enough level that we could be trusted not to squeal, even if we should somehow be captured by North Koreans. One thing I was sure of: any North Korean interrogating me would have to speak English.

Once a month this young guy with long blond hair would drive up to our building in a red Corvette. He had the green

badge with a gold diamond, making him the only other person
in Korea who could enter our locked vault. He'd say, "Yo-po,
Yo-po, you guys, it's the bookmobile," as if that were an official
password. Then we'd let him in. He wore no name plate, but
Kiesler told me the guy was an Army captain who played golf
with the Korean generals. They probably thought he was CIA.
He delivered illicit photos and code books into the vault, what
he had bought from the generals. Stayed long enough to
mumble a top-secret weather report, give Kiesler a ceremonial
poke on the upper arm, salute both of us sarcastically, and then
take off in a cloud of dust. I didn't know his name then, but I
would later get to know him almost as well as anybody I ever
met in my life. Because of what that guy taught me, I would lose
five hundred dollars in a poker game, catch a severe case of the
clap, and almost have my security clearance taken away. No, I'm
not completely bitter about it; I just want to set things straight,
figure out whether I paid too much for my Korean lessons from
the guy.

January, the last month of his tour in Korea, Specialist Kiesler
said, "I think I finally got you trained."
Training had taken three months. Three weeks would have
been sufficient. The job entailed two hours of real work per day.
The rest of the time we would read North Korean magazines
(pictures of the "beloved and respected leader" Kim Il-Sung
visiting a fertilizer plant or hydro-electric project), or we'd talk
American politics. Turned out both of us were Republicans,
though on opposite ends of that limited spectrum. Kiesler was
really obsessed with putting Daniel Ellsberg behind bars when
he got back—the "greatest traitor in American history," he
called him. He brought American magazines and newspapers
into the vault, which he later ran through the shredder, as if our
use in that room had contaminated them. He told me if
Ellsberg had been a soldier, he would be doing time in
Leavenworth right now. He told me about this one guy he
knew in Texas who wrote a code-word on a latrine wall and was
serving a twenty-year sentence in some military prison. For
nothing more than taking out a magic marker and scribbling
one word. It wasn't even a four-letter one. "What kind of

damage could one little word do," he wondered, "as opposed to the million words in the Pentagon Papers?"

"I wouldn't know."

"It ain't gonna change history. None of this low-level stuff means crap. It just keeps you and me off the unemployment lines."

When Koreans came into our building to do maintenance, we were required to guard them with M-16's. One time I had to hold an M-16 on a frail, elderly man while he fixed a toilet in the officers' latrine, and the old guy smiled at me, and muttered short phrases in Korean which had something to do with his admiration for the M-16, though I couldn't be sure.

Kiesler and I were always cold in our vault. Sometimes we jumped up and down, calisthenics, trying to keep warm. The only source of heat in our locked vault was a Gold Star electric space heater, which smelled like burnt hair—or like rubber when we held our boots close to the heating coils.

"This is such a shitty place," Kiesler said. "I should take you out to P'yong-Taek to meet the wife, now that the main gate is open. We could ride out by bus. You ever done that?"

"Nope." I had only taken the military buses up to Osan Air Base and Seoul, once a month if I felt adventurous. It was a four-hour ride up to Seoul. I'd walk around the Yongsan post in the middle of town, marvelling at how closely it resembled the small town I grew up in, with its maple trees, American high school, colonial churches, blond women driving around in Buicks. Blond women in parking lots calling out, "Brian, I told you not to run ahead of me."

Kiesler crossed out today's date on his calendar, as if it were quitting time. "You can ride out with me after work. Brenda wants to play bridge and we need a fourth." That was the first time I ever heard him speak her name. I looked at her photo and said to myself, "You're still Judy to me." Though the eyes became less intense, the voice less husky.

"Jack will be there," he said. The name meant nothing to me. I knew nobody by that name.

The ticket to P'yong-Taek cost the equivalent of ten cents. We rode in a bus not much larger than a VW van, but it had seats for twenty. A young woman in a blue uniform hung out the front door and yelled "Stop" in English whenever she saw a potential passenger, and "All Right," when it was okay for the driver to start up again. This was at a time when most Koreans did not have cars, and the rural buses were the only way to get around if you couldn't afford cab fare. In the village, the driver stopped at nearly every corner, and entire families would climb on, lugging boxes of eight-track tapes, blenders, toasters, that kind of thing. There was no heat in the bus, but the bodies kept it warm, and the people all smelled like sour cabbage.

The landscape from An-Jong-Ri to P'yong-Taek was mostly rice paddies and small villages. One monument broke the monotony and began to haunt my imagination, the tall concrete skeleton of an unfinished church on a bare hillside, visible for half the journey. It made me think that the local people had given up church-building when the Americans came to town. Thereafter they had channeled all their energy into night clubs and tailor shops and black-market electronics boutiques.

When the bus stopped at a tiny crossroads, I saw two words spray-painted on a brick wall. "Gae Cho-shim"—like some kind of political slogan. Then I suddenly remembered that it meant "Beware of dog." I turned to Kiesler. "Beware of dog."

"I don't see any dog."

"On the wall."

"Picture of a dog?"

"No, it's written out in han-gul."

"Then it's Greek to me," he said with a laugh. "If it ain't on the list, I don't know it. I forgot all that other crap."

"I was just thinking, you know, it was nice to be able to understand something like 'Beware of dog.' "

"You need to know more than that, you get stranded out here in the boonies, soldier. Can't make much headway goin' around yelling, 'Beware of dog.' They'd put you away."

"I have other phrases. I haven't forgotten everything we learned at language school."

"But they taught you North Korean there. All those teachers came down from the north. That's why we can't follow what the gooks are saying, and that's why, when we try to speak to them, they curse us."

"It's nice to be able to read something."

Kiesler looked back through the rear window. "The Koreans eat dogs. Maybe it's the name of a restaurant."

I should not have laughed. A white-haired woman sitting in front of us turned around and scowled. To the woman sitting next to her, she said in Korean, very slowly, "Americans are worse than dogs"—as if she knew the exact speed of my listening comprehension.

I looked at Kiesler. He had not understood. Perhaps, by the end of my tour, I would revert to complete ignorance of the language. Only one week after we had finished the Korean course, and they were still cutting orders for me to go down to Security School in Texas, I ran into one of my teachers in downtown Monterey. He asked me a simple question in Korean, "How are you today?" and I answered him in French.

"You ever eat dog?" Kiesler asked. I shook my head. "How about monkey? Listen to this. Brenda and I once went to this restaurant over in Ansong. We were the only Americans. Anyway, the house specialty was monkey. Monkey brains, actually. We didn't order it but we watched the people at the next table. This restaurant had a special kind of table where the monkey— a live monkey, by the way—where this monkey sits on some kind of stove with his head sticking up through the middle of the table. Can you picture that?" With his hands he made a tabletop around his neck, then imitated how a nervous monkey might look around, his mouth making an O shape. "The people sit around the table waiting for the monkey to get hot, then they start whacking it on the head with these long wooden spoons and the brains go flying. Kind of noisy—until the monkey finally dies."

We stepped off the bus near the train station and walked the last mile. Kiesler told me I had to pick up the return bus here before midnight. "I don't think you want to stay over. The spare bed is broken. And the hotels in this town, I think you'd have to speak Korean to be understood, to get a decent room and such."

P'yong-Taek had tree-lined streets and nice houses—or, at least, nice walls, nothing spray-painted on them, behind which

I assumed the houses would be nice. It could have been America except for the flavor of smoke coming out the chimneys—a kind of charcoal peculiar to Korea. The Kieslers lived at the end of a cul-de-sac, a house larger than the others, with a television antenna protruding above the red tile roof. But what threw me most of all was the red Corvette parked in the driveway. It had military plates and a cardboard sign in the window—some kind of curse written in broken Korean, certain letters backwards, others upside down. Inside the house, Brenda and Jack were laughing, watching TV.

"Sonofabitch got here first," Kiesler said.

It was that blond CIA guy, of course, who sat on the living room couch next to Brenda. "Father Knows Best" was on TV, dubbed in Korean. The father sounded like Robert Young, though a bit gruff, and the actress who had dubbed Jane Wyatt's lines seemed much too hysterical, saying "Ai-Goo" ("Oh dear") every other word. I guess Jack and Brenda were laughing about that. The youngest child in that TV family— Cathy?—cried out, "Ah-bo-jee! Ah-bo-jee!" in such a pathetic and hopeless way that one could picture, just listening to the sound track, some dirty-faced urchin running through the streets of An-Jong-Ri wailing for her father.

At first, Jack didn't seem to know who I was, and we had never been formally introduced. He must not have recognized me in civilian clothes.

Jack wore a mixture: blue jeans and a green fatigue shirt, with the name ripped off above the right picket, unbuttoned halfway down his chest so I could see his gold chains. Sunglasses. He was smoking Korean cigarettes, and from the looks of the ash tray, he had already gone through several packs.

Then his mind clicked as to who I was, and he said, "Yo-po, yo-po, soldier, you buy those pants in An-Jong-Ri?"

"No, I bought them back in the States."

"Maybe you lost weight or something?"

"Could be," I said.

"I got an *excellent* tailor in An-Jong-Ri." He tugged on his shirt collar. "For those occasions when I have to dress up."

"I can't think of any occasions when I might have to," I said.

"Then I'll keep my tailor's name a secret."

By the end of "Leave It to Beaver," a dozen empty beer bottles crowded the colonial coffee table. The place looked as if it had been furnished out of a Sears catalog. At least there was no round table with a hole in the middle, for a monkey's head to stick out of.

I asked Brenda where the nice furniture came from.

"My father shipped it from California. It wasn't that much."

"What will you do with it when you leave?"

"Who said we were leaving?" She was smashed, a happy drunk. The bridge game was a joke. Brenda didn't know when to lead from the board or from her hand. Most of the time she skewed the bidding so that she could be the dummy, and she stood behind Jack and rubbed his shoulders and played with her hair while he wasted his high cards early in the hand. Kiesler and I took almost every trick, and he seemed too involved in the game to care what Brenda and Jack were doing.

The blond guy never said anything in English, except "I play the ROK generals for money." He must have been in debt to them.

Brenda laughed and said, "Funny money or real money?"

Jack took off his sunglasses and squinted at me. "Never mind. It's classified."

Brenda rubbed her eyes, and blue eye shadow came off on her knuckles. Her face was tanned and wrinkled. She looked ten years older than her picture, which made her a good fifteen years older than her husband, or he had preserved his unwrinkled looks by remaining forever poker-faced.

Jack left at ten and we played three-handed bridge for a while. I showed them how, for I had played this version with my parents after my grandfather died. Brenda kept laying down her cards, face up. She fiddled with her dark brown hair, twisted it up in a bun, then let it fall to her shoulders. Finally she went to bed, and Kiesler walked me to the bus stop.

"I know it stops here at eleven-fifteen. I used to ride this baby six nights a week—commuting in for the midnight shift."

"I don't see why you'd work the midnight shift."

"First three months, they had me on the headphones." He slapped the side of his head. "Then I told them I was losing my hearing. In both ears. What was really going on was, I was losing my fuckin' *mind*, brain cells dripping out the ears. Anyway, for whatever reason, I was screwing up the numbers half the time. Five numbers, then two seconds dead air, then five more. OH-YUKE-EE-PAL-OH. SA-OH-EEL-YUKE-EE. All fuckin' night listening to those fuckin' Martians. Sometimes it was a woman's voice. Sometimes a man. Sometimes you couldn't tell. But I kept thinking, I could have learned what I needed for this goddamn job *in one weekend*. Fuckin' Army. And when they shifted me over to the vault, I found out the guys with the headphones were being doubled by Korean nationals over in the next building. And we were only using *our* guys' numbers for back-up, so my headphone job never really meant nothing, and they never had to rely on my numbers to break the code. All those fuckin' five-digit numbers. Jack told me all that."

"No wonder those guys drink so much."

"I try to tell them, 'It don't mean nothing,' but they're too far gone, those guys with the headphones. Just remember the next time you're wondering why you're sitting in that fucking vault—*It don't mean nothing.*"

An old Datsun drove by slowly. We could hear the car radio going, tuned to an American station.

"Where did Brenda learn her Korean?"

"Born here."

"What?"

"Only kidding. But don't you think she looks Korean?"

"Not particularly."

"She has gone native and passed. She gets a kick out of it, strolling around the city in her kyong-bok gown. She loads up her eyes with a ton of goo, so you can't really tell her apart from the slants." I was surprised to hear him speak of her that way, but of course, he had had plenty to drink, and she had possibly provoked him.

"But where did she learn her Korean?" I was almost certain that Jack had taught her, but I kept my theory to myself.

"What happened was she learned it from living out here in P'yong-Taek. It was just a practical thing. She watched Korean TV all day while I was at work and it sunk in somehow.

Otherwise, she's actually illiterate. So's Jack. He's always getting lost because he can't read the signs. He spent a weekend in Pusan once, thinking he was in Inchon." Kiesler stopped to look at the bus-stop sign. "At least I can read the goddamn signs."

"I'd think he'd do all right asking directions. He spits it out like a native."

"Now this is the craziest story. You can believe it if you want, or check it out later with Big Daddy. But this is what Jack told me. He grew up in L.A. in some ghetto. He thought all the kids he was playing with were Chinese. I mean, his family was really ignorant, Okies or something. He didn't know the difference. The people in the ghetto spoke something called Han-Goo-Mal. He thought that was just a weird Chinese dialect. He got pretty good at it, better than his English, in fact, which he could barely read or write. So about ten years ago, he enlists right out of high school and they send him to Korea, and he finds out he's totally fluent in Korean. When he re-enlists, they send him to OCS and then somehow, he never told me exactly how, he got turned into a spy. He's got this country by the short hairs."

"Do you envy him?"

"No. I hate Korea. Glad to be going home."

I had all kinds of questions. And Kiesler seemed in an answering mood, loosened up by all those bottles of Crown Maek-joo. But then the jitney bus stopped in front of us, and Kiesler banged on the glass door. The driver laughed, finally opened it. There were no other passengers.

"Yo-po-say-o," Kiesler said. "Looky here, Pak-Sang, you take care of my number one friend here, he gotta go home and work the midnight shift and keep ol' Han-gook safe for democracy."

Pak-Sang smiled. No teeth. "No problem, Captain."

"I go shopping for you in PX next Saturday, okay?"

"No problem, Captain, Number hana."

"Kamsa-hamneeda," Kiesler said, thanking him.

When we passed the train station, Pak-Sang stopped the bus and honked but the old man standing there waved—or gave some kind of power salute—then sat down on a bench. "He gonna catch cold out there." The old man's feet were tied up in burlap.

We drove through the outskirts of town, then picked up speed on the main road to An-Jong-Ri.

"I live in An-Jong-Ri," Pak-Sang said. "Nice big house, three bedrooms and one indoor bathroom, American style. I used to work where you work. Retired now, U.S. government pension. I know what you do for work." He laughed.

"Okay, what do I do?"

He pointed to his ear and shook his head.

"What is that supposed to mean?"

"Big secret."

He kept driving, and I could see his face in the rear-view mirror. He was chewing some kind of tobacco. "Snowing hard now," he said, and turned on the wipers. Though he knew I was a "linguist," he spoke nothing but English to me.

To the east, the lights of An-Jong-Ri saturated the snow, giving it an orange tint far up into the sky. We were three miles from the village, and I could see the skeleton of the church on the hillside off to the left, a dinosaur profile against the orange glow. "What is that?" I asked my driver. "Methodist church," he said. "But they all gone now. Too bad. They move to Ansong, I think. We don't got no church in An-Jong-Ri." As we circled the bottom of the hill, I kept looking up towards the church. At the first crossroads in the village, two people stood on the corner, and Pak-Song stopped to let them on. When he got a closer look, he decided not to open the door. A Korean woman and a black American soldier. The young woman pounded on the glass door, screaming curses in Korean. Pak-Sang laughed and peeled out, spraying gravel and slush. "They can walk. They're lazy people, all of them."

I said, "Stop," and Pak-Sang let me out at the next corner, more than a half mile from the main gate. I wished to orient myself towards the skeleton church, but it was a good mile in the other direction.

I climbed a different hill, angling through a neighborhood of shanties. One of them seemed cobbled together entirely from old signs—on the largest, I could see the smiling face of a young woman, and then some words that meant nothing to me, and I could hear people talking inside. I understood nothing but

isolated fragments: "I" and "you" and "thank you" and perhaps "tomorrow." At the edge of this poor settlement, I had to
duck under barbed wire, and I turned around and looked out
over the village. The clubs that catered to American soldiers
were still lit up, their signs blurred through the snow. I could
just barely make out the neon palm tree of the Doral Club, the
red dice of The Sands, and I worried that I would lose my sense
of direction, never get back inside the gate, so I came back
down the hill, following a different path through the club
district.

Now I worked alone in the vault. Kiesler had gone back to
the States two weeks ago, presumably to enroll in law school in
California, where he would train himself to go after the likes of
Daniel Ellsberg. Without Kiesler's company, the vault work
took less than a half hour a day, and I read novels the rest of the
time. I didn't get out much, though the weather had turned
warmer and everybody talked about spring.

It was about time for Jack to drop by with his illicit photos;
you could never predict the exact day. Brenda's picture still sat
on the desk, as if Kiesler had packed in a hurry. In fact, he hadn't
packed at all, simply did not show up for work one day, and then
I looked at the Rocky Mountain calendar and saw that all the
days had been crossed off, and I supposed it was my turn to start
counting, although you never said anything about being "short"
until you were under a hundred and I was closer to two
hundred.

Sometimes I got so cold in there I kept the vault door open
a crack, and I could listen to the guys in the main listening
room, their typewriters clicking five digits at a time. Two-
second pause, five more digits, then another pause, all of the
typewriters synchronized, as if all the headphone guys were
tuned to the same station. I rolled my chair to the doorway and
looked out into the room. Occasionally one of the MP's would
come by and say something like, "Please be more careful," and
then close the vault door for me.

I dusted Brenda's photo. I took it out of the frame and
looked at the back. Someone had written, JUNE 1965.

There was a knock on the door and then, "Yo-po, yo-po, you

guys, the fuckin' bookmobile is makin' its monthly rounds."

"Come on in, Jack." I tossed the book I was reading into a desk drawer.

"Just the one of you, huh?"

"For now, anyway. Supposed to be some guy coming out of language school in a month. Or security school."

"How do you know it's a guy? They got girls now in language school. I seen their pictures."

He picked up Brenda's photo and turned it over so that it faced up. Laid down the packet of photos. "Not much in here this time, just a couple of heads blasted off and one set of memory-code generators. Not much activity. Must be all of them staying home to celebrate Kim II-Sung's birthday. Budget cuts, possibly. We got budget cuts, too. They cut off my credit card for gas. Can you believe that shit?"

He sat down in the chair at Kiesler's old desk. "Your ex-buddy always kept this desk perfectly clean. You gotta be careful you don't keep your desk too clean. Some officer comes in here and sees a neat desk, he figures you spend too much time on your housekeeping duties."

"No officers ever come in here," I said. "Except for you, of course."

"Who ever told you I was an officer?"

"Kiesler did."

"You guys were never busy enough, you had to gossip."

"Then tell me, Jack, are you even a soldier? I mean what the heck *are* you anyway?"

"Classified."

"Where the heck do you live? Seoul? P'yong-T'aek?'

"Why don't you shut your big fat mouth, soldier. Don't you know this place is wired, every fuckin' square inch of it?" Somewhere, Jack had learned "command voice," and to hear him speak that way shook me up. I stared at him for a good minute.

"I can't talk in here," he finally whispered, cupping his hand over my ear.

THEN, LET'S MEET IN A CLUB, I wrote on a scrap of paper.

T'MOROW NITE AT 8, THE DORAL, he scribbled his

answer, smiled, whispered good-bye, got up, and slipped through the crack in the door.

The Doral was supposed to look like a fancy American night club, but the mirrored globe above the bar was missing a dozen pieces of glass, the vinyl chairs smelled like benzene, the barmaids needed major dental work, and the potted palms had been dead three years.

There was this black-haired guy waving at me from one of the tables. I couldn't tell if he was Korean or American until I was ten feet away, and then I could see it was Jack wearing a wig.

I sat down across from him.

"This the usual get-up?" I asked.

"There's nothing I can do about the eyes, except wear sunglasses, and the gooks don't go for that. They think it's a black American custom, so they detest it."

He slipped on a pair of shades anyway.

"You still don't look Korean," I said. I had no idea why he needed to look Korean. His nose was too long.

"But maybe a half-breed, huh? Left behind after the Korean War? Raised in an orphanage."

"I suppose. As long as you kept your wig on, though it's a pretty obvious wig, if you ask me."

He reached across the table and grabbed my arm. "Hey, man, this is just a lark, you know? I don't need to look Korean. I'm okay with the way I look."

He whipped off his wig. His real hair was only an inch long now, almost shaved to the bone on the sides.

"Whoa!" I said. "They force you to do that?"

"*Who* force me?"

"I dunno. Whoever forces you to do anything. . . ."

"Well, somebody does, though I haven't met the man as of yet. Starting next Monday, I work out of HQ company right here in Humphreys. In an office, *in* uniform."

"You unhappy about that?"

"No. I'm a lifer. I do what they ask."

He put the wig back on. "Lots of guys have wigs. I know where I can get a better one."

"Where?"

"Sorry, soldier, but that's classified. Anyway, you don't need a wig the way I do."

We sipped our drinks, mostly ice now. Jack surveyed the bar, watching the waitresses do their work. A tall, big-breasted girl came on duty. She wore a white silk blouse and short black skirt, and her abundant hair was piled on top of her head in a huge French twist. Jack grabbed my arm. "That one," he said. "You know who I think she looks like?"

"Connie Francis?"

"Who the hell is that?"

"A singer, a movie star."

"No, I'm talkin' about somebody you know, an old friend of yours. Brenda Kiesler."

"I barely know the woman. Knew the woman."

"Of course, that girl is not really Brenda," he said. "I think she's named Julie. But let's suppose our old friend Brenda hadn't gone home with Frankie. Let's just suppose."

"What are you talking about?"

"Nothing important. But let's suppose Brenda wanted to stay in the country, for whatever reason. Let's say she took a liking to it. Can't you just picture her sashaying around the Doral, servin' drinks to the Mee-Gook soldiers?"

"Why would she wanna do that?"

"Money. These girls make damn good money."

"I meant, why would she wanna stay in Korea?"

He was looking at me with his shades on. He started picking his teeth with one of those cellophane-decorated toothpicks, and I could see he had not taken advantage of his dental benefits. His teeth were tan colored, with several broken off, others missing. "You know, soldier," he said, "I'm not gonna be stoppin' by the vault anymore. There ain't no more doubled agents comin' on line. I hope you got some kind of scam figured out, so the officers think you're busy, otherwise you gonna be sittin' in the next room with headphones on, takin' down five-digit code. That kind of shit. They trained you for that contingency, didn't they?"

"I have very poor hearing," I said.

"Ha, ha!"

"I can't understand Korean."

"Just a waste of taxpayers' money. You and old Kiesler. Can't even count to ten. How much time you got left in the service?"

"Five, six months."

"You might make it. But I pity the next guy who has to go into the vault. They trained him to do nothin', poor sucker." His face was expressionless. His pity was entirely rhetorical.

I stared him down. "Why would she wanna stay in Korea?"

"Who? Oh, Brenda. What do *you* know? What do you really know about anybody in the world? You don't know Kiesler. What kind of guy do you think he was? Did you think he was cool? Or did you think he was a complete asshole?"

I didn't answer.

"Brenda was cool," he said. "Let's just leave it at that." He summoned the large waitress, who did look a lot like Connie Francis, though under all that eye makeup, she still had oriental eyes. Jack started talking to her in rapid-fire Korean, looking at me, pointing at me, then tapping her on the arm. She walked away a couple steps, then turned around and laughed. She looked at me, shook her head.

"What was that all about?"

"I told her you thought she was a big movie star."

I said nothing.

"Five, six months," He shook his head. "I don't know. You might make it. But you got big problems, man. I think I gonna have to take you out every night and teach you some real Korean."

Recapitulation

BY PERRY GLASSER

Dorothy's father went mute. Linguini slid from his fork to his plate, the fork suspended in the general vicinity of his ear. His gray eyes glazed, then glowed, and his lips wrestled with a smile that would not go down.

Dorothy twisted to look, but through the dim jungle of ferns and coleus saw only candles, couples, stained beams, aproned waitresses and sweating silver wine buckets. Daddy's New York restaurants always were down or up a flight of stairs, lush caves off street level, places you could dump your drink into the soil of something that grew.

His napkin stabbed at his lips. "You see that woman over there? In the blue suit? I haven't seen her in fifteen, maybe sixteen years. Look at her, you'd never guess she'd once been a star in the circus."

The woman sipped white wine and listened intently to the man with her. Gems—nothing gaudy—decorated her neck and fingers. She wore just a hint of makeup. A woman who knew the difference between style and fashion, she could be thirty, she could be fifty. Like a stone on her chest, Dorothy felt the crushing inadequacy of her youth.

Naturally, at that precise moment, the woman's eyes found them.

But Daddy was already up and tugging at Dorothy, giving her no chance to release the Diet Pepsi served with a twist of lime, a mocktail for the kid.

The woman's delicate hand folded about Daddy's. "Michael,

it's been too long." Her voice was more cultured than her pearls. Her hair was perfect. Absolutely jet black eyes. The palest pink nail polish. Maybe, right after Daddy brought her back to the dorm, Dorothy would throw herself off the roof.

"Is this . . . you must be Dorothy."

Dorothy gave a little wave, wiggled her fingers, felt like an idiot, and put her hands behind her back. She nodded, smiled, and wondered why on God's green earth Daddy couldn't have given her the smallest hint about this place, maybe she'd have worn anything but this stupid T-shirt and ratty razor-slit jeans. She might at least have tied back her hair, which, loose, looked as if small furry things spent winters curled behind her ears.

"Dorothy, this is Tricia Walters."

Tricia Walters introduced her friend whose silk shirt was white on white. Daddy explained to "Trish" that for a few days he was visiting Dorothy, his Columbia sophomore. "No one calls it Barnard, anymore," Dorothy said, felt lame, and took a vow of silence.

Little questions were asked. Tricia Walters had knocked around, then came to rest. Daddy had settled in St. Paul, mourned, and remarried. After a while, Trish said, "It's been a real treat seeing you, Michael. You look the same."

Daddy laughed.

"No, Michael. You look terrific."

And then the first funny thing happened. Daddy, who liked to laugh, stopped laughing. He became solemn.

The second funny thing happened as they returned to their table. Trish and her friend stood, and that sultry, cultured voice, maybe an octave above Jackie Onassis's, but rougher, called, "Dorothy," and when Dorothy turned, Trish thrust a cocktail napkin into her hand. "That's my phone number," she said. The woman in blue smiled at her. Those black eyes could surely kill.

The third funny thing happened half an hour later over dessert, which neither Daddy nor Dorothy ever ate but Daddy nevertheless always ordered. Dorothy said, "She knew Mother, didn't she? She must have. From the time when we were a family in New York. When I was a baby." And Daddy said, "In a way. But not really. They never met." He stirred his coffee, one sugar, no cream. Dorothy withdrew the cocktail napkin from her shirt pocket. The phone number had been written with a fountain pen, and the black ink had bled. "Do you want this?" she said.

"No. I don't want it. Absolutely don't want it. No way."

His unprovoked sharpness told it all. "You were lovers," she blurted out.

Daddy's baleful gray eyes snagged her. "Boy, Dor, you are some piece of work for nineteen."

Mother died the clear April afternoon her unimpeded car had taken flight off a two-lane blacktop Minnesota road into a wall of unyielding pine trees. Suicide? Recklessness? Maybe she'd swerved to avoid a deer. Her death was inexplicable. Dorothy had been four.

Mother's only legacy was Dorothy's anger and her fuzzy memories of blankets, warmth, a soft voice, an emerald green dress, and an aroma Dorothy thought special, until at twelve she disgustedly discovered it was nothing more exotic than Johnson and Johnson's Baby Powder. That had seemed Mother's final betrayal.

At thirteen, a dark, lonely time, Dorothy studied old photographs. In the photos lay hints of her future. Her height would be that; her bust would be so; her face's shape would finally settle there.

The history professor's precious daughter was gifted with a good mind, but school sucked to the roots. At fourteen Dorothy came home at two in the morning and her guts sprayed a six-pack of Budweiser over the living room rug. Daddy called it experimentation—he always indulged her—but had he known everything, he might have been less complacent. Being grounded now and then never inhibited visits by Bobby Williams, who bicycled to her house, scrambled over the ledge of her ground floor window, smoked a little dope, and got his brains screwed out.

But Daddy believed his daughter was a princess savant, and so, two years ago, Daddy had made phone calls. The old-boy network extended into Columbia, at least for a provisional admission. Dorothy learned the advantages of extended sobriety and chastity. She'd surprised everyone but herself by making dean's list.

So now that she was nearly at peace with herself, and now that she had grown into believing Daddy was no fool and so must have known more about her than she ever thought, and now that she could actually *like* her father for giving her the rope she'd needed, now a hitherto completely unknown factor in the funnel of events that V'ed down to creating the finished and final Dorothy had been made available to her.

It was disturbing.

Dorothy felt no loyalty to her mother, no sense of outrage. Other than die, what had Mother ever done?

Cold-lit words like fireflies flitted through her head. *Paramour. Tryste. Rendez-vous.* Delicious words. Here was boring Daddy the professor running around with the Girl on the Flying Trapeze. As an amusement, meeting Tricia Walters would beat all hollow sophomore acne cases who want to read poetry naked. And though Daddy wouldn't know, Tricia Walters and Mother might once have met. Courageous women did that.

Could Dorothy learn such courage? The moment she doubted it, Dorothy became absolutely certain that she was destined to do so. She saw immediately that in the absence of her mother the coward, this woman her father had once loved, this Trish Walters, was the key to that realm of confidence, self-possession, and certainty that opened only to those who willingly stared unflinchingly into the unadorned face of their own motives.

A call to the cocktail napkin number was answered by a secretary. Dorothy immediately hung up. Tricia Walters was Sultana Jewelry.

That same afternoon, boldly, with no appointment, Dorothy popped into Sultana. She was dressed for anything, a yellow dress and black belt, black shoes, black sweater. She felt like a hornet.

Tricia Walters took her in and cancelled the rest of her day.

The huge windows of Tricia Walter's corner office overlooked most of Manhattan, river to river, facing north. An opalescent sky dripped cranky rain. Rich ice-blue carpet covered all the floor except for a humming air vent. An isolated, scrawny plant barely survived in its terra cotta pot; a white sofa faced the desk and a low mahogany table. The desk itself was antique, French provincial. The room was cold and stark, Dorothy thought.

They spoke, and Dorothy's resolve to confront this woman and by force of will require her to reveal all evaporated in the faint sandalwood scent floating on the office air. When Dorothy exhausted her store of college anecdotes, in her battery-acid voice Tricia talked about business, her factory in Queens, and how she'd come to be here. It sounded like the canned speech it surely was. Ten years had taken her from pinky rings made from bent silver spoons peddled on street corners to the twenty-ninth floor.

The office became murky and gray. In the gathering shadows beyond a high intensity lamp's narrow cone of illumination, they sat, each invisible to the other.

"But what I miss is the circus," Tricia Walters said suddenly. Her chair spun slightly, and Dorothy would not have been surprised if the woman had thrown herself back, kicked off her spike heels, and thrown her bare feet onto her desk. "I suppose your father never mentioned me."

Dorothy needed to say nothing.

"That's not surprising." From her desk she took a Balkan Sobraine cigarette. The flame of her lighter flared a globe of golden illumination on the older woman's face, but then she leaned back into the shadows. An unblinking firefly, the burning ember of her cigarette floated in the darkness. Her ashtray whirred and sucked in smoke. "Right after your father got the job in Minneapolis, that's a year or so after you were born, I joined the circus. That sounds ridiculous, I know, but it was an accident, something that came and took me away more than I sought it out. I'd quit college—which was where I'd met your father, he was my teacher—and I started making jewelry. I sold the stuff out of a suitcase on street-corners, at fairs. You know, the Feast of Saint This or the Blessed That. Fried sausages. Fried dough. Beer. And the little waspy kid who was a throwback to the sixties and sold trinkets. One of the fairs hired a carnival troupe, the guys with the rides and the fun houses, and I decided to go with them. I'd have been about your age, maybe a little older. I think I was twenty-two.

"We were in Rochester, New York, when the carnival hooked up with a circus, a real flea-bite outfit. We all traveled together. A few trailers, a bus, and two trucks. One tent, one tiger, three clowns, eight horses, and an elephant. We were doing a night in some church yard when the Amazing Mario, our knife thrower, came to me and explained that Loretta, his wife, partner, and target, was throwing up. Did I want to stand in? Catch a few knives?

"I tell Mario he is crazy, what do I know about it? But he says all I have to do is look pretty and he'll walk me through the act. Fifteen minutes. I tie back my hair and I squeeze into Loretta's outfit, all rhinestones and spangles, fish-net stockings, a pom-pom on my butt, and enough herring bone to push my boobs over my head. I swear, you could set dinner service for two on my chest when I wore that thing. I'd breathe again when the act was finished.

"The music comes up—we didn't have an orchestra but a tape-deck and big speakers, that's how rinky-dink this show was—Mario grabs my hand, and the next thing I know I'm smiling at a few hundred people, my hands in the air, my feet in sawdust, and Mario is juggling knives. In case you ever wondered, kid, I am here to tell you those things are real. They weigh about two pounds each, nine inches of tempered steel. I don't know what to do with myself except smile and dance around, which it turns out is exactly what I'm supposed to be doing. Mario turns me sideways, sticks a cigarette between my teeth, and like a shadow I feel the knife go by. Thunk. It's in the wood backstop and I've got tobacco shreds on my lips.

"Mario grabs my hand and we bow, and I am sure I have lost my mind. I have seen Mario and Loretta do this and I know what the finale is. We build to it. Mario throws knives with his lip. He throws knives with his foot. He throws knives blind-folded. He throws big knives. He throws small knives. Mostly what I am doing is setting up balloons and candles as targets when I am not pointing at Mario, but even though I am smiling until my cheeks hurt, there's a part of me that wants to run off and hide. See, I know how this ends.

"The act goes on and on and then Mario cues the drum roll. The house lights dim, and two guys in white tights come out.

"They boost me onto the circular backstop and strap me in. It's a grooved oak table top splintered where knives have hit it. They fasten a leather strap across my waist, another at each ankle, and one more for each wrist. My arms are stretched over my head. The straps are stained dark, and I think how Loretta has sweated here eight or ten shows a week. I look like a rhinestone saint ready for martyrdom. One of the stage hands who will turn the wheel whispers to me to keep smiling, and not to worry because all the stays are controlled by a single release. 'Keep your eyes closed, kid, you'll be fine,' he says.

"But I can't do that. I try, and my eyes pop right open. I'm not nervous. I'm excited. This is great! I think. This is the greatest thing that ever happened to me. They tilt the thing totally vertical and light sparklers all along the rim. Rubes don't know that because the thing spins, the fire is no danger. I'm in the center, and the flash and heat go out from centrifugal force.

"Mario begins to throw. Our shills in the audience start it off, but the rubes get the idea quick enough. They count. 'One,' he places the toughest knife early, before the thing spins too fast, right between my thighs. Then he slips on the blindfold. The world is whirling. All the people in the seats are a blur, upside-down and then right-side up. The tent lights spin around me. Colors run. Spotlights turn in orbits. Pink spots. Red spots. White spots. Music so loud, the bass vibrates through me. 'Two.' 'Three.' And there are two more knives, one at each side of my head. Mario throws them two at a time. I smile like a lunatic, all a target can do. I smell horse piss and the iron-stink of the sparklers, and I hear the groan and creaks of the backstop's axle. 'Four.' 'Five.' And now there are knives bracketing my hips. Faster and faster the backstop spins. I'm riding The Wheel of Death. Blood fills my head. I can't close my eyes. Knives six and seven surround my left ankle, but by now I am a marble in a kaleidoscope, and I don't hear the audience roar or count because it seems to me the colors make the noise. I'm at the bottom of a roaring whirlpool that has caught the rainbow. But I can hear my own heartbeat, because my heart has lodged in my skull. Thump-thump. Thump-thump. I think, 'Am I screaming?' I want to, but can't. Screaming is not part of the act. People howl for us. The sparklers flare. I'm held in a hot red spot. I never hear or see the eighth and ninth knives. Faster and faster, the world goes round and round."

She paused and lit a second cigarette. Her slim hand hesitated over her partly unbuttoned silk blouse before finally resting at the base of her delicate throat. "One night, I climbed up on a spinning table and a mad Armenian threw knives at me."

Later that week in an overheated room of the Butler Library, Dorothy pondered Strindberg's *Ghosts,* looked up, and across the table peering at her from beneath the emerald shade of the table lamp were a man's two eyes. Two scenes and a dozen pages later, the eyes still examined her. Bottle-green, they sucked in light.

A graduate student at Teacher's College, Psych and Counselling, Damon was twenty-six, was pleased to be back at school full-time after three years of elementary school teaching, five years of marriage, and six months of divorce. Dorothy learned that much walking through rain to the West End Bar, and during three cups of coffee she learned more, all of it insignificant beside the fact that she felt within her something absolutely new, something that for her had no name and no precedent, something that had ridden on the aroma of wet wool emanating from his coat. His beard curled, and, incredibly, along with sparkling droplets of rain held a wisp of gray. Here was a man shaped by sadness, so different from what she'd known—boys, eager and shallow. He talked about pipe briars treated with whiskey, his thick hands before his face shaping air into gnarled wood.

That evening in his apartment redolent with tobacco, they drank wine and listened to the measured strains of a violin concerto, and since he never made any move toward her, never so much as brushed her arm, barely shook her hand at the dormitory lobby when he took her home, since nothing she expected had happened, she found herself more and more impatient to hear from him again.

Friday, she was strangled by Othello. Bent backward off a

plank resting on two sawhorses, an actor's hands at her bared throat, his body massive over hers, Dorothy's eyes rolled as she protested Desdemona's innocence, and when her coach urged, "*Scream*," blood filled her head. She was swept away in the flood of Desdemona's final terror made her own. She shrieked, gurgled, and totally surrendered to the moment, finding within herself black wells from which she drew despair and passion unlike any she had any right to know. Flushed, exhausted, drained, she finished to applause, vaguely frightened by the inner alien she had summoned and unleashed.

That same night Damon found her. Hours later, she took him, so savage, fierce, and desperate an act that she astonished herself. In the morning, by the thin light filtered through her lover's bathroom's opaque window, in his mirror she examined the red places on her hip, chest and throat where his beard had rubbed her skin. She dressed quickly, left, and never awakened him.

Damon called three times more, but Dorothy arranged to be unavailable. The whole thing was entirely too dangerous.

For years, she drifted at the perimeter of theater, eventually boring in to a niche as an administrator. She became passionate about well-designed posters, press releases, and unions. Actors were inexplicable. Marvelous, wonderful, talented, but inexplicable.

Her father's childless second marriage ended in acrimony. Dorothy was unsurprised, but she was sorry for Daddy's troubles. When a time came that he was to be honored by his university, Dorothy did the dutiful thing. Arriving at the airport gate, as his arms enfolded her, through his coat's bulk she immediately felt precisely why his colleagues hastened to grant the honors ordinarily reserved for a man more senior.

At his home, not the house where Dorothy had grown up, as Daddy poured brandy, Dorothy set a hardwood fire. The alcohol warmed them. Faint color seeped into Daddy's face. "Cancer," he said, "I can live with it." And he smiled wanly and added, "For a while." They watched the fire.

The day after the testimonial dinner, Dorothy phoned New York. She would stay a month more.

Winter in Minnesota means early darkness. Brandy before the fire became a ritual. She told him about her career, her advancement, the occasional man who visited her life, none special. Yes, she thought herself fulfilled, as fulfilled as she could be. Daddy listened, his head nodding, falling to his chest, jerking upright, his fluttering eyelids losing the struggle until he slipped into deeper sleep, his legs wrapped in Canadian blankets, Daddy small in his big chair.

"You need to know more about your mother," he said the week before Dorothy's life would return her to New York. "There's a story or two from the time before we were married."

"We were part of a circle of friends, mostly men, boys, really, younger than you are now. Dating. We were students. She still lived with your grandparents. I lived alone. Once or twice a month these friends got together, in this one's house or in that one's. We played cards, poker mostly, but sometimes bridge or hearts.

"Your mother was a very serious card-player. She never allowed me to be her partner at bridge because she knew she'd be furious with me if we lost. Losing was unacceptable for her.

"And she was proud of being 'one of the guys.' This is before 'feminism' was an ism. Your mother adored being told she played poker as well as a man. And she did. Better, mostly.

"The end of one night we got a little punchy, a little crazy, and so someone dealt Acey-Deucey. Do you know the game?"

Dorothy shook her head.

Daddy sighed. "In poker you bet as you go, a certain amount each card, and you play against the other players. But in Acey-Deucey you play against the pot. Everyone puts up one dollar. The pack is shuffled, two cards are turned face up to each player in turn, and the player bets any amount up to the whole pot that the next card will fall between the first two. The best chance is an ace and a deuce, the highest and lowest cards. That's Acey-Deucey."

Dorothy nodded. It made no sense at all to her. His tired voice slurred, but he continued as though he were not fatigued.

"Some hands are simply unwinnable. You can't draw a third card between a five and a six, for example, but you still have to make a minimum bet. And the game can go forever because there's a player who never gets tired—the pot. If you decide to go home, even if everybody decides to go home, whose money is that in the middle of the table?

"That night the cards were treacherous. Someone would be dealt a king and a four, bet five dollars on what seemed a sure thing, and the next card would turn up a three. Four separate times a player was dealt ace-deuce, called 'pot,' which meant they bet the whole thing, and lost because another ace or deuce turned up. A tie doesn't win this game. The pot doubled, doubled and doubled again. We became grim. Lots of smoke. Quiet. Just the snap of the cards. The pot, you see, was winning.

"That was when your mother was dealt an ace and a deuce. She said, 'Pot,' right away, didn't even think about it, didn't count the money to see if she could afford it. That was her way. But the fellow who was dealing the cards, Bill, didn't turn the next card over. Instead, he said, 'Where's your money?'

"Your mom laughed. She thought Bill was joking. After all, we'd been playing poker with each others for years. 'I'll write you an I.O.U.,' she said.

" 'Nothing doing,' Bill said. You see, if he could make your mother bet less than the whole thing, why then he still had a chance at some of the money himself. All the other players agreed with Bill. They insisted your mother either have the money or bet less. They counted it. One hundred and twelve dollars. A lot of money for us then. I didn't have enough to lend her. No one else was willing to lend it to her.

" 'All right,' she said. 'If you want to be like that, I'll get it. No way am I letting this go by.' She said to me, 'Michael, watch that deck of cards,' swung on her pea-coat, and charged out the door. We heard her car start. She burned rubber all the way down the block. Nearly two o'clock in the morning but your mother went out into the night, leaving us to stare at each other and the tiny pack of cards at the table's center.

"Forty-five minutes later she returned. Her hair drooped over her eyes and she had six twenty dollar bills in her fist. Her face was flushed, her collar was around her ears, she had the final stub of a cigarette between her thumb and index finger, and her eyes were hard as marbles. She must have gone to her father, awakened him, told him the story, and he'd given her the money—he was a sport, your grandfather. To ask her father for a loan must have cost your mother a lot, a lot more than money. She'd spent years, her whole life, trying to prove to herself and the world that she was not 'Daddy's little girl.' I don't suppose you know anyone like that, do you?"

Daddy's laugh bubbled into a wet cough. He pulled his blankets tighter around his legs. Staring into the fire, he spoke slowly, savoring the memory being replayed before his eyes in the flames.

"She ground her cigarette into an ashtray, slapped the bills down on the table and said, 'Pot. The whole damn pot.' Bill turned up a nine. Your mother didn't smile. She didn't whoop. Nothing. Like she expected it, was entitled to it, knew it all along, and was angry with us for requiring her to demonstrate what was so plainly obvious. She stuffed big bunches of crumpled money, mostly ones and fives, into her pockets. Your mother never carried a purse.

"And then she left as abruptly as she'd returned. We heard her car engine, her tires squeal, and we sort of stupidly looked at each other.

"That night your mother and I stopped being boyfriend and girlfriend because that night I realized I'd have to marry her. She had a kind of strength I needed. That's a long, long time ago. Thirty years? More. I've never told you that story, have I?"

His unshaved chin fell to his chest. The brandy glass slowly slipped from his fingers and bounced on the thin carpet. His eyes were closed when, talking as much to the dying fire as to her, Daddy said, "Win or lose, no one with that much tenacity would drive off a road on purpose."

That summer, among Daddy's final effects, in the garage Dorothy found a sealed crate. One side had been crushed from the weight of book cartons that had rested on top of it. The box smelled of mildew and age. Sitting cross-legged on the concrete floor, she peeled the masking tape from the seams.

Photographs, the very same she'd studied when she was nine and ten and predicting her future. At twenty-seven, Dorothy had fulfilled her own worst adolescent expectations. She had grown into the form. Dorothy could have passed for her mother.

But when her mother had been her age, her mother had been dead.

Beside the photographs in the box, Dorothy found letters from her mother to her father. The historian could discard no written record. They were filed in chronological order. All were written before they were married. The pack of letters was bound with a black velvet hair ribbon.

Dorothy read three adolescent gushing avowals of devotion, became embarrassed, returned the three to their place in the pack, and then destroyed them all. It was easier to do than she could have imagined.

Everything she could do for Daddy was done. His ashes scattered, Dorothy drove her father's Buick—now hers—to the cemetery. She could no longer avoid the obligatory visit to her mother's grave.

Isolated, the plot somewhat separated from the others, it was not well-tended, though wild purple and white alyssum among the spare grass gave the site a settled look. She'd brought no flowers, wished she had, and promised herself she would when next she returned even as she acknowledged no such time would ever occur.

The midwestern August air was laden with the smell of dust and cut hay. The strong sun cast sharp shadows. Lowering herself to one knee, Dorothy brushed a dry twig from the small marker. Her fingertips traced the shallow letters etched in the smooth marble—name, dates, and "Loving Mother"—and Dorothy's lips moved soundlessly, bestowing on her mother her pardon.

Hours later, driving east, for no reason she understood she steered the Buick off the interstate. She found herself on a winding two-lane blacktop road lined on each side by towering pine trees. Her window down, fragrant summer air cooled by the forest's shadows washed over her. The Buick gathered speed. The roar of passing air grew. The unchanging horizon between the rows of trees rushed faster and faster toward her, drew closer and closer, while beside her what had been separate trees blurred to solid, narrowing walls. She was a leaf afloat on the waters in a steep flume, and the exhilarating rush and plunge quickened her heart. The world grew more and more dark, and then she shot forward into the dazzling light of a vast rolling plain. She allowed the car to coast to a stop, cut the engine, and stood in the dust by the side of the road. As far as she could see, fields of growing corn beneath the summer sun stretched to a horizon now limitless.

Wild Hearts

BY KAREN PETERSON

One time Maurita sang for six hundred miles. She was driving an old Buick across a plain of mesquite and creosote scrub. She kept the windows rolled down and she smoked cigarettes. She sang "Two More Bottles of Wine," she sang "Never Like This Before," she sang "Drown in My Own Tears." It was one of those days when the highway reflects the color of sky, when cars go floating over a blue shimmer before disappearing into the horizon. Maurita sang to keep the Buick's gray hood pointed straight at the shimmer.

She wore silver bracelets, three smooth circlets on her right arm and an engraved snake coiled around her left arm, the flattened head with its sliver of forked tongue at her wrist. This bracelet repelled men or else attracted them. A man's eyes might stop on the snake, or they might move up Maurita's arm, giving her a sense of its shape and its slenderness, a sense of her own tanned skin and dark hair, of her long neck, and the space she occupied, the way she filled a T-shirt, a tight denim skirt. She would wait for this to happen. Otherwise, she was just there—the way she was just there in the Buick, on the highway. In the Buick, with its red vinyl upholstery, which gave off its own heat.

Maurita was driving to meet Farley. Farley, who had lived with her before he took off in his van on a run across the border. Farley, who once told her, "Until we die, our lives hold possibility. What kind of possibility do you like best—the unreal weirdness or the random kind?" So when the envelope came in

102

the mail, she wondered what kind of possibility he was sending, along with the key and the address, written in black ink on a sheet of white paper. Two-forty-one Tortuga, in a city six hundred miles away. No matter how long Maurita stared at the squared-off letters of Farley's handwriting, at the paper and the way the paper had been folded, none of it told her anything.

She couldn't see any reason not to go. Her horoscope in the newspaper read: "By focussing on matters of communication, you can lift your life to a new plateau." She still had the money Farley gave her, and her choice of wheels—Farley's pick-up and his Buick parked in the front yard. Maurita packed up her clothes in pillow cases and paper bags. She took the boom box and tapes. The Buick had half a tank of gas, more than the pick-up.

She was singing "Anything for Love" as she drove across the wide, bleached-out plain.

It was dusk when Maurita drove into town, past the liquor stores, the fast-food restaurants and adult bookstores, their signs lit up in red and pink and yellow. She stopped at a gas station to ask for directions, her left arm resting on the rolled-down window, and the attendant—a soft-faced kid—staring at the silver snake. When she turned off the commercial strip, she drove down streets lined with dusty cottonwood trees, quiet streets where kids played ball, long-legged kids who stopped their games, moved to the curb to let her by, their shrill voices following after her.

Two-forty-one Tortuga was a small, box-like stucco house, its square of dried-up lawn enclosed by a chain-link fence. Farley's van was not parked in front. There were no lights on inside.

The latch on the gate rang against the metal post. The gate scraped the pavement. A dog barked in the neighbor's yard, a stubby white dog with a dark spot over one eye. He hurled himself against the chain-link fence, yapping frantically as Maurita came up the walk to the house. The key slid into the lock, turned easily. Maurita groped for a switch on the wall, then the room sprang into light, the couch and chair in slick black imitation leather, the frayed green carpet. She went through every room, looking for a sign of Farley. He had left no note. The bedroom closet and dresser drawers were empty. There was nothing on the kitchen counter, on the red formica table. No food in the refrigerator or cupboards. Nothing, except an empty beer bottle on the rim of the bathtub.

By the time Maurita went back outside, the lawn lay in deep shadow, the street lamp's yellow circle of light reaching only to its edge. The white dog barked again. Maurita was at the gate before she noticed the men in the yard on the other side. Two men, who might have been there when she drove up, only now stepping forward.

"Good evening," said one of them. "You looking for Farley?"

"You seen him around?" she asked.

"Not today." He stepped onto the sidewalk, a thin man wearing jeans, a wide belt, and no shirt. His skin was pale, chest smooth, almost hairless, and he kept up a patter, introducing himself, so glad to meet her, his name Terry and his friend—he waved towards the taller man—his friend's name was Clay, and they were sorry they didn't know where Farley might be, neither one of them having seen Farley for maybe a couple days.

Maurita opened the Buick's trunk. Then the taller man—Clay—was there at her elbow, scooping up paper bags and pillow cases in his long arms, helping her to carry everything in one trip, following her into the house, where he set her things down on the green carpet. She looked up at him, into eyes that were blue, the same pale shimmering blue she had seen on the highway all afternoon, the blue she now finally caught up to, stepped into, his eyes not stopping on the snake but taking her in all at once, like light on her skin. He was a big man, with big shoulders, his face planes and angles, high cheekbones, strong jaw. He reached out his hand, not quite touching her face, his fingers holding a shimmer of touch to her face.

"Farley's a lucky man," he said.

That was all. The screen door banged shut behind him. The dog barked. The gate scraped on pavement.

Maurita's horoscope read: "Take time to do everything thoroughly. The best part of your career is still to come." She read it in the newspaper that she bought every morning from the box on the corner. She had to walk past Terry's house to get to the corner. She noticed that his curtains were always drawn closed.

She read the article in the newspaper about the rash of dog killings by a person or persons unknown—five dogs found poisoned, an Irish setter shot through the head, a dalmatian hanged by his own leash from a tree. Dog owners were warned to avoid leaving their pets outside unattended. She read the article about a sharp increase in violent crimes committed in the city during the past month. The police chief was quoted. "People are not satisfied with their lives," he said. "There is a lot of pent-up frustration."

Maurita listened to tapes on the boom box while she waited for Farley. She sang along with "Burn That Candle." She sang "Heat Wave." For hours she sat on the slick black couch, looking out at the street. She watched the family next door, owners of the white dog and a battered red Plymouth with tailfins. She watched the kids throw sticks for the dog to chase.

One night, while she sat on the couch with the light turned off, the drapes and windows open, two men walked past on the sidewalk. Two men, the tall one dressed in dark clothes—no more than an outline against the dark street, but Maurita recognized him. It was Clay, walking next to Terry, whose bare chest shone pale in the darkness. They were laughing, and the white dog in the yard next door barked at them. Maurita saw Terry stumble, and Clay reach out his hand to Terry's shoulder. Clay lifted his other hand, a glint of bottle to his mouth. The words he said to Terry came to Maurita through the open window, like a line in a song. "You'll see what I'll do."

She watched them walk past her yard, stepping into the street lamp's circle of light before they passed out of sight. Then she took off her shirt. She let the night air move over her skin.

Her horoscope read: "You will have uncanny luck in finding lost objects."

She read an article in the paper about the arrest of Clayton Bartlett for the murder of his former girlfriend. Police said that Aileen Ross had been beaten and strangled, her body discovered shortly before midnight by an unidentified male friend who entered the apartment through an open door. Bartlett was arrested the next morning at the gas station where he was employed.

For days Maurita watched Terry's house. Then one morning, on her way back from the newspaper stand—the neighbor's white dog barking at her and wagging his tail—she saw Terry out on his front step, bare feet in the dust, a beer can in his hand.

"Hello," she called to him.

He lifted his beer in her direction, as if to toast her.

She hesitated, then walked up to him. "Your friend," she said.

"What about him? You want to know if he did it? Well, let me tell you something. He was too drunk to know if he did it or not. He don't remember a thing. He was probably too drunk to have done it, and he might even have been too fucking drunk to know if he *wanted* to do it." He stared down at his beer, tracing the rim of the can with one finger. "See, I was with him earlier that night. We'd been drinking all day. Tequila and beer. The lawyer asks how much, but I don't know. We had a bottle. We had a couple six-packs. The lawyer says it might make a difference. Only how the hell should I know how much? All I know is, I was supposed to go to work. I was on my way when I realized I was too wasted. I came home and crashed. Next thing I know, he's on the news."

"I saw him that night," said Maurita. "You too. Walking by."

Terry looked up at her, squinting against the light. "You saw us?"

"You looked drunk, all right. Both of you. And I heard you laughing. You sounded drunk."

Terry set his beer can down on the step. "You wouldn't be willing to testify to that, would you?"

The lawyer told her that her story would never stand up in court. He was a young man, big and blond, with a fleshy face, a fleshy, prominent chin. He wore glasses, and the eyes behind the glasses kept shifting from the papers on his desk to the silver snake on Maurita's arm. He counted off the reasons on his fingers. "You'd have to convince the jury you were able to recognize two men from a distance at night," he told her. "Two men you spoke to only once in a brief, casual conversation. You'd have to convince the jury you could tell from a distance that Clay was so drunk as to be not legally responsible for his actions. And you'd have to establish your credibility as a witness, even though you have no idea what time it was when you saw all this."

"I don't have a watch," said Maurita. "But I know what I saw."

The lawyer held up both hands, palms towards her. "I believe you, okay? It just won't play. A good cross-examination could raise too many doubts for the jury. You didn't see how much Clay actually drank. You didn't speak to him, so you don't know if he was incoherent or not. Maybe he and Terry were only a little drunk and they happened to stumble over some irregularity in the sidewalk. Or they might have appeared to be drunk because they were laughing. Maybe it was hours after they walked by your house when you looked out and saw two men who resembled them enough to be mistaken for them in the dark."

Maurita stood up. "Look, I don't have any stake in this. If you don't like what I saw, then I guess that's it."

"There is one more thing." The lawyer's eyes shifted back to the papers on his desk. "I talked to Clay after you called, and he asked to see you. He doesn't have family in town, so he hasn't been allowed any visitors yet. But if I say that you're helping me with the case, I could get you in—."

In the visiting room of the County Detention Center, Clay's eyes locked onto Maurita's. His eyes seized hold and took her with him, right out of the room, away from the pale green walls, the long steel green table with chairs on either side and the lawyer discreetly busy with his papers, away from corridors with loud footsteps, clanging doors, and into the light, the open air. "I can't tell you what it meant to me," Clay said to her. "That this beautiful woman I only met once came forward to offer her help. See, there's all these people I know, people who know me and some of them even owe me for something, and all of them are ready to testify against me. I'm not talking about Terry, but the rest of them, not giving me any benefit of the doubt. Hell, some of them will come right out and lie."

He was leaning towards her, hands flat on the table. That night in her living room, he had touched, almost touched, her face. Now his hands stayed on the table.

"I don't understand why they can't use your testimony," he said. "You know, it's like some kind of measure of how screwed up this world is, that a jury wouldn't believe you, who has nothing to gain by telling what you saw, and they would believe the people speaking and lying against me. Only—I don't want to waste time talking about that now. I mean, that's not what really matters. What's important to me is that you came forward. When I heard that you had, it was like a sign that I shouldn't give up hope. Which is why I asked my lawyer to bring you here. So I could thank you."

The light held that same pale blue shimmer. And she held his gaze—she was letting herself be held by his gaze with a sheer fall beneath them.

"I know I'm blurting everything out," he said. "Just when I don't want to come on too strong. See, when you're locked up all these hours—I mean, I know I'm in a serious situation. And now you're here, and there isn't much time, so I want to cut through the bullshit and tell you straight out. I hope you don't mind. But to me, you're like some pure, clear crystal with the light shining through. Look, don't get me wrong. Terry told me about this guy Farley. And he must've come back by now."

"Not yet," said Maurita.

"You haven't heard from him?" he asked. He leaned closer, over the table. "Well, he'll be back. He's not crazy."

Maurita smiled at him.

"I want to ask you something," he said. "But before I ask it, I think you have a right to know—well, it's true. What I told my lawyer. What I told Terry on the phone. I can't remember a thing about that night. I try to remember, but I can't. I'd tell you if I could. See, I couldn't lie to you. Because you're my crystal. And when I look at you, I don't know how to say this— I want to feel myself clear and pure next to you. Does that sound corny?"

She shook her head, still smiling.

"Listen," he said. "I don't want to put any pressure on you

to answer one way or another right now. I just want you to know how much it would mean to me if you could come back to see me again."

There was no reason for her to stop smiling, to take her eyes off his, to look down from where his eyes held her. No reason for her to refuse.

"Sure," she said. "I could come back."

She read that more dogs had been killed—four poisoned by hamburger laced with rat poison, two shot, and a dachshund knifed, slit open. An official at the Animal Control Board was quoted. "It might be an individual or maybe a group with a grievance against dogs," he said. "It might be someone with a sick mind. Whoever it is, they're preying on animals who are helpless to escape because they've been fenced in or staked. Please, if you love your pets, don't leave them outdoors unattended."

Maurita sat on the slick black couch, listening to tapes, singing along with the songs. She sang "A Thousand Times," and "If Anyone Falls." She was waiting for Farley, or else for a sign, so she listened and watched.

When she and the lawyer went back to see Clay, he told her that he thought about her at night. "I hope you don't mind," he said. "See, you've given me an image to hold onto. Something to keep me from sinking. Remember that night I first met you? How I brought your bags into your house and stood there, in your living room? I keep thinking, if I could just go back there, before any of this happened."

The next time she came to see him, he hardly seemed to notice she was there. He was telling the lawyer about the psychiatric evaluation testing. "That horseshit," he complained, his eyes darting in quick glances about the room, his fingers tapping on the table. "That multiphasic, that bipolar. They've been running these tests on me since I was eleven years old. They think I haven't figured them out by now? If I wanted to, I could make those fuckers think I'm a raving lunatic. But I'm not gonna play it that way."

"You know," said the lawyer. "It wouldn't hurt your case."

"What happened when you were eleven years old?" Maurita asked.

His eyes lifted to her then, the blue flashing at her, dazzling her. "See, I never could stay out of trouble," he said. "I always had to be trying stuff out. Like the time I set fire to my mother's kitchen curtains. I was four years old when I did that. I still remember those curtains. They were made out of some kind of shiny fabric, with a pattern of roosters. Rows and rows of little roosters, some of them right side up and some of them upside down. I just held a match to them and they went up. Weird. You know what I mean? You do some simple little thing and so much happens. All of a sudden, those curtains were like two sheets of flame, blowing out at me. Then my mother came in screaming. They finally sent me away when I was eleven."

He reached across to Maurita, his fingers to her left arm, moving over her skin to the silver snake, pressing the head of the snake down into her wrist. "You know what I'd like to do to you," he said.

"Clay," said the lawyer. "If she comes here with me under the pretext of helping with your case—"

"Okay, okay." He moved his hand away. Then suddenly he was smiling. "You know what else I'd like to do? I'd like to take you for a drive in your Buick. For a long drive, somewhere up in the mountains. I like cars. That's why I got a job at a gas station. Not because I couldn't get anything better. I just like to see people riding around in their cars. Where'd you get that Buick of yours anyway?"

"It's Farley's," she said.

"One time I hot-wired a Buick just like yours," he said. "Took it for a little ride. Didn't even get caught. Sometimes it seems like I got caught for everything I ever did. But I didn't get caught for that one."

His words came to her like the sign she'd been waiting for. A hot-wired Buick, just like hers. A Buick that opened up a tunnel between them, Clay's eyes pulling her into the tunnel. "You know, that night," he was saying. "That first night, when I was there in your house. I didn't really leave you that night. I didn't go out the door. I stayed with you. That's what I wanted anyway. You could tell, couldn't you?"

Maurita smiled at him through the tunnel.

She smoked cigarettes and listened to tapes on the boom box. She sang along with "Hold Me." With "Don't Stop." She sat on the couch and looked out the window at the neighbor's white dog. She watched him walk along the chain-link fence, stop to sniff the ground, circle a spot, lift his leg.

In the evening, Terry came by with a six-pack of beer. He sat down at one end of the couch, Maurita at the other, one beer for her and one for himself, the four cans between them sweating onto the black imitation leather.

"How is he?"

"About the same," said Maurita.

"He hasn't got depressed?" Terry asked. "Man, I hope he don't get depressed. He's a good dude. The best. I mean that. But when he gets depressed, watch out." He paused to take a drink. "Now, Aileen," he went on. "Aileen had a way of getting him depressed. Don't get me wrong. I'm not saying he did a thing to that bitch, but she was asking for it. She was stepping out on him and everyone knew it."

Maurita stared out the window as darkness came over the street and into the house, the lights left out, and Terry going on about Clay from the other end of the couch, until the beer was finished and Terry went home. She watched him go, then she took off her clothes. She lay on the couch, bare skin against slick imitation leather. She listened to "Soul On Fire," singing along, the words like something she could feel on her skin, like Clay's fingers.

After a while, the neighbor's dog barked. The gate scraped against pavement, footsteps coming up the front walk. That night, that first night, it would have been Clay. Clay, who had not really left. He might have gone out the front door, gone as far as the gate—even opened the gate before he turned around and came back, footsteps on the walk, the dog barking more frantically.

The key turned in the lock, the door pushed open. A man's voice called her name. When the light switched on, she covered her eyes with one arm, peering out from under the arm.

It was Farley. Farley, who was shorter than Clay, and on his way to paunch and baldness, the dome of his forehead sun-burned, also his nose. Farley, who was laughing as he said, "Oh, babe. This is just how I've been thinking of you. I've been driving for days with a stash in the van and a magic lizard in my pocket."

In the bedroom, on the mattress in the dark, the fingers were still Clay's. The mouth that pressed down on Maurita's was his, and the blind, battering need that pushed into her.

In the morning, Maurita sat in the kitchen, at the red formica table, while Farley drank a cup of instant coffee. "Let's put it this way," he said. "I made enough on this trip to buy us some time. So where would you like to go?"

She opened the newspaper. Her horoscope read: "Take time to develop your talents. Capitalize on your assets."

"Why can't we stay here?" she asked Farley.

"Here? Babe, I'm talking about Guaymas or Mazatlan. You want Boca Raton? La Jolla?"

She looked down at the table, at the pattern in the formica— faces with mouths open wide, as if in warning. "I don't know if this is the right time for me to go anywhere," she said.

"Well, think about it," he said. "We got the rest of the summer to burn."

Later on he asked her again, while they sat on the couch, smoking a joint. One of his hands rested on the back of her neck. "What about Laguna Beach?" he asked. "Or Pensacola. The beach, babe. We got to go listen to the waves."

"Your sunburn will get worse," she told him.

"Sunburn," he said. "Gonna let the sun and white sand bleach out my synapses. You holding out for Belize? Or Vera Cruz?"

She stared out the window, watched the neighbor's white dog dig a hole at the fence. "I don't know," she told Farley.

He took his hand off her neck. "Look, babe. I'm going to the beach. I get the feeling you don't want to come with me."

The dog moved off, out of sight. Maurita looked down at her bracelet, at the tongue of the silver snake. "It just doesn't seem like the right time for me," she said.

After Farley drove off in his van, Maurita looked through the Help Wanted section of the newspaper. She answered the first ad in the first column—secretary wanted, light office duties at A-Active Vehicle Insurance Agency.

The office was in a squat cinderblock building. The sign in the plate glass window read: "Cancelled or Drunk Drivers— Accidents—Convictions—Teens—Pay As You Drive—E-Z Budget Terms—We Defy Comparison."

The boss, Lon Seguros, was an aging, pot-bellied man, with a blue coiled snake tattooed on his right forearm. He did not even glance at Maurita's bracelet. "When can you start?" he asked.

"Right now," said Maurita.

"Okay, kid," he said. "We'll see how it goes. Now listen. This is what you say when you answer the phone. 'A-Active, all risks, low low rates,' Got it?"

Maurita answered the phone and took messages. She typed up invoices and accident reports. She filed estimates.

There was a blue Ford Toronado, sideswiped on Los Lobos. A Chevy Beretta, vandalized and stripped. A pale yellow Lincoln Mark VII, rear-ended by an uninsured driver.

Maurita made arrangements with the lawyer to go visit Clay. She sat at the steel green table, watching Clay clench and unclench his fists while the lawyer went on about mitigation, diminished responsibility, duress. After the lawyer finished talking and moved off down the table with his briefcase and papers, Maurita told Clay about her job. She did not mention Farley.

"I wish you didn't have to work," Clay said.

"It's not a bad job."

"What I mean is," he said, "I wish I was out of here. I wish I could take care of you." Then he told her about his brother who lived in Connecticut. "He's coming out here to see me. As soon as he can get away. See, he's got things to do. Business to take care of. He's an incredible guy. He's got money. A big house. A sailboat, and a Fiero. Once he gets here, he's gonna straighten out my situation."

"So when is he coming?"

"Soon. He'll be here soon. He just got tied up." Clay stared across at her, his eyes holding that same pale blue shimmer, his eyes holding something else too. "Hell," he said. "I don't even know if I want you to meet him. You'd fall for him in a minute. Everybody does." He looked over at the lawyer, then he leaned forward. "You know that night," he said softly. "That first night, when I met you. After I brought your stuff into your house, I took hold of your hand. I was looking at you. Moving my eyes over every part of you. And we did—what each of us wanted. We did things we'd never done with anyone else. All night long, until sunrise, when you fell asleep and I tiptoed out of your room. That's how it happened. How it really happened. You remember, don't you?"

When Maurita drove home, Tortuga Street lay in darkness, the street lamp reaching only to the edge of her lawn. She pushed open the gate, started up the front walk before she realized that something was wrong—the white dog wasn't barking, and the next moment she saw him, the white belly, short legs dangling in air—the dog hanging from the neighbor's tree, from the low branch extending over the fence and into her yard.

Maurita went back to the Buick and drove away from the dog. Down quiet streets, where the windows of houses were lit by blue television lights, and then down streets with signs flashing yellow and pink. She circled and doubled back over her route, driving miles through town, seven times past the County Detention Center. She was singing "Wild Heart," and "Don't You Know I Love You."

Maurita looked in the newspaper for any mention of another dog killing, but she could find none. She asked Terry about it.

"No shit," he said. "Well, good riddance. I might of shut the little fucker up myself, if I'd thought of it."

Maurita laughed, but she knew that the white dog was a bad sign. She looked over at the neighbors, the kids chasing each other through the yard, the father out working on his red Plymouth, leaning under the hood.

In the parking lot of the El Alba Cafe and Mesquite Grill, the windows of a white Maloney Stretch Cadillac were smashed. A Pontiac Firebird was totalled in a three-car collision, the driver not injured but two others in the hospital.

"You know what it is," Lon Seguros told Maurita. "People

just are not careful."

When she went back to see Clay, nothing moved in his eyes.

"I heard from my brother," he told her. "There's no way he can get here before the trial. Something's come up. Something to do with his business."

His hands lay open on the table, palms up. Maurita fingered her snake bracelet, traced its curve of neck.

"Can you tell me what's important?" he asked. "I mean, come on. Business or family? Seems like you can't count on nobody."

He was whispering, his words moving across the table to her, moving the air that touched her face. "It makes me crazy that I can't touch you. How can that be too much to ask? Just to touch your hand. Touch my crystal, so I can feel strong. My trial's coming up. And I know I don't have much of a chance. If my brother had been able to get here—well, who knows?"

Now something came into his eyes, something that pulled at her. "You know, they could put me away without ever giving me one minute alone with you," he said. "That's all I want. A little time alone. I mean without a lawyer or anyone else. I asked him if we could have a few minutes after the trial or the sentencing, or whatever. He said the only way would be . . . well, I shouldn't be saying this."

She was leaning towards him, the tunnel opening between them. "The only way would be what?"

"The only way would be—if we got married."

She asked Lon Seguros for time off so she could go to Clay's trial. "Why not," he said. "But let me tell you something. A kid like you should be going with some guy who's in a position to take you places. To give you nice things . . . "

She sat in the court room, on the bench behind Clay. She stared at his shoulders, at the shape of his shoulders beneath his blue blazer, and the back of his neck above his white shirt collar. The lawyers were talking, the witnesses answering questions, but Maurita watched Clay. If she leaned forward and reached out her hand, she could touch him. She could put her mouth to the back of his neck, to the soft skin behind his earlobes. They had done what each of them wanted, things they'd never done

with anyone else. That night—that first night—he had gone
out the door, then turned back. He was still turning, and his
turning pushed the lawyers and witnesses to the edge of
Maurita's sight. The voices she heard were the voices of those
who were ready to testify against him, who would not give him
any benefit of the doubt, who might even be lying.

There was the voice of a woman who lived in an apartment
down the hall from Aileen Ross. This woman claimed to have
seen Clay in the lobby of the building on the night of the
murder. She described Clay as a jealous, possessive man with an
uncontrollable temper.

There was the voice of a man who had come to see Aileen
Ross at midnight and found the front door wide open, the
apartment a mess, chairs and lamps knocked over, and Aileen
lying on the kitchen floor.

Then there was the voice of the psychiatrist who testified that
Clay's level of alcohol consumption could not have impaired his
ability to distinguish between right and wrong. The psychiatrist
went on to say that Clay's partial amnesia regarding the events
of that night seemed rather too convenient and circumspect to
be convincing.

There was the voice of the medical examiner who testified
about the bruises on the decedent's neck, also a large bruise on
the back of her head, most likely caused by impact against the
wall, and smaller bruises on the right leg, caused by a blunt
object, possibly a chair. But the bruises, Maurita knew, were
those on a woman who'd had a way of getting Clay depressed,
a woman who Clay hadn't done a thing to, even if she had been
asking for it.

For two days, the voices testified against Clay, until the
prosecution rested and the defense brought Terry to the stand.
Terry, dressed up in a plaid sports jacket and red tie, with his
hair slicked back. Whenever the lawyer asked him a question, he
ducked his head down and then answered slowly, as if carefully
choosing his words. He testified that he and Clay had been
drinking all afternoon and evening on the day of the murder.
"You know how it is," he said. "You have a couple—I mean, we
had a couple beers and we sat around, and then we went out for
more six-packs and a fifth of tequila—"

Then Clay was on the stand, dressed in his blue blazer, his white shirt and dark tie—his face all planes and angles, high cheekbones and strong jaw, his face with its tan faded now, but his eyes, still that same blue shimmer in his eyes. He was staring across at Maurita when he answered the lawyer's questions. Every word he spoke to her, telling the truth.

"Now, Clay," said the lawyer. "Can you tell us what you did after Terry left to go to work?"

"I don't know," Clay said to Maurita. "I don't remember. I don't remember that he left. The last thing I know was that we were walking down the street. Down Tortuga Street."

He had gone walking past Maurita's dark windows. The white dog had been barking. Clay had lifted the bottle of tequila to his mouth. He was laughing. Drunken laughter, his words slurred and incoherent. If the lawyer had let Maurita testify, she could have told them that he had been far too drunk to have done anything, to have wanted to do anything. She could have told them that he wasn't even thinking about Aileen—

If Maurita had been outside in the yard, he would not have walked past. He would have stopped and come into her house. She would have testified to it—how Terry had gone on, and Clay had come in. He had stayed with her that night, while they did what each of them wanted. Things they'd never done with anyone else, all night until sunrise, when he tiptoed out of her house to go to his car, which was where he found himself when he woke up.

The ring was a narrow filigree of silver. He promised, she promised to take each other, to have and to hold—Clay, who was wearing a blue prison jumpsuit, having just been sentenced to twenty years, and Maurita in a white cotton dress, a blue gauze scarf tied around her waist—the courtroom cleared, with only Terry and the lawyer left as witnesses, and the minister brought in by the lawyer, since the judge had refused to marry them.

Then Clay was kissing her. They were alone in the courtroom, a few minutes alone. Clay's fingers were moving under her white cotton dress, his fingers and his mouth pulling at her, giving her a sense of herself in the air, the sheer air and light, where her new ring was shining, along with her bracelets, her coiled snake. A few minutes alone, before the state patrolmen came in with their handcuffs. Then Terry was next to Maurita, pulling her through a crowd of reporters. "How does it feel—" someone asked.

"I have nothing to say to any of you," she said.

In the newspaper article, she was quoted as saying more. She read the article over and over, the description of her dress, and how she had told them, "We might be apart for a long time, but someday we'll be together. If other people don't understand, I have nothing more to say to them." Even though she knew she hadn't said this, it began to seem like something she might have said. And she liked knowing that other people were reading about her and Clay.

On Sundays, she drove to the State Pen. She sat in a booth, looking through a thick-paned window into Clay's eyes. She talked to him through a phone. "What's it like?" she asked.

"It ain't county jail," Clay said into his phone. "And it ain't reform school. I haven't got it figured out yet. There's a kind of balance, if you know what I mean. The way I see it, you got to be here as a force, but not one that's pushing against anything."

Maurita put one hand to the window, fingertips pressed to the glass. Clay put his fingers to hers—with only a layer of glass between them.

She went back to work at A-Active. She filed estimates and sent cancellation notices. The first time she agreed to go out for a drink after work, Lon Seguros took her to La Manzanilla Cocktail Lounge. He bought her a pineapple daiquiri and introduced her to his cousin Rafe, a slender young man dressed in a loose-fitting white suit and snakeskin shoes with pointed toes, who danced with her and led her flawlessly through the calypso, the mambo, and other steps she'd never known how to do. She let him take her home, let him whisper that she was beautiful, that she was just what he wanted. His hands were not Clay's. Clay was far away, behind glass and concrete and bars. Clay might have been thinking about her, he might have been going crazy from wanting to touch her while she was lying with

Rafe in the dark.

A few nights later, Lon Seguros took Maurita to Jimmy's El Gato. He introduced her to Vincent, who talked her into going to the dog races with him. Maurita stood close to Vincent when he placed his bets. She drank beer and watched the lean dogs streak by. Vincent won a handful of bills. Before he took her home, he stopped at a jewelry store and bought a tiny silver heart on a chain.

Her horoscope read: "Be meticulous about finances. Fulfill a nutritional need."

At night, she lay on the slick, black couch. She heard the gate scrape on pavement, then footsteps up the front walk. No dog was barking—the white dog was gone—and the footsteps were not Clay's, but Vincent's. Vincent, who brought her one long-stemmed red rose and a bottle of champagne.

On the highway east of town, a cherry-red comet Caliente skidded over a concrete divider into oncoming traffic and hit a Chevette, killing the driver. Someone slashed the white wall tires of the sea-green Pontiac Bonneville that belonged to Lon Seguros.

"Who would do this to me?" he asked Maurita.

Maurita typed invoices and answered the phone. "A-Active," she said. "All risks, low low rates."

"It's me," said the voice. "Your husband. I got to ask you something. You have any idea what it is?"

"How would I know?" she asked.

"Terry says he's seen guys leaving your house late at night."

Maurita waited, hanging onto the phone.

"Are you gonna say it's not true?" he asked.

"Clay—"

Suddenly he was screaming. "I'm locked up here. You think I won't know, but I know. You want to see what it means to me? You want me to show you? You just wait and see what I do."

"Clay, wait a minute—"

But he had hung up. There was only the dial tone.

Early the next morning, before Maurita left for work, two cops came to her door to tell her that Clay had been found dead in his cell, hanging from a towel. They said that it looked like suicide, but Corrections Department officials would contact her after the autopsy.

She sat on the black couch, slipping her ring off, then back onto her finger. She pressed the head of the silver snake into her wrist.

She waited until dark, then she packed up her clothes and tapes in pillowcases and paper bags. She took everything, except for the white dress which she left hanging in the closet. If Terry was watching from his window when she carried her things out to the Buick, she saw no sign of him.

When she drove west out of town, she was singing "Think About Me." She was singing to keep Clay and a white dog from coming to her as she drove. Clay, with a noose made out of a towel, not intending to kill himself—she was sure that he only meant to show how he wanted her. To pull her back to him, out of pity this time.

After she had been driving for a while, a woman's face appeared at the side of the road. Maurita had never seen the face of the murdered woman, but she recognized it. And she knew it for a sign, a sign that would stay with her until sunrise, when she would see once again the blue shimmer of open road.

Wildlife

BY JOANN KOBIN

I'm the early bird on the lot this morning and at first I don't notice. I unlock the doors to the showroom and miss the fact that the two main windows are crashed open like broken eggs. Take it from the top. Chunks of glass on the lot and showroom floor. Splinters of glass sprayed across the roof of a teal blue four-door Accord. I don't believe my eyes. I'm standing in a puddle of blood. Murder. And I'm the next victim.

A thin, twisting inkline of blood weaves around the cars on the showroom floor. Vandals? Thieves? But no car is missing, no car damaged. I move closer to the smashed windows and see hair stuck on the jagged edges. Apeman crashes Orangedale Honda? I reach for a phone to call the police and see a deer standing behind the red Prelude. It's spying on me. Trembling. Its eyes are dark circles of light. Golden creature, I want to shout, I'll help you. And then seconds later another deer, a smaller one, trots out of the back office, a gash on its shoulder, its eyes shining with terror. 911.

I'm explaining it all to 911—they think I'm nuts—when Frank, the manager, comes in. "What the hell goes on here?" and then he gets the picture. The doe trots around the show-room, dragging its bleeding flank past the rear fender of a Civic wagon.

Listening to my band's demo tape on the way home that raw April evening, I decided that the piece needed more percussion, needed something. I couldn't concentrate. What was on my

121

mind was how to tell Laurie what happened in the showroom this morning. I had the feeling my wife was beginning to think I was a liar. Not exactly a liar but a bullshitter. Was the band really going to make a record? Was I getting anywhere? Why didn't I put my energy into selling cars at Orangedale Honda?

Tonight Laurie should have no problem believing me. The incident was splashed across the local newspaper. I should have bought the paper but Laurie doesn't like reading or watching the news. She has enough life and death all day. She's a nurse in premie unit of the West Benton hospital. I kid her about being in the micro-chip industry. Some of those babies weigh in at barely over a pound.

At home I found Laurie in the den watching her favorite program—the video of our wedding. One hour and fifty minutes of that dazzling event, which took place over a year and a half ago. Curled up at the end of the couch, she was staring at the screen, trying to figure something out—me, or at least that's what I thought.

"You're home early, hon," she said. She'd just taken a shower and had on a pink terry cloth bathrobe and a towel around her head. Her voice was muffled in terry cloth. She was at the part of the tape where the camera goes from table to table and every guest has a turn with the mike. I kissed the top of her towel turban and slid next to her on the couch. She reached for my hand and squeezed it. Usually I like when she does that, but sometimes I don't. Sometimes when she touches me it feels like she's trying to tell me how to think—by osmosis. Within seconds the tape cut to the dance floor. I was dancing with my five-year-old niece, Melissa, the flower girl. I'm crazy about that kid.

Laurie said, "You know, Gary, there's no serious footage of you on the whole tape."

"What about our first dance?"

"You're grinning."

I asked her to rewind. "*I* think I look serious," I said. She turned back to the beginning, to the part where her mother, all misty-eyed, was fussing around her, fixing her veil. A while later she arrived in front of the minister on her father's arm, not letting go of it all that fast either, I thought.

The ceremony was over. We were at the reception now. The guy we hired to do the video was telling us what to do. Hold up your drinks. Kiss the bride. Kiss the bride's mother. The wedding proceeded. My mind wandered to the scene at the showroom at 8:00 o'clock this morning. The jagged glass smeared with blood and hair. It took me minutes until I spotted the doe on the other side of the red Prelude. I've seen deer before, but why does wildlife seem so large and dangerous when it's trapped inside? Once when I was thirteen, a chipmunk got into our kitchen and ran across the counters and stove. "Gary," my mother said, "it's like a lion's in the house. Please Gary, help—help me get it out of here."

"It was a beautiful wedding," Laurie said.

We'd got to the part where the video cameraman was filming the woman photographer who was taking stills. Everyone at the wedding had a camera. Even my five-year-old niece had her own Polaroid. I kept thinking—then and now, too—that this isn't the way a wedding should be. A wedding should be outdoors, under trees or on a stretch of lawn, or in a clearing of a forest. There should be no cameras of any kind.

"Don't you think it was a beautiful wedding?" Laurie asked.

"I'm sorry, honey," I said, "if it seems like I'm not concentrating. Something happened at work this morning."

She pressed the pause button, stopped the tape. "What happened, Gary?"

"Don't worry Laurie. I didn't get canned." I told her about the two deer that crashed through the showroom windows. I told her about the look in the doe's eyes, and how the smaller deer suddenly trotted out of the back office where it seemed to have been nuzzling the computer terminal.

"It sounds so sad," she said, and then asked whether anyone else had been in the showroom at the time and seen the deer too.

Closing my eyes for an instant. I saw the golden creature staring at me with those eyes which were full of terror but not full of hate. In that moment when its eyes were on me I was as much an animal as it was.

I told Laurie how at 9:15 three police officers showed up and one state environmental police officer. I had never heard of environmental police officers until this morning. I told Laurie how the doe was bleeding more and more, and Sweeney, the environmental cop, told Officer Brazeau to put it out of its misery. The little one too. Later a pick-up truck arrived and transported the deer to the County Jail: venison supper for the prisoners.

"It's so unbelievable . . ." she said softly.

"Unbelievable—like you think I'm making this up?"

"No, unbelievable as in strange. A baby on the unit died this morning around the same time."

"I'm sorry," I said after a couple of seconds. I knew how attached Laurie got to some of those mini-babies. "Was it on the unit for a while?"

"For more than three weeks, and we all thought she was thriving. She seemed so bright and responsive."

"That's how I felt about the doe," I said.

She stared at me. "Gary, you're comparing an animal that people hunt and shoot—and that you've known for less than an hour—to a baby whose parents love it and have been planning for for months, and have dreamed about . . ." She stopped, and with an edge of weariness clicked on the video and in silence we watched the end of the wedding. Her mood picked up and I got depressed. The band that Laurie's folks hired played too loud. That's unusual for a rock musician to say, but it was true in this case.

There was something about the wedding that wasn't right. But what exactly did I have in mind? Our wedding wasn't any different than the five or six other weddings I'd been to in my life. My friend Richard's wedding came spiraling out of my memory, a wedding where the bride arrived on a horse-drawn cart, and the groom galloped in bareback on a black horse—at a school in Vermont that I'd been to for a few months years ago, when I was seventeen. Almost half my lifetime ago.

I was sent to that place because I was flunking out of high school. You see, I couldn't read until the fourth grade. My spelling was and is still totally original, and what exactly a sentence is is a mystery to me; paragraphs too. But at any rate, in my second or third year of high school I got into heavy-duty trouble. It was the early seventies and I was smoking a lot of dope and dropping acid. One day my dad found me barking like a dog and lapping water from a bowl on the floor. Then I lapped applesauce. That got to him. Eventually the guidance counsellor told my folks about a school in Vermont, and my home state, Rhode Island, would help pay the tuition. It was *not* a school for the retarded, they swore to me.

I haven't thought about that place in ages. I wonder if it's still in operation. I wonder if Mark and Carmen still run it. Pine Hill School, that was what it was called. Mark was a weirdo—but strict about not using drugs. Carmen was younger, pretty, with one thick dark braid down to her waist.

It ended up that I was at the school for barely three months because when my folks came to pick me up for Thanksgiving break they decided they didn't like the place. My mom wanted to report the kitchen to the board of health. My dad took a good look around and said it looked like a hippie commune. He called the place "a free love school," and in fact you could get laid there without too much difficulty.

Those memories cheered me up as I watched the end of the video: a long sequence of Laurie and me waving good-bye. Off to the Bahamas for a week, Laurie in a fancy pink suit. She looked strange to me. The longer we're together—and we lived together for almost three years before we got married—the more unfamiliar she gets. The Laurie I knew best is the one who sang country western with my best friend's band, in a pair of silver cowboy boots and a shirt that looked like it was made of tinfoil.

"Laurie, did I ever tell you about that school in Vermont? It was a farm. Pine Hill." Laurie was brushing her damp hair. Dinner in the oven was beginning to smell good.

A shadow passed over my wife's face. "Gary, was it really a school?"

"It was a farm-school," I explained, "with cows and sheep and pigs and chickens, even ducks. The animals got slaughtered for food. Every student had a job. It was my job to gather eggs." I told her how rich-tasting the duck eggs were, like eating a prime steak.

Dinner was ready. We moved into the kitchen. Round blue magnets held snapshots of Laurie's mini-babies—the success stories from the unit—on the refrigerator door. In the middle of the table was a wire basket with ketchup and vitamin pills and a stack of paper napkins. I took a napkin and put it next to my fork. Laurie wanted to know what the other students at the school were like. Right then I could only remember this kid called Tony. He was always tapping people on their heads and saying, "Good day, kind sir," or to the girls, "Good day, foxy lady." He was harmless. Okay, once in a while he'd say, "Hello fuckhead!" and the pat would be more like a smack. I decided not to tell Laurie about him.

Laurie filled our wine glasses and made a toast: "To a hard day. Glad that it's over." She sipped a little wine and then twisted pepper out of the pepper mill onto her stew. "Gary, what kind of school was it exactly?"

I got mad. Lately, she kept trying to get me to admit, in one way or another, that I had problems. Because I wasn't sure about wanting a baby. Wasn't sure about living in a condo townhouse or staying in the car business. It's partly true, the way we were living didn't feel right to me, but who was living any different? I got mad and told her that Pine Hill was a school for ordinary kids, plain everyday teenagers. A few problems here and there.

"I wonder if the place is still in existence," she said.

"I wonder that too," I replied, and when we were done with supper and I finished washing the dishes, I stuck my head out the kitchen window, pulled the three-quarter moon into view, and took a good deep drag on the spring night. The moon looked skimpy tonight—dull, the color of ash.

That night and for many others Laurie and I tried to make a baby. Her suspicions about me quieted down until she got her period some weeks later. "You're not enthusiastic about having a baby," she said, as though enthusiasm was the problem. I told her I was willing to slide home, so to speak, on her enthusiasm.

In May with a stretch of good weather, Hondas started selling like hotcakes. I let customers take me on long test drives far away from Orangedale. I was selling cars but remembering more and more about that school in Vermont. People I hadn't given a thought to in years. This kid Warren—how he stole Mark's World War II bolt action rifle and cornered one of the teachers at the end of a math class at eleven o'clock in the morning. Kept him hostage all through lunchtime. The teacher managed to talk him out of the main event, and Warren was shipped home with his mom and dad that afternoon. Talk buzzed around the school that a kid like Warren should never have been allowed to watch a pig get slaughtered. What I remember is that I actually dug Warren. We hiked up a mountain and at the top he stood inches away from the edge of the rock outcropping. He wanted to fly—like flap his arms and fly. He told me he was a goddamn eagle. I told him he wasn't.

In mid-June Laurie still wasn't pregnant. She was discouraged but not hopeless. She never gets hopeless, she gets curious instead. We decided to take a weekend trip and try to find Pine Hill. In the car on the way up to Vermont, she said, "If you just had a hard time with school work, why didn't your folks get you extra help or tutoring? Why'd they send you away?"

"I guess I was in a demoralized state." Questions get me nervous: I'm not good at answers.

"Were you emotionally disturbed?" she finally asked point-blank.

"Sure, I was a total mental case," I told her, and made a weird face and curled my tongue and let it stick out of my mouth. She glared at me and I glared at her, and then we broke down and laughed a little.

When we were a couple of miles from the motel where we were going to stay that night, Laurie touched my arm and said, "Gary, I'm sorry. I always forget what a terrible time you had in school."

"It wasn't that terrible," I said. "I always had friends."

The next morning we set out to find the school. Automatically I seemed to know which fork in the road led to Pine Hill. "Now the scene opens up after the waterfall on the right," I said, steering between the ruts and the soft shoulders. I drove slowly. In the distance I could make out a fenced-in garden and the path to the stone lodge where Mark and Carmen used to live. I pulled the car off the road, and we got out and gazed across the hayfields. I took a deep breath and pointed the length of the enormous field, to a small hill. "That's where the wedding was. On that rise."

"What wedding?" Laurie asked.

"Two teachers were married there. Right after I got here—in September. The fields were still green. It was beautiful. After the ceremony there was a sauna and after that there was a *feast*—that's what Mark called a party." I could picture the tables covered with the bright colors of Indian bedspreads and the platters of food. Staring out at the hill, I remembered the bride in her silky iridescent dress. I remember even now how all I could think about then were her breasts—their softness and whiteness. She never wore a bra. A couple of days before the wedding I had seen her naked in the sauna and her nipples stood out like little pink erasers at the ends of brand-new pencils. When the ceremony was over, after they had kissed, the bridegroom helped the bride up onto the black horse and then hoisted himself up, and off they galloped down the length of this field.

"What do you think?" I asked Laurie. She was gazing up at the rocky, corrugated face of the mountain. Her silence seemed spiteful.

Finally she said, "It's beautiful, but it doesn't look like a school. Where were the classes held?" I told her I didn't remember, and I didn't.

I took Laurie's hand and tugged her in the direction of the stone lodge. Her hand was damp. The place was a ghost town. Skirting the garden, we followed a dirt path behind the barn and past a large pen, or corral. There was something about this spot: it was where Mark had killed the pig. I had never seen an animal die. There were two or three earpiercing shots and the pig was lying on the ground. Mark made quick work of slitting its throat and cutting off its head. The headless, mud-smeared body strained to stand on its legs. The legs pawed the air. The damn pig wouldn't die. That kid, Warren, screamed, "Croak, you motherfucker." He kept screaming that until one of the teachers led him away.

"Why'd you stop here?" Laurie asked and I told her I was just thinking about all the animals that used to be in the barn—horses and cows and pigs and sheep. She smiled and we started walking again. It was uphill now.

The door of the stone lodge was constructed from wide planks of wood. I was tempted to turn around. Why spoil a nice dream? I knocked, my knuckles scraping against the splintery boards. All was quiet. I knocked again. "Be right there," a woman's voice called. Laurie hid behind me. In a few seconds the door opened and Carmen appeared. She looked almost the same: she wore her hair loose now; good shape. Soft dark eyes, suntanned skin, dangling rainbow earrings. "Shhh . . . , don't tell me your names," she said; "they'll come to me in a minute. You're old Pine Hill students—or at least one of you is. Give me a moment . . ." She studied us closely, ushering us in at the same time.

"Don't give me any clues," she warned when I was about to speak. "I like doing this and I'm very good at it." Now she was staring only at me. "Gary," she said quietly. "Gary Lucas." Her smile was a winner's smile.

"I was only here for three months," I began.

"That was a shame, as I recall," she said. "I remember that we thought you should have stayed longer. I was sorry to see you leave. Mark was too. You carried so much pain."

Something about that remark made me sick; I wanted to run; the idea that she said that to every student who ever came back here to visit. *You carried so much pain.* It was a kind of generic-brand statement. How could you miss? How could you go wrong? She went on, "I remember we advised your parents to let you stay. It's a shame you couldn't have stayed the full year, or maybe even two." Her voice was gentle, and it was true what she said—I'd been hurt. I tried so hard when I was a kid to do well in school and I was so ashamed that I couldn't. For years I made believe I could read, and hoped the teachers wouldn't catch on, but they always did. "I remember your dad," Carmen continued; "he didn't want his son son living in a hippie commune."

Carmen took a pitcher of iced tea out of the refrigerator. Laurie was hanging on her words and her manner of speaking, which was soft and sweet, yet professional. Carmen gave us our drinks and led us outside to a small deck, which hadn't been there in 1973. "I built this last year," she said. "I built it all by myself."

"It's terrific," Laurie said. I could tell she was a little in awe of Carmen.

"Tell me, Gary, what happened after you left Pine Hill?"

"I guess age cured me," I said.

"Were your folks able to arrange the kind of tutoring I recommended?"

"Some," I said, uncomfortable with the topic. I honestly don't like remembering school or anything about it. I moved the conversation around to what Laurie and I do now. I like telling people about Laurie's work. I like describing the size of some of those babies, and the miracles the nursing staff perform.

"I think it's the nurses that keep a lot of those babies going," I said.

"The nurses and technology," Laurie added.

Carmen asked Laurie about the financial burden of caring for those tiny babies, but Laurie had questions for Carmen, questions about me. "Carmen, how come Gary was sent to Pine Hill?"

Carmen thought for a moment or two. "No one really understood the seriousness of Gary's learning problems until right before he came here, and back then schools didn't have special programs for students like Gary. When he got here he believed he was lazy or stupid or both." Carmen glanced at me to see whether she was getting it right. That was how she remembered it. I nodded, embarrassed to be the topic of discussion. "Look," Carmen said, "why don't you two stay and have lunch with me." Laurie accepted the invitation and I asked where Mark was.

"We got divorced right after the school closed about ten years ago," she said, and then, "No, I'm not lonely . . ." She turned her face away from us, and her eyes swept the view. I followed her eyes up the valley. The road cut the valley like an arrow going through a heart, diagonally. I could make out my car parked on the side of the road far in the distance.

Carmen wanted us to help her pick lettuce for lunch, and guided us down the hill to her garden. She walked between us and reached her arms around each of our waists. I remembered that about her—that she touched people, and that sometimes I liked it and sometimes I didn't. Laurie seemed nervous with Carmen wedged between us. In the garden I watched Carmen crouch next to the lettuce and almost daintily pick a few leaves from each plant.

"Do a lot of old students come back?" Laurie asked later when we were eating lunch on the deck. Carmen told us that it always amazed her how over the years she heard from so many students. Also, in the nice weather a few always drifted by in person. "Like you, Gary," she said, touching the top of my hand. Laurie and I put on our expensive sunglasses; Carmen seemed happy to squint. We drank more wine, and I asked, "What about Warren Tudryn? Ever hear from him?" Warren's last name came to me out of the blue.

"Warren Tudryn." She sighed. "That's a sad story. He was in the state hospital for a number of years and then when he was let out, he killed himself." She paused to let me absorb that sad piece of news. "It was a shame he couldn't have stayed here," Carmen said, "but he was too sick."

I was sad, but also uneasy with the turn of conversation. Laurie had a faraway look on her face. Carmen went on about other students, most of whom I'd never heard of and didn't want to hear about, even the ones who were doing well: Janie So-and-so became a lawyer; Randy Ellis was gay but lucky: he didn't have AIDS. "That's great," I said. I was about to tell Carmen about my band, but I changed my mind. I could tell that Laurie wanted to leave.

After lunch Carmen walked us back to the car. She strolled along slowly, smiling up at the mountains. A couple of times she kneeled down on the side of the road and examined stones or sticks. She mentioned wanting to get goats. "I'm glad you came up," Carmen said warmly. "You're doing well, Gary." She hugged me and patted me, I hugged her back, and she hugged Laurie, who took a small step back from that hug.

When we reached the highway Laurie wanted to take the wheel. For a couple of hours we barely spoke. What was going on in my mind was that I was heading in the wrong direction. I had a pretty good idea of what Laurie was thinking.

"There were some sick kids at that school," she said after a while.

"I wouldn't have known it then," I answered.

"How come?" she wondered aloud. I shrugged. "Couldn't you tell that that boy, Warren, could have been an ax-mur-derer?" Laurie said.

I shook my head NO. "He wanted to be an eagle," I murmured.

There was a heat wave in the beginning of July and a long holiday weekend. Cars, even Hondas, weren't moving and my band took a vacation from playing, and Laurie and I weren't getting along. We stopped sleeping together. She accused me of always dreaming of some other life, of not putting any energy into *us*. "It's like you think there's some better movie at another theater," she said. I knew she wasn't all wrong.

On a boiling hot Sunday morning she wanted to go for a drive to the reservoir. I thought she wanted to lace into me about my problems, but actually her mood was fine. I was the grouch. I wanted to move in with Carmen. I was half-in-love with her. I kept seeing her in the garden, I pictured her with the goats. I saw myself in the fields riding the tractor, mowing. I saw myself climbing the trail to the rocky ledges on top of the mountain, gulping pure air.

"Gary, what actually happened after your parents didn't let you stay at Pine Hill?"

"I went back to public high school. I think I had a math tutor. I stopped doing drugs. I graduated."

"It seems that just being at Pine Hill for three months helped you," she said.

"I never thought about it that way but I think you're right. I got into music."

"Your were lucky," she said, putting her arm around my waist. We strolled alongside the water, which was a flat brown color. The reservoir was low. It had been a dry year, a snowless winter. "What'd you think of Vermont?" I asked. "Did you like that valley with the stream winding its way through it, and the mountains kinda holding it in place?"

"I liked it, but I can't picture living there," Laurie said. A little while later she said, "Gary, I don't think you know how lucky you were."

"I guess I never think of myself as lucky," I answered.

For the next couple of weeks I daydreamed about Carmen. She was only thirteen years older than I was, about forty-six. Laurie was a year older than me. In my mind's eye, like some day-glo video, there was Carmen harvesting in the green peppers and string beans from her garden, milking goats. She was attracted to me, I knew. Every day I told myself I'd call her, plan a little excursion to visit her, see how it felt being up there without Laurie, but I kept postponing the actual call. The car business had picked up, and the band started rehearsing again and we had a few gigs. Our agent almost had the recording contract in hand.

One night after rehearsal I came home and opened the door, and there were no smells, no little sounds, no damp cloud floating out of the bathroom. When I turned on the lights I could see that the plants were gone, and so were the pictures of Laurie's family. The coat closet had none of her coats. In the kitchen the photos of the micro-babies were striped off the refrigerator door. The vitamin pills were gone from the wire basket on the table. Laurie was gone. I mean she had packed up and pulled out, without even a fight. There was a note on the kitchen counter: "I'll call later." Cold as ice, I thought. If only it had read, I'll call *you* later.

I held the note and turned it over and over, expecting to discover more writing, some not so serious reason for her taking off like this. Was she going to come back? I figured that if she had taken the video of our wedding with her, then there was hope: it would mean she was still trying to figure me out. I searched in the cabinet in the den, rummaging around making believe I couldn't find it. The video, however, was there. At first I didn't want to touch it, but when I did, like a howling burglar alarm, the phone rang. "I have only one thing I want to say," Laurie announced: "What kills me is that you don't know anything about the pain *I've* been going through."

"What pain? Please don't hang up!" I begged. "Explain it to me." She hung up.

I could have cried, I think. Instead I clicked in the video and slumped into the coach. A good fifteen minutes of the tape consisted of Laurie getting dressed. Then came the ceremony and party. I could see how miserable I felt at my own wedding, how jittery, how scared, how stupid and out-of-place—except when I was dancing with my five-year-old niece, Melissa. I'm crazy about that kid. I watched the tape from beginning to end, one hour and fifty-two long minutes, to be exact, and when it was over—after we waved good-bye to family and friends and left for the Bahamas—I thought about what Laurie told me on the phone. About who was the one carrying the pain. I got pissed.

Henrietta

BY MARY TROY

Henrietta Marschand was not, in the self-sacrificing, giving sense, a nice woman; and indeed, had never in all of her eighty-nine years tried to please someone other than herself, unless of course it was convenient for her as well, or unless it was her son Henry who had paid her back, when he returned from the war in the Pacific boys his age fought, by marrying a woman so dumb she probably thought Angola was a type of sweater. No, if given the choice—and one always was—Henrietta chose herself. And that had been fine with her, just natural and smart. And it still was okay, she thought, because she was probably as good as anyone else, had probably been entertaining or interesting to some others along the way. Besides, she had seldom hurt anyone, that is, not on purpose, just for the hurting.

In fact, every now and then Henrietta felt positively saintly, and knew that was partly because she lived in a germ- and dirt-free apartment in South Saint Louis next to St. Anthony's Catholic Church, and mainly because it was easier to be a saint at eighty-nine than it had been at nineteen, or thirty-nine, or even sixty-nine. And she was a sweet-looking old woman who knew it, counted on it when she asked the man at the market across the street to help her with her bags, when she waited for younger men—and older ones if she saw any—to open doors for her, when she expected to be offered one of the two armchairs in her internist's waiting room. Her hair, at one time so black it was almost blue and shiny from the egg she washed it with once a week, was white and, though thin, still had

135

enough body that Beatrice and the beauty shop two blocks away could get it to curl in around her face. And her face was smooth, smooth as a peach, she thought when she looked at it, smoother than the faces of any of the other women in her senior citizen apartment building, even those just barely seventy. And her voice was not weak, quavery, like most of the others, and her eyesight was better than she had any right to expect.

Old Ruth Eisele up there at the lectern, reading from the Book of Kings, couldn't see well enough to tell dominion from domination, couldn't speak clearly enough anyway to keep from sounding like a radio you were almost out of range of, was an insult to those like Henrietta who took the trouble to get up early and come to mass, and who would have offered her still clear and full voice for the epistle had she known there was a need. So much for feeling saintly. Anyone, even a sweet-looking thing like herself, who could be irritated by Ruth Eisele during the offertory of the mass when she should be offering herself to God, was not a saint. So be it.

She had despised Ruth, had been plagued by Ruth for what seemed forever, for most of what the insurance brochures called her declining years anyway, but it had begun long before. When Ruth's husband, Ted, had taken a job as ticket taker on the passenger train and made the run from St. Peters, Missouri, to St. Louis, stopping at Union Station—now a shopping mall—and staying overnight three nights in an inexpensive downtown hotel, that had not been Henrietta's fault. And the fact that Henrietta's husband of less than a year operated one of the fruit stands in Union Station, and Henrietta herself with her black hair hanging down her back sold Ted an apple each time he passed as he made jokes about Eve and temptation until she had to join him in his hotel room after her husband left her in the evenings to visit his widowed mother, was not Henrietta's fault either. Not really. If Jack, the husband, had stayed home, if his mother had not been both ill and clinging, if Henrietta had not been beautiful, if Ted had not been that kind of man, and if poor silly Ruth had been a more exciting woman, nothing would have happened. And nothing very much did happen, either, just a little flattery and flirting followed by some quick sex, which she liked for the urgency and excitement until the time she decided she may rather have Ted all the time than Jack, and Ted laughed.

"I don't think my wife would go for that," he said, and began to talk about Ruth, showering her with loving testimonials—"a good woman," "a real feminine woman," "a true partner," "a terrific mother"—which made Henrietta mean, mean enough to write to Ruth in care of St. Peters, Missouri, thirty miles away and tell her all.

Well, Henrietta did not and had not considered the sex immoral, no matter what the church taught—though she confessed anyway as soon as it was clear that Ted had transferred to another route or taken a different job altogether, and what the priest called her "near occasion of sin" was gone. And she did not consider it wrong to sneak out, deceive dear Jack like that. He was a sweet boy, though quiet and somewhat boring, and if she had not loved him, she would not have married him. The war was to blame. Before he went to France, he had been a flirt, laughing and teasing all the girls, and she knew the prestige she enjoyed for being the prettiest was enhanced by his choosing her. After France, he still loved her and she him, too, but as an old friend of the family, as a slightly addled cousin. Still, she was his wife, and had he wanted her in that way often, she would have stayed home. He had, in a sense, dibs on her. But as it turned out, she took nothing from him that he wanted. Nor did she think it was wrong because of Ted, for he was certainly not the victim and had known all along what he was about.

But it had been wrong to write to Ruth, probably immoral, surely unethical. Henrietta had known it then, and she knew it now, but the letter from Ruth was mean, too, was a way of rubbing in Henrietta's wrongness. "I'm praying for you," Ruth wrote in red ink on pink stationery. "We weak human beings need both strength and forgiveness. I pray for us all." Then the Christmas card later that year from Ted, Ruth, Charlene, and Henrietta (the French poodle Ruth gave Ted for his birthday right after the letter) made Henrietta wish for the collapse of the bridge over the Missouri River and the permanent isolation of St. Peters from civilized society.

And now as punishment for her sins, Henrietta walked from

daily mass with Ruth, helping Ruth by holding her steady when she felt faint on extremely warm days and by guiding her in winter down the cleared narrow path in the sidewalk. "Be careful. Step where I do," she would say, because with her poor vision, Ruth was just as likely to step on a patch of ice as not. As Henrietta helped and befriended Ruth, she considered it a penance stiffer than the Our Fathers the priests gave in confession, a reparation for her whole life, a way of racking up points toward her own salvation. At eighty-nine, it was not too early to start storing up indulgences and good marks for the future.

"It's going to be another hot one," Ruth said now as they walked the half-block to their building.

"I'm surprised," Henrietta said, "that after living ninety-two years in the Midwest, you still consider the heat of July worthy of comment. You act like it's a news flash."

"We should live in Yosemite. Josie was there for two weeks, and she said she had to wear a jacket at night," Ruth said. "What a wonderful trip she had, too." Josie was Charlene's eldest daughter, and Henrietta often heard about Josie's travels, promotions, experiences. No matter where Josie went, even if just to a high school play one of her children (Ruth's great-grandchildren) was in, it was the best place possible, was exceptional. Henrietta, on the other hand, spoke to her own granddaughter, Patsy, when Patsy wanted to borrow money to get another degree, go to another school to become a licensed insurance salesperson, business manager, or pre-school teacher. Henrietta always said no, too, but not without a lecture that included telling Patsy to get rid of the bum she was living with, the so-called freelance artist who claimed he was trying to get jobs but never did. "When you were twenty, you preached to me about freedom and love," Henrietta always said. "Now that you're beyond forty, I hope you see that hard work and sacrifice and goals are more important."

"The mayor of Yosemite is a friend of theirs, you know," Ruth was saying as they entered the air-conditioned lobby. "Of course, he's loaded. His family had money, I think. But anyway, Josie said they stayed with him, and he has a great big mansion, just a big old building with three floors and wings and what not. It had whatchacallit, thirty-foot ceilings, and one wall was all windows from top to bottom."

"No one knows what whatchacallit is, and if you have to
babble, at least talk to me about people I know," Henrietta said
and thought that if she could only manage to get along with
Patsy, listening to Ruth and going to mass wouldn't comprise
all her social activities.

"Her husband didn't go with her at first, even though the
mayor is his friend from the Navy. Josie went by herself and her
husband joined her later because his mother is sick. She's a
Garner, you know."

"Who? I don't know any Garners."

"A cousin of the Garners who live on Delor, I think. Anyway,
she's in terrible shape with strokes and blood clots, and now
she's being fed by tubes through her nose. That's the only way.
But Josie stayed two weeks and said he had a white grand piano,
the mayor did, and he would play it at night, and he's just a card,
I guess. A real kidder. So one night, he was playing—this was
when Josie's husband was there so it must have been near the
end—and he put his hands whatchacall on his head and kept
playing. He had made it into a player, see? Well, Josie said that
was really something. They all got a big kick out of that."

"Why would anyone want to be fed through the nose?"
Henrietta said. "I mean it, Ruth." She was concerned about the
so-called advances in medicine, had been for a while. A ninety-
year-old from the apartment had had a foot amputated recently
so she could live another two months, not long enough to learn
to handle her wheel chair. After that Henrietta had made both
Patsy and Ruth swear on Bibles that they would not let her be
cut up, end up with tubes in all kinds of odd places, not dead but
not too alive, either.

"Unzip me," Ruth said. "I'm going up and take this dress off.
Charlene always buys me dresses that zip up the back, and I
don't know why."

Henrietta unzipped Ruth's dress, and Ruth walked slowly
into the elevator, displaying an expanse of damp, white skin.
"Are you coming?" she said. "Yesterday, I forgot to press four,
so I rode up to eight and back again, twice, before I remembered." She laughed. "But then, it's not like I'm in a hurry."

"You make me crazy," Henrietta said. "I think I'll sit down

here alone. Maybe I'll call Josie and tell her you need a keeper."

The apartment building they lived in was not a nursing home, but was exclusively for senior citizens, those fifty-five and older. Henrietta was saddened whenever she realized if Henry were still alive, he wouldn't be eligible for ten years. But Henry died of a heart attack while playing touch football, the game John Kennedy had just then made so popular, in Forest Park with some clients and employees. He was just Patsy's age, forty-two, but was also the father of a nineteen-year-old—who Henrietta believed desperately needed his guidance—and on his way to becoming wealthy through his food brokerage business. But he had been burdened by a money-crazed wife, one who was not satisfied even with the Persian lamb coat and the Thunderbird, one who also wanted a condo on the lake a few hours to the southwest that was misnamed Lake of the Ozarks. It was common knowledge that stress caused heart attacks, and living with Tricia, whose attitude Henrietta described as slightly more selfish than "gimmee, gimmee," had to have been stressful.

Nevertheless, the senior citizen apartment was perfect for someone like Henrietta who liked her privacy without the fear of living in a separate house, without having to triple bolt her door and put bars on her windows to guard against the evil the television and newspapers convinced her was rampant in the rest of the population. And though there was no nursing care, the residents watched out for and checked up on one another, ready to push the help buttons—two in each apartment—that would bring EMS teams. But of course Henrietta knew everything was okay only as long as the buttons were not pushed. She even had petitioned unsuccessfully to have hers disconnected.

She and Ruth had come to the apartments together, moved in within weeks of each other three years ago. Sixty-five years earlier when they had been only names to each other, one the wicked other woman, the other a drab, lifeless mother of the year, neither could have predicted they would spend their old age together. Ted would surely get a hoot out of it, Henrietta thought, but he had died of stomach cancer so many years ago, almost thirty, and besides she remembered so little about him, she wasn't certain he even had a sense of the ironic.

Henrietta finally left the lobby, noticing that just the physical act of standing and then of walking to the elevator tired her more than usual. She should rest for a while, take a nap before lunch, she thought, or she could just skip lunch altogether—today was meatloaf, which wasn't that good anyway—and sleep all afternoon. From her apartment on the seventh floor, from the sliding glass door that opened to the narrow balcony, she could see the house she and Jack had lived in, the one he died in while sitting at the dinner table when only fifty years old, falling face down into the peach cobbler. And she stayed in that house as Henry and his family, including Patsy who was only three when her grandfather died, lived a few blocks away. She stayed until the late sixties, until Henry was dead, too, and the neighborhood filled up with people who put fake wood paneling on the tall, cool plaster walls, lowered the ten-foot ceilings, boarded up and bricked over the fan lights and transoms and stained glass windows, put aluminum siding over the bricks, and put astro-turf on their front stoops. It was what she told Patsy amounted to hoosier remodeling. And once a neighborhood was full of hoosiers, women with rollers in their hair who scream, "Get your ass in here," at their children who soon learn to shout vulgarities, too, the others, the ones Patsy told her to call blacks, with their beat-up cars and loud radios, would be next.

So she moved west in the direction of St. Peters, actually, but south of that to an area of instant neighborhoods and luxury townhouses. She bought a luxury townhouse, and Patsy helped her settle in, but refused, she said the whole time, to condone her grandmother's white flight. "I guess I can live anywhere I want," Henrietta said. "I've saved my money for nice things, and now I have this nice kitchen with a dishwasher and an icemaker. Besides," she added to make Patsy angry. "I'm not bigoted. I sold to that whole hoosier family with the pick-up truck only because I couldn't find any blacks."

The year she moved into her townhouse with plush rust-colored carpet and central air, the year she decided she did not miss cracked plaster and foot-wide baseboards that always needed dusting or painting or both, was the year Patsy took up with that artist. No doubt about it, Henrietta thought now as she looked out at the roof, actually the television antennae of her old house, Patsy and the artist had been together a long time, twenty years so far, just as Patsy had predicted. "We are committed," she had said then. "Even without a piece of paper." Still, if the artist ever sold anything, got any kind of job at all, Henrietta knew he would be gone. Patsy supported him—not too well at that—and was being taken for a ride. When she got to be fifty or so, the artist would find a younger woman to support him. That was the way it worked. Why couldn't she make Patsy see that she wasn't concerned about the immorality of the situation; that it was the stupidity of her own kin she couldn't take?

It was her first Christmas in the townhouse that the artist gave her a pen-and-ink sketch of her old home with its mansard roof and double-doored entrance, but Henrietta knew it was a peace offering, and refused. It was Christmas Eve when they brought it over, smiling at themselves for bearing the perfect gift, and she said, "It's okay, sort of like the house." Then to let them know she did not approve of their arrangement, did not recognize the artist as a person with a right to give her anything, she told them to take it home. And that was that. She spent her holidays alone for a while until Ruth started insisting she join her at Charlene's, or in later years, at Josie's. And even then, Henrietta fixed her own holiday dinner and ate it beforehand because, as she told Ruth over and over, neither Charlene nor Josie could earn their livings as cooks, not even for the bums who ate at the Salvation Army mission downtown.

Henrietta met Ruth at the first bingo party she attended at that fancy new church in West County that looked like a bank, and when Ruth recognized the name, Henrietta said, "How's the poodle?"

"If you want to fight," Ruth said, "let's do it in private. Come over for lunch tomorrow. Ted's dead, and I want to protect his name in public."

At lunch the next day, over chicken salad with too much mayonnaise, Ruth graciously forgave Henrietta, acted the victorious woman who had held on to her man, placed Henrietta in the category of also-ran. It was too much for Henrietta to take. "I could have had Ted if I'd wanted him," she said and pushed her plate to the side. "We had fun. Have you ever wondered how much? Have you ever, in your whole life I mean, had as much fun?" That she couldn't really remember any fun did not deter or even slow her attack. "If you had been better, he wouldn't have strayed. Your mother should have told you that before you were married." She stood, picked up her purse and the beige gloves no one but she wore anymore. "I doubt if Ted ever had much of a good name, though he may have had a reputation on his route. And I do not want to be your friend."

But Ruth was hard to insult. When Henrietta was down with the Hong Kong flu a few months later, Ruth brought soup, aspirin, hot toddies, and Henrietta was grateful initially but annoyed later, annoyed mainly that Ruth had realized she had no one else. Henrietta had not spoken to Tricia since Tricia had talked Henry into selling the market he had inherited from Jack, the one Henrietta had worked her fanny off in just to keep it from going under during the Depression. And Henry, out of misplaced loyalty, had stopped all but the basic communication with his own mother a few years before his death. And for so many years, Patsy had been busy marching for Civil Rights, Women's Rights, Gay Rights, whatever, and when Henrietta reminded her she was a troublemaker and should earn some money and dump the artist instead, Patsy would sulk and stay away until she wanted money.

When Henrietta was seventy-three, four years after her move to the new parish, she was accused of not turning in all the bingo profits—the job of selling cards had been hers for most of the four years—and Ruth defended her, even when it was clear to all that Henrietta had been paying herself, as she admitted, "just a few dollars a day. After all," she said, "I am not one to steal, but if the Catholic Church is so concerned with justice and charity, why would it expect me to work on Saturdays and Wednesdays for nothing?"

"That's exactly right," Ruth had said to those, including the pastor, who wanted to bar Henrietta from all future games. "Henrietta has always done only what she thought right." And at that, Henrietta told Ruth to shut up, told the priest she was quitting her job, and tried to insult him, though he continued to smile indulgently, by saying he and Ruth were two of a kind.

Still, Ruth remained loyal and true, remained Henrietta's only friend, so when it was time to move into an easier-to-handle place, Henrietta chose the old neighborhood, one where she could walk to church, to the market, and told Ruth she could come along if she wanted to. No sooner was the invitation given, though, than it was regretted. Henrietta hoped Ruth had not been listening, had not understood. What possessed her, how could she have been so unthinking, Henrietta wondered, but remained confused about. Anyway, it was too late. Ruth put her name on the waiting list even before Henrietta did, sold her house before Henrietta sold hers, and lucked into one of the nicer corner apartments above the quiet streets. "Why, oh Lord," Henrietta prayed, feeling more Jewish than Catholic, "am I so cursed?"

As Henrietta was unzipping her own dress—she was not nearly as decrepit as Ruth—in preparation for her nap, there was a knock and then, as none of the senior citizens locked their doors, hers opened. "Grandma?" Patsy said. "Are you here?"

"Where would I be?" Henrietta said, surprise and fatigue making her crabby, heading her toward a fight. "Why are you here?"

"I wanted to see you."

"You should have called first. I'm tired."

"Thank you, I'd love to sit," Patsy said, and did. "And it's great to see you, too."

"You want money," Henrietta said, zipping herself again for her visitor. "How much?"

"How much will you give me?"

"Nothing."

"How much will you lend me then?"

Henrietta sat, too, and put her feet up on the coffee table, an act she considered a prerogative of age. She no longer had to protect her furniture, keep it good indefinitely. "At my age, I don't make loans." Her age. It wasn't impossible she would outlive Patsy after all, but eighty-nine was pushing it. "Do me a favor," Henrietta said. "Do something for me, and I may do something for you."

"Look," Patsy said. "Am I in your will?"

"Hello," Ruth said and entered the small living room before

Henrietta could answer Patsy. "Can you give me a zip? I'm going down to lunch."

"Why don't you keep your clothes on for a whole day?" Henrietta said, and started to stand.

"I'll do it," Patsy said. She stood and Ruth presented her back. "I'm Patsy," she said. "I know you're Ruth."

"What a lovely surprise your visit must be," Ruth said.

"What makes you think it's a surprise?" Henrietta said, still leaning forward as if she could not remember whether she was getting up or sitting back down.

"I've heard a lot about you," Patsy said to Ruth, shouted actually in one of her ears as young people tend to do with the elderly, as she zipped the dress. Ruth wore a blue and white check, not the one she had worn to mass that morning, and Henrietta knew why. Ruth wore it to lunch because it was relatively new and someone who had not seen it yet might comment, and Ruth would be able to puff up like a refrigerator biscuit and say Josie gave it to her. Henrietta had already given Ruth her opinion of the dress, that that color blue made the liver spots on her face stand out more. And that was the truth.

"If it wasn't a surprise, you'd have told me," Ruth said to Henrietta.

"I don't tell you everything," Henrietta said. "Go downstairs and show off your dress."

"That's a nice dress," Patsy said. "What favor do you want of me, Grandma?"

"Her darling granddaughter bought it for her," Henrietta said, sinking back down in her chair. "Too bad she can't work zippers."

"You look fresh and energetic," Ruth said to Patsy. "Are you on your way to work?"

"I just bought this," Patsy said, stepping back to give Ruth a better view of her shiny red leotard covered below the waist by a black wrap-around skirt.

"Hah," Henrietta said. "She probably doesn't have a job. She's here for money."

"It's part of my new profession. I'm going to be an aerobics exercise instructor."

"Josie has a friend who teaches exercise classes. A man. One she almost married years ago, but she wasn't really in love with him. Not like she is with her husband. He lives in Denver, the exercise teacher, not her husband."

"I want you to grow up," Henrietta said to Patsy. "Act as if you have some sense, can see the writing on the wall, as if you take after your father instead of your mother. At least make him marry you." Henrietta sat with her head back and her eyes closed. She had spoken loudly to interrupt Ruth. "And Ruth, no one wants to hear about Josie's friend or Yosemite. Patsy wants to know if she's in my will."

"Denver," Ruth said.

"Am I, Grandma? Because if I am, I thought I may as well use it to buy into an exercise corporation now. Why wait until you're dead?"

"Ask your rich mother," Henrietta said.

"I don't speak to people who wear dead animals," Patsy said. "I wouldn't stoop so low."

"Just as low as me, huh? Just low enough to torment me, to steal from me, to anticipate my death." She stood suddenly, quicker than she had in at least the last ten years, and continued, though the room darkened and her left arm jerked. "I never did anything so horrible to you that you have to smack your lips at the thought of my death." But she doubted she had done anything so wonderful as to deserve friendship, either. A pain in her chest was burning, piercing, so she sat back down. "I am going to do my best to spend all my money before I go. I would hate like hell to leave you any," she said, and fell over on her side.

Two weeks and two operations later, a fragile woman who could not or would not talk, who was fed through a vein in her arm that had once been in her thigh but had been grafted just for the feeding, was moved from Incarnate Word Hospital where they had done all they could do, to Gardenview nursing home. "It's not the most expensive," Patsy told the artist she lived with, "but it still costs a bunch. Anyway, she doesn't need luxuries now."

Patsy arranged the move for 9:00 P.M., right after she taught her first exercise class, and Ruth insisted on going along, seeing that Henrietta was settled in, in peace.

"It's funny," Patsy said. She spoke to Ruth, but she looked at Henrietta, at the wide-opened but blank brown eyes which seemed pasted on the peach-smooth face of the woman who rested (or so it seemed) in her new and final bed. "Grandma always said she didn't want to go through this. I don't think I would have pushed the button for the medics."

"Oh, my," Ruth said, plumping a stiff, thin pillow under the thinning white hair. "Your grandma said a lot of things in her day, but I didn't pay much attention to any of it. I expect she knew that."

Weigh Station

BY BARBARA ASCH CAMILLO

The circus caravan moved into a fine rain that peppered her window with a light spray. Lil dimmed the brights on her semi and switched on the wipers. The passenger blade whined and shook, but never gave the windshield a single swipe. Lil glanced at Grandpa. The green glow from the dashboard cut deep into his wrinkles. Outside, the road wound by a river, and into patches of fog the headlights hit like fat fists plunged into a pillow. Drizzle collected and was then brushed away by the single windshield wiper blade. "Let's pray we get a heavy ran," Lil said. "The farmers are a long way from being out of the drought."

"Bite your tongue, girl. It's bad luck to wish out loud. What if you wished up a worse drought, or a tornado to blow down the tent? What if a lightning bolt stampeded the elephants?"

Lil bit the corner of her nail and stared through the windshield. Grandpa put his empty coffee cup between his knees and took the new route slip from his pocket. He extended his arm under the dashboard lights and squeezed his eyelids together. "Want me to read it to you?" she asked.

"You think I can't read? I can read just fine. Keep an eye out for Route Sixty-two North." Grandpa coughed and swallowed. "Has Scotty left his brains in his hat? It says here he's routed us right by a weigh station!"

"He'd better not have," Lil told him. "We have too many trucks down. We're overloaded, under-repaired and tied together with a ball of twine."

"Well, it says so right here, 'Weigh station.'"

"Maybe Scotty knows it's closed." Lil wished that the wiper could go faster. Water smeared across her window like Vaseline.

Grandpa dumped his empty breakfast wrappers and cartons onto the floor and let his head slide onto his shoulder. Soon, his mouth hung open. His dentures picked up an emerald glow from the dash.

Lil drove through miles of flat fields, endless rows of stunted corn and withered soybeans. Squalls lunged and receded, running topsoil onto the road in a dark, watery soup. The wiper couldn't keep up with the wash of water. Lil down shifted, leaning forward, staring at the fat globes of rain battering their way through her headlights. Grandpa stirred when the rig slowed, and stared out his window. "This is some pain in the ass morning," he said. "You know as well as I do the rain's too late for most of the farmers. Hardly a one will harvest enough to pay for a single ticket." Grandpa pinched the end of his nose. "We have to think about next season. Without enough ground water, one or two storms isn't worth a cricket's turd."

Lil shifted her hips, all pins and needles from Thirty-two's lumpy seat. She knew about groundwater. What the farmers needed was days and days of summer rain and days and days of winter snow, or, come spring, the corn seeds wouldn't stand a chance of going from sprout to healthy plant. Lil could picture the spring planting and all those tiny little corn seeds lined up kernel after kernel after kernel in row after row from Kansas to Ohio. Curled, their first sprouts bent like fresh white knees, they looked like golden fetuses waiting to be born.

For now, she'd have to count on "Skro" Houston hustling the circus through the rest of the season, scrambling for ticket sales, staving off bankruptcy week by week in the hope of long days of rain and long days of snow building up huge, spreading pools of water that waited deep underground for spring.

Her head ached from staring into the rain. The coffee had made her mouth dry. Two fresh sticks of Juicy Fruit would taste good right now, she decided, but she knew there'd be a fight if she started to chew. Grandpa wouldn't miss a chance to remind her that she looked like a camel with green slobber and long, floppy lips.

Now that he had had his nap, he was getting restless. His right hand tightened and loosened as if itching to shift the truck's gears. His feet did a tiny two-step, as he pushed down imaginary clutch and gas pedals. The hell with it, she thought, and pulled out a pack of gum and popped two sticks into her mouth. "Lil," Grandpa told her, "you look like a slobbering camel. You know you . . ." She felt Grandpa's hand on her arm. "Weigh station!" he shouted. "The coops are open!" Lil leaned forward, staring at a large metal sign.

WEIGH STATION
OPEN

She followed the arrows up a drive that ran off the road at an angle and stopped behind the cat truck, a seat truck, and an elephant truck that was idling on the scales. Ten yards beyond the elephant truck, a dozen show rigs were lined up along the borders of a field. When she stopped, she looked at her watch. Shit, she thought. We're running late and here we are with twelve overloads. Probably only a quarter of the caravan, maybe fifteen or twenty trucks and trailers, had passed through the weigh station.

I'm in for it, she thought, figuring that she had at least three bald tires and half a dozen clearance lights out. The rain sieved past the spotlights. The overload would be the worst. Besides horses, ponies, and the pile of poles, there were the bales of hay stacked on the roof. By now they would have sucked up enough rain to water ten herds of elephants.

The elephant truck moved off the scales and Lil eased Number Thirty-two forward, behind the cat truck, next to a glass door that led into the station building. Lil looked through the glass toward a cement block wall that was lit pale blue by two rows of fluorescent bulbs. It was a backdrop for desks, chairs, and maps that might have been part of her brother Jordie's old pop-up book, *Policemen Are My Friends.* In front of a large desk, Mr. Houston stood stiff as a stuffed walrus Lil had seen in a museum one year when the circus played Santa Barbara, California. His face was rumpled, as if he'd put in the wrong false teeth. Behind him, a half-dozen show drivers leaned against a relief map of Iowa. All of them faced a

Department of Transportation officer who stood with both arms resting on the desk.

A pile of ragged folders, most of them bound by rubber bands or old string, lay on a green blotter in the center of a gray desk. Lil had the same kind of folder. It was filled with her log book, cab card, chauffeur's license, medical card, and bills of lading. The officer turned and glanced out the window. His face was tired. His eyebrows sagged across his forehead. For a moment, Lil was tempted to ask Grandpa how bad he thought the fines would be. Grandpa claimed to know the fines from most of the continental states, and carried a mental rundown on every one of the rigs. Everybody knew that his figures had once been correct, but now they'd be years out of date.

Their breath had begun to fog up the windshield and Lil turned on the defroster. She decided not to look at her watch. There was a steady beating on the roof that rose to a roar. Part rain, part Sampson, Lil decided. Sampson or one of the other lions in the cat truck was roaring. Maybe rain had seeped into his cage, maybe he was irritated with the change in the weather. He sounded mad as a cement mixer choking on gravel. The familiar voice of lion, the warmth of the truck, and the sound of the rain comforted Lil and she leaned back in the seat feeling more hopeful. It would be tight, she told herself, but there still was leeway to get to the lot in time for the early show. The important thing was that last night at dinner, Front Office Lois had said that the advance sales were good. A couple of full houses would go a long way to make up for the morning's fines.

When the cat truck left the scales and parked behind the other semis next to the field, Lil shifted into first and rolled her rig a truck length, stopping just behind the seat semi. She sometimes wished Grandpa still drove his horse truck and she could return to the old days when Mom pulled the trailer and he let her ride with him in the truck. She used to stuff her pajamas in her jeans and eat donuts until she fell asleep with her head on his lap, rocked by the jolting of the truck and the shifting of his thigh muscles when he rode the gas.

She leaned forward, trying to make out if the seat truck had been slapped with violations. Grandpa waved his forefinger in front of Lil's face. "Lil!" He pointed out the window. "The monkey wrench. Get rid of it quick!"

She rolled down the glass. The rain hit cold and hard enough to soak her pink shirt to the color of grape juice. She hung out the window to her waist, trying to unscrew the wrench. A week ago, when the mechanics were too busy to fix her side mirror, she'd borrowed Grandpa's old monkey wrench, tightened the grip, and left it in place of a missing bolt.

"Hurry. Lil, Hurry!"

She scraped her knuckles against a nut and licked the blood away. The screw spun between her fingers but the grip didn't loosen. Damn. The teeth were rusted in place.

Now don't get frazzled, she told herself. Pretend you're a calm person. She thought about Rafael, the new wire walker. If he had a motto, it would be, "Never let them know what you're thinking."

"Hurry it up, Lil!"

"*Madre de Dios,*" she whispered, figuring that was what Rafael would say if he finally got mad. "*Hijo de madre de Dios.*" She yanked with both hands. The wrench gave way and her torn knuckles slid across a rusted nut. She slipped back into the seat and wiped her face with a McDonald's napkin. The mirror remained in place, suspended from its one remaining screw.

"Can I see that wrench, Miss!"

An officer stood below Lil's window. His hands on his hips. If his hair was dry, it would probably be auburn. Now it was dark and slicked down in the rain, smooth as a wood duck's feathers. He watched her with the kind of look that towner men sometimes wore when she walked into the big top in not much more than her Passion Pink lipstick and a few inches of cloth covered with sequins.

"Anything you say, Red," Lil told him. With his big, gray admiring eyes, it was easy to smile back at him.

"Nice wrench," he said, when she handed it to him, "but a little rusty." He passed it back through the window. "Are you a show girl?"

"I'm the bareback rider," she told him, figuring it would be too much to explain that she worked five acts plus the spec parade. She widened her smile and held his stare. Hell, turn it on a little more and maybe he'd wave her right through.

Red drew his slicker tight around his neck with one hand, with the other he wiped the rain from his eyes and eyebrows. He stepped back and bent in a deep bow and gestured her forward. It was Lil's turn on the scales.

She closed the window and gave him a thumbs up sign, then pulled forward, lining up her wheels. She waited for the reading, drumming her fingers on the steering wheel, and stared into a dime store mirror that she'd stuck to the visor with white adhesive tape. It always irritated her that her face didn't look properly adult. Going without make-up made her features seem tinier and more childish. Only her eyes were grown-up, but they looked old enough to be borrowed from her mother. Her hair stuck to her head as if it were held in place with glue, except for her pigtails that tried to curl but only poked out like spikes. Her features slid from the mirror when a truck pulled behind her and its headlights swept her image away. She looked into the rain and her face reappeared in the window glass, a white reflection against the dark sky.

"You have a weight violation," the speaker barked. "Park your vehicle and come on in for a scale reading."

Lil pulled forward, pulled behind the seat truck, and stared out of the window. She wondered how her mother was doing. Was she still on the road with their trailer? Was Jordie her brother asleep with his head on her lap? Mom had been after her to replace the broken taillight and the front clearance lights. Mr. Houston only paid the fines on show rigs. If Mom was fined, the family would have to borrow from Skro and he'd dock their salaries come payday.

"You want I should go in with you?" Grandpa asked. "Do you want me to argue about the violations?"

"No, thanks. Skro is taking care of things." She reached in front of Grandpa and took her blue folder from the glove compartment.

"O.K.," Grandpa said. "You go on in. I'll sit here and figure fines."

"Have fun," she said and patted his arm. She pulled a new box of trash bags from beneath the seat. She bit a hole halfway down either side and one in the middle of the bottom, then stretched each hole wide enough for her face and arms to poke through. She slipped the bag over her hair and peered out.

Once she stepped out, rain pounded against the plastic. She held the folder inside the bag, in her right hand. Her left hand poked out like a flipper. She made a dash for the overhanging roof of the cement block building; the bag slipped from her head and settled onto her shoulders. Her pigtails dripped against her neck.

A few yards ahead, someone ran toward the office. "Rafael!" Lil shouted, and squeezed next to him under the roof's over-hang. They huddled together. Water collected in a stream at their feet. The rain had plastered Rafael's hair into two neat black wings pressed tightly against his skull. He looked like a silent movie star, starting out of a black and white photo, wearing a smile and Brylcreem in his hair. Rafael reached out. His fingers plucked at Lil's trash bag. "Nice raincoat," he said, "Who's your tailor?"

Lil looked down at her watch. It was after seven o'clock and they still had another hundred miles to cover. If the big top crew didn't start setup on time, there might not be a first performance.

One of the show's blue school buses turned off the scales and then pulled behind the row of parked trucks. Lil pointed with her chin. There's your Papa. They've got him on a violation."

"It must be the tires," Rafael said. "It's always the tires." He touched her hand, then ran toward the door, shoulders hunched, moving in a graceful lope that reminded Lil of his high wire finale—the last run across the tightrope before the forty-five degree descent down the guy wire.

She ran after him and slid through the half-opened door. A rush of warmth and the sound of Skro Houston's voice flowed over her. The group of drivers lining the wall seemed to have doubled. They were staring at the back of the uniformed officer who still stood behind his metal desk talking to Skro. Houston's hand closed into a fist and punched the air above his silver belt buckle.

"Damn it! Son of a bitch! Who do you work for, Al Capone!" Lil's breath stopped below her throat. In the old days, there wasn't anyone better at velveting an official. Lil always thought that the lines on Skro's face made him seem strong. He still looked tough, but now he had the look of an Iowa farmer who'd been out in the sun, watching the drought kill his crop year after year.

"One 'damn,' and one 'son of a bitch,' " the officer said. "Let's see, I think we have one, no, *two* more bald tires. That's twenty-five dollars, plus fifteen percent surcharge and court costs. That comes to thirty-eight seventy-five for each violation. Thirty-eight seventy-five times two is, uh, that's another seventy-seven dollars and fifty cents." Lil followed Rafael and stood with the others against the wall. She watched the agent's profile reflected in the window that faced the scales. The rain ran down the glass, pulling his reflection with it, like a picture painted on melting wax. Next to her, the drivers shifted their weight in slow, awkward movements. Lil stared at her own reflection and pushed her hand through the bag to the elbow. Her image disintegrated into a puddle at the bottom of the glass. Beyond her reflection, the cook house truck rested on the scales, a dark shadow in the downpour.

"You sniveling bastard!"

"Sniveling bastard," the agent repeated, "sounds like another safety violation." Please God, Lil prayed. Don't let Skro run up more violations than he can pay for. Houston's pale face grew paler and his cheeks shivered, as if a new stream of profanity was fighting itself free.

"Son of a bitch!" Skro said, "I'll take you all to court."

"Son of a bitch," the agent repeated in a monotone, writing on his pad. A waxy, blue vein crawled, throbbing across Skro's temple. His mouth opened. His dentures clicked. Lil could see the tender pink of his gums.

And then the door opened and Red stood in the entry way. "Captain. You'd better come quick. They're rearranging the cargo on those overloaded trucks, and . . ."

The captain turned slowly. "Lowell," he said with exaggerated care, "*I am busy.*"

"But . . ."

He slammed his fist on the desk. A glass paperweight encasing a preserved scorpion jolted into the air, then landed with a faint rat-ta-tat. "*I am busy.*"

Red's face flushed. He glanced at Lil, as if she were the only witness to his humiliation.

"Ye-s-s-s, sir!" Red said, and walked out of the door.

"Mister. You-wait-right-here." The officer jerked a raincoat from a coat rack and stamped into the rain behind Red.

"Hold my folder," Lil told Rafael. She pushed out the door, running across the cement behind the two officers. Their black shapes quivered under the first slashes of lightning. Rain fell like cold knuckles against her scalp. It filled her eyes. The sky was still dark, the rising sun shrouded by the gathering of fierce thunderheads. She pulled the bag over her head and peered through the slit. The air shivered, then trembled with the sound of thunder. One of the elephants trumpeted.

The row of trucks lined up by the edge of the field had grown longer. Their metal sides were thick with running water. A second bolt of lightning cracked the sky like a broken mirror. It froze Hortence, the elephant, as she eased out of the truck's open door, shiny and slick with dark rivulets running along the crevasses of her skin. "Move up," Shmutsihk, the head elephant man, barked. Half the herd had lined up next to the camels, two zebras, and Alfredo the donkey. Behind Lil, rigs were backed up from the scales clear to the road.

The officers stood facing the elephant trucks, on either side of a steaming, bucket-sized dropping. Another streak of lightning, and another—the rain came in squalls across the cement. What's in their minds? Lil wondered. Are they thinking, How strong are the bars on a lion's cage? Are they wondering, Can an elephant break her chains?

Their unease made Lil feel strong. She felt clean and light; the rain, the wind, the animals seemed invented, a magic trick that brought the agents onto her turf. They were strangers on their own ground. The storm still blotted out the morning except for a faint glow along the edge of the clouds, and Lil felt linked to the tethered bison, to the camels, and to their handlers.

Another stroke of lightning. The ground shook with the pull of thunder. Lil wished they'd hurry up and reload the elephants. If the lightning got much worse, they might run.

The captain took a half step forward. He waved his arms in a stuttering arc, and then backed up. He was shouting.

Lil could see Red sidle up to Shmutsihk, say something, then edge away.

Shmutsihk walked near Lil without seeing her. "We're re-loading," he shouted to his men. "Tail 'em up!" A bolt of lightning seemed to rise from the ground to the sky, lighting a mountain of cloud that a moment before had been as black as the black morning sky. The bulls' skin glistened like mud-covered hills. They filled the morning with their restless bodies linked trunk to tail. Their trumpeting ran up and down the line, vibrating with the thunder. "Tail up! Tail up! Tail up!" the elephant men shouted. Lil could feel their weight shift the ground under her, could smell their odor as it washed from their bodies and swirled in the puddles at her feet. She felt their fear.

"Tail up!" the handlers shouted. Their voices made her body feel cold under the damp inner skin of her plastic trash bag. "Please God, don't let them run," she whispered, waiting for the men to order the elephants down into the mud on their sides, the safest place for elephants with minds to bolt. The squalls came on steadily, but the lightning held off. One by one, elephants lunged up the ramps and into their trucks. Their trumpeting quieted to low, throbbing coos. She could hear them rocking, safe in the familiar darkness of their trailers, warbling one to another.

The captain and Red trotted toward the office with Lil following a few yards behind. Beyond the agents, through the window, Lil could see Rafael, dry and distant in the rectangle of light bordered by the station window. His hands were spread, palms out in front of Houston. He's trying to talk some sense into him, she thought. Skro stood opposite Rafael, tight-shouldered and stiff-legged.

She skirted her truck and glanced into the cab, thinking that maybe Grandpa would have some influence with Houston. But he had dozed off again, his forehead and cheek outlined by a street lamp. His hair rose foamy and white around his skull, bleached by the light to the halo of the very old. Lil felt weak with the urge to protect him. She'd once seen a photo of a painting of Great-great-great-great-great-grandpa Vallotton, his hair as wild and white as Grandpa's, his face as stubborn. She turned away from the truck and broke into a run, entering the building just behind the agents.

The room seemed warmer and steamier than she remembered. The captain's raincoat shed a tattoo of water onto the black and white tiles of the linoleum floor. Houston's gray face was stained with red splotches like flowers of ink on a wet page. His lips were thin and white.

For one moment, the fate of the circus seemed frozen in his unspoken words. "Skro!" Lil shouted. She stared into his face. "You—you're damned lucky that Mr. Murillo hasn't fired you long before this!"

Houston and Rafael stared at her with identical black slate eyes. Both men's mouths appeared to hesitate over the same, startled thoughts.

Slowly, Rafael looked from Lil to Houston and then he nodded. "Old man," he said, haltingly. "This behavior has gone far enough." He glanced at the captain. "How do you do, sir," he said, and his voice grew firmer and louder. "I'm Rafael Enrique Murillo y Ponce de León, the general manager of Houston Brothers Circus. I am here . . ." he paused and looked once more in Lil's direction, ". . . to apologize for this man."

The captain turned to Rafael.

Rafael rushed on. "You," he said, leaning forward, pressing his palm against Skro's chest, "you are fired."

Shifting so that he blocked Houston from the officer's view, he met Lil's eye, then exchanged a quick glance with Skro.

Rafael nodded his head toward the captain. "I not only apologize for this man's behavior," he said, and his rich voice held barely a hint of an accent. "But I will give you my word that he will never again work for the Houston Brothers Circus." He leaned back on his heels and folded his arms. "Do you hear me, old man? Pack your gear. You will be paid and left in the next town."

Lil edged forward. She walked behind Skro and put her hands on his shoulders. "Let's go," she said and gave him a little push. He moved forward slowly, without lifting his eyes. "March," she repeated, resting her hand on his shoulder, guiding him forward under a clock that hung above the door. It was almost nine. The circus might make it to the lot in time for the early show.

"Year after year we return to Iowa," Rafael was saying, his

voice firm. "I intend to see that we continue to be welcome visitors." Lil kept Skro moving. Rafael's voice flowed with them through the half closed door. "Houston Brothers Circus is anxious to pay any fines that you deem fair."

"Who are you again!"

"Murillo. Rafael Enrique Murillo y Ponce de Leon, the manager of Houston Brothers Circus." Skro kept his head down and stepped into the rain. The wind blew the door shut behind them with a final thud. The rain had eased to a faint mist that brushed like velvet against Lil's cheek. She breathed deeply, then exhaled. Her next breath brought the acid, sweet smell of lion and the comforting, ginger-hay scent of elephant.

The sky was filling with light. She noticed Number Thirty-two parked nose to tail with the other rigs, linked in a long chain along the verge of cement. For the first time in weeks, the red and white stripes on the trucks were washed clean. The caravan looked like a freight train waylaid by a storm, stopping briefly on a journey through a foreign land.

Pictures of Silver,
Pictures of Gold

BY JONATHAN MANEY

"They'd let anybody in," Jerry said. "A Russian."

"They let *us* in," my mother said softly.

Jerry was talking about the old man who had moved to the other side of the trailer park. We'd all heard that the man was a Russian—or used to be.

"Hey Ric," Jerry called.

I pretended to look up and notice Jerry for the first time. I hated him. I was going on sixteen and blamed him for keeping us in such a crummy place. I'd been looking at the back of his head; his hair was long enough to part at his shirt collar and show the whiteness of his neck.

Jerry leaned against the kitchen counter. He stroked his beard. I grinned back at him.

"I'll get my shoes," I said.

I told him I'd go over there and see what the old man was hiding. It was what I always did with someone new.

"Just let us know what he's got," Jerry said as I went to the door. "Me and Maria need to do some figuring."

I caught a glimpse of my mother behind him. She had been to the refrigerator and had a beer in each hand. I saw her nod at me, and I had a feeling she wanted me to check things out for her, too.

The trailers close to the main road were the oldest of the

bunch; some were at least fifteen or twenty years old. These were the ones that rented out cheap. As you went into the park, the trailers were newer and had mostly old people in them and windows with flowerboxes. In the very back the trees began— aspen and some trashy-looking pines— and in a spot at the end of everything the Russian had parked his trailer.

I walked right up to it. Jerry told me that this was the way to avoid looking suspicious; it was sneaking around that got you caught. I knocked hard, but before I could hear anything the door swung in and I jumped.

"Hallo," the old man said, pushing up his glasses.

His eyes took time to focus on me. Up close his face looked transparent, with the veins in his cheeks showing through, and over his bald head a few white hairs stuck straight up or fell down to where his eyebrows bushed out. He was tall and his head seemed heavy; his whole body leaned as if he was tired of carrying it. But it was the eyebrows I noticed most; they were wispy, like wings.

"Who are *you?*" he said.

I blurted out my real name, not the one I'd meant to use.

"Please, please come in," he said.

He held the door open. His voice was deep and slow, and reminded me of movies on television after midnight.

"Sit down, please," he said as I went inside; then I watched him go into the kitchen where he put something in his mouth. When he came back he had teeth. He smiled and said he'd met my mother at the mailboxes. I kept my mouth shut and looked around at the old man's things. His trailer was a lot bigger than ours, but the furniture was old and looked lived-in. He had a clock that might have been worth something.

"So, you like to push pieces around?"

"Huh?" I said, staring at him.

"Chess"—he stretched the word to a hiss. "Your mother said."

My mother. A long time ago one of her boyfriends, Chuck, had taught me to play. We had started out with checkers and when I was good at it Chuck decided to teach me chess. "A real game," he used to say before I began to beat him—"the only one you hate to lose." When Chuck left, I had a full set of checkers that I marked as kings and queens and rooks and pawns. They were mine that way, and with no one else to play I began to think that the whole game was mine and always had been—like I'd made it up myself.

"Yeah, I play," I said

"Good," he said. "So which do you choose, the black or the white?"

"Black," I said; white was what Chuck always took.

The old man smiled.

"All right," he said. "We begin."

He went into another room, a bedroom maybe, and came back with a big board. He set it down on the table by the window. I took a chair there and saw the view of the trailer park and the road down to Grantsville. I was surprised what a good view it was. But I didn't look very long, because the old man was laying out his side, and I had never seen such amazing pieces—ivory, he said, and mine, ebony—they were carved like the statues in a church my mother and I used to go to when we lived in Arizona.

The old man made his move. I could see what he was up to: the pawn in front of his king was now two squares ahead, making way for his bishop and queen. I did the same. Everything was fine until I lifted my carved black knight.

The old man shook his head.

"No, not that one," he said. "This is not the best, this move."

I grinned.

"I can take your queen."

"Yes, yes. But do that and you uncover yourself. Here. And here."

He pointed to a rook and my own queen. He raised his eyebrows.

I put the knight down. I was stuck. I looked at a whole lot of combinations and still I couldn't decide what to do. Before, with Chuck, I could see the future; I knew what would happen every move we'd make. But now I couldn't see a thing. I looked up and saw the old man watching me.

"So what would *you* do?" I said.

He sat back in his chair. His glasses had come down his nose and he tipped his head to look through them.

"Call me Mr. Chernov," he said in his slow, monster-movie voice: "Then I'll show you what to do."

At home, my mother had a dreamy look on her face. Jerry was gone and she was wearing his blue bathrobe. The place reeked of dope, and Ancient Age was spilled on the counter.

"What if I had friends?" I said.

My mother stopped smiling and tucked the robe in tighter around her waist. She gave me a sour look.

"What's wrong, Ric?" she said, sitting down at the kitchen table. "This isn't good enough for you?"

"When are we going to leave?"

She pushed a strand of hair out of her face. "What?" she said.

"Are we going to get out of here?"

She reached for a package of cigarettes, shook one out and lit it with the lighter Jerry had given her. After the first drag she said, "I'm not going anywhere."

"Yes you are."

"Don't hold your breath," she said, and I could see that she wasn't serious, that if I kept at her she would come out of the place in her mind she was always going off to. And things would be like they were before, when we talked about which cities we'd go to and how we'd get there and the better life that would naturally follow.

"I'm not going anywhere," she said again, and her eyes shifted away from me.

"Like hell," I said.

I watched her shuffle out of the kitchen and disappear into her room at the end of the trailer. I began to panic. Summer was almost over. I sat down and thought about the places we'd been—Arizona, New Mexico, and now Utah—and how every time we moved it was because of Gordon or Tom or Chuck saying so, and not because *we* made a decision.

"All right then, *I'll* go! You hear me?" I said, and listened: "I'll go by myself." But I don't think she heard me.

"Well, anything good over there?"

Jerry was back again. He had a part-time job mowing lawns down in Grantsville, but I never knew where exactly. He said he moved around a lot and rode tractors. His shoes were never stained; somehow he kept himself clean. It was past seven o'clock by then and my mother was still asleep.

"Nothing," I lied. "The old man doesn't have much."

Jerry gave me a disgusted look.

"Got to be something in there. Color TV?"

"No," I said, and I was glad to tell the truth; the Russian didn't have a TV that I knew of, just an old Zenith radio.

"Microwave?" Jerry asked, and narrowed his eyes.

"Built-in," I said.

"Any furniture?" he said, bearing down on me.

"Just regular stuff," I told him. "Nothing new."

"He's got a new trailer, though," Jerry said. "A Golden West. But his car's no good—you think maybe he shot his wad on the trailer and moved in here because it's cheap?"

His eyes moved off me for a second.

"Maybe," I said, and then Jerry looked at me again and stroked his beard; he liked to pull the long hairs growing just below his mouth.

"Maybe," he repeated. "But maybe not. Either way, we're dipped in shit."

He lowered his voice and glanced at the shut door to my mother's room.

"Must be *hot* in there," he whispered, and he smiled at me and nodded his head. "Ric," he said, wiping the sweat from his forehead, "we got trouble. I don't have the money for groceries."

He let this sink in.

"The new Albertson's," I said. "We haven't been in there yet."

In Grantsville we drove by houses where people were out hosing their lawns, and when they looked up, Jerry waved. He had a Waylon Jennings tape that he sang along with. He called me "partner" once or twice and kept grinning, and I could see why people liked him.

We pulled over a block from Albertson's. I would go in first, then in a few minutes Jerry would follow. He was going to head over to the meat department and see if he could get a steak or two.

"Rib-eye," Jerry sang. "Tenderloin, sirloin, T-bone; you can taste the sound."

Jawbreakers were the best. Fireballs were good, too—either one I could hide in my cheek while I held my throat and pretended to choke. Then, after a clerk and maybe one of the managers started over to me, I'd spit it out and cough hard as if I'd almost gagged to death.

I saw Jerry.

The new Albertson's was pretty big so I was careful to keep an eye on him. I'd already swiped a jawbreaker; this one was purple, and I was sucking on it to get it down to size. Jerry wandered over to the meat department after looking at the bread and pastries. He caught a glimpse of me and I knew this was the signal to go between the first two aisles. But the jawbreaker was still too big. I was trying to mash it up with my teeth when it flipped down my throat and I couldn't swallow.

By the time I made it home it was dark. Jerry's truck was off to the side. I could see a blue light in the living room; the TV was on and when I walked in Jerry and my mother were sitting together on the couch, holding hands. My mother smiled.

"There's some meat left on the stove," she said. "It might be a little dry by now."

"Where you been, partner?"

"Took a walk," I told Jerry.

He gave a nod and looked back at the TV. What else could I say? He didn't even wait for me. I still felt light as a balloon in my head, and my throat hurt where the checker had jammed her fingers inside. Her nails were sharp, and between her and the manager squeezing my gut from behind, the jawbreaker had popped out.

As soon as I sat down in the living room, my mother got up.

"Night," she said.

Jerry let his hand brush against my shoulder on his way behind her. I found a roach in the ashtray and reached over to turn up the TV. Even with the bedroom door shut I wanted to drown out their gluey voices.

A science special was on; it was about this woman who was trying to decide whether apes had a language. Watching it I decided they did, but it was a secret language nobody else could understand. Looking at their faces I could tell that something was going on, but you had to be them to be the expert.

"So, you come to play chess," the old man said.

"Sure," I said, but there was another reason.

"Excuse me," he said, touching his chin; the stubble on his cheeks made the bottom half of his face seem frosted.

I figured he was going off to get the chessboard. While he was gone I looked at the cuckoo clock and decided that even broken it had to be worth something. At the top was an elk's head with curved yellow horns, and draped at either side of the dial were rabbits and ducks and quail, and each had glass eyes that looked as real up close as anything dead I'd seen. Above the dial was a door, and I was trying to open it when Chernov came back.

"What are you doing?" he said.

His face was pink and wet and his chin had a spot of blood where he'd cut himself.

"Now," he said. "We begin." He held his arm out toward the table by the window.

The chessboard was already there.

This time I took white. He didn't seem to care. And I started a different way: I put my queen's pawn forward two squares. I would get him with my queen, the most powerful piece on the board.

The old man flexed his eyebrows; he made the same move.

After that it got worse. As the game went on I noticed how the afternoon sun came through the kitchen window and threw lines across the backs of Chernov's books—there were bookshelves in the living room—and how it made their titles shine.

"You would be better to watch here," Chernov said, disgusted. "You're not making sense."

"Where'd you get these?"—I was still looking at the books.

Chernov shrugged. "Oh, souvenirs," he said.

I got up to pick one out. The pages were filled with words made of letters like capital B's or A's but with horns attached. You could tell it was from someplace far away.

"So, you have found something," he said.

He took off his glasses and wiped them with a tissue. His eyes looked raw.

I put the book back on the shelf. Already I felt like I was stealing.

"They are from a long time ago," he said.

He leaned forward and put his hands on his knees and looked at me with his sore eyes. I thought he was going to yell at me,

"Maybe you would like to see some Russian people. Some real Russian people. Maybe you would like to see some pictures I have."

He put his glasses back on and went to one of his rooms. I wondered if "real Russians" lived in trailers. He'd cleaned things up since the last time I was here: the newspapers were gone, and the calendar on the kitchen wall now said August. When the old man came back he had three books in his arms.

"Push it over—the chessboard, please," he said in his heavy voice, and when I moved the chessboard he set the books down on the table between us.

He took a seat and flipped the top one open; it was an old photo album, huge, with a red velvet cover.

"These were my cousins in Vladivostok," he said, pointing to the first picture.

I saw three women in long white dresses sitting at a table. The table was heaped with flowers. The women had their hands in their laps. Their faces were silver—as if each had a light inside.

The old man turned the page. As he went on I saw that all the pictures had that same silver light in them—like something you would remember from a dream. And I began to feel like *I* was in that strange place until I heard a backfire from the road.

"I am boring you," said Mr. Chernov.

I couldn't pull my eyes from the window. I knew that sound: it was Jerry's truck shifting into second. I watched the truck move fast down the road and then turn from Grantsville, I had no idea where Jerry was going, but seeing him drive out like that I envied him.

"You should be glad he's gone," I said to my mother. "I am."

It was almost a week since Jerry had left. My mother told me that Jerry was in Southern California, where he had friends and would stay a while. Already the sheriff had been here to look for him.

She was wearing the green dress she put on for special occasions. We were sitting in the living room after dinner with the TV turned down. She looked nice just then and I wished we could be someplace else where people could see us. She reached for the ashtray to snub out her cigarette.

"He'll be back," she said.

"You know the Russian," I said. "He's got some things I think we could sell."

My mother had her hands in her lap where she twisted a ring. "Like what?"

I told her about the chess set and the cuckoo clock and said he had other things in drawers.

"Don't you like him?" she said. "I thought you two might be friends."

"I don't want any more friends," I said, getting up. "I've had enough of your friends."

"You don't have to get mad," she said and looked at me.

"Listen," I said, "how much have you saved?"

I saw her eyes move toward the TV, where some woman in a bathing suit was jumping up and down.

"No," she said. "I told you. I'm not going anywhere right now."

I sat down in the torn-up chair across from her.

"Why?" I said. "This is perfect. We can get out. We don't have to live like this."

"Live like what?" she said hoarsely. "You think it's so much better anywhere else? You think things will be different? You think you'll find some perfect place in that goddamned crazy quilt out there?"

I just stared at her.

"Look, hon," she said. "I haven't got the money to buy the gas for the car we haven't got to take us where we can't afford to go. You understand?"

"We'd take off if you wanted to," I said.

"To where? Where *is* this wonderful place?"

We had talked about a lot of places—Spokane, where she had a brother; Phoenix, where she'd been a hairdresser; New Mexico, where she had a friend who still wrote to her—but all I finally said was, "I don't know, California maybe?"

My mother swept back the hair that had fallen over her eyes. She looked at me as if I was dumb and pathetic.

"The more you expect, Ric, the more you'll be disappointed."

I tried to swallow. My throat was still raw where the jawbreaker had caught in it. All this time I'd been blaming Jerry. But it wasn't Jerry. It was her. She would stay here and wait for him, and if he didn't show, she'd find someone else. Someone worse. She wasn't going anywhere with me.

I went to the door. She didn't look pretty anymore, not in the way I'd imagined. She looked like she was getting ready to go out again, and that's all.

"You don't look so good," said Mr. Chernov.

I forced a smile. "I want to see your pictures," I said.

"Bictures?" he mumbled. He wiped his mouth with a napkin and kept chewing. "Ah, you mean my family."

He had just finished dinner. The albums were still there, pushed off to the side of the table. The old man cleared things away and we sat down and opened the one with a dark green cover. I was glad I'd asked about them—it gave me time to think.

He flipped through the first few pictures, tapped his finger and said, "Here was very good building. . . . This was old Russian church. . . . This was taken the day I discovered that if you mix vodka with tea, you have a very different drink."

On the next page there was only one photograph. He touched it but didn't say a word.

"Who's this?" I asked.

"Her," he said and cleared his throat. "She was my mother."

The photograph showed a big woman sitting in a chair. She wasn't smiling, but you could tell from her eyes that she would. Her dress was like the ones I'd seen in the first album, but even fancier: this had lacy stuff hanging from the front, all the way down to the tips of her pointed shoes. I remembered my mother drunk in Jerry's bathrobe.

Mr. Chernov turned the page.

"You see this boy," he said, pointing to a head shaped like a kidney bean. "Kidnapped, right out of his home!"

"Yeah?"

"They came to his house and rang the bell. He went to answer the door." Mr. Chernov clicked his fingers. "That was it—disappeared. You like that, don't you."

I nodded.

"I'll tell you a little story. I can't remember if his parents paid a ransom; I think they did. Anyway, he was a friend of mine. He told me the kidnappers were three or four fellows, ex-officers maybe. The way they talked they were well-educated, you see. And while they held him, they let him read good literature, some Tolstoy and Turgenev.

"One day one of them slipped up and left a pistol on the table. So this friend of mine, he picked it up and said, 'Okay. I'm going to shoot you.' 'Nah,' said the other guy, 'you're not going to shoot me. I wouldn't hurt you.' So my friend put the gun down."

Mr. Chernov belched. He turned the page and went through each of the milky-gray pictures, the men in tall boots and fur hats, the women in white with jewels around their necks, and then to sleighs, horses, and dogs, and a harbor full of ships which he called "The Golden Horn"—and the whole time I was beginning to think of his "Russian people" as a weird place I'd go to if I had a chance, though just then any place was better than where I was.

"Hah!" he said, rubbing his finger on the wavy, almost white hair of a kid who looked out from the album page. "That was me, here, with blond hair."

The old man caught me glancing at his head: the stray hairs had fallen to his eyebrows again. His eyes glimmered behind his glasses, and he passed his hand over the checker pattern of pictures on the black page—the faces there, the houses with twisted columns and tall porches and window frames as carved as his cuckoo clock, which ticked quietly on the wall.

It was the last page. Mr. Chernov closed the album.

"So, you want more?"

"Sure," I said. I couldn't decide what to do. If I took the clock or the chess set, who would buy it from me? How much would I get? Would I have to beat the old man up? Would I have to hurt him somehow?

"This was a long time ago," he said, reaching for the third album. "First," he said, "why don't you tell me what you see in these that is so interesting?"

I didn't like the way he was looking at me. It was as if he could read my mind, and I wasn't used to anyone doing that.

"Tell me the truth," he said. "You want to get out of here, don't you?"

I stared at him. The old man brought his face up close to mine.

"You think I have something here?" he asked. "Diamonds maybe? A pot of gold?" He waved his hand in front of his face and sat back. "Stupid—stupid!" he said.

My eyes slid from him to the junk in the room. I didn't make my move. Not yet.

"All right," Mr. Chernov said. "We go to the next part. The next part is not quite so nice." He opened the album and thumped a finger on someone's head.

"Yelena. She was quite the pianist. She used to play classical music. Chopin. Schubert. I used to come to her house and she would be practicing. And I wonder. I didn't pay attention, you know, to what she was playing."

The old man was quiet a minute. "Sometimes I hear this music," he said.

"And here, we were lying on these blankets, she and I. Her hair was blond but her eyebrows dark; do you see it? She was half-Jewish. She and I, we were quite the naturalists."

I stopped looking. I was tired of pictures. My legs tingled and I was mad because I hadn't done anything.

"You left," I said. "You left that place."

"Ah ha," said Mr. Chernov. "A little story, just so you know. In Vladivostok when I was in gymnasia—that is like your high school—they had just kicked the Bolsheviks out, and the Bolsheviks, they had some three-inch guns and were trying to get back in. You do not know what a Bolshevik is, do you?"

The old man's eyes shone. I said no.

"They had pretty good slogan: 'All land to peasants, all factories and mines to workers.' Problem was, if anybody owned a business or property, they knew they were going to get it in the neck. But let me tell you the truth about these things.

"It was the time of my examinations that I am talking about. I took sixteen subjects in two or three days. We had our own mortars in the park by the school, and they would set them off, like this: ONE-TWO-THREE, and the teacher, he would hold up his hand while they went off; but he'd timed it so he'd already asked the question. So I had time to think. His hand would come down and I would answer.

"There were fires all over the place and I had to cross town to get home. I was wearing a uniform, my school uniform—so I had to be careful. I ran around corners, through people's yards, over gates. And then there was this big yard where the Bolsheviks were hiding. One of them said, 'Come here.' He grabbed me and pushed me against a fence. I could feel his breath in my face. He wanted to know which side was winning. They were changing from their uniforms into civilian clothes. I said I didn't know, I had to go home. But when I came to my street, I saw that everything was smashed to pieces.

"You see, the town was partly destroyed while I took my examinations. My whole family, two of my cousins, even the cook—they all were wiped out while I waited for that teacher's hand to fall."

Mr. Chernov stared beyond me through the window.

"What happened then?"

"So what happens when the Bolsheviks take over?" he said. "They have a big parade. I dressed up like a bum to see them. You couldn't go out in good clothes. It was dangerous to look like an aristocrat. In this parade they had red armbands, sabres, stolen horses. Beautiful horses. And this one guy comes along, I notice him wobble all around. I say out loud to someone next to me how drunk he is. Naturally the man on the horse, he hears me. He turns the horse around with his sabre raised."

Mr. Chernov's hand flew up over his head, where it shook but stayed in the air. His eyes were wide and staring.

"What did you do?"

The old man looked at me over his glasses for a long minute. In his eyes I could see how hard he was holding himself together—how hard it was now and always would be.

His hand swooped down at my face. I flinched; it missed me and crashed on the table.

"I ran away," he said.

Mr. Chernov got up then. For the first time I noticed how dirty his clothes were: his shirt was stiff with sweat, and his pants had pee stains. I followed him to the door. Beyond him the sky was gold. I could see over the trailer tops, the road to Grantsville, and even a piece of the Great Salt Lake ten miles away. I felt my own life move past me into the open air, into what my mother called the "crazy quilt," which wasn't crazy at all—just woods and fields and bare spots stitched together, light and dark, like chessboard squares.

"You can go now," Mr. Chernov said. "You can go."

Rituals

BY MARILYN K. KRUEGER

An early frost hit two years ago, just when deer hunting season was about to begin. We pulled the tomato plants and hung them from the rafters of the garage, hoping the fruit would ripen. We always had plenty of green ones, but a person can eat just so many green tomato pickles and green tomato pies. The days were still sunny and warm, but the sky held a gauze of cloud and the breeze ruffled gooseflesh along my arms. Tamarack needles flamed orange among the pine and fir. They were always a surprise.

Thirty head of deer fed in a big draw behind the main house on our ranch. Four big bucks were in the herd, and two little forked-horns. The cool days of fall had brought them down from the high country, shiny and fat from alpine grazing. My husband and I loved to take walks along the fence line to watch them. We counted heads together, and looked for horns. Charlie would play-act that he had a rifle. BAM . . . BAM . . . he'd say, and laugh.

Charlie was an experienced hunter. He had started at the hip of his father when he was seven. They packed the camp boxes and sheepherder stove, man-tied the tent, loaded the gear on a couple of mules, and disappeared into the mountains for a week. After Dad got too old to enjoy the hard ground and cold nights, Charlie hunted with four buddies he'd logged with in earlier years. Dad treated me to dinners at the Elks while Charlie was gone, and we danced every waltz the piano player could remember. It became a fall ritual, broken only once. That was the time big red Jake didn't want to be packed. He hammered a hoof print into Charlie's chest and laid him out flat. We did without venison that fall, and Dad and I missed our dances. Charlie got a permanent dent under his heart, and an old Basque sheepherder got the mule.

Charlie never hunted on the home ranch. It was too easy, he said. He ran cattle among the deer there, watched them graze, knew where they'd be. Not much sport in that, he'd say. I saw it differently. Charlie took his hunt to other grounds for me. I don't like guns or the noise they make, or the thought of those animals not jumping our fences anymore.

Two days before the opening of buck season he got a call from his friend LeRoy whose ranch ran along the breaks of the John Day River. Every October the deer came out of the Rudio Mountain country to nibble on the last of LeRoy's alfalfa. Even wary trophy bucks were tempted by the sweet leafy greens.

"Get your rifle sighted in. I counted sixteen of them buggers, three with horns twenty-eight inches or better. You can set your camp on the back ridge."

I could hear LeRoy's voice, even though I was in the kitchen fixing dinner and Charlie had the phone in the den. LeRoy lost most of his hearing cutting logs—just like Charlie. They'd shout at each other, and hear just fine. Both got aggravated as hell when everyone else only mumbled.

Charlie started to pack his supplies after the call. His old German shorthair pointer, Daisy, got excited. She had accompanied him on bird hunts for over fourteen years, making them partners twice as long as our marriage.

Daisy claimed Charlie as her territory, but she was gracious enough to allow me a share. She never hesitated, though, to remind me of who was first in my husband's affections. She'd amble to his side and lean against his leg. Gazing at him through doe eyes, she'd flip his hand to the top of her head with her nose. Stop whatever you're doing and pet me, she demanded. They had occasional bad times, too. Daisy's habit of chasing deer, and Charlie's tendency to miss the chukar she held on point could ruin an afternoon for both of them. But, by evening, Daisy would lay at Charlie's feet by the fireplace while he scratched her ears. I envied the easy way they forgave each other.

Because Daisy liked to run deer she was left behind on Charlie's hunting trip. She whined as he packed, and followed him from room to room, not letting him out of her sight. He loaded the stove and tent, a couple of folding chairs—he and LeRoy had back problems these days—his cot, and a sleeping bag. Most of his dried food supply was good from the previous pack trip. Some meat and fresh fruit would fill out the list. By ten o'clock all he had left to do was to work on his hat.

Charlie's favorite Stetson had fit his knobby head perfectly. Gathering sweat and smoke through the years, it had achieved a crusty, weathered look appropriate to the man who owned it. The hat was as essential as a pair of well-worn Levi's or broken-in boots—more so. Charlie named it Billy, though I never knew exactly why. Unfortunately, Billy was lost in a poker game the spring before, during a sixth round of Jack Daniels. Charlie replaced the hat with a John Deere cap through the summer, but it wouldn't do for hunting. Neither would the purple wool Arctic Cat cap he used against the bitter times that could come quickly in the mountains. A new hat would be worse, according to Charlie, since a clean Stetson caused more glare than his bald head.

He filled my cast iron teapot with water, and turned the gas up high until steam billowed out. He held a tan felt hat I bought for his birthday, the one he wore once to a funeral, over the moist heat rising from where the teapot's lid should have been. As the felt softened, wilting over the teapot's girth, Charlie worked the brim with grimy hands he purposely failed to wash. The dirt and oil from his skin bled into the fabric, leaving make-believe stains of age and experience. He molded the brim in a downward motion like a potter forming the lip of a bowl, dipping the front and back edges more deeply than the sides. He set the hat on an overturned Tupperware bowl, dimpled the crown just so, and left it to dry overnight.

The next morning, I took my daily walk with our dogs through the juniper stand. The path led to the big draw on the back end of our place. It's about two and a half miles, there and back. I had kissed Charlie good-bye just in case he finished packing and left before I returned. The "old" felt hat sat on the hot metal hood of his pick-up bleaching in the sun.

I was nearly through the junipers when I saw a four-point buck standing in a small clearing, head lowered, watching the dogs that had run impatiently ahead of me. Bax and Jip, our male cow dogs, stood on either side of the deer, each about fifteen feet away. They wiggled and yipped with excitement, but made no move toward the buck. The old pointer, Daisy, was in front of the deer, sniffing the ground and closing the gap between them. Her senses worked well only at dinner time, so I wasn't sure if she saw the deer or not.

The buck was nervous. He lurched toward the old pointer, his shanks dropping nearly to the ground. That was when I saw that his right back leg was dangling from the knee joint, bloody and mangled. A hunter had taken careless aim. The younger dogs barked, sending the buck in frenzied pivots. His three legs danced and balanced the bulk of his body while the fourth leg scribbled crazy arcs in the dirt behind. The old dog was slow. The buck panicked. He caught her with his antlers and pinned her to the ground. She screamed as the sharp points of horn pierced her rib cage. I ran straight at the deer. He sprang to the side away from Daisy, and crashed through the junipers toward a shallow, brushy ravine. A trail of blood marked his path. Daisy rasped, her body stuck in a convulsion of shivers.

We were all in motion in one way or another: Daisy fighting death, the young dogs chasing the crippled buck, me racing home, hoping to find my hunter. The pick-up idled in the driveway. It was packed, with a green tarp tied securely over the gear. Charlie was brushing out dirt and gravel that had collected in the grooves of the floormats.

"Charlie, you need to get your gun." I choked on the words. I told him what had happened as best I could. I was crying so hard I didn't get a good look at Charlie's face, just the top of his shiny head as he bent to pick a stem of hay off the ground.

He pulled his rifle out of the rack on the pick-up's rear window, and placed one bullet in the chamber, some more in his pocket along with the deer tag. Twenty feet up the lane he yelled back at me, "Call LeRoy and tell him I won't be coming." I leaned against the pick-up door, waiting to hear two shots. I remember seeing that perfectly molded felt hat on the front seat, barely visible beneath his sleeping bag.

The next October, just last year, Charlie's dad died. He was eighty-nine and frail, but his death still caught us unprepared. Charlie tended to the necessary matters of Dad's estate, and arranged the funeral. For years they'd agreed on the vileness of painted corpses, brass-railed caskets, and dank holes in the ground, but something must have changed Dad's mind. He was laid beside Charlie's mother who'd died thirty years ahead of her man.

The church that day smelled of gladiolas and roses, Dad's favorites, and the perspiration of too many people in too little space. The minister thanked Dad for being such a fine host to bring so many friends and family together on a sunny fall day in God's country. He said he hoped Dad was still walking along the mountain creeks that he loved, that we'd watch for him at the willow patch and Buttercup Meadows. Charlie'd held up pretty well until then.

By the time Charlie packed and stored Dad's belongings—the antique gun collection, trophy mounts, heavy canvas camp gear—and found renters for the house, he'd missed another hunting season. He said it wouldn't have felt right going, but to me it wasn't right that he stayed home. Rituals that I thought were reoccurring benchmarks in Charlie's life had lost their place, and in some related way, I feared losing mine.

This year when buck season began, Charlie bought a deer tag at Shell's Mercantile just before they closed for the night. He didn't make plans with LeRoy. "Maybe I'll go up South Fork by myself," he said at dinner. While I washed the dishes, he pulled out his bivouac tent and camp stove from the storage room, some bread, hard cheese, and instant cocoa to put in his backpack. I put the cast iron pot on to boil water for tea as Charlie piled his gear against the wall by the front door.

I ached for the rowdy enthusiasm—phone calls back and forth between Charlie and LeRoy, nephews, brothers, and neighbors wanting to know his plans. This time there were no menus, no grocery lists, no fights over who should pay for what. I said I'd go with him, my voice husky from not speaking for a while, but Charlie just shook his head. He said he'd make coffee for himself in the morning, and leave. I held my hands around a steaming mug of tea, and watched Charlie sift through odds and ends in the coat closet. He rubbed his thumb across the brim of his tan felt hat, but didn't take it off the shelf. Instead he grabbed the purple knit cap with the Arctic Cat emblem. "It might be cold tomorrow night," he said, and stuffed it in his pack.

Water in the Aquarium

BY ANNE CALCAGNO

Back and forth, along the green tiles of the pool's edge, Jennifer Peersall pursued and corrected her swimmers every day. Tall, lean, and punctual, she changed her bathing suit twice a day, refreshing her dedication. She believed it was unnecessary for swimming instructors to descend into the water. She grew irritated with "experimental" teaching methods demanding that teacher and student "share" the experience. A cowardly approach, she said. The students were going to be in the water alone when they left her, so why should they need her now?

Two weeks ago, the pool director, Mrs. Chanson, introduced her to Jason McCurver. "Jason very much wants to learn how to swim. I want him to come to your Monday/Wednesday group." These were Jennifer's thirteen-year-olds, the oldest group. "Give him your best. Jason, she's likely to have you walking on water."

Jennifer did not trust Mrs. Chanson's reason for allowing him to register. Jennifer wasn't hired to teach adults. Mother had said: "Don't trust another woman when it comes to a man. Use those eyes in the back of your head."

The man stared at her with a discomfiting glint, his fists clenched tightly in his pants' pockets, protruding like knobs on the side of each leg, but he returned later that evening for the course. Jennifer proceeded to direct the class, walking along the rim of the pool, as usual, ordering the students to go toward the deep end, requiring them to blow into the water and collect

180

coins from the shallow bottom. He hung back, stranded, a tree in a flood. After a while, he inched himself along the pool wall, muttering. "You must step down to help me, Ms. Peersall."

"Mr. McCurver, swimming is an individual skill. You won't learn if I'm with you."

Mr. McCurver's nostrils flared. "Well, then I better change my mind about this course." All at once, he said, "Listen, Ms. Peersall, I am an adult. I don't ask for help when I don't need it. But I know my own limits. So when I ask for your assistance, I don't deserve a two-cent lecture. You get me?"

Jennifer felt unusually warm. This ridiculous man used his power to obligate her; Mrs. Chanson would expect her to acquiesce. Teenagers were clutching their coins, all ears, their hair dripping. "All right, Mr. McCurver. I'll assist you and you'll learn how to float on your back. I won't do this again."

She had stepped into the pool, laid him on his back, and slid her arms under his shoulders and pelvic bones. "Relax, relax, tilt your head back." Though he was buoyant in the water, he felt heavy to her. He would not shut his eyes and continued to watch her. There was fear in his composure. Then, unexpectedly, she understood his anger. She felt him dependent in her arms, not unlike a child, and a startling affection swelled in her for this man. He had pleaded for her help. His eyes shut for an instant and she gently supported his shoulder blades, keeping him afloat. Her face tilted close to his. The water lapped and bounced around her waist. Suddenly he flashed his eyes on her, harsh and suspicious. She snatched her hands away, dropped him. Twisting and floundering, he smashed the water with his arms. But he stood up.

"You bitch," he screamed. "I didn't deserve that!"

She stared at him, transfixed. She must disguise this professionally. The students began giggling, watching this man whose fingers squeezed against one eye then the other, desperate to clear the water.

"This is how we test our students, Mr. McCurver. If you fall out of a boat, this is what will happen. But if you feel the treatment is unfair, you can leave." She grabbed her wits like laundry from the rain. He leapt out of the pool.

When the class was over, the students gone, she stood still

listening to the faint churn of water from the cleaning filters. Each evening, alone, she crossed the pool for forty laps. She sprung into a dive, aligned, sharp as a knife, anticipating her body's cut into the water, the water's quick way of containing then lifting her. There was silent blue all around: healing, cool, flickering. Then it filled up with him. Each armstroke barely missed his hammering face; infuriated, she jumped out of the water and went home.

Jason McCurver returned to the next class. "My severe teacher," he said, then he added quietly, "I owe you an apology. Please let me buy you a cup of coffee after work—if you have any extra time. I need to talk to you."

"If it relates to your lessons," she replied.

The coffee shop had dark walls with red lamps. They glowed like small delicious hearts. "Fear changes a person," he begun without hesitation. "I sell for a pharmaceutical company. We're hot with a new product for rheumatism. A few of us topped the sales quota and won ourselves a cruise to a conference in New Orleans. I speak French." He stuck out his open palm and pursed his lips. "*J'ai pour vous un produit fantastique!*" She smiled.

"Ms. Peersall, the sea is a nightmare for me. I spent summers alone as a boy hiding from friends who invited me to the shore. I must break out of this. I'm going on that ship. No one knows I'm in that Godforsaken teenage course of yours. Please teach me to swim."

"You should have told someone. Your behavior was inexcusable in the last class," she said.

"Will you help me?" He looked at her nervously.

Coffee waited in her cup, and she pressed her fingers tightly on the curved handle. Seven years of living independently had so taught her to occupy her time that she had never been chosen as a confidante. She always told herself that solitude made her wise, unlike those distracted by many friends. She knew about bitter worries, keen secrets. She tended a garden inside her, only no one walked in it.

As Jason McCurver drove her home, she found herself talking. "I was born outside Charleston. My mother was a lifeguard and taught me how to swim when I was three. She just threw me in the water; some children will paddle instinctively. Mother said that if you knew air *and* water you had a greater sense of God."

"What did your father say?"

"He wasn't a swimmer." Her cheeks flushed.

"Six o'clock will do, won't it?" Jason had said.

The sky was dimming, moist and even, changing colors at the horizon. The pure air and simplicity of it made her hold her breath. Now she startled herself by almost walking past her building. She moved in a reverie, filled with fertile reconstructions. Jennifer greeted the manager, who was knitting pink booties for her grandchild, then climbed up four flights of steps to her apartment. When she opened the door, she felt pleased. It was partially the clothes on the bed, lying crisply ironed, that made the difference. Her anticipation of the evening almost relied on the dress itself.

After showering, she doused herself in a cream scented of carnations, stretched a comb through her short blond curls, and painstakingly etched blue eyeliner on her lower lids. Only a few years back, she had ignored her appearance. "You can't find your spirit in a mirror," Mother would say. "Everything visible is this world's disguise. So don't be primping around here." But it was your body that made concrete the lessons life slapped you with; you stood there, face pink, mortified, implanted. She could remember when she was sixteen, very sheltered, Ian Simpson had kissed her. His tongue was sweet and ugly and curious like a small frog in her mouth.

Now Jennifer had come to see that she was trim and young-looking: thirty-one, straight back, firm breasts. She slipped on shimmery hose and her periwinkle dress. She filled a glass with seltzer water and went into the living room to wait. She ran her fingers over her dress; it was flesh-warm and silky. She noticed herself touching things with curious abandon, as if they extended from her, and grew.

Jason said, "Why'd you cut your hair like this? It's like a Japanese sponge. Tell you what: let it grow long. . . . " He put his hand behind her head, drew her forcefully, and kissed her.

She sat paralyzed in the seat, inept and immobile, not knowing how to want. Jason's hand touched her knee, then he said this about her hair. She slapped his hand away roughly. He clutched it to his breast. And she felt horrible, apologized. He had only made a light comment.

"Don't men tell you what they like? Well, I won't tell you if that's what you want."

"I don't like you to tell me what to look like. I didn't know you were going to kiss me."

She sat straight, feeling every part of her turn gray, and thought she better go home.

A week and a half ago, he had said, "It's quite a coincidence, Ms. Peersall. The studio apartment I'm renting has an aquarium. I think you would like it; the fish are so graceful. Unfortunately, I have a dinner appointment, but would you stop for a quick visit?"

His door was to the right, off a long hallway. She kept her distance. When the lights did not work, he guessed there was a main switch his weekly cleaning lady had shut off, yet he couldn't find it. An eerie green light danced in the room. "At least the aquarium's working," he exclaimed. Then in an awkward voice he said, "You see, that green light is a little like your eyes. Ms. Peersall, your eyes are mysterious fishes."

He left her alone, seated on a double bed next to the aquarium. Strange, nimble water reflections fell on her skirt. When he returned, he sat next to her and gazed at the fish. Then he took her hand evenly and tenderly and held it awhile. Inside, she began throbbing; the noise intensified and battered against the green, lapping patterns. His face, with green ribbons, twisted and bounced before her. He called her curls "tendrils" and touched them. His hand became strong and playful and another hand crossed over to her waist. She kept her eyes open, her back a column. The green waves shimmered over his neck and ears and he kissed her throat and leaned her back so fast on the bed, and she was fighting him but he was speaking, "Green eyes . . . my lovely strong woman."

Jennifer had fled down the hall.

She had worried throughout the night and morning. She did

not eat lunch. She went for a walk. What kind of fool did he want to make of her? She knew that once a man got you naked, he thought he had won and you had lost and it always seemed to her, too, that not to lose you ought to hold your body high and tight as a wall. She had put her hands to her face, resolving never to go near him again.

But when he next arrived at the pool, he took her hand and said, "I'm ready for my lesson. Can I see you tonight?"

"You aren't tired, my lovely?" Jennifer heard herself agree to see him.

Tonight she would meet his companions. He had said, "You're important to me so you ought to meet them. Most of them are local. That's why you can't mention swimming. And just to be safe, I thought we ought to play out a disguise. It'll be more fun for you, too." He laughed.

She was thinking she would hold fast as a buoy in Jason's mind when he overcame his fear of water; patiently she would walk through his anxieties with him. "I could be a cashier," she said, imagining it. It occurred to her that cashiers often wore too much makeup.

"Why is it I can always count on you?" Jason grinned.

The buzzer rang. She said, "Hello" into the intercom.

"Jennifer, do you mind if I don't come up? The car is running and we're late."

She walked into her room, twirling herself from side to side in front of the mirror, watching her dress glide. She felt as if she had a small flower in her throat, and gathered up her coat, wrapped it close.

"Jennifer, you're beautiful!" he exclaimed as she sat down. "How am I going to stand letting you talk to other men?"

"We'll just see," she replied, and smiled at him.

He touched her thigh. His fingernails were neatly clipped. "For God's sake, don't talk about swimming."

"You don't have to say that." She looked at him, her eyes growing hot quickly. "Why shouldn't you trust me?"

"I should," he said.

He kissed her and turned on the radio and they drove swiftly past stoplights and neon announcements. The city glittered with decorations, signals, and faint stars in the sky.

As they entered the restaurant, Jason waved his arm at a table of men. There were no other women with them. "You're going to be our Queen Bee," Jason whispered in her ear.

She walked rigid and proper at his side. When they reached the table, one man leaned forward, raising his glass. "Ah, a victim for Casanova," he said. He was squat with a neck the same thickness as most of his head, his blond hair cropped. The rest of the men stood up and nodded in a reserved way as Jason introduced Jennifer Peersall to them.

The squat man interrupted, "I'm just the clown around here. No harm intended. Pleased to meet you." He stretched his hand.

"Of course," she said, smiled pleasantly, and shook his hand.

"Where did you find this pretty lady?" a dark-faced young man asked, leaning close.

"Jenny's my cousin, twice removed. She's a cashier."

"What a becoming dress, Miss Peersall," the young man said warmly.

Jason said, "All right, Jennifer, this admirer's name is 'Slim.' Listen, we always go by nicknames. Don't worry if you can't remember them all. You've already met 'Butch,' the loud-mouth. 'French Fry' is over here." A man with a wide-nostrilled red nose shot her a quick grin. " 'Tubes' father was a plumber, George is 'G.' "

The men drank beer, but Jason chose a bottle of white wine for Jennifer and, with each toast, filled her glass. They ordered their meals, then spoke boisterously, gregariously; she concentrated until the bones at her ears and temples ached, then she loosened and let the voices swim around her. Smoke and wine made her heady: little fish seemed to flick and tingle her skin, pursuing currents along her capillaries. She watched Jason, the men's affection for him. His name was "Baby." They laughed hard at his jokes. He bought a round of beers. Her limbs began to feel rubbery.

"If I *did* have to choose a roommate on that ship, I'd pick Baby," Slim confided in her.

Butch interrupted. "Never trust a man until you meet his

company. Am I right?" He grinned. She tried to hold something close to herself while he ran his eyes up and down her like a metal detector, but she didn't know what. She remembered expecting the dress to make her feel free but she felt a lack of control.

Smiling brightly at her, Slim said, "We all have your pretty company, and that's a pleasure!" He added, in a whisper, "Butch has no manners."

Jason flicked his hand to her knee, under the table. The wine became hot inside her, her head felt fat. The men ordered more beer. They discussed their work. A few doubted the ship's success. Slim asked Jennifer if she met many types, while cashiering. Carefully, she explained that in every country of the world you could find the same types; you had to have a set of rules and act on principle.

Slim said, "You're a very perceptive cashier."

She smiled back, and imagined wearing ruby-red lipstick as a cashier. They wore tight sweaters you had to have a straight back for. She straightened herself in her chair, pushed herself slightly forward over the table. Then she was lifting her hands up and down on the table.

"Hey, are you playing checkers?" Butch asked.

"Checkmate!" she cried.

"Mating! Now we're talking," he said.

"Watch your mouth." Jason raised his voice.

"Watch mine," Jennifer interrupted, making clicking sounds, then pouted. She started to laugh and laugh and then felt strange as if suddenly it was brilliant daylight and her skin had turned utterly white. Her eyes wide, she turned to Jason.

"Sweet, you'd better not drink any more wine," he said. The men looked away.

When the meal was finished, the plates in disarray pushed to the center of the table, the room had become quiet. The conversation began to flag, and Jason said, "I must take this young lady home."

Jason's friends shook her hand and bowed, said they hoped to see her again. Jennifer murmured, "But I hope so also." Jason winked at them and waved.

In the car, she asked, "Did I drink too much?" She toyed with her scarf, her legs clenched so tightly they hurt.

"You did, but darling, that's fine. Everything went wonderfully." He put his palm lightly on her leg. "Now you come home with me and I'll make you some coffee." Her nervousness increased. She wondered if she'd failed him. In her mind, a great wind seemed to be rushing, and she felt she was trying to collect scattering leaves.

Jason opened the door and switched on a lamp. The orange glow spread through the room. The eerie green aquarium waves almost disappeared. He took off his coat and pulled her next to him on the bed, turning off the light. He pushed her down. Jennifer pummeled his back but he was on her, insistent and hurried, and she wanted him so near her and then for a moment she felt the skin on her belly being tugged upwards and she became aware her dress was crumpling. He said, "Jennifer, I want you."

Suddenly, she was crying. She had never wept in front of a man before. And yet she embraced him while she cried, and told him he was the finest swimmer, and she would wait for him and write letters to the ports . . .

Jason hushed her abruptly. He said, "Listen!" They could hear shuffling noises in the hall, then voices. "It's them," he whispered in her ear. "They know I'm home. Lie quiet and they'll leave."

They rang the doorbell. He clenched her arm. She pressed into the mattress to disappear, but the sheet tangled, clinging to her like wet, ruined paper.

"Leaving your friends out in the cold, Baby?" they shouted. Jason held her wrist tightly. Their voices gradually melted down the hall though she still listened, feeling the hallway was a huge empty ear.

"Come kiss me. They're gone," Jason whispered. "And we have something to complete." He tugged at her leg; she pushed him off. He stared at her blankly.

"Jason, hush! They'll know I'm here." They pressed on top of her. Her heart was about to crack inside her. "Jason, they found us," she whispered, grabbing his arm.

"No," Jason said. "They're gone. Come on now." He put his arms around her and pulled her close. Jason breathed violently and said many things. And Jennifer clutched him. And now, when they were finished, they lay in the darkness for some minutes. She smoothed his hair and kissed his ears.

"My hero-swimmer," she called him.

He stepped out of bed and pulled his pants on. "I'll think of you," he said and walked into the bathroom. She glided her legs along the smooth expanse of the mattress.

"Quite a lover, don't you think?" The walls spoke. She grabbed the sheets to her, saw light streaming from under the hallway door. Along its border, shadows began to move. "Everyone gets their share." Fists began pounding on the door. "Come on, Baby. Don't be stingy," someone cried. She shut her eyes. She did not trust this, as if it were a dream; she would suddenly be saved. The doorknob was rattling. She screamed. Jason burst out of the bathroom, half-squatting like a wrestler. "I want mine," a voice yelled into the wall. "Hey, back in line!" She recognized Slim's voice. "No cuts!" She thought she saw Jason smirk. She tried to scream. Her mouth was open, her mind crying, Jason staring at her now.

"That's enough, you assholes," he yelled. "Get the hell out or I'm calling the police right now! Oh, Jennifer," he murmured, sitting down. "Pay no attention to them. They're drunk, that's all. Ignore them."

"Jason, they heard! They were listening to us! To everything!"

"Jennifer. Calm down, Jennifer. They're gone. It was only meant as a joke. They got carried away."

"Is that what it is?" she said.

He ran his fingers through her hair and they became like little animals scrambling and scratching at her. She tried to remember all that he had said to her.

"Jason, did you know they were there?" she demanded.

"Don't be ridiculous," he said. "Sleep now."

She could not lie still. Echoes boomeranged against the walls of her skull. Her hand began to grow and swelled and soared over her head, leaden, like a wild pendulum, and careened down onto Jason's cheek, slapping the bone. His whole body jerked. Then he slithered off the bed, stood up, and walked into the bathroom. The water began running. There were no other sounds. He returned, undid his pants, and climbed into bed again. "I put cold water on that," he said.

He turned his back to her. She remained still. Eventually even his breathing abated. Then she dressed herself, but could not leave; could not counteract the stern logic that said *adjust*, that included this as part of the earth and night, and what she had never received from loneliness. Then, not knowing what she expected of their intimacy, she crept back into bed, in her clothes, removing only her shoes.

In the Name of Love

BY EDWIN MOSES

Through his spyhole in the leaves, he stared at the house. The back door stood wide open to whatever breeze might blow. Upstairs, the windows of his grandmother's bedroom were open too, but shrouded with heavy white drapes. What *must* be his grandmother's room. It had been so long since he'd been allowed in there, he couldn't quite remember. What you'd see if you looked out—the big backyard maple, the honeysuckle bush in which he now crouched. He didn't remember the drapes, he couldn't make anything connect. The house told him nothing more than his mother and father and aunt had, since that day months and months ago now, long before school let out, when Gram had not come down for dinner.

They had sat down at the table that evening at six o'clock sharp, as always, the three adults and Michael and Sara. Then . . . well, what? Start eating? But they weren't allowed until Gram had said grace. He glanced at his sister; Sara, three years older, didn't seem to know either. Finally, his father muttered something, head ducked—*Bless oh Lord* it might have been, nothing more—and reached for the bread: an awkward lefthanded swipe at it, his elbow a good yard wide of the face that was not there. Gram took it first, always, and passed the plate, but only the ghost of her in his father's gesture was present that night. Aunt Laurel, knowing some unimaginable thing, had not set her place at the head of the table. Michael took the bread as it came to him and found it dry as dust in his mouth. Sara, bolder, asked the question: "Where is she? What's

191

wrong with her?"

At once his mother replied, "Why, nothing, honey, nothing, she's up in her room, resting, a little under the weather, just what happens when you get older"—an explanation too ready, too long, too earnest, and from the wrong person, his mother not being the one who knew things. His father, who didn't know things either, chimed in: "Just a little under the weather. You took her up a tray, Laurel, didn't you?" And the children listened, a little breathless. It was Aunt Laurel who knew. But she just nodded, said nothing, carved precisely right-angled bites out of her cutlet as on any ordinary Thursday evening.

To the others, afterwards, maybe that was what it was— Michael's father in his big reclining armchair in the corner of the living room, chuckling at something in the *Kansas City Star*, his mother humming and wandering her aimless way about the house; but not into the kitchen, Laurel's place. So they weren't talking about it, even to each other. Sara had gone out. Gram was up there in her room, alone. After a little while he ventured up the stairs. The bathroom was up there, so he could say that was why if anyone—Laurel—asked him. Her door, on this mild spring evening, was shut tight. He had his book under his arm, *Mother West Wind's Children*. *Who's going to read to me?* he thought, and flushed with shame.

Because she had read to him every single night at bedtime since he was old enough to remember. In his pajamas after his bath, he'd find her on the sofa in the living room without having to look, an unspoken appointment they had there. She'd be knitting in bold colors, reds and blues and bright grass greens, which matched her determined progress through life. Had raised four children alone, after her husband left her for another woman. Never a word of complaint—in the family that was legend. She would look up at the slight sound of his bare or slippered feet on the oak floor, peer over her glasses which would have slid down her hawk's beak of a nose, and mock-grumble: "You? Again? I'm to read? *Again?* Such a boy for books. About the crow? Now what's that rascal up to this time?" With Michael curled up close, gently inhaling the sourish, pleasing old-woman scent of her, she read in a vein of alert, humorous inquiry. Blacky the Crow, master trickster of the Green Forest, held no secrets from his Gram. *Stole that egg when he ought to have been home asleep, did he? Frightened out of his wits by Hooty the Owl? Serves him just right.* Bright eyes in her cocked head searching him when he stood to go, arms round him soft as wings, voice sibilant in his ear—

Who loves you, child?

You, Gram.

Who loves you best?

You.

Who's going to love you forever and ever?

You—

She might have been a bird herself.

He came back downstairs that evening and wandered forlornly around the house with his book, but nobody noticed except Aunt Laurel, the second time he passed by the kitchen. Her voice arrested him: "Bedtime, child." Then as he hesitated she saw, she who like Gram saw everything even if she failed to understand it, what he was about, and added, "You may read yourself a story from that in bed." So he did. He was most of the way through first grade, after all. He read about how Striped Chipmunk got the pockets in his cheeks, which Gram had read last night, to bring last night back. And so she would not have missed anything. The next story in the book, about how Johnny Chuck ran away, was one of her favorites.

But from that day on it was never the same. The next evening when she did come down, he and Sara sat watching their mother, watching her not eat. *A little of this nice chicken. So good. Do try some.*

Oh yes, thank you, Katherine, So kind . . .

But sat there not eating. Everyone ate, always, sick or well. Putting a nice meal on the table was hard work. Katherine's eyes flickered everywhere, pretending not to see. Swept past the still faces of her son and daughter to the china cupboard in the corner, whose glass front gave her back only her own pale, lovely, distracted face; and up, but nothing to see on the ceiling which Laurel swept off weekly. . . . They had no spiders, hadn't for years. Word must have gotten around. Then she caught her sister's eye, or Laurel caught hers rather and drew it down to her own right hand . . . which she snatched up and away as if the table had turned red hot. The tips of her first three fingers tingled, from tapping them on the hard oak.

* * *

Gram read to him about Johnny Chuck, but she left out the best part. *That rascal,* she was supposed to have said, *running away from his poor mother like that. Oh, now who's this coming? Reddy Fox? So is Johnny going to get what's coming to him this time? What's that shadow? Redtail the Hawk? Now that little rascal's in for it!* But no, she just read, flatly, with no sign of understanding or enjoyment. *Who loves you?* she asked. *Who loves you best? Who will love you always?*—but merely out of habit, it seemed, because she was looking at him strangely, as if she couldn't quite remember who he was.

The day after that, when he came home from school, she was gone. She had gone to the hospital for tests, they said. Routine tests. *It's nothing,* they said—to themselves, when they thought Michael was not close enough to hear. (But then they hardly seemed to notice him unless he was right underfoot.) She's getting old, she does too much, she's just a little tired. After three days she came back, but again she was not at the dinner table. Nobody said anything about the tests. They were important, apparently—more important even than the tests in arithmetic he took, and always got a hundred on, in the first grade at school—but he could not imagine what they were or what they were for. Sara didn't know either, or anyway wouldn't say, and she was nine and knew almost as much as the grownups. She was carrying an old Raggedy Ann around that she'd given up a long time ago.

* * *

The front porch was bordered by forsythia bushes, bright yellow now in early April. Playing under them the next day, he heard something.

She wants Ollie here.

What for? It's a routine operation.

Still, Laurel. She's an old woman. She's scared. Hadn't we better call him?

If they got along together, yes. If it would help. But you know how they are with each other. She needs quiet, a chance to rest.

But what if.

You worry too much, Katherine. You always have. Don't you believe what the doctor told you?

Yes, but.

She's strong. Stronger than you know. If anything happens, we'll call.

Then he heard the screen door open and close. For a long time he crouched there, seeing nothing through the yellow haze. His heart was pounding, and he was sweating, and faintly queasy, as if he had run too far and too fast under a blinding yellow sun. *Birds*, he remembered. Large black birds against a deep blue sky.

* * *

This operation she has to have. What is it? What's it for?

I don't know. Something they have to cut out of her.

Cut out of her? Why? Sara, don't go. Tell me why.

In her stomach. That if they don't cut it out, it will make her sick. Listen, Michael. Ask Aunt Laurel. Ask somebody that knows.

She wouldn't tell me.

That's your problem. If you wouldn't snoop around in the bushes, you wouldn't hear things and you wouldn't know anything and you'd be happy.

Where are you going?

To Judy's. And I don't want you tagging along.

I could play with Susan.

Susan doesn't want to play with you anymore. She said boys are dumb. Listen, go find some boys to play with.

There aren't any boys around here.

So? Is that my fault?

* * *

She was gone for a long time. They cut open her stomach and a black bird flew out.

* * *

One day after school his mother was waiting for him on the porch. She said, "Michael, your Gram came home this morning."

"Oh."

She was waiting for him to say something, some particular thing like the answer to a question in school. What was the question? What was the matter with him? In school he always knew the answer.

"Michael, honey?"

"Is she? Is she all right?"

"Yes, oh yes, they say they got all of it. But what I wanted to tell you. She needs rest. She won't be leaving her room for a while. Laurel and I will look after her. And so we need for you and Sara to be very, very quiet when you're in the house. Could you? Do that for us?"

"All right. Could I see her?"

"Honey, not quite yet. In a little while. You see, well, she loves you so much. Too much stimulation . . ."

"What's that?"

"Excitement. Too much excitement . . . it's not good for her just now. Honey, you understand? Do you?"

Crying. She was crying. If Gram was all right, then why?

"Michael . . . "

"What?"

"Would you like me to read to you?"

* * *

Her door was closed. He listened with his ear against it, but he couldn't hear anything. There was no way of knowing if she was really in there.

* * *

On the get-well card he drew her a picture from her favorite Mother West Wind story. Under a big yellow sun, Hooty the Owl sat on a branch of the Lone Pine. He was too big, somehow, a quarter of the height of the tree, but he had to be for his yellow eyes to show. You could see him snapping his strong curved beak. Around him flew Blacky the Crow and Sammy Jay, though you couldn't see Sammy very well against the blue sky, and all their friends and relations—dozens of them, diminishing in the distance to small black and blue V's. He wished he could give her a picture of the part she liked best, how Hooty punished Blacky that night when it got dark, but that would have been nothing but black. All the way across the top he wrote, in red, *caw caw caw caw caw;* and inside, in green, *Get well soon Lov Michael.*

After dinner that evening he stole up the stairs to her bedroom, slipped the card under the door, and waited. In a minute or two Laurel came out and shut the door behind her. He knew at once that he'd done something wrong, though for a long moment she said nothing; just stared as if, unimaginably, she herself were frightened.

Finally she said, her voice hoarse as he'd never heard it before, "Thank you, Michael. It's a lovely card."

"Did she like it?"

"She's sleeping. I'll give it to her when she wakes up. She needs a lot of rest just now."

"That's why we have to be quiet?"

"Yes. Yes, you see we have to help her, however we can. Just in little things . . ."

Suddenly she was kneeling in front of him. "It's all right," she whispered. "Michael, it will be all right," and she crushed him in her strong, gaunt arms. Brushing his face, directly in front of his eyes, were wisps of the graying hair she would not touch up, despite his mother's urging. When at last she released him, he said—whispered rather, awed by her strength and passion and the tears on her cheeks—"Would you read to me?"

"I can't. I have to stay with Mother. With your Gram. Do you understand?"

"Yes, I guess so."

"When she wakes up, someone should be with her, in case she should be . . ."

Frightened, he thought she was going to say, as he himself had been in dreams, waking in a house profoundly empty. But this was Gram, afraid of nothing. His mother had told about it since before he could remember, how Gram's husband had left her one day with no warning and no money and four young children to raise; and how when Katherine, nine then, asked her what they would do, she simply replied: *Go on, bravely, as we always have.* And so, until now, they had.

"In case she needs something," Aunt Laurel said, and added, "When she gets well again, things will be different."

* * *

But she didn't get well. She was in and out of the hospital all that spring and summer, and every time she came home she was worse. Michael himself saw almost nothing of her—fugitive glimpses of a figure increasingly frail and gray, lifted bodily up the stairs now by his mother and aunt on each of her homecomings—but he heard the whisperings. He heard the sighs and saw the shaken heads. Silence enveloped the house, spreading like a dark fog from his grandmother's room, up and down the hall, down the stairs, until at last, if Aunt Laurel had had her way, it would have encompassed the entire neighborhood: she railed under her breath at the occasional motorcycle or delivery truck. It spread to school, where Michael, formerly the first to raise his hand, sat mute. Miss Marshall knew. She never called on him, and on the last day of school she kept him after the others and hugged him tight.

"You be good," she said. "Be brave. You're a big boy now."

He felt very small. His father, who had rarely failed to find something in the newspaper to laugh at out loud, no longer came straight home from work; sometimes he even missed dinner, once in a while was out past Michael's bedtime. His mother and aunt kept vigil. Sara spent most of her time down the block at her friend Judy's house. But Judy's sister Susan, until a few months ago Michael's best friend, would now have nothing to do with him—and so he played alone for hours, silently, in his fort under the big honeysuckle bush in the back yard.

Then, one morning in late August, Uncle Oliver came. Michael heard the car pull up, then when he peeked through his spyhole in the leaves he could see it in the driveway. It was a long gray car—a Packard—and there was something about it that made Aunt Laurel mad. Then Uncle Oliver got out, in gray too with a pink necktie, and walked around and opened the trunk and lifted out a suitcase. Then, before slamming the lid, he yawned and stretched and gazed around. He must have driven all the way from where he lived in Denver, Colorado, almost six hundred miles, during the night.

He seemed in no hurry to go in the house. He didn't see Michael hiding in the honeysuckle, nor did Michael come out and show himself. In the old days he would have, because he liked his uncle. Oliver took him somewhere every time he came, three or four times a year—to the natural history museum at the university in town, or the zoo in Topeka or even Kansas City, and once (though this was a never-to-be-revealed secret between them) to his Aunt Elizabeth's farm. Michael watched as Oliver at last picked up his suitcase—picked it up, a big Gladstone bag, as if it were empty, but then Oliver was the strongest man Michael knew—and disappeared around the corner of the house, toward the front door. The boy stood still for a long minute, watching, the leaves tickly-cool against his face. Then he dropped to his knees and poked his head out of the bush. There was no one in sight. Crouching low, zigzagging all the way, he ran to the back door and into the kitchen. He could hear a murmur of voices in the living room. He crept down the long hall and put his ear to the door.

Laurel said, "Well, so you got here."

"I got here," Oliver said. "Here I am."

"You had to drive that car? Why didn't you fly? You could have been too late."

"Too *late?* Wait a minute. Just how sick is she, anyway?"

The voices got too low for Michael to hear clearly. *Inoperable*, he thought his mother said, a word he didn't know, and then from his uncle, shockingly loud: "Goddamnit. *Goddamnit*, how long have you known she was dying?"

Michael ran back up the hall and out the kitchen door and across the yard, forgetting to zigzag this time, and into his fort. It had rained during the night, a light shower, and the ground was still a little damp. It was cool where he lay curled up, his arms around his knees.

* * *

He woke to the sound of his name. When he looked up he saw his uncle on his hands and knees, his shoulders filling the entrance, one hand holding the pink tie up out of the dirt.

"Nice place you've got here," Oliver said. He backed out and stood up, brushing at his knees. "Private and quiet." Michael had not yet moved. "Mind if we talk?"

Now the boy scrambled out in his turn, feeling ashamed as he always did when any adult, even Oliver, intruded in his private world. It was not a fort. It was only a honeysuckle bush.

Oliver yawned. "Long drive over here," he said. "Only way I'd do it, in summer like this, is at night. Once you roll down onto the flatlands on 24, why you just plain fly. Ninety-five, a hundred miles an hour all the way, and all you see is the black road and the white line in your headlights like the longest tunnel in the world. Stopped at an all-night joint somewhere west of Salina and sat down at the counter next to a man that runs two thousand head of Black Angus cattle. Now that is one hell of a lot of beef on the hoof. He knew for a fact I was strange and I was pretty sure he was, but we got along, Michael. We got along. It's what you call the spirit of the road. Anybody tell you what's going on around here?"

It took a second or two for the question to register. The boy was remembering the drive back from his Aunt Elizabeth's, half-dozing in the dark to the sound of the rushing wind. Finally he ventured, "Gram is sick."

Oliver nodded. "She's real sick," he said. He had been standing as he spoke of the road, gazing off across the back fence. Now he squatted on his heels, his eyes level with Michael's. "Real sick. I imagine you figured that much out for yourself. Anybody *talk* to you about it?"

"Aunt Laurel said I had to be quiet."

"Sure, she would. That sounds about like her. They never said a thing to Sara either. Mike, what your Gram has is called cancer. I'm not sure myself just how it works, but it grows inside you until some of your organs get to where they don't work anymore, and then you die. And by that time it's better that you die. Gram's going to die real soon."

The boy was silent. Oliver added, "What does that mean to

you? I mean, what do you think happens when people die?"

Michael shrugged, staring at his feet. "Their souls go to heaven?"

"Laurel tell you that?"

"Yeah."

"I couldn't say myself. I've never been there. You understand she won't be around anymore. You won't see her the way you see me now, right here in front of you. You know what happens to her body?"

"No. I wish . . . "

"What, son?"

But he couldn't say what he wished. That his uncle would go away and leave him alone.

Oliver said, "Remember when Sara used to bring home dead birds, and you'd put them in a cigar box and dig a hole and bury them? And she'd say something over them? One time she said, 'Little bird, may your spirit fly straight to heaven.' Well, those were funerals, and that's what they're going to have for your grandmother."

But those were just birds. That was just a game. How could it have anything to do with what was happening to Gram?

"The thing you have to remember," Oliver went on, "is— see, I don't exactly know what happens to her spirit when she dies, but I do know that it's gone out of her body. That body you always thought of as *her*, it's not anymore. What they bury is not *her*. The burial, that's just a way of showing decent respect to the dead. What matters is what she meant to you, to all of us, what she taught us and what we remember. That way, she lives in us, no matter whether it's true or not about heaven. You understand any of this?"

Michael nodded. He couldn't remember a thing Gram had taught him. A single thing about her, not even what she looked like. She was slipping, slipping, gone. He swayed on his feet and felt his uncle's hand on his arm. Oliver said, "That was a lot to hit you with all at once. You all right?"

"I'm okay."

"I was supposed to tell you, she wants to see you."

"Right now?"

"Actually, about fifteen minutes ago. Are you scared?"

The boy didn't answer. *Be brave. You're a big boy now.* Oliver said, "I could go back in there and tell them I couldn't find you. Thing is, we might not feel so good if we lied about that, when it's too late to do anything about it. You want my hand?"

Michael took it and they walked slowly toward the house. "She wants to tell you goodbye," Oliver said. "That's natural, considering how much she loves you. You love her too?"

The boy nodded. He began to cry, and felt himself swung up into his uncle's arms. Then he was sitting in his lap on the back step. "We'll just sit here for a little while," Oliver said, "till you get to feeling better. Then, afterwards, maybe we'll go out for an ice cream, just you and me. Would you like that?"

"In the car?"

"Sure in the car."

Michael nodded mutely. He rubbed the tears off his cheeks with his knuckles. Oliver set him on his feet, and they walked together into the silent house.

* * *

Oliver tapped on Gram's door, once, twice—it sounded loud, but any sound did then. After a moment Laurel opened it and without a word walked back to her chair and took up her knitting. She was knitting something red—the only splash of color in that whole dim room, Oliver thought at first, until, as they walked closer, he saw Michael's blue and green and black and red get-well card on the bedside table. There was a Bible next to it. The only sound, besides the faint clicking of Laurel's needles, was the curtain rustling in the light south breeze.

Michael glanced at Gram's bed and then away again. He had not been able to make her out at all; an indistinct mound under the white coverlet, merely, as if the thing inside that was killing her had worn away also the planes and angles that said to him *Gram.* Now as his uncle led him to the bed he could see her face, very pale, the skin almost transparent, familiar and yet strange, so that it said to him, *This is just Gram, who reads to me and hugs me and loves me,* and at the same time, *Where is she? What is this thing in her bed, in her body?* The thing smelled, Gram's smell but not quite familiar, yet strange. Her voice had always been strong, piercing, strident almost. Now she whispered, and it was no voice that Michael had ever heard: "I want to talk to him alone."

Oliver's hand tightened on Michael's for a moment. The boy looked up and saw his uncle gazing, uneasily, not at him but at his grandmother. "He's scared," Oliver said. "Who wouldn't be, his age? Why don't I stay?"

"I want to talk to him alone."

Laurel had not heard, or pretended she hadn't, so that, when Oliver gave the boy's hand a final squeeze and turned toward the door, she made no move to follow. What was she knitting— a sweater for her niece? A crimson shroud? He said, "She wants just Michael."

For a long moment Laurel still did not move. Maybe she thought her mother would not be so rude as to die in her presence; it would be like dropping off to sleep in company. Or some secret would be told—what secret, to a six-year-old boy? But finally she did set her knitting in the basket on the floor and followed Oliver out.

* * *

"Come close," Gram said. "Close so you can hear me. You can sit on the bed."

He sat awkwardly, first tailor-style with his legs crossed, then with his knees against his chest. Then he remembered and was afraid to move. His Aunt Laurel, when he wriggled too much in church, would squeeze his arm until he thought her fingers would meet at the bone. Gram's eyes were closed. He sat hugging himself, his face tight against his knees, his eyes squeezed shut against the growing certainty that she was dead.

She said—whispered—"You will never know how much I love you. You the best of all of them. Michael, do you know I will watch over you always? I will watch over and guard you all the days of your life, until we meet again in heaven."

He opened his eyes now and saw that she was staring at him. Staring into him. Whatever he did, forever, she would know. She said, "You are my only grandson. You must carry on the name. Now tell me you love me."

He tried. He opened his mouth, but no sound came out.

"I must have that to take with me," she said. "Tell me you love me and you will always love me." And still he could not, nor, awed by the enormity of his betrayal, could he even look at her any longer. "Kiss me," she said. "Michael, won't you even give me that?" But he could not kiss her from where he was without lying down on top of her and crushing the life out of her. He scrambled to the floor and stood three feet away, rigid, transfixed by her terrible, pale, demanding eyes.

"Kiss me!" she said. And on the instant, almost in the same breath, he cried, "I hate you!"

He stood and she lay for a moment in silence, and then he saw a tear well up under each eye. *"I hate you!"* he cried again and ran to the door, wrenched it open, slammed it behind him, and stood cowering against it. But the hallway was empty.

Then his aunt appeared from the bathroom, almost running on tiptoe. She grabbed him by the arm. "What have I told you about noise? I can't believe you'd do that! Go on, get out of here!"

Without pausing for an answer, she opened the door and stalked into Gram's room and closed it again. Closed it silently, even in the heat of her anger, as if God might forget to come for her mother if no attention were drawn to her.

Michael remained trembling in the hall. She hadn't heard, then. She had been in the bathroom at just that crucial moment, and she hadn't heard.

But Gram would tell her. Was telling her right now, and the door would fly open, and the boy ran. He crouched on the landing where he could watch and bolt at the first sign. Gram would tell, unless he had killed her. He almost must have, saying that. For a terrible moment he hoped he had. Then he would be safe. No one would ever know. But Gram would know, and she had said she would watch over him forever. She would never forgive him. And Aunt Laurel would think it was him slamming the door that did it, and tell everyone. If Gram was alive she would tell, and if she was dead Aunt Laurel would tell.

He heard a voice from below. "Michael, what are you doing there?" His mother. "Go on out and play. No, tell me first, what did your grandmother say to you?"

He couldn't speak.

His mother looked at him for a moment, then shook her head and passed on up the stairs. Down the hall. Her hand on the door. Michael ran, down and out the back door and across the yard to his fort. But that was no good. They would find him there. At once, hardly pushing, he ran on back and scrambled over the fence, scratching his bare legs on the wire. There was a tangle of unstaked tomato vines back there, and he put his foot down heavily on a ripe tomato, tripped, squashed another as he fell. The sharp smell made him suddenly aware that he was hungry. He put his sticky forearm to his mouth and licked at the juice. Then he was in the alley with a tomato in each hand. He glanced back at the house, formerly his house, the shrouded windows of Gram's room staring blankly down at him.

* * *

He was in a park somewhere. A playground. He went down the slide. Something sour rose in his throat. Sat in a swing . . . what was that? A flicker of blue and white in a little tree, but Sammy Jay was dead. Buried in a cigar box. *Don't ever let me catch you playing with dead birds again!*

It's not playing. It's . . . you have to.

And what is that mess on your nice clean clothes?

I don't know.

What is that frightful mess on your hands?

I don't know I hate you *wash it off.*

He turned the handle on the drinking fountain; it turned hard, but before he could get his hands up to wash them the water was gone. He wet them one at a time and scrubbed them together and wiped them on his shorts, but they were still filthy, and then he saw her. The washcloth in her hand, beckoning him where he sat with his listless fingers in the dust. "Little boy?"

No.

"Goodness, how did you get so dirty?"

Coming with the washcloth. He tasted . . . soap. Run. At the edge of the park there was a dead bird in the grass by the sidewalk. Sara, look. Look what I found!

Hey, neat. Quick, go ask Dad . . .

* * *

He had a very hard time getting a shovel. He thought he had
one almost right away, but then some woman came out the
back door and glared at him, so he had to leave it and run.
Down the alley. There were garbage cans and cinderblocks and
broken pop bottles, even a couple not broken worth two cents
each, but he couldn't stop. Dogs barking at him. A patch of
tomatoes, right there in reach against a rotting board fence, but
he didn't want any. He opened a garage door and found
nothing, a second and a big yellow cat darted out past him into
the weeds. There was a strong smell of gasoline, and, growing
in the foot-wide strip of waste ground between the garbage and
the alley, a sunflower twice as tall as he was. The shovel was
leaning against the back wall of a garden shed, where, from the
pile of turned-up earth, someone kept it to dig worms. It was so
heavy, or he had grown so weak, that for an awful moment he
thought he would not be able to lift it. The blade was rusted
red. But it was a shovel. He ran with it, stumbling, the blade
banging his shins at every other step, for half a block before he
had to stop. He stood it upright on the ground and put his
sneaker on the blade and shoved. Nothing happened. He
needed a hose to water the ground. And a box. He reached the
corner and turned down a street. After a few steps it seemed to
him that he must be going the wrong way, so he turned around
and went back. Which way? Lost. He had lost her.
    Then she was right there in front of him, blocking his way.
"Little boy?"
    No.
    "Goodness, how did you get all the way down here?"
    "Little boy? What are you doing with that shovel?"
    Don't ever let me catch you playing with dead birds again, and
he remembered birds. The place his uncle took him.

* * *

"Son, could I ask you what that thing is for? Suppose you
leave it with me. You won't have any use for it in there, will

you?"

He felt light without it, as if it had been the only thing holding him to the ground. A long time finding her with the eyes everywhere, glaring at him. All dead, every single one. And then when he did find her, he couldn't think for a minute why he wanted to. Then he remembered.

But he didn't have the shovel. He couldn't see how to get her out, even if he did have it. How could she breathe in there? How could she see, without her glasses? Then in the middle of her face he saw it. Sharp hooked beak. It opened, snapped, opened. *Why do you hate me?*

"Michael?"

No.

"Michael, are you all right?"

Why did you kill me?

Gram, no.

"Michael, Christ, do you know who I am?"

The eyes gone, where?

Michael?

*   *   *

Here, in the Dyche Museum of Natural History, it was cool. The limestone walls were two feet thick. Still, Oliver was sweating, the boy so quiet and light in his arms. What had he been staring at, so drawn by it he had not heard his own name? Oliver looked into the display case himself, but all he saw was *Bubo virginianus,* the great horned owl. Bright blind eyes, hooked beak and talons, nothing more. He carried the silent boy back out to the reception desk. The attendant said, "I take it he's with you?"

"He is now."

"He came in here with this," and the man produced from behind the counter a heavy long-handled shovel. "I didn't want him taking it in, with all that glass in there."

"I can understand that."

"What do you suppose he wanted it for?"

Oliver shrugged and walked on out, and it was not until the sunlight hit him that he knew. *Little bird, may your spirit fly straight to heaven.* But an owl? A silent night-time killer. He shivered. Eased the boy down onto the steps and sat down beside him. "Michael? Are you all right?"

The boy nodded.

"What's that all over your hands and shirt? Not blood?"

"I don't know."

"You must be hungry, anyway. You want to go get something to eat?"

"Ice cream?"

"Whatever you want."

They rose, blinking in the sunlight as if they had just emerged from a dark movie theatre or a cave. Whatever she did, she did in the name of love, Oliver thought.

"Come on," he said. "Let's go eat."

Naked Woman

BY JOY TREMEWAN

At first, Eileen thought the woman wore one of those flesh brown pantsuits, but when she glanced across the street again, she realized the woman was naked. It was a Sunday morning—11:55, really. Eileen dropped her watering can and it clattered down the porch stairs.

The naked woman walked down the sidewalk and was almost in front of First Baptist Church. In the street beside her crept an old brown car. Eileen could hear a man's voice—"Get in the car, baby—GET IN THE CAR!"—but she couldn't see the driver. The naked woman looked steadily at her own feet, as if she couldn't hear the man at all.

Eileen ran into her house, grabbed the quilt off her sofa and ran back out.

The naked woman was passing by the foot of the church steps when bells rang and the doors opened.

Eileen draped the quilt over the naked woman and gasped for breath. She hadn't run in many years.

Tires screeched. The brown car sped away.

The naked woman shut her eyes and leaned into the cloth against Eileen. She looked young. How young? Eileen couldn't tell anymore. Was she a teenager or a thirty-year-old woman? "Why, you're no more than a girl," Eileen finally said. "Who was that? Was he trying to rape you? Did you get away? I mean before he did? Come on now, come to my house, it's just across the street, we'll call the police. Can't let him get away with that!"

Sweat trickled from the naked woman's forehead. She twisted the quilt tighter around her. "No, I'm fine," she said. "I have to go now. I have to go."

"You come on now, you can't go nowhere, not like this." Eileen put her arm around the young woman to guide her across the street.

A man ran out in front of them. Eileen read the gold pin on his lapel—Deacon Jones.

"What's going on here?" he demanded.

"Why . . . why this poor child just escaped from a rapist and I'm taking her to call the police!"

Deacon Jones studied the young woman. "This girl's in shock," he said. "You better let me take her, ma'am. We can call the police from the church office."

Eileen felt the gawking eyes of the congregation on them and pulled the young woman closer.

"Let me take her," said the deacon. He grabbed the young woman's arm and made to pull her from Eileen.

"What's going on?" a voice from the church steps shouted. "Deacon Jones, what in the world's going on out there?"

It was the pastor. Eileen saw the whole congregation would follow him down. When Deacon Jones turned to answer, Eileen quickly guided the young woman across the street and up the stairs to the house.

The deacon yelled, "Come back!" But he didn't follow.

"Busybody!" said Eileen as she locked the deadbolt. She laughed, felt victorious. She had never liked that church or its members. There used to be a neighborhood there, populated with red brick bungalows like her own. The church had bought it all out.

Eileen's eyes were slow to adjust to changes in light. When she could see again, she saw the young woman wrapped up like furniture on moving day. She made the room look dirty. She stared at Eileen.

I'll have to vacuum after this, thought Eileen.

"He'll be back. He'll come for me. He'll come for you, too."

"Why, I'll call the police!" Eileen intended to take care of this mess as quickly as possible. She watched the news, she knew how ugly this could get. The young woman was lucky she was alive. Shots could've come from that car as quick as pleas. Eileen picked up the receiver and punched in the numbers.

"Oh, dear," she said. "I didn't get his license number, did you? Did you get his name? It was a brown Pontiac, wasn't it?"

"He's my husband."

"Oh. Oh dear." Eileen hung up the phone.

"He'll be back."

The young woman hugged herself and stared at the door. Eileen worried her hands together.

Years ago, Eileen's mother told her what to do with worry. Don't wallow in it, look around, you'll see something needs to be done. See that pile of dishes, wash them. See that dust, get it out. Look behind the furniture. Scrub the bathroom. Get on outside and fix up your yard. By the time you go to bed, worry will let you be, work will have run it down.

Eileen saw there was a lot to be done in that room. She had to finish watering the plants, her precious geraniums, too. The young woman, she looked bony, her face was ashen. Eileen figured she wasn't eating right.

"Are you hungry? I can make you a sandwich. It's time for me to fix lunch." Eileen moved closer to the young woman. "Yeah, it looks like you haven't been getting enough iron. I got some tonic, do you good."

"I don't love him. He said I could never leave him. He said he loves me. He's going to kill me. He locked up all my clothes. He took my dog."

Eileen felt cold. She crossed her arms, trying to keep the warmth. "I can still call the police. Just tell me, I'll do it. Swear out a warrant. You can do that. Man like that, treat his wife like that, he ought to be horsewhipped. And you no more than a child. Want me to call the police?"

"But I did leave." The woman giggled.

"Do you want me to call the police, dear?"

"The shelter. I want to go to the shelter."

"The shelter. Okay. Fine. I can give you a ride. What's your name? I can drive as long as it's daylight. Can't see at night. You wouldn't know about that, young girl like you. You ought to leave that husband. Make a new life. You're so young. What shelter? Where is it?"

"I have the address here in my pocket," the young woman said and reached down.

"Oh, dear, well, can you remember the name?"

The young woman didn't answer. Her face emptied. Eileen had seen that look before. The woman just stared at the door and wrapped herself tighter in the quilt.

Eileen got aggravated, afraid they might stand there forever, the two of them suspended in silence in her living room. Why, they'd hardly moved since they came in.

The garden in the backyard would need water too. And the weeds—you had to get them quick or they'd take over.

Eileen wanted to put the quilt back on her sofa. It was such a pretty one, dark blue flowers bursting out of a sky blue background, it made the sofa look new, not like the same old thing she'd been sitting on for forty years.

"Camille," said the woman.

"Excuse me?"

"My name, it's Camille."

"Well, now, that's a pretty name. My name's Eileen. What's your last name?"

Again, the woman didn't answer. Eileen sighed. Why had she run out like a fool to get this woman when the deacon of First Baptist could have and would have, too? Eileen walked over to the window, lifted the shade and looked out. When her eyes adjusted to the brightness, she saw the church lot was empty. Camille was her problem.

A brown Pontiac cruised by. Eileen dropped the shade.

"I'm going to the shelter," Camille said. "I won't stay here. I heard my dog, my Blackie, her cries. He had me locked in my room. I tried to get out. He let me out and there was a stain on the carpet. He told me I could never leave. I had brushed her and walked her and she looked at me—looked out for me. But I left. I haven't loved him. Not for a long time. I have to go!"

Reaching for the door, Camille let the quilt fall behind her. The sight embarrassed Eileen, she had forgotten Camille was naked.

Camille pulled on the door.

"No, dear, no," Eileen said, and put her hands on Camille's. "It's locked. I've got it locked."

Camille grabbed Eileen's shoulders. "You have to let me go! You have to let me out!"

"Yes, dear, yes, but you're naked. Let me loan you a dress. Let me take you there. Just tell me the name. I can look it up in the phone book. Just tell me where you want to go."

Camille grabbed her own face, pushed her palms into her cheeks and breathed in loud, quick gasps. Eileen put her arm around Camille and led her to the sofa. "Just sit down, dear." Camille collapsed on the sofa, her head in her hands.

Under *Women* in the Yellow Pages there was only Apparel. There was no listing for Shelter.

"The name of the place, dear, can you remember it?"

"Wife Abuse. YWCA Wife Abuse Services."

Eileen couldn't find it in the Yellow Pages, but finally located it in the business section of the White Pages.

"Good. It's not too far. I can take you there."

Camille stood up and went to the door.

"No, dear, wait! Now I've got a lot of old dresses. I'm sure I can find one for you." She led Camille to the bedroom. "Won't you sit down?"

But Camille stood. Eileen stared at her. Years ago, Eileen found her husband's magazines, a huge pile all filled with bodies. Naked ladies. She had looked inside and was sickened. Flesh and lips. Everything open. She ground her teeth, thinking about him looking, looking at them all.

This was different. This body of Camille's. Eileen stared. The breasts sloped forward, the waist curved inward. Her hips and thighs enveloped a triangle of curls that emerged from between her legs. Eileen felt her own skin humming. She wondered if her body had ever looked that way. She tried to think of a time when she had seen it, but even when she was bathing she looked up and washed herself by touch.

Her calves, her feet, her hands—she could see those. Her face she checked in the mirror. These were hers. Her shape was the shape of the dress. What was under her dress belonged to someone else—to nature, perhaps. To something. That something sent messages. There were aches. There was blood. There had been cycles. But it wasn't hers. It belonged to the same dark force that soiled the world with violence. She watched the news.

To the same force that blew dirt in waves over everything. There was always something to clean. It wasn't her body.

Then Eileen noticed the large bruise on Camille's right arm. Another seemed to appear under Camille's nipple, and another, a blue lake on her rib cage. Pale bruises, they would blacken soon. Eileen ducked her head in shame. Why hadn't she noticed them before?

"I have, I have to get you some clothes."

Eileen had gotten increasingly stout over the years. She'd kept all her dresses, though. At first she told herself she'd be able to wear them again. She never shrank back, but she kept the dresses, kept them all.

When she opened her closet, Eileen was bathed in the smell of old fabric. Sometimes, she'd go in there, push her way in and let the dresses cocoon around her. After the early news, Eileen always watched the comedies. There was an hour-long drama on, then more news. After that, she was sleepy. She made herself a snack and watched Perry Mason solve a crime. Then she could sleep, usually. But some nights, she'd lie awake, unable to close her eyes, unable to make out the shapes in her own bedroom. Those nights she felt her way into her closet, no light, and pushed her body against the soft resistance of all those dresses, the pressure of all that fabric steadied her, rocked her to sleep.

Eileen burrowed back twenty years to find a dress that might fit Camille. Then Eileen wore reds, greens and blues. The newer clothes were prints and pastels. When she saw a shimmering green shoulder, she grabbed it and emerged.

"There! I bet you can wear this. This used to be my favorite!"

Camille looked at the dress but said nothing. Eileen could see whatever made the fabric shimmer before had dulled.

"Well, anyway, it should fit you."

Eileen sifted through her dresser for underwear.

"I'm not even going to try to get you in one of my bras. Your ah—breasts—are too small. I suppose you wear panties, but I never did like them. You'll have to be satisfied with these drawers."

Eileen laid the clothes on the bed. Camille regarded them but made no move.

"Well, get dressed, dear. Get dressed and I'll give you a ride over to the Y."

Camille stared at Eileen. Eileen recognized that stare.

"Phew! I never knew I was getting into all this!" Eileen shook Camille a little, but the young woman didn't respond.

"All right! I'll dress you! I used to dress my husband, he was sick for—God—years—before he passed. He stood there and stared, just like you are, except he was sick and you—you're—well, I don't know what you are. Heavens! By the time I water those poor flowers, they'll be cooked. I'll powder you first. It's a hot day. Can't have you getting prickly heat."

Eileen was surprised at how easily she'd shifted back into her nurse's voice. She got the powder box and started dabbing the puff on Camille's neck and back. Camille said nothing.

Eileen hated dressing her husband. She'd learned to dress him quickly, talking to him in that sweet nurse voice, but not looking until she was done, then she'd straighten and smooth his clothes and lead him out for his walk.

She blended the talc into Camille's back. She bent to rub the powder on Camille's buttocks and thighs, then stroked down to her calves and ankles.

When she stood up, Eileen was dizzied by the quick movement.

No matter which way she turned Camille, there was no resistance. Eileen felt she could keep turning Camille until the young woman spun like a top across the room. Instead, Eileen powdered, gently pressing the puff across the young woman's breasts.

Talc smoked around their faces.

"You don't see me, do you?" Eileen asked. She sighed, dipped the puff back into the powder box and dusted the bruise on Camille's ribcage. Eileen powdered Camille's belly, avoided the triangle, stoked the front of her thighs, down her leg, all the way to her toes.

As she put the puff back in its box, Eileen looked at herself in the mirror. She felt so plain. And her skin—it looked so old. She wanted to unzip it and pull a new one out of the closet. All her nerves hummed. Under her skin, she felt fluids moving through hollow tunnels. What did her body look like? She felt her rib cage. Was it also tender and blue?

She'd been glad when her husband died. Glad when her children left for bigger cities, nothing to care for but weekly letters. They were proud she never needed anything. People should take care of themselves. She took care of things. Cleaned the house and it stayed that way. She liked her plants, how well they did with just water and dirt. They never cried out at night. They died without pain.

Eileen glanced back in the mirror at Camille. Her skin was paled by all that powder, like a child's skin, but Camille was no child. She was bruised. She came with whoever drove that brown car.

Eileen shuddered. Nerves, she thought. And she hadn't eaten. How long had that woman been there? She was still naked.

"I got to get you on down to the shelter." Eileen picked up and put back down every item on her dresser, before she turned to Camille and took up the dress. "Now, here, lift up your arms. Come on now, dear, lift your arms up and I'll slip this on you."

Slowly Camille's arms went up and Eileen tugged the dress over the young woman.

It was as if a spell had been broken. The naked woman was gone. Eileen knew it would be only a matter of minutes before Camille was gone, altogether. Eileen would fix a big dinner.

The green dress made Camille's face look ghostly, showed the dark circles under her eyes.

"You look anemic."

Eileen held out the nylon drawers. "Let's get finished now. Let's get these on. Step on in." Camille stepped in the drawers and Eileen pulled them up to Camille's waist, but they fell right back down.

"Lord!" said Eileen.

But Camille giggled.

"Well, now, maybe you're coming to," said Eileen. She safety-pinned the drawers snuggly around Camille's waist and pulled the dress down again. The only shoes she had to give were entirely too big. "They'll protect your feet till you get there."

Eileen stood back. Camille looked ugly in that dress and her legs stuck up like twigs from the big shoes.

Eileen grabbed her purse, her car keys and Camille's arm. When Eileen unlocked the door, Camille stepped out and took a deep breath. It was hot and muggy, but it felt fresh to both women.

As they walked down the steps, a brown Pontiac cruised by. Eileen couldn't see the driver.

Camille stopped moving. "He'll be back."

"That's why we got to get you down to the shelter, where they can protect you."

"He'll be back for you, too."

The street was quiet. Eileen couldn't hear the car's motor anymore.

"He isn't after me. Once you're where they can protect you, I'll be fine. I'll tell him you left. Tell him I put you on a bus." She grabbed Camille's arm and forced her down the porch steps, across the yard and into the car.

Fear. Or was it heat? Eileen was sweating when she started the car. Nothing to do but get that girl gone.

It wasn't a very far drive to the Wife Abuse Shelter, but it was in a part of town Eileen didn't like to go in anymore. The sign was small but she found the building. What was once a fine Victorian two-story had been converted; part of the porch was closed in for additional space. Eileen waited for Camille to get out.

"I won't be going in, dear, I'll just let you out here. I got to get on back to my work."

Camille sat there, scrunched over, gripping the door handle. The dress could be a janitor's uniform.

"Come on now, dear, this is where you wanted to go, this is the shelter."

"The shelter?"

"The wife abuse shelter. Where you wanted to go."

"The address is in my pocket." Camille made to reach in her pocket. "He locked up my clothes." Eileen was tired of the whine in Camille's voice, was tired of her, wanted to sweep her out, sweep her out to join all the dust outdoors.

"You're here now. I got the address for you."

"Out of my pocket?"

Eileen rolled her eyes and looked over the steering wheel to the road. "Yes, out of your pocket. Now, please, go on in. They can help you there."

Camille laughed. "He didn't expect that." She opened the door, stepped out, then reeled back around. "I'm not always this way, you know. You can come back and see me. You've been very kind. Will you come see me?"

"I don't know. I'm busy these days."

"Yes, well, thank you. Thank you for the clothes."

Camille closed the car door and walked up the steps to the wife abuse shelter. Eileen's shoes clopped with each step the young woman took. Eileen watched, half amused, half relieved, when a memory jabbed her.

She had run to her mother's house. She couldn't remember what she'd done to make her husband so angry. She remembered she never did it again. It only happened once. How many years ago was that? She did what he said, stayed busy, and when he was sick, she tended him. What was it? She thought back and back but couldn't remember why he'd hit her, couldn't even remember the fight, the hand that released the blood. All she could remember was running to her mother's house. Her mother opened the door. Her mother stood there, had a rag to press on Eileen's bloody nose. Her mother stood in the door, ready, expecting Eileen's arrival.

An alarm buzzed briefly when Camille entered the shelter. The sun was setting; Eileen had to get home soon or she wouldn't be able to see. She drove faster than usual. Handling the speed comforted her, took her mind off the wasted day, off old memories better left forgotten.

Her street was busy with cars going to the evening service at First Baptist. Eileen saw the brown car pull away from her house. Someone in the church lot was yelling. A man dashed across the street and met her in the driveway.

"I saw him. He was like a madman. I tried to get over here, but he ran when he saw your car." The name in gold was Deacon Smith.

Dirt was strewn all over the porch and down the stairs. The pots she had scrubbed and reused year after year were smashed. Eileen picked up one of the White Beauty geraniums she stored every winter and replanted every spring. It had grown bigger than most people had ever seen a geranium—practically the size of a bush. The stem was crushed, frayed really, but the flowers and leaves had not yet wilted. He must have stepped on it as he fled.

"Who'd do such a thing?" asked the Deacon Smith. "Why, it's just plain meanness. You need me to help you? Want me to call the police? I didn't get his license, but it was an old model Pontiac."

Eileen tossed down the geranium, stepped over the dirt and pottery fragments, and unlocked the door.

"Ma'am? Ma'am?" yelled the deacon, but Eileen locked the door on his voice.

When her eyes adjusted, she saw the quilt still heaped on the floor where Camille had tossed it off. She picked it up, shook it out and draped it back over the sofa.

A naked woman. A naked woman.

Eileen had seen the scratches in the wood around the dead bolt. He could get in. He could break windows. She watched the news. Sixty-one was not too old to be found murdered. Why had she run, the blue quilt flapping behind her? Were the comedies about to start? Would Camille walk back in his house, an empty suitcase, a paper bag, trying to get her clothes?

Eileen went to the storage room and got the biggest box she could find and took it to the bedroom.

The box was bulging with dresses when she dragged it down the steps and into her car. She dragged it through the potting soil and dirt covered her hands, clothes and car seat. The street was quiet again. Church was in service. She could hear the organ, but she couldn't see the church. Already her night blindness blurred everything.

She got in the car and turned on her bright lights. She could only see what was directly before her. She backed out of the driveway fast, faster than she would have yesterday. She would get those dresses to Camille. And if she couldn't stop the rapid beating of her heart, she'd stay there, she'd stay all night.

The Museum of Ordinary People

BY LEWIS TURCO

They had been making these trips ever since their children had disappeared. Now, almost ten years later, they were on the road once more, driving through yet another little town they had never before seen. It was spring, the sun was warm. The pain had diminished over time until it was a dreary ache, but it was there, always. Every now and again it would put out a blossom of poison and then fade. It was the same for both of them.

"Look," Janet said, reaching over and touching Howard's hand as it rested on the steering wheel. She pointed through the windshield at a billboard.

"*The Museum of Ordinary People*," Howard read aloud, "*Five Miles Ahead on Route 12A.*" He blinked and frowned. His eyelids appeared to be paper thin, and the skin on his forehead not much thicker. One had the impression that the iris shone through, or the bone, but it was an illusion. His was a common sort of face.

So was Janet's. Both of them were beginning to gray, Howard more than his wife, but they were still on the farther edge of young adulthood. If they appeared to be older than they were, no doubt that was owing to their situation.

"Let's stop when we get there," Janet said. "We can take the time." She frowned also and covered her eyes briefly with her long fingers, then she smoothed her dress, which was blue and wrinkling under the seat belt.

Howard braked suddenly and leaned across his wife to peer out the right window. "What is it?" Janet looked too—a boy and girl were playing in the front yard of a house with a moderate-sized lawn. He appeared to be about eleven and she seven or so.

Janet sighed. "It can't be, Howard. You know that." She shook her head. "They're too young. When are you going to realize that?"

"Sorry," he said, sitting up straight and easing down on the accelerator. "Good thing there was nobody behind us." He glanced into the rear-view mirror as they moved slowly forward down the street of anonymous houses.

"They'd be ten years older," she said. "Billy would be a junior in college and Beth would be just out of high school."

"My mind knows that," Howard said, "but my guts don't."

They drove in silence for a few minutes, remembering the day the children hadn't come home from school.

There had been nothing unusual about it. All four of them had gotten up at seven in the morning, dressed, and had breakfast. "What are you going to do today?" Howard had asked the table at large. Billy had shrugged and his pompadour had fallen down across his eyes. "Nothing much," he said, reaching for the butter. "We're having a spelling test is all."

"I think you need a haircut," Howard said to his son. "How about you?" He sent a droll wink in his daughter's direction and she giggled.

"Eat your cereal, Beth," Janet said. "You're just moving it around with your spoon. Don't you like it?"

"You put too much sugar in it."

"Okay, give it to me." Janet took the bowl over to the sink, poured some of the milk out of the cornflakes, which were beginning to look a little soggy, and added some fresh from the bottle on the counter.

"Okay, Mom's fixed it," Howard said. "Now eat it up and let's go."

Beth began to scoop the cereal into her mouth. Billy got up

and grabbed his backpack. "See you!" he yelled.

"Wait for your sister!" Janet said.

"Wait for me!" Beth squealed, grabbing her lunch box.

"Whoa!" Howard called as the front door slammed.

It opened again, briefly. "Bye!" Billy called and slammed it again.

And that was the last time anyone had ever seen either of the children.

"There's another one," Janet said, pointing ahead through the windshield.

The Museum of Ordinary People, read the sign, *Three Miles Ahead. Largest Wax Museum in the Midwest.*

"How many do you suppose there are?" Janet asked

"Not all that many, I wouldn't think." Howard had to bend to look as they passed.

They Move! They talk! The Experience of a Lifetime! Don't Miss it!

A red light stopped them. "We need gas," Howard said.

"There's a place." Janet pointed again—it was a 7-Eleven station up a half-block.

The light turned green and Howard pulled in and stopped at the pumps. "Fill it, please." he said to the attendant and got out of the car to stretch.

"Nice day," the attendant said as he unscrewed the gas cap and inserted the nozzle.

"Really nice." Howard put his hands on his hips and arched his back. The sun was warm on his face. "What's the name of this town?"

"Midville. Not from around here?" The pump hummed.

"Not so far away—a hundred miles or so. Lived here long?"

"All my life—twenty-one years." The tank was full, and the attendant rattled the nozzle against the rim and recapped it.

Howard reached into his pocket for his wallet, pulled out a bill and handed it over. His fingers hesitated, then he flipped to a picture of the children. He showed it to the young man. "Ever seen these two kids? They might have shown up in town when you were, oh, about eleven years old."

The attendant peered at the faces smiling out of the photograph. He hesitated, then he shook his head. "Can't say as I have," he said. He gave Howard a look as though he were going to ask a question but had decided against it.

Howard nodded. "Well, thanks." He took his change and put his wallet away. As he opened the door to get back into the car he said "By the way, how's this Museum of Ordinary People up the road? Ever been there?"

"Oh, sure," The attendant turned to look up the street. "But not lately. Everybody's been there once, I guess. If you haven't, you ought to try it. It's good for a laugh." He nodded and turned to go back into the station. "Have a nice ride," he said.

Janet and Howard got back into the car and re-entered traffic. They were quiet for a few minutes. The trees along the curb were turning green quickly—it seemed almost as though spring had accelerated as they'd driven, but no doubt that was because the season was further along this far to the south. And then, as the houses began to grow sparser, the front yards to grow larger, and the trees to thicken, suddenly it was country-side and there were fields and few houses except at considerable distances.

Janet reached down and turned on the radio. She searched for a while and found a station they liked. For a few minutes they listened to golden oldies. And then they saw it. "There it is," Janet said.

Howard slowed down. "Are you sure?" he asked.

"Why not?" she said.

" 'Admission $5.00,' " Howard said.

"Oh, I guess we can afford ten dollars, can't we?" Janet looked at her husband. "And it's not as though we're in a hurry," she added quietly, almost under her breath.

He smiled and nodded. "Sure we can." He pulled into the small parking lot and they sat in their seats for a moment or two listening to one of the old songs, then Howard turned off the motor.

When the children hadn't shown up by suppertime Janet and Howard had really begun to worry. They phoned around to the homes of schoolmates and friends and discovered that Beth and Billy hadn't been to school at all that day. The police had been notified then, and soon it was apparent that the kids had never even made it to their buses. They'd simply vanished between the house and the bus stop a block away.

The police canvassed the neighborhood, but no one remembered seeing the boy and girl in particular. Kids walking the streets in the morning were such a common sight that, even when someone thought he might have glimpsed the missing children, he wasn't sure it had been that particular day.

When at last Howard had been able to stop pacing or running to the door or driving around in the car peering out the windows into the shadows gathering and thickening among the houses of his neighbors, he joined his wife sitting next to the phone with a haunted stare in her eyes and a handkerchief in her fist. They had sat there like that all night long, waiting, jumping when the phone rang or the doorbell sounded, slumping when it turned out that there was no news. As the search went on, neighbors and friends came and went with food and consolation, with assurances that Beth and Billy would turn up, that all would turn out well, that there would be a reasonable explanation for what had happened.

But they had been wrong, and a strange sort of emptiness began to occupy Janet and Howard from that point onward. The rooms of their dwelling filled with a silence that cried out for quick movement and loud music. A veil of anxiety settled itself between the parents and their home—nothing seemed to be real, to be solid or stable, not even their marriage, although they drew closer together after an initial repulsion, like magnets reversed, for each wanted at first to blame the other for what had happened. Common sense had prevailed, however; they saw that nothing could have been done to prevent the loss of Billy and Beth, for it could not have been foreseen.

When at last the police had no leads left to follow, when the story faded from the back pages of the newspapers, when even a private investigator could offer no more hope, on the weekends and on their vacations Howard and Janet would drive in any direction, show their pictures, ask their questions.

"Are we going in?" Janet asked.
Howard roused himself and shivered a little. "Oh, sure, hon"

he said and got out. By the time he'd walked around the car Janet had gotten out herself and stood waiting. Together, they walked to the door of the museum and went in.

It was a large old Victorian house. Just inside the door, in a wide hallway, there stood an oak table where an old woman sat selling tickets. "Welcome to the Museum of Ordinary People," she said, nodding mechanically and leaning forward. "That will be five dollars apiece." Howard gave her the money. She opened a drawer in the table, deposited it inside, and handed him two tickets. "Please take a brochure," she said in her odd monotone. "It will explain the museum. Please walk straight ahead." She sat back, blinked her eyes slowly, and said no more.

As they walked down the corridor toward the first door Janet leaned close to Howard and whispered, "Doesn't she remind you of someone?"

Howard paused, glanced over his shoulder, frowned, and said, "You're right, but I can't think who."

"Let's look at the brochure," Janet said.

The museum of ordinary people is a unique exhibit, it began, *in that there is nothing extraordinary about it except its premise. Here the visitor will find the people he knows saying the things he would expect them to say. The waxwork figures are completely lifelike, even to their movements, for they are animated by extremely sophisticated electronic components which are capable of smoothly imitating natural muscle action. The recorded voices are those of real people responding to real situations and dialogue. Please enter and enjoy yourself in an imitation of the real world that is so convincing as to be astonishing. If the exhibit is successful, it will make reality seem fresh and new—it will give you a new perspective on your own life.*

Howard looked at Janet with eyebrows arched high on his papery forehead. She stared back at him, the phantom of a smile playing across her mouth. "Well," he said, "let's give it a try. I'm willing to be amazed."

"It sounds like fun."

He opened the door and they entered.

"Well, hello there!" said a woman on the other side. "It's real nice to see you, hon," she said. She had on a waitress's uniform; there was a pencil stuck behind her ear and a sales pad slipped through her belt. "Geez, when was the last time you was in here? Musta been a long time."

"We've never been here before," Janet said. "We didn't realize this was a restaurant too."

"Oh, never mind, just let me tell you what's good today. The soup's good—minestrone they call it, but it's just vegetable soup. And then our specials . . . "

"Thanks," Howard said, "But we're not hungry. We'll just look at the rest of the exhibits." He smiled politely, his hand gentle but firm on Janet's back as they moved past.

". . . are liver 'n onions with bacon, chicken fried steak. . . . " and then she stopped talking and stood still, facing toward the door.

"Look, Howard," Janet said, nodding toward a beam of light through which they had stepped. "She's one of the wax figures."

"We tripped an electric eye," Howard said, sticking his finger into the ray. "Unbelievable."

"Well, sir," an elderly male voice said behind them, "that was back in 'sixty-six as I recall, and I never caught a better fish since." They turned quickly and saw the replica of a dock with a boathouse where an old man sat leaning forward in his rocking chair whittling a piece of wood. "Sure would like to run into a fighter like that big-mouth again." He nodded and chuckled.

"Straight out of my childhood," Howard said. "That looks just like the boatkeeper at Huntington Lake."

Janet laughed uneasily. "I feel like telling you to be quiet because he'll hear you," she said. "They really are lifelike." She walked on.

"Sorry, folks," the policeman said. He stood with his hands behind him and shook his head. "There's been an accident down this street and you'll have to keep clear. The fire department's laying down some foam over the spilled gasoline." He pointed with his nightstick. "It's not much farther if you go that way."

"Thank you, officer," Janet said before she could catch

herself.

Howard grinned. "Probably the accident's in the living room," he said. Janet laughed and flushed.

They lost track of time. Every room held a crowd of ordinary people who spoke to them, offered advice, asked directions, complained—like the fat woman on the mock-up of a bus who said, "Oh, my feet ache. I been on my tootsies all day long, and now I gotta go home and make supper for my old man. Will he appreciate it? Oh, no," she said, shaking her head, making her chins wiggle and her red hair with the brown roots jounce, "he'll just sit there after supper with a beer watching Monday Night Football while I do the dishes." She snorted. "Boy, I could do with a beer myself, come to think of it."

And there was the journalist sitting at his word-processor typing a story. "Fred Foyle," he said, turning around as they entered his office. "What can I do for you?" He had a thin face and a shock of pale hair that fell down over his eye. "Want ads? That's over there at the classified desk," he said, pointing. "Can't help you." He turned back to his screen. Janet and Howard heard him sigh. "Obits!" he snorted. "This week I'm on obits. Next week I'll be on garden parties." He hunched forward and began to type, still mumbling.

"I'm starting to get hungry," Howard said. They were standing in an upstairs hallway looking out a bay window over the countryside. The sun was beginning to settle into the fields and appearing redder as it did so. There was a wind, too, that could be seen but not heard, riffling through the few trees visible in the landscape.

"That was a lot fun," Janet said. "It was like walking through a whole town full of people that you feel you know."

"I wonder who got the idea for such a museum." Howard mused a moment and then said, "Well, I guess that's about it. What say we hunt up some food and then head home?" A gust of wind rattled the window behind them as they turned toward the stairway. "Too bad that waitress downstairs isn't real."

"Oh, look," Janet said, "there's a doorway we missed." She walked across the carpet and paused with her hand on the knob of a door that looked out of place in the old Victorian building. Out of place but familiar, like almost everything else in the

Museum of Ordinary People.

"Never mind it," Howard said. "I've seen enough, haven't you?"

"Oh, let's just have a peek," Janet replied, but before she could turn the knob Howard put his hand over hers.

"It's late," he said. "I'm hungry." He smiled. "I've had enough, haven't you?"

Janet hesitated, then she smiled back at him and let her hand fold into his as together they walked away from the last door.

A Carnival of Animals

BY EMILY MEIER

When the first truck came in from the freeway, it was dusk. Lights gleamed on the fast food restaurants and the gas stations along the access road, and, in the western sky, a rim of pink sank away behind the hills. It was hot out. There were girls in halter tops in line at the Dairy Queen and boys stripped to the waist, and toddlers, in printed tennis shoes and diapers, holding onto the straps of their mother's purses. When the trucks rolled by, everyone turned to stare at the garish pictures on the semis—of ferris wheels and distorting mirrors—and eyed the bulging canvases that were tied down the length of the flatbed trucks.

"There's a bunch of them," said a boy at the back of the line who was half a head taller than anyone else. The girl who was holding his hand in his back pocket nodded and brushed away beads of sweat that glinted on her midriff.

"There's supposed to be. I heard they're having their own animals this year."

"They are animals," the man in front of her said, and a thin ripple of laughter ran through the line. The girl turned back from staring at the road and looked at him, but the man didn't say anything more.

Just after midnight, the last stragglers of trucks pulled through the stoplights and headed for the fairgrounds, which made a camp now, with trucks and vans ringing the perimeter in the style of a wagon train stopped for the night. The girl, who had tiptoed past her parents' room when she came in, listened for her dad to yell she was five minutes late and make her mad all over again that she had a curfew when nobody else in the whole high school did. But she heard him snoring instead, and she went on into the bathroom and washed out an ice cream stain on her halter and then got ready for bed. She crouched down in front of the open window in her bedroom. She was looking after the trucks, trying to follow the lights all the way to the fairgrounds. A mosquito hummed near her ear and then bit her in the leg and she swatted at it and thought she heard one last backing rumble of a truck in the distance. But the lights she saw now through the window were all street lights. They were stationary, every one of them, and she pushed the covers over the end of the bed and lay down.

She was not sure, not really, what it was the man in line had meant. She'd been wondering about it and the different things that might make somebody think a person was like an animal, but the only thing that seemed very close was what Jerry Henderson had wanted her to do in his car the night before he went to the Navy and even that didn't seem like quite enough. She scratched her leg and straightened her nightgown behind her back. She closed her eyes. She scratched on her arm and, in a while with her mind jumbling tattoos and broken teeth and the thick paint of grease on the gears of carnival rides, she fell asleep.

In the morning, a little after dawn, the first horse vans and livestock trucks pulled through the fairground gates. The camp was already up. There was a line of people filling containers with water at the faucet in front of the grandstand, and two children were rolling marbles in the dust and another was hanging on the door of a camper, his knees tucked up under the doorknob while he swung out over a stubble of grass. There were trucks backing into place to unload machinery for rides, and a man yelling and a noise of metal—the hard grating clash of steel on steel and a jarring ping of hammers striking nailheads. The men in the John Deere hats driving through to the animal bars drove slowly, staring through the windows of their trucks past their wives, who were pink and rounded and staring, too, to see the carnival people, to see if it was fact they were all dark and leather with muscles as hard as metal shanks they bolted together. Gravel crunched under the wheels of the trucks and, inside the

unloading pen, a pig fight started up with an enormous bellow-
ing and squeal.

Just after nine, the girl, whose name was Suelinda Elly,
brought her younger brother and the two neighbor children
she watched in through the gates to have a look. They had
walked up the street pulling a wagon with a doll in it and now
Daisy, the three-year-old climbed in on top of the doll and said
her feet hurt.

"Well, I can't help it your feet hurt," Suelinda said. "You can
just sit there if Joey won't pull you. Go ahead and bawl. I'm not
going to listen to you." Suelinda straightened the cuff on her
shorts and squared her shoulders back. "You come on now,"
she said without turning around. "We get where those tractors
are and you're not behaved, *you're in for it!*" She started
walking slowly, waiting for the wagon to start, but she was only
half listening, her real attention centered on the carnival loop,
where the people sitting in the dust or revving the motors on
the rides had their eyes on her. She tilted her chin up and pulled
her stomach tight.

"Hey there. Suelinda!" The wagon started up behind her and
Suelinda looked over at the machinery display and saw her
cousin Tim sitting on a spreader, waving.

"Go on and talk to him, Joey," she said out of the corner of
her mouth, waving back. "Tell him I got hoarse yelling at the
ballgame and I got these children to take care of. Daisy, don't
leave that doll in the dirt." Suelinda picked the doll up and
dumped it in the wagon. "Go on, Joey," she said. She was
feeling let down and cheated all at once, as it she'd been
dreaming a good dream and gotten yanked awake. "How come
we have to live somewhere that everybody acts like a relative—
or *is?*" Suelinda took hold of Daisy with one hand and the
wagon handle with the other. "Now where did Todd get to?"
She shaded her eyes looking around. "Daisy, you see where
your brother went?" There was a minuscule twitch started in
Suelinda, like a tiny alarm bell going off, and she looked after
Joey and in the farm machinery and across the road where the
merry-go-round horses were all stretched out at gallop.

"There," said Daisy pointing, and Suelinda spotted him now,
next to a ticket booth—Todd with the same blond curls his

sister had but the longer legs, the laziness of his body. He was watching something, his weight forward on one foot as if he'd been walking somewhere and forgot to keep going.

Todd David Grenager you trying to get yourself lost with all these strangers here? Suelinda had the words all set and she was ready to grab Todd by the waistband of his shorts and pull his heels up off the ground, but when she got to him, she tugged at his shirt without looking at it and whispered at him: "Come on, you."

There were two men standing beyond him, one she'd seen somewhere before, who had a camera around his neck, and the other a carnival man—clearly—with a giant buckle on his belt and hair that was a sheeny black like the high polish on a shoe. They were arguing, the carnival man with his eyes glaring and his hand gripping the other man's arm so it showed white.

"Come on, Todd," Suelinda whispered again, and the carnival man looked at her, his eyes dropping in an instant from her neck to the ground and then riveting back hard on the man in front of him.

"There's people here with their face in the post office that don't look to have their picture took. I said you can give me that film."

Suelinda was backing up, pulling on Todd and she pushed him and Daisy into the wagon and picked up the handle again. "If Tim's here, Uncle Ez must be. Let's find his baby calves." She was dragging the wagon across the road, walking fast. But she couldn't get over it, the surprise of what the man had said. It was very nearly thrilling as if the newspapers and TV were coming to actual life.

"Uncle Ez, are you here?" Suelinda looked in the cow shed where the calves were tethered, and then she pulled the wagon down the middle aisle, letting Daisy and Todd rub on the calves' ears, and all the while she was wondering what it would be like for somebody with his picture in the post office, what he would have done in the line of murder or robbing banks. She was thinking of people in striped uniforms. She was thinking of a man with his head smashed into a toilet, the way she'd seen somebody in a movie once.

In the evening, when she'd done the supper dishes, listening the whole time to her parents argue on the back porch about whose fault it was her brother was getting divorced already, Suelinda went upstairs to take a shower. The fan was blowing in the hall and she stood awhile in front of it, trying to cool off. She was going back to the fairgrounds again. She had a date for 7:30 with Joel Krieke, who was pretty much her boyfriend now that Jerry Henderson had gone to the Navy and her mother said she was too young to wait (Suelinda figured *she* was paying for whatever it was they thought her brother'd done wrong), and she felt halfway as if she were already there. In her room with her clothes off on the bed and her robe on and Smokey Robinson playing on the record player, she was as good as in one of those campers. With her eyes shut, she could see the flowered curtains on the window. There was a silk wrapper flung over a chair and the smell of fingernail polish and there were coffee cups with rings in them and a start of mold and there were ashtrays full of cigarette butts. Suelinda made her hips go back and forth, swaying to the music. They were different in the carnival. That's what excited her. They were different from anything she knew.

In the shower, with the shampoo suds running down her neck, she thought she smelled cotton candy. She'd taken Todd and Daisy again when the rides started up at two and, in the afternoon heat, the whole fairgrounds had smelled like hogs and caramel corn. There was a girl there no older than she was selling tickets in a booth and a baby, that had to be hers, lying asleep on the floor. It had startled Suelinda, seeing the baby there, with a pacifier in its mouth, and its hair damp on its neck.

Not that she didn't know girls her age that had babies. She knew girls who were sixteen and had babies just to get out on their own. But what it was that seemed hard to get a grasp of was to be *that* girl you'd have a baby, *and* you'd travel with the carnival. Suelinda couldn't fathom it. She couldn't make what that would be like come clear in her mind. She shut the shower off and toweled herself dry and took the hairdryer into her bedroom.

When she was dressed, when she'd finished with her hair, she went out and looked at herself sideways in the hall mirror. She had on her pink sandals and her best shorts and the pink tank top she'd bought on Saturday and she knew from the mirror just what kind of once-over she'd get from Joel when he saw her. She looked good. She looked terrific, in fact, and she went in and sat down on the bed and did her toenails in "Racy Plum," waiting, and went through a stack of movie magazines until the doorbell rang.

He was two minutes early. Boys were always early or on time until they were sure of you, and she put a Kleenex and four dollars in her shorts pocket and went downstairs to let him look at her. He seemed like a boy to her, standing at the door—the funny way he grinned at her without meeting her eyes. He seemed like a boy even more than Jerry did, and it came to her all at once how the man at the carnival had taken her in—totally—with just a flicker of his eyes and she wondered what in the world it was a man like that could do to you that a boy—even a boy like Jerry Henderson—had never even thought of.

"You ready for the skydive?"

"I am," Suelinda said, and they went down the front steps and waited for Todd to shoot by them on his Hot Wheel.

At the fairgrounds, all the rides were going, and Dolly Parton was blaring out on the loudspeaker at the radio booth.

"Wait a minute. Wait, I like this record," Suelinda said, pulling on Joel's arm, and she put her hands on her hips, listening. "Oh, she can sing."

"There you are. Miss Dolly Parton," the announcer said. "And you all know how she gets dressed. *In nothing flat!*"

Joel was laughing and Suelinda pushed her arm through his and hooked her finger in the belt loop of his jeans. "Oh, you men sure like a joke," she said, turning her eyes up at him. "I thought we were taking the skydive."

It was when they were at the top of it, ready for the car to plummet toward the earth, and she was hanging onto Joel and he had his arm tight around her, that she saw the girl from the ticket booth again. She was leaning on the door of a trailer and fanning herself with a towel.

"See that girl?" Suelinda asked, and then the car dropped and the air rushed up over her windpipe and she screamed.

"She was there," she said afterwards, when they were walking past the booth with the toy pandas in it. She pointed toward the trailer.

"Who was there?" Joel said, and Suelinda waved at her Aunt Sue who was the bigger part of who she was named for and had on a painted felt hat with gold tassels hanging from it.

"Just this girl my age that was selling tickets before. She had a baby. Can you imagine traveling with a carnival?"

Joel shrugged his shoulders, and Suelinda kept her eyes on the trailer while she waited for him to get her a snow cone. The girl was inside there right this minute, she thought. Maybe she washed her baby up in a plastic washtub and put it to bed. Maybe she was getting ready to go back to work. Maybe she was in there talking to who she was married to or whoever it was that baby's father was.

Suelinda took the snow cone and tilted it up and drank out of the side. Joel was shooting an air rifle now, trying to win her a stuffed dog, and she had one eye on him and the other on the trailer. Maybe that man was in there with the girl. Maybe what he was was an escaped convict himself who'd forced the girl to go in the carnival with him. Maybe he was a man with a wife somewhere else he couldn't see because of a stakeout or maybe that girl had just plain stolen him from another woman.

The last idea seemed like a fact, all at once, and a picture flashed into Suelinda's mind that was like a picture on TV or in the movies, of a girl stretched out on a bed with a man towering above her and another woman, with hard eyes appearing suddenly in the doorway and the girl grabbing at the sheets to pull them over her. Suelinda could see the whole thing, but where she was looking from was the bed and the woman in the doorway with the hard eyes was the girl with the baby.

"Well I won it for you. Where's my thank you?" Joel said, and Suelinda took the dog from him and gave him a squeeze around the waist and kissed his cheek.

"I guess I get it later," he said into her ear, and Suelinda took his hand and started off for the crafts and flowers building.

"Come on," she said. "I got cousins that win blue ribbons, don't you? There's no living with them if you don't look."

Walking through the weaving display, she thought she talked to half the people in town: "I don't know if they set the court date yet." "Well, he's been real busy, Mr. Henry. It's his busy season at the shop, so maybe that's why it's late. I can tell him to call you when I get home." "They were pretty good, except Todd tried to get himself lost." "No. I had a postcard, but that's all."

Suelinda headed for the flowers, and Joel picked up a big bouquet and stuck it on his head, fanning out the gladioli like feathers.

"Hey, set that down!" Eunice Price straightened up in the middle of the tables, all at once, her garden club tag glittering in the light and her finger wagging at them. "Joel Krieke and Suelinda Elly, I'm surprised at you."

"Sorry, Miss Price," Suelinda said and Joel tickled her in the back and she half choked to death to keep herself from laughing.

"I suppose you want to see all the chickens. You want to see every rabbit and little pig?" Joel said when they got outside, and Suelinda glanced at the trailer and shook her head.

"I don't care. We could go on the octopus. Did you see if they brought those animals they were talking about?"

"There're some birds down there. You can hear them," Joel said, and they started walking down the row of booths, past the man with the oiled chest who was playing the shell game and the beckoning woman with the bracelets all the way up both arms (Suelinda had already stared at her awhile and decided she was a washed-up belly dancer or a retired madam), past the floating ducks and glittering T-shirts, the canned screams booth and the three-minute charcoal portraits.

"Well, is this it?" Suelinda asked, disappointed. They had stopped in front of the last booth, which was empty except for a pair of blue and gold parrots in a cage and a greenish-yellow canary.

"So who said they were having animals?"

"Animals? You want animals, sweetie?"

"It's that bird talking," Suelinda said, startled.

"You betcha, sweetie. Hey Pete, come on out. Hey Petie, we got you an audience."

Suelinda had her hands on Joel's arms, watching. There was a door at the back of the booth and it was opening now and a monkey scampered out with a cup on its hand. "Pay her. Pay her," the parrot screamed, and a boy next to them dropped a quarter in the cup.

"Folding money, buster," the parrot said, and Suelinda took out one of her dollar bills and waved it at the parrot and then put it in the cup. "What a looker! *Sweet*-heart," the parrot said, and Suelinda laughed and noticed there was a man standing in the doorway now, an old man in a felt hat and suspenders who was eating a sandwich.

"Slept through supper," he said. His voice had an odd, gravelly accent, and it seemed directed mostly at himself. "Princess!"

Suelinda looked back at the monkey.

"Princess is a dog!" the parrot howled.

"She is a dog," Suelinda said. She could just see a tiny, gray poodle with earrings and a satin bow peeking out from behind the man's legs.

"Come on, Princess," the man said. He had finished his sandwich and he walked out and stood in the center of the floor with a hoop in his hand. "Princess," he said again, and the dog jumped through the hoop which seemed about eight times her height, and Suelinda decided the old man looked grumpy but sweet, with lines in his face as deep as her great grandfather had when he died.

"Oh," she said, sucking her breath in.

"What?" Joel asked, and she shook her head. *The old man had numbers on his arm!* She had perfectly sharp eyes and she could see them on his skin, a long row of numbers that started with a letter. That meant he'd been a prisoner. From somewhere she knew that meant he'd been a prisoner someplace.

Suelinda stared. So here was an old dog trainer, and even *he* must have been a prisoner—even someone like him! Maybe he'd been a safecracker when he was young. Maybe he still was. Maybe he was one of those people that lean up against the lock of a safe door, while they turn the knob, and listen to hear it click.

There was a small crowd gathered in front of the booth now, and the dog started to prance on its hind legs, and the monkey bowed in front of them with the cup.

"Joel, look at those numbers. There on his arm. See? He

must've been in jail," she whispered.

Joel shook his head. "No," he said in her ear. "Maybe in Auschwitz. Maybe someplace like that," he said, but then the parrot was talking again.

"Pay her. Pay her, sweetie. Oh, what a looker! *Sweet*-heart."

"Let's go," Joel said, and Suelinda went after him through the crowd and nodded at her sister-in-law who was trying to look over the top of her head.

So leave it to Joel, she figured, to think he got something she didn't. Auschwitz what? If she knew anything, this old birdman had killed somebody. She couldn't picture him with a gun in his hand, but she could see him with a knife. She could see him sneaking up on somebody with the blade glinting in the sun.

"You want good seats for that race, we better head for the grandstand," Joel said.

"They're racing? I thought it was the demolition derby."

"Sure they're racing. They been practicing for it all week. The demolition part's for after," Joel said, and he paid at the window.

When the cars were in the middle of their warmup laps, Suelinda was thirsty. "Don't you think they have somebody selling Coke here on a hot night like this?" she said, looking around. "Well, I'll get us one. No, you sit there. I can do it." She got up and she was halfway to the exit when she saw the man again. He was leaning against the railing about two feet from where she had to walk, and she thought he was looking straight at her.

"Oh, God," she said under her breath. Her stomach was balled up in a hard knot, and she turned her head to one side, pretending she was hunting for someone in the crowd, and she kept on walking, hoping she hadn't turned as pink all over as her clothes were. She could hear him breathing when she went by.

Outside the grandstand, she ran. It was as if some excitement had boiled up inside her and made her run. She ran all the way to the hot dog stand and then she forced herself to stand in line.

"Two Cokes—large," she told the vendor. For as much as the Coke sign seemed perched on the cook's head, what she was really looking at was in her mind, the man with the out-sized belt buckle and the sheeny hair. She knew he'd eyed her with a look that was, for all the world, like a man in a movie who was burning up at the sight of a woman and straining to keep his hands off of her.

Suelinda paid for the Cokes and picked them up and started slowly back across the fairgrounds. She couldn't think of what a man like that would talk about. She couldn't think, when he wasn't talking about pictures in the post office, what he would say. She pried the cap of her cup up with her teeth and took a swallow. She had this scene in her mind. It was this dark night and it was still hot out and she was standing with the man behind the trailer and he had his arm straight-armed out to her shoulder and he was staring at her and she was waiting.

"Get out!" She could hear what he was saying all at once. She was reading his lips but she could hear him at the same time. He was spitting the words at her. "Get out. What is this, a setup? Get!"

Suelinda pushed the cap down on the Coke. Her hand had jerked a little to the side and some of the Coke had spilled down the cup. She could hear the man yelling at her exactly as if he were, but what struck her even more, what she hadn't thought of until now, was what his hands would be like. She could see them moving in the darkness. All lit up like hands in a horror show, and they were bony, oddly elongated, and the nails were covered, as though they had to be, with grease.

Suelinda shook her head, trying to clear it. *I got too much of this heat*, she thought, and she licked at the dribble of Coke on the bottom of the cup. Well she was going to look at the man straight on. She was going to give him the same kind of stare he'd given her and see just exactly what it was he looked like. She put one of the Cokes on top of the other and held her hand up so the stamp showed. She could hear the crowd yelling and the cars roaring around the track. Somewhere over to the left, Dolly Parton was singing again, but the song that was going through her own head, the song that was making her feel a little giddy and giggly was, "Just one look, da, da, da, da, THAT'S ALL IT TOOK! Yeah!" Suelinda pushed her shoulders back and started into the grandstand.

She was making her way around a knot of people when a shout went through the crowd. It seemed to come right up from the bleachers, rising over the noise of the cars, and then there was an enormous, collective gasp. Suelinda jumped and squeezed the Cokes so the top lid popped off. "What?" she said. The man was gone and everyone was standing up in front of her and there were screams all over the place and then, as if somebody had slammed a door shut, it was quiet.

"What happened?" Suelinda hurried up the steps to Joel. She squeezed beside him.

"Eighty-four." Joel's eyes were fixed on the track, and she saw the car now. It was on fire just inside the infield and it was split nearly in two. A siren had started up in the distance and the other cars were stopped at crazy angles on the track and people were running everywhere.

"So who's eighty-four?" she asked.

Joel craned at the program the man in front of them had. "LaVern Cobb. I never heard of him."

"He must be from away. They stopping the race then?"

"I guess they'll pull him out if they can."

A siren was screaming outside on the road and the fire truck roared onto the track and the firemen were scrambling around, working at the hoses, and an ambulance pulled up behind them. Suelinda's eyes roved through the crowd. She couldn't see the man. She couldn't find him anywhere. "Here's your Coke," she said, remembering, and she drank hers and kept looking around.

"They're getting him out now." Joel was like he had his breath sucked away. "I wish I brought my binoculars."

"How come you'd want to look for?" Suelinda put her Coke cup down and crushed it with her foot. "You think they'll race anymore?"

"It looks like his leg's half off."

Suelinda glanced down the row. She thought she'd spotted the girl with the baby and she kept watching out of the corner of her eyes, but when the person she was looking at turned around, it was somebody else. She scratched her leg. "You got any of your Coke left?"

"I don't think he even moved. Here."

The car was still smoking and the drivers from the other cars were out leaning on their cars, looking.

"Well it must be over, Joel," Suelinda said. The ambulance siren had started up again toward the hospital. "Look. The track's all ripped up there. Did he roll? What happened to the loudspeaker? They for sure won't race any more tonight. We might as well go. Look. Those people are leaving there."

"Did you see him? I think his face was charred. All right, we can go. But where to? It's not even nine-thirty yet."

"The ferris wheel's running." Suelinda pointed at the top arc of cars that were curving through the air behind the grandstand. "We didn't ride that yet. We could ride it and we never tried the octopus. I guess they won't give you your money back for this but they should." Suelinda had Joel's hand and she kept searching through the crowd while they walked down to the exit.

In the night outside the grandstand, all the rides were lit up and moving like giant sparklers writing in the sky.

"It's pretty," Suelinda said, pushing the stuffed dog up higher under Joel's arm, "even if it is still hot. I think a carnival's pretty. Let's just walk around." She was looking at the booths, hunting through the people running the rides.

"What was his name again?" Joe said.

"Who?"

"Eighty-four."

"LaVern Cobb—you said it was."

"I think he was dead."

"Well, who'd want to race one of those cars anyway? It's dumb." Suelinda rattled the change in her pocket. They'd stopped walking and they were in the darkness only a little way off from the trailer where she'd seen the girl in the afternoon.

"I really do think he was dead."

"Well, maybe he is." Suelinda could see the curtain in the trailer moving faintly in the air. "Look at that trailer. It's got stickers from all over. There's Florida and California. What's that bottom one? Is it Texas?"

Suelinda closed her eyes, listening to the sounds around her—the music from the merry-go-round and the long wail of a cow from the animal barns. She was seeing something different in her mind now—some Texas night and a shootout and drugs—she thought there'd be drugs—and the old safecracker, turned in by the madam, dying with a contorted grin on his face in a hail of bullets and the carnival man escaping somehow— paying for his freedom by forcing the girl on another man.

Suelinda felt a shiver along her spine.

"Can you feel what it's like here, Joel?" she said, opening her eyes and curling herself into his shoulder. She bit the tip of his earlobe and ran her tongue behind her ear.

"They're all dangerous, dangerous people," she said. She held onto his wrists and stared hard into his eyes. She could feel the blood surging up to her temples and her heart racing. "I *love* it. Joel," she said, whispering against his shirt collar, "I'm scared to death."

The Empire Beauty Salon

BY ANNE WHITNEY PIERCE

On an August day in New York City, a woman's yearning comes full circle. The morning begins like any other. She opens her beauty parlor, tilts up the hairdryers, sweeps no more than night dust from the floor, smoothes the sand in the sand tray, and rearranges the shells on the shelf. As the eight o'clock news comes on the radio, the Waikiki poster on the wall catches her eye. The muscled surfer hovers on the crest of a giant wave while the coffee perks. Three people have been found murdered in the night, the announcer says, and the air is bad. The telephone operators are back on strike and there will be Shakespeare in the park that night. City pride, a street study reveals, has never been higher.

Out of the woman's yearning comes a wry laugh. She fills a bucket and goes out to splash water on the sidewalk, scrubbing it clean with a wire brush. She is forty-eight years old and not unhappy. She owns the Oceana Beauty Salon on West 112th Street and business is good. The mortgage is paid and she has health galore, more, perhaps, than she will ever be able to use. She hasn't been sick but that one day when she lost the baby, a baby she never really expected to make it anyway. Her policeman friend, Brett, walks her beat and her friend Tony owns the best Italian restaurant on the East Side. The woman is a New Yorker born and bred, but if affection and pride are the measures, she has never really felt that she belongs here.

The woman has always loved the ocean from a distance, in books and photographs and TV shows, and the feel of it on her toes on trips to Coney Island or the spray from the Staten Island Ferry on a windy day. Over the years, she has amassed a large collection of travel books and posters and brochures on sea-bordered lands, having combed the city's bookstores and travel agencies to find them. All of the ocean paraphernalia—the shells, the anchor, the sand—has been bought in New York City, it being a place where one can buy anything, even the stuff, if not the essence, of dreams. Her beauty parlor is something of a landmark, its front face covered with shells stuck on stucco, its twin potted palm trees standing guard out front, defying cold, smog and vandals alike. The ocean music she plays has lulled more than one customer to sleep under the hairdryers, and stops passersby on the warm days, when the sounds of waves roll out onto the street.

The woman's customers are regular and loyal. Many of them are elderly, although she will cut anyone's hair and considers this just to be chance. They all share with her a yen, if not for the sea, for something equally as compelling. In the woman's beauty parlor, they are free to dream. Even Mr. Hurlehee, one of the woman's few male customers, keeps coming back with his receding hairline, although she often suggests that he call the toll free number and speak to the hair specialist who jabbers with a lisp on late night TV. Mr. Hurlehee won't hear of it. He has searched the city far and wide for the feel of hands as soft as the women's on what is left of his hair, for an ear as keen and a chair as comfortable. He comes more often than is necessary for a trim and some "poofing," as he calls it, and is most often lost in a book which the woman picked up once at a church sale, a book called *The Magical Island of Fiji*, with full-page color photographs.

"A man could really hang his hat over there in Fiji, Roxanne," Mr. Hurlehee has been known to say.

And Roxanne—for that is the woman's name—has been known to reply as she snips off tiny bits of his hair and the traffic snarls outside, "Could hang it right on a cloud, Mr. Hurlehee. Watch it ride away." She and Mr. Hurlehee have chuckled to think of hat racks in hatless lands. They've even had lunch a few times, once with martinis.

Mrs. Agnes Pepperdine, who owns the dry cleaners a few

doors down, has come to the Oceana Beauty Salon every Thursday for thirteen years after her palm reading session with Madame Angela, sure that Roxanne can somehow recreate the aqua color of the Mediterranean Sea in her limp gray curls, and make all of Madame Angela's predictions for her come true. Mrs. Pepperdine has spent many an hour in Roxanne's chair, studying the brown-skinned girls in hula skirts and bikini tops walking the beach on the Bora Bora poster on the wall. "No wonder they look so good," she has often speculated, blowing on wet, red fingernails while Roxanne does her up in curlers. "No winter. No carbon monoxide. No MSG. Now that, Roxanne, would be a good life."

And Roxanne has often replied in a solemn voice for the dream that they share. "No subway trains. No lines at the supermarket. No traffic jams. No wonder those girls look so good."

It is, in fact, on the very day that Roxanne learns of Mrs. Pepperdine's death, that she finally reckons with the yearning. "Agnes was found stone cold," Mrs. Bensonhurst—a customer and mutual acquaintance—tells Roxanne. "Three days after the fact and not by that millionaire son of hers."

"Who found her?" Roxanne asks, starting to comb out Mrs. Bensonhurst's wet, tangled hair.

"The *Christian Science Monitors* started to pile up on the doorstep," Mrs. Bensonhurst explains. "A neighbor went for the super."

"Is she gone?" Roxanne asks, thinking in a crazy moment that maybe it's not too late to stop Mrs. Pepperdine from going to the grave with dingy curls.

"You don't get much deader than dead, Roxanne," Mrs. Bensonhurst says.

"I meant has she been buried yet?" Roxanne says.

"Today," says Mrs. Bensonhurst, turning her face this way and that, to see herself at different angles in the mirror. "Over at the Soldiers Field next to her husband, not that he was ever very good company."

"I never met him," Roxanne murmurs, reaching for a comb. Ms. Bensonhurst's hair has never really needed her. It is like steel wool, holds its curl at all costs and never seems to grow. Roxanne tugs away, upset that Mrs. Pepperdine will have to leave the world with sour milk in her refrigerator and so many dreams unfulfilled, with only an ungrateful son left to see to things. An unspeakable distress fills Roxanne, as the waves crash through the speaker on the wall—maybe an anger.

"Did you hear me, Roxanne?" Mrs. Bensonhurst is asking, suddenly aware that Roxanne's hands are still. Roxanne starts to comb again and Mrs. Bensonhurst goes on, "I was saying how even a million dollars can't bring back a dead mother."

At this moment, Roxanne bends to the yearning's will. She sees how there will be more ends now than beginnings, how all of them will be swallowed up by one horror or another, and taken away, one by one. She sees that she has no real obligations or ties, how alone she really is. She understands, be it a curse or a blessing, that she will be on the earth for a long, long time. She sees that she alone is the maker of her fate and how that makes fate easier to mold. All of this comes to her not with self-pity or sadness, but with relief. Roxanne decides that she has had enough of her city, any city, and that she will move to a seacoast town.

Roxanne chooses Maine because a trip to Camden with an old lover once made a dent in her heart somewhere, because it's not too far away, but far enough. In Maine, she will know the language and the hair and the TV stations and the cuts of meat at the supermarket. She would not be good in the places on the travel posters—Tahiti or the Riviera or Puerto Escondido. Her white skin would burn and her thick ankles would never learn to dance on the hot sand. Truth be known, she can't even swim. Nor would she know what to do with the dark, slippery hair of the brown beach girls, if they ever came to her with it. But surely in Maine, where there is fast food, hardship, and a cold, cold ocean, the hair is still in need of a Roxanne.

Out of an atlas, Roxanne settles on the town of Morocco, Maine, as her new home, satisfied to seek the exotic only in a name. It is the dot on the tip of a jagged spit of land north of Damariscotta, and only a bus can take her there. She takes the ten-hour bus ride, three of them spent winding down tiny roads from Augusta to the coast, and finds the perfect storefront for her beauty parlor, sandwiched on Morocco's Main Street between Albow's Drug Store and a knick-knack shop which sells the kind of things which line the shelves of Roxanne's New York salon—sea glass and fishing net, seagull pins and sand dollar paperweights. Back stairs lead up to a two-room apartment overlooking the lobster pound and Morocco's harbor. The walls are freshly painted and the floors are of wide pine. She signs a lease that day.

Roxanne hires a local carpenter and discusses her plans for the beauty parlor. He is swarthy and silent, with the blackest of hair and a rumbling voice. He is neither lobster fisherman like his father nor carpenter, really, he explains, but an aspring pharmacist. Having been rejected once from the Bangor College of Pharmacy, he is doing odd jobs while he studies and waits for the next application deadline to roll around. "Can you do this and that?" Roxanne asks him, needing a person of specific temperament and skills. The boy can do this and that. He can do most anything she wants, he assures her, understanding right away that Roxanne is a person who knows what she wants.

In late September, Roxanne returns to Morocco on the bus with the matching luggage set she picked up at Causeway's Bargain Basement on West 44th. The beauty supplies have come ahead of her in a cushioned truck and the shop is ready. Frederick, the young carpenter, has done more than a fine job. The Empire Beauty Salon is as much a sight on Main Street, Morocco, as the Oceana was on west 112th. The store sign is just how she pictured it—a plywood face of the Empire State Building rising above the floor. Frederick has installed plate glass behind the cut-out windows and painted in the sills and moldings carefully. Inside, on the wall across from the hairdryers, hangs a blown-up photograph of Times Square at night, with blurry lights and street signs, the neon streamers of moving cars, the clock stuck forever at 11:59 on a forgotten New Year's Eve. On the opposite wall, stretching from one corner to the other, is a mural on canvas that one of Roxanne's New York customers painted for her. It is of the Hudson River, first as it might have been in days gone by, filled with clear water and fish and swimming children, its banks dotted with small houses and trees. Farther along, the skyline rises and the trees fall. The fish and the children disappear and the water fills with oil swirls and tin cans. As smoke and dirt obscure water and air, all life is removed.

Roxanne works alongside Frederick for hours, unpacking boxes of books, maps, and photographs of New York, which she has bartered for the sea stuff back in the city. Roxanne puts a model of the Statue of Liberty in the window, a garland of fresh flowers resting on its crown. Frederick hangs up posters of ice skaters at Rockefeller Center and the U.N. Building and the Staten Island Ferry. Together, they prop up the literature on a magazine rack that Roxanne got once from a man in the concession stand business.

"Where d'you ever find a thing like this?" Frederick asks her.

"I got that rack from a friend," she tells Frederick. "For a midnight song."

At the end of the day, Frederick and Roxanne spend a long time admiring the finished shop, which is redolent of fresh-cut pine, musty books, shampoo and satisfaction. Both have made note of the other's persistence and strong, unbending arms.

Roxanne settles easily in Morocco, Maine, mostly because she is a person without a need for importance or absoluteness, someone who doesn't necessarily have to be who she has always been before. When Carrie Eaton says flatly, "More off in the back, Roxanne. I won't be back until spring," Roxanne is glad to oblige. She never thinks to try and change a person's mind or look, having eschewed the alchemist tasks of beauticians. The whims and desires of her customers are nothing and everything to her. She simply applies her expertise to their desires, just as the shoemaker would fix her shoes the way she asked him to.

Roxanne is not a showboat or a gossip, as the town had feared when they watched the Empire State Building sign rise and her shop take shape in Frederick's hands. She is a good business-woman and neighbor, competent and sensible. "Nothing extra about her," the smitten mailman reports, spreading the news on his rounds. "She won't be a half bad fit, round here."

In early October, a small man with a crease of authority in his brow stops by Roxanne's shop. "Mr. Doug," he says, introducing himself with a twist of his bull neck. "Town manager. 'Fraid I have to close you down for a few days."

"Why?" Roxanne asks.

"Trouble in the sewer," he says. "Could be two, maybe three days."

Roxanne nods her head as a bad smell rises up from the street and creeps into her shop. She doesn't fuss about lost business or the stink, but instead studies Mr. Doug's strange pointed ears and ringless fingers, and invites him in for coffee, remarking, as she ushers him to a chair, "Broken sewer doesn't do anyone much good."

Roxanne is always on the lookout for a beau, as she likes to call that man that she may someday find, rather than a lover. In her mind, love has only a little to do with what she might finally do with such a man—raise a glass of milk, choose a brand of cleaning fluid, read chapters aloud from a book. She would keep this man at a distance; he would want it that way, too. At thirty-nine, when she met her husband, Frank, Roxanne had just about given up on love. Frank played the banjo and sold subway tokens underground for the uptown trains. He died at the age of fifty-one, after seven years of their marriage, just when Roxanne was beginning to figure out what love was—something akin to letting go, comfort stung by resignation. Roxanne thinks Frank died from the darkness and the fumes which spewed from the trains, although it went down on the death certificate as a liver disease set to galloping by Frank's love of whiskey. Frank used to say that Roxanne was the best thing that ever happened to him, and though she'd pshawed him every time, it had made her feel good. Roxanne doesn't blame herself for Frank's death. She only thinks that another woman might have kicked him up the subway stairs and into the clean air, might have poured his whiskey down the drain and insisted on some conversation and a softer beverage. But Frank liked his life so well—his sports page and his slippers and his bottle and his wife. Roxanne had thought no more of changing him than she ever had a customer's hairstyle. And when they lost the baby, it had made even more sense to let one another and well enough alone.

Roxanne is a good-enough looking woman, with strong features which will survive when the rest of her starts to crumble. She is not tall, though there is a tallness about her. In middle age, she is solid. In old age, she will be regal. Her velvety, unlined skin is her best asset, and her stringy brown hair, ironically, her worst—unwilling to take a curl or a tint or a twist or a wave or a curve or a slant or any suggestion at all—refusing to do anything but hang lifelessly at her broad shoulders.

Sometimes, during those first fall days in Morocco, although she realizes it is crazy, Roxanne imagines that Frederick might be the beau. He is young, but he might just as well be old. He is self-contained and seemingly unattached, to any person or any age. Frederick spends a lot of time in the Empire Beauty Salon with Roxanne, becomes a fixture which comes to surprise no one. There is a peaceful, unspoken understanding between Frederick and Roxanne. When he's not studying or working on his application to pharmacy college, perfecting every word of his Personal-Statement-in-Four-Hundred-Words-or-Less, he takes out his tools and putters around the shop, keeping things in good repair. He washes the windows and touches up the paint, rearranges the books and magazines on the rack. Idle in November, he collects 114 signatures of approval and puts a red flashing light on the top of the Empire State Building sign. Roxanne calls a halt as December sets in and Frederick appears one day with a bucket of yellow paint and the intention of painting highway driver lines on the floor. "The East Side Highway," he explains. "Right here in Morocco."

"Next you'll be setting up a toll booth at the door," she says, filling with a hopeless affection for him, as some snow melts on his busy eyebrows. "Palming quarters from the customers and giving directions to Shea Stadium."

"What happens there?' he asks

"It's where the Mets play," Roxanne says. She could really love a boy who doesn't even know where the Mets play. "Baseball."

"Toll booth's not a bad idea," Frederick says.

"Why not make a model of the Brooklyn Bridge instead?" Roxanne asks him. It is on this cold day that she finally gives in to the urge to touch Frederick, laying a hand on the arm which swings the gallon bucket of paint. "There's room over in that corner." She has already sent for prints of the bridge's design from a New York librarian friend, and bought dowel and lathing and glue. She knows that the Brooklyn Bridge will keep Frederick busy and nearby for a while. Whether or not he is the beau, she likes his presence, and sometimes hopes, perhaps as a mother does in some back reach of her mind, that Frederick's application to pharmacy college will be turned down again, that she will be his champion and his consoler, and that he will stay with her forever in the Empire Beauty Salon.

By the end of the first spring, Roxanne wants to know whether or not she will spend the rest of her days in Morocco, Maine. At forty-eight, there may not be time for another epiphany or move. She closes down the shop Wednesday, stopping everything to consider. In the very early morning of an April day, Roxanne wakes to the darkness and can sleep no more. As the light rises from the dawn, she sits in her rocking chair and looks out over the harbor to the islands, searching the screech of the gulls for an answer. When she starts feeling sleepy from the rocking and the sunlight, she gets up to rummage in some unpacked boxes. She reads some old letters from Frank, not so much letters of love, she decides, but satisfaction. She finds a song he once wrote her on a napkin at an outdoor cafe. It went, "Roxanne/I'm your fan/Hope to be your man/ Someday." He'd already been her man by then, but left the words because they'd come out that way. Roxanne tosses out the letters but holds on to the song, for a song, no matter how bad, should always be saved.

Roxanne sits by the hour in the rocker, shaken from her trance by a rumble of thunder. The sky suddenly darkens and the wind shifts to the northeast, swinging the sterns of the lobster boats around. Roxanne gets up, stiff from the sitting, and puts the kettle on the stove. The doorbell rings and Roxanne answers it in her bathrobe and slippers. The town manager stands before her, looking like a Martian with his clean-shaven face and crew cut haircut and pointed ears.

"Mr. Doug," Roxanne says, still not sure whether this is his first or last name. "More trouble in the sewer?"

"Shop's been closed three days now," he says. The Moroccans seem to prefer to call it a shop. "Everything all right, Roxanne?"

"Everything's fine," Roxanne tells him.

"You're not sick, are you?"

"No," she says. "I'm not the least bit sick."

"I thought we might take the air," Mr. Doug says authoritatively, as if she were sick and the air might cure her.

"The weather doesn't look so good," Roxanne says, pointing up to the nearly black sky.

"May take a while," Mr. Doug says. "For the sky to overflow."

"I can't leave just now," she says, gesturing without aim back to her living room. "I'm in the middle of something."

"Well, if you ever come to the end of it," Mr. Doug says, peering into the empty room, all business once more. "Just let me know."

After Mr. Doug leaves, Roxanne goes back to her thinking with hot tea and a new sadness. There is an unfamiliar emptiness inside her now, always plugged up before, she guesses, by the old yearning. As a gull swoops down to dive for a fish, a new lump of feeling drops down into the hole, clanging as a bead would in an empty tin. With a pang, she remembers how Frank used to bang up the stairs with bread and whiskey in a bag, calling out, "I'm home, Rox. The goddamned world ain't licked me yet." Frank's swearing and bad grammar used to embarrass Roxanne. Now his ain'ts seem like sweet, skewed poetry.

This, Roxanne guesses in her rocker, is loneliness come to call. And like Mr. Doug, who came at a bad moment, it must be shown the door. I am forty-eight years old, she goes fiercely back to her thinking. Widowed. Working. The 573rd inhabitant of Morocco, Maine, not counting the winter batch of babies. I did not come in search of an Eden. There is a chaos there, born of isolation, a hardness born of limitation, a hopelessness that laps up on shore from the impassable sea. But there is also a peacefulness, a great feeling of space and possibility.

There is hard winter here, but also soft summer. There is good sense, and there is nonsense. There is kindness and there is greed. There are children. And dogs. And mothers. And men. The final balance would be the same in New York or the real Morocco or Timbuktu. There is no reason, Roxanne decides, not to stay here where she has plunked herself.

Later, as the thunder rumbles and lightning streaks the sky, Roxanne dozes in the rocker. She returns to New York in a dream, wandering aimlessly through its streets in a blinding rain, calling out the names of her old customers, "Mrs. Muriel Throckmorton! Miss Bella Bernstein! Mrs. Agnes Pepperdine!" The women appear out of tenement house windows with wild and messy hair and flop their hands at her. "You deserted us, Roxanne," They hiss. "You flew the coop." When Roxanne wakes, the storm has passed. As the peach of twilight falls back into the harbor, she waits for the shadows of the women to disappear back into their windows. She has no regrets, only memories and dreams. The gulls retire to the shore with echoing squawks and Mr. Ablow closes up the pharmacy next door. Roxanne hears Frederick's voice. He has taken to spending time with Mr. Ablow, as he used to before Roxanne came. She opens the window and calls out, inviting them both for dinner. It is only logical that Frederick would seek out the town pharmacist as a mentor. And who is to say that Mr. Ablow, a widower and a kind man, is not the beau?

A year goes by. Roxanne's beauty salon fills with regular customers. She gains a few pounds, which, people say, do her well. Frederick gets turned down from the pharmacy college again but loses neither face nor heart. The Personal Statement, now raised to 500-Words-or-Less, takes new leaps toward perfection. The salon has never looked more ship or shape, now a monument to her old city. More space has been found on the crowded walls for pictures of Central Park and Chinatown and the Macy's Day Parade. The magazine rack is lined and brochures and books detailing historic monuments and city walks and tourist attractions. One corner of the ceiling has been made into a planetarium and Frederick's model of the Brooklyn Bridge stands tall on a corner table. The people of Morocco give these things a glance with polite but not feigned interest, because they speak of Roxanne. Roxanne doesn't often talk about her past. She doesn't reminisce or compare or glorify or tell her customers how she got to here and from where, or how it used to be, when Morocco meant no more to her then a hot, faraway land of veiled women and camels, bordered by a cool sea.

But comes the day when Frannie Haskell sits down in the chair and asks Roxanne, "What's it like, that city you came from?"

"It's just a place," Roxanne says, lifting up Frannie's blond hair and tying the cape around her shoulders.

"Oh, come on, Roxanne," Frannie has a beautiful retarded baby and runs the movie house up on the hill. "You don't expect me to believe that."

"Well . . ." Roxanne considers. "You should see the Manhattan Yellow Pages. It's the thickest book you'll ever come across. A kid come into my parlor once. Jimmy Crane. He was fifteen, tiny and quick as a cat. He did flips on skateboards in the park near my house and passed the hat. He told me he wanted a mohawk. All the kids had them, he said. It was true. I sat him down on the Yellow Pages and talked him into a crew cut. Next day his mother came in to thank me, said as long as she was there, was there anything I could do with her hair. She'd just come through chemo and had some patches. It was a tough job."

"Patches?" The light in Frannie's eyes gets Roxanne going for a while. She layers and snips Frannie's bangs and gets out the blowdryer. "I did some teasing and stretching," Roxanne tells Frannie. "That woman fought that cancer like a demon and her hair came back in beautifully. She ran one of the elevators over at the Empire State Building."

"Ever been there?" Frannie asks.

Roxanne shakes her head. "No," she says. "I kept meaning to. But there was this building near my old shop, thirty stories high and only one room on each of them. Looks two-dimensional, just like the sign out front." She dusts the hair from Frannie's neck, gives her a hand mirror, and swivels her around in the chair to have a look. Nodding approval, Frannie gets up and wanders over to the magazine rack, picking up a pamphlet on *Architectural Wonders in the Big Apple.*"

"Whad'you say that building was called?" she asks Roxanne.

"The Flat Iron Building," Roxanne says, bending to sweep Frannie's hair into the dustpan. "It was some architect's idea of how to keep something ordinary from getting lost in a big, crowded place."

"I'd like to meet that person," says Frannie.

"I looked him up in the phone book once," Roxanne says. "Thought about giving him a call, just to tell him I liked his building. But in the end, I didn't. I'd built him up so much, I figured it wasn't really fair to hold a wonder up to its maker."

Frannie nods. "Best just to leave a good thing be," she says.

The next winter, after a few bitter nights in January, the harbor freezes over for the first time in twenty-seven years. Roxanne is forty-nine and wears long underwear, top and bottom, under her dime-store print dresses. Her added weight has settled becomingly. Touched by the sea air, her hair has grown mysteriously thick and reddish, and taken on a slight curl. Mr. Doug asks Mr. Fister, who runs the lumber yard, if he's noticed that Roxanne's no strain on the eyes these days. The long-smitten mailman lingers at the salon, stopping for a cup of Roxanne's coffee and cream, when invited. In her pile of mail one morning, sandwiched between the electric bill and a Museum of Fine Arts Catalog, Roxanne finds a postcard from an old customer. It shows a woman with ruby lips and hands on shapely hips standing on a sandy beach wearing an old-fashioned polka-dotted bathing suit. Underneath her, in letters meant to look like waves, reads the message, GREETINGS FROM THE JERSEY SHORE! Seeing Mr. Hurlehee's cramped, neat handwriting embarrasses Roxanne, as if she has come upon him shaving in his underwear.

"Dear Roxanne," the postcard reads. "Finally made it to the ocean myself. Joined my brother in the dry cleaning business. I haven't had my hair cut since you left. Hope you are well. Love, Morris Hurlehee."

Mr. Hurlehee's distant, curlequed, *love* makes Roxanne cry on this cold, cold day, and she doesn't cry often. The mailman sneaks away, leaving his coffee half finished by the door. Mrs. Betty Link comes in for her appointment and notices Roxanne's red eyes. Roxanne slips the postcard into her work apron pocket and blows her nose. Mrs. Link announces that this kind of weather breeds nothing but drunkards and colds, and suggests a hot rum potion. As Roxanne is getting Mrs. Link ready for her perm, Frederick comes rushing into the shop. Jumping up as if to dunk a basketball, he crashes into his model of the Brooklyn Bridge, sending hunks of it flying into the air. He bends down to pick up the pieces lovingly, but without the sorrow he would have felt the day before.

"What is it?" Roxanne asks. "What happened, Frederick?"

"I got in," he whoops with a Cheshire cat grin. "Third time around. They just couldn't say no."

Frederick is the warmest, most joyous thing in Morocco that day, and later Roxanne invites him up to her room for a celebration, pulling out from under her bed the gift she has been saving for this day, an old book, bound in leather and lettered in gold leaf. *A Carpenter's Guide*, written in 1869, an almost useless thing of great beauty, which only Frederick could love. He studies the book for a long time while Roxanne sips at a vodka gimlet and makes a sort-of soufflé for dinner.

"Never had eggs for dinner," Frederick says, finally closing the book. He pulls the card table over to the bay window and lights the candles. They spear peas with their forks and watch the water lap the boats as the lights of distant houses flicker. After dinner, Frederick comes around to Roxanne's side of the table and reaches out a square hand.

"How'd this happen," Roxanne says, taking his hand and smoothing the blackened thumbnail with her finger.

"Never been much of a hammerer," he says.

Roxanne pulls him forward and he sinks down on his knees. She runs her fingers through his thick hair and murmurs into it, "A hammerer you'll always be to me."

Later in the night, Frederick slips out of bed and starts to get dressed. Eyes open a crack, Roxanne watches him, his body solid and smooth from years of hauling lobster traps from the sea at his father's side. When he's done, he stands at the foot of the bed, with his shoes in his hands. Thinking her to be asleep, he whispers. "Thanks, Roxanne."

"Don't thank me, Frederick," Roxanne says sleepily, propping herself up on a pillow. "For such a small thing."

"I'm not talking about the book," he says.

All lingering sleep leaves Roxanne then. She feels suddenly lost and shriveled, an old crone who has lured a boy into her bed in a strange land, a boy who will take the last bits of her dignity and her youth away with him, soon tossing both aside, because he has more than enough of his own. The pleasure Roxanne has felt in Frederick's uncertain arms turns to shame, a feeling that is strange to her, like a new taste in a baby's mouth. She tries to picture Frederick a baby in his father's arms. And for the first time, Roxanne thinks of the baby she lost as one that might have filled her arms, or a hard and empty moment such as this.

"My old man isn't going to be too thrilled," Frederick says with a wry smile.

"About what?" Confused, she thinks Frederick is still talking about her.

"About my good news," Frederick says.

"Does he expect you to stay and help with the lobstering?" Roxanne asks. She wonders why she has never asked this question before, realizes that she has never even met Frederick's parents, though she has often mistaken herself for his mother.

"No," Frederick says. "He's gotten over that. He just doesn't think much of a career in a drug store."

"Why do you want to go to pharmacy college, Frederick?" Curiosity comes to Roxanne late, as it has so often before.

"It's a good profession," Frederick says. "I get to use my head. To help people. And it's a way out of this town."

"You don't like this town?" Roxanne is truly surprised.

"I like this town all right," he says cautiously. "I just don't like this kind of town." He struggles with the zipper on his jacket and shakes his head. "I'll never understand how you ended up in a place like this, Roxanne." Frederick's question is fearful of an answer.

"Luck mostly," she tells him, leaving it at that. "I like it here."

"Grass is always greener, I guess," Frederick says. His hand twitches on the doorknob. He is eager to be off and spread his news. "I'll never forget you, Roxanne," he says, slipping sideways out of the half-opened door. His eyes plead with her not to try and stop him. "Thanks again."

Roxanne can only pull the sheet up tight around her and say to Frederick that he is more than welcome.

When Roxanne turns fifty that summer, the people of Morocco give her a surprise party. They rent the town hall on a Friday night and Mrs. Weed, Roxanne's last appointment of the day, lures her there with a story of a pot-luck dinner. Roxanne has taken to attending such gatherings, finding them practical for a person of her situation. No one hides or jumps out at her, but Roxanne has truly never been more surprised. The hall is decorated with streamers and a big sign on a sheet reading HAPPY BIRTHDAY ROXANNE. HAIR'S TO YOU! A band plays old-folk music and Roxanne dances on the parquet floor with every man in town, not one jealous wife's eye upon her. Frederick's mother, soon to be a customer of Roxanne's, introduces herself. She has just had a letter from Frederick, with news of an aced exam and a pharmaceutical girlfriend.

"He said he'd enclosed a photo of her," she says. "But I couldn't find it. Frederick asked me to send his best to you."

Roxanne searches her eyes for suspicion or disgust but finds only Frederick's cool kindness. "Frederick's a good kid," she tells his mother. "Really, one of a kind."

Dinner is roast beef, rarish, corn on the cob, a bean casserole and a jello mold, not so much for the eating as the looking, with miniature imbedded marshmallows which spell out Roxanne's name. Mr. Doug, with skin so grazed by sun and sea it's almost purple, sits at the head of the banquet table and tries to think up a toast while Edna Creel, the postmistress, brings out a huge Betty Crocker cake, made in the shape of a skyscraper. Mr. Doug remembers the feel of Roxanne's hands on his back and the sweet smell to her wispy hair from one night the autumn before. All of his calls have gone politely unanswered since then. When it comes time to speak, he can only say wistfully, raising his glass of champagne. "Here's to you, Roxanne. Here's to fifty more."

On this starless night, near midnight, Roxanne is the only

sober one to leave the hall, and not because she hasn't been drinking. She feels light headed and ageless, both touched and justified. In her hands, she carries a party hat, some cake wrapped in a napkin, and a gold locket with a scrolling R, her gift from the townspeople. Roxanne thanks the friends who mill about her outside on the grass. Declining all offers of a ride, wanting to stretch her legs and the good feeling of the night, she starts to walk home.

It's a soft night and the air is thick with the smells of road dust and bay leaves. From time to time as Roxanne walks on the unlit road, she senses something following her. But each time she turns around, there is only her disappearing shadow and the swallowed curve of the road. She is spooked in a way that she has never been before, even in the city, where she was mugged once, shaken and bruised and taken for a few dollars. She screamed till she was hoarse at those punks, sent them running at least. At home she treated her scrapes with iodine and set her bruised self to soak in a hot epsom salt bath. Here, with no danger to touch, and no one to hear her cry, she can only breathe deeply and push the wind behind her. Roxanne breaks into so much of a run as she can remember from the old days of roaming the streets of Brooklyn as a child, thinking with anguish that if she can no longer run, she's lost everything. A bird's hoot makes her stumble and she skins her knees. Sweat ekes from her temples and her palms, as she pushes her aching legs on to Main Street. There, she falls back breathless into a walk on the familiar, cracked sidewalk, smoothing her hair and her checkered work apron, which she never bothered to take off during the party. Finishing off the cake in the napkin, Roxanne ambles up past the shops to the Empire Beauty Salon, the flashing red light on the sign her beacon. She peers with satisfaction into her dark, spotless parlor, then cuts down the side path, stopping abruptly before she reaches her stairs. Sitting on the bottom step, in the loose crouch of a city stoop sitter, is Mr. Hurlehee, of Yonkers, and more recently of the Jersey Shore. He tips off his Yankees cap to her and they laugh together as they used to, for he has grown completely bald.

"So why did you come?" Roxanne asks, clutching her party hat and crumpled napkin in one hand and the gold locket in another.

"Dry cleaning's not for me," Mr. Hurlehee says. "It's too . . Well, it's just too . . ."

"Clean?" Roxanne says.

He laughs. "I thought you might understand," he says.

"Well," she says, sitting down beside him on the step. "Maybe it's not such a bad thing."

They look out over the harbor, watching the lobster boats bob gently in the blue-gray night.

"I've just come from the city," he says. "They tore down your beauty parlor," he says.

Roxanne nods. It would pain her more if they'd left it tomblike, untouched, or if someone else had come in and tried to make it another kind of place. She pictures the bulldozers crushing the shells and levelling the palms. "What else could they do?" she says.

"Pretty place you found here," Mr. Hurlehee says, pulling up weeds from the ground in a bunch. "But it's no more Fiji than the Jersey Shore, is it?"

"It's the same water," Roxanne says, rising to her feet in some small, unexplained anger. "It's all the part of the earth that's not the land."

Mr. Hurlehee's knees crack as he rises to soothe her. "It's nice,'" he says. "It's really nice, Roxanne."

"You must be tired," Roxanne says. "Come on up. I'll make you coffee."

Mr. Hurlehee hasn't brought a suitcase or a warm coat, Roxanne notices. Fletcher's Upstreet has a good man's jacket on sale. As they climb the steps, the locket falls from Roxanne's hand. She stops and stoops to peer through the cracks in the stairs to the ground below. The champagne catches up with her as she bends over and lights dazzle the sides of her eyes. Blinking, she tries to clear away its fog. Mr. Hurlehee waits for her at the top of the stairs.

"What is it, Roxanne?" He speaks with a soft frog in his throat, as he used to after he'd settled his big feet on the silver footrest at the Oceana. "Have you lost your key?"

The glitter of the locket on the ground catches Roxanne's eye and she starts back down the stairs to fetch it, as relieved as if she'd come upon some of the dignity she lost with Frederick on that cold winter night, or a bittersweet memory of Frank, or one shell she wishes she had kept from the old salon, with a curved mother-of-pearl lining, soft as a baby's skin. Having retrieved her gift, Roxanne has only one task left for what is left of the night—to convince Mr. Hurlehee that the sea is forever the sea. Holding the locket in her hand, she looks up past Mr. Hurlehee to the black sky, where one faint star has been let loose to wander. The harbor lies like glass. The town is empty and only the street lights hum. Even the gulls have given up the ghost. Roxanne is startled by the shrillness of a voice meant to be soft. "We don't use keys, Mr. Hurlehee," she hears herself say. "Here in Morocco, Maine."

Bird Watching

BY DIANE STELZER MORROW

The winter I was eleven Tom Gordon's son, David, killed himself. He hanged himself in his bedroom closet while his parents were at church on a Wednesday night. Though it has been more than twenty years I remember the night perfectly. The siren. Going out to the front yard. The way the stretcher slipped, jerking down, when the men lifted it onto the ambulance. And then afterwards, when the ambulance had gone, Mrs. Bianco, one of the neighbors, walking over and telling us what had happened: the shock of it. This was in Sunset Hills, one of the calmer suburbs of St. Louis, and David was not the kind of boy anyone expected that of. He was only fifteen, my brother Mark's age, not even old enough to drive. In the mornings he used to ride his ten-speed past our house on his way to school. He wore white oxford shirts and clean blue jeans, and in the winter a blue down jacket. He played saxophone for the high school marching band. Just a week before he killed himself he'd come by our house selling light bulbs. I'd answered the door and then gone to get my father. David told us if they could sell enough of those light bulbs the band was going to get to take a trip to New Orleans. As he spoke he looked my father in the eye, and twice that I can remember he called him sir. My father was impressed. He ended up buying several boxes.

My parents were not by any means close friends with the Gordons. We were new in the neighborhood and had lived in the house only two years at the time David died. The few people my parents knew were all from our church—the Catholic church, St. Augustine's. The Gordons went to Stone Baptist. (My mother had grown up in Clinton, a small town over on the western side of the state, and she knew all about Baptists. She'd told me how in Clinton one of them was always coming up to the door demanding to know whether or not a person had been saved. This happened occasionally in St. Louis as well, and she said it made her blood rise—the intrusion of it. I figured the thought of stepping inside a Baptist church might make her blood rise too.) But the Gordons were our next-door neighbors. And, as my father put it, when it came to something as important as a funeral they had no choice.

The funeral was on a Saturday morning. My mother wore a navy blue dress and Mark wore a tie. My father said he'd rather I didn't go, but if I wanted I could ride along in the car and he would drop me off at a school playground behind the church. I didn't mind him doing that. I liked playgrounds better than I thought I would like the funeral. After he drove off I tried out each of the swings. Then I climbed up on the monkey bars. From the top I could see the church and the sky and the street behind it, cars going past and a boy on a bicycle—everything ordinary. Then the singing started, a deep wailing like nothing I'd ever heard before; it seemed to pass from the church straight into my bones. I froze there, both my hands gripping the top rung. Then I jumped down, ran across the playground, climbed over the fence, and stood behind the church, where the dumpsters were, and some empty boxes. I leaned back against the bricks; it was as if the music was inside me, a hot liquid in my legs and arms, and I stayed there, until the very end—that moment when the door opened and the first people started coming out, and I ran back to the playground.

That night after supper my father told me he'd seen me.

"Saw me where?" I asked him. We were watching television in the den. My mother was in the kitchen finishing the supper dishes. I had the same feeling I'd had one time in the first grade when I'd pulled back the heavy curtain from the confessional to look inside and one of the nuns had caught me.

"It's okay, Janie," he said. "I probably should have let you come. You're old enough."

He got up and turned off the television set. "We could go for a walk?"

It was dark outside, and cold, but I didn't hesitate. I ran to the front closet to get my boots. Walks with my father since we'd moved to the new house were as rare as hen's teeth.

Before we'd moved to that house we'd lived in Kirkwood, an older suburb of St. Louis where the houses were small and close together and where my parents knew everyone in the neighborhood. At night there my father loved to go for walks. Most nights I would go with him. In the spring and summer the other fathers would be working in their yards and he'd stop and talk with them about dandelions or how much rain we'd had, tilting his head back and squinting up at the sky. In the winter neighbors would stop him and ask him to come in for coffee.

People liked my father. He was a tall man, and heavy, with an ordinary face except for a birthmark which covered most of his cheek. The birthmark was a part of him, like his nose or his hands; I hardly noticed it, except at the grocery store when I would see strangers looking at it, or, more rarely, when he was bewildered and the birthmark would darken into a deep violet. My mother had told me once she thought the birthmark was one of the reasons people were so quick to like him. I think now she must have meant that the birthmark put people at ease— that they could see right away there was something imperfect about my father, right on the surface, and then they weren't afraid of him. But at the time I thought she meant that the mark was beautiful.

In Kirkwood my parents went to cocktail parties on Saturday nights. Before the parties I would sit on my parents' bed and watch my mother get dressed. There would be the smell of perfume on those nights, and the sound of her heels on the bedroom floor, and the smell of soap too from my father's shower. Just before he left she would tie his tie. He was a full head taller than she was and she had to reach up to tie it. When she was finished he'd look in the mirror and check the knot. I thought being an adult must be a wonderful thing.

I must have been pretty young then—six and seven and eight. By the time I was nine I'd begun to worry about my parents. Something had happened. It had to do with my father and a single woman who'd come to our church whose name was Miss Gunther. Though no one in my hearing ever told this particular story, it had become, in a way, the main story in our family.

Miss Gunther was a homely woman—thin and freckled with a kind of horn-rimmed glasses that made her look like a middle-aged woman, though I think she was probably in her twenties, thirty at the most. She had just left the convent, and, because we knew that, she looked naked to us in street clothes. She wore tweed skirts and dark cardigan sweaters and black sensible shoes. A wig too. Sometimes we'd be sitting behind her at mass and Mark would point to the back of her head, and I'd see how one or two strands of her own brown hair were sticking out of it in the back. After mass it was a custom at that parish to have coffee and doughnuts in the gym. While the mothers stood talking together in small groups and the fathers stood by the door, waiting, Miss Gunther stood next to the doughnuts, eating one after the other. She especially liked jelly doughnuts, the kind covered with powdered sugar. It amazed me the way she could eat them and not gain weight. During the whole year that we knew her she was a skinny woman, her legs protruding from beneath her tweed skirts like sticks.

She'd been there about a month when my father befriended her. It started one Sunday when one of the other fathers referred to her as Olive Oyl. The truth was Miss Gunther did look a little like Olive Oyl—something about the shape of her face, and those legs. Maybe that's one of the reasons my father reacted the way he did. Though he didn't say anything in front of the men, on the way home he looked at Mark and me in the rearview mirror and told us it was easy enough to be cruel to someone who couldn't defend themselves, and wrong. The next Sunday he crossed the gym for a doughnut and stayed to talk to her. I followed him. It seemed to me any conversation between my father and Miss Gunther would be weighted with significance. This one, as it turned out, wasn't. She was a sixth grade teacher at the public school; they were mostly talking about her students. Later, as my father was walking out of the

AMERICAN FICTION

gym the other fathers teased him. He shrugged. I was embarrassed for him and proud at the same time. After that week he must have talked to her every Sunday.

On Sunday afternoons in Kirkwood we had big dinners. My mother laid out the linen tablecloth, and the china, a centerpiece in the middle of the table that she reworked every season. The fall that Miss Gunther started coming to our house on Sundays the centerpiece had its usual harvest theme: a basket with Indian corn and squash, and in the center my mother had put a small pumpkin. Miss Gunther said it was about the prettiest arrangement she'd ever seen. This was the kind of thing she was always saying. As she spoke she'd tip her head down and press her lips together, waiting, a look that made it seem as if the whole purpose of her life was to please. In any case she wasn't pleasing my mother. Though Miss Gunther offered each Sunday to help and often set the table, I could see right away my mother didn't like her much. It seemed odd to me. My mother had clear white skin and thick dark hair and she always took care with her appearance. On the surface, it made no sense at all for her to be jealous of Miss Gunther.

My father was in the habit after dinner of asking who wanted to go for a drive. Before Miss Gunther began coming over this was only a formality. He would wait at the front door, his hand deep in his pocket, jangling his keys. The four of us always went. We'd leave the dishes sitting on the table, and we'd drive out to the country west of St. Louis, or, more often, we'd drive through some of the newer and more expensive suburbs, my father pointing out houses he'd buy for us when his ship came in. My mother loved these drives. She seemed her most lighthearted then, her most hopeful; at some point along the way she could always be counted on to turn around, her arm across the seat, and inform us all how lucky we were.

The first Sunday Miss Gunther came, my father was already at the door after dinner, his hand in his pocket, the door open, when my mother shook her head. She started clearing the table. "I have too much to do," she said. "Besides, there isn't room in the car."

My father closed the door and stepped back into the front hall. "What?"

We had a large Pontiac then with lots of room in the back seat, and he didn't know what she meant—or he pretended not to—but I thought I did know. She only meant there wasn't room for Miss Gunther there. I felt the same. But I felt my father's surprise too.

Miss Gunther stood up, looking back and forth between my mother and father. "I don't need to go. Really. I have papers I could be grading."

But my mother was insistent. "No. You go on." It was as if already the damage had been done. She stacked the dishes, balancing the silverware on top, and carried them into the kitchen.

Then Mark was on his feet. He announced he had a touch football game he couldn't miss and, having said that, walked past my father out the front door. That was the hard thing about being a daughter. You couldn't just go off like that.

My father took his keys out of his pocket and tossed them from one hand to the other. "Miss Gunther," he said. "We would very much like for you to come with us." Then he looked at me. I was sitting on the floor putting on my tennis shoes. "Janie. You coming, or are you going to sit there like a log all day?" It was a perfect fall afternoon—clear and blue and cold. I wanted to go with him. But by this time, my mother was rinsing off the dishes, the silverware clattering against the plates. I couldn't leave her like that. When I'd finished putting on my shoes, I got up and started clearing the table. Which is how it happened that my father and Miss Gunther began going for drives on Sunday afternoons.

What eventually took place seems inevitable to me now, and somehow less important; what was going to happen had begun already on that Sunday. Two months later my father and Miss Gunther stayed out one night past midnight, and the next morning my parents announced we would be moving to a new house.

We moved in June. One day school was letting out and the next morning I came downstairs to find two men in the kitchen wrapping glasses in newsprint and laying them in boxes.

The house itself was five or six years old, but because it was new to us it had, like all new houses, the unfamiliar smells to contend with, and the bareness—the feeling of space. If I stood at one end of my room and spoke, I could have sworn my voice echoed, and when I looked out my back window, instead of looking out at houses, I looked out onto trees. The trees surrounded a pond which I couldn't see from my window, but sometimes if the breeze was right I could smell it—fresh water and cattails and the way the ducks smelled there when you got up close to them. Behind the pond was a highway. At night the trucks going past sounded like trains, or a foghorn.

Everything was new. The way the house creaked in the wind and the smells of it and the neighbors and the way my parents were with each other; and my father, he had changed too. Instead of going out into the neighborhood in the evenings he'd settle himself on the couch after supper; by nine o'clock he'd be making the soft sputtering sounds that meant he'd gone to sleep.

The night of David's funeral I was thrilled when he said he wanted to go for a walk. I practically pulled him out the door. It was a cold night with some old snow on the ground and patches of thick gray ice on the sidewalk. A couple of times I slipped and he had to catch me under both arms to keep me from falling. After the second time he took my hand. I asked him what the funeral had been like—inside.

He thought for a second. "It was sad, Janie."

I shook my head. That wasn't what I'd meant. "Did you see the body?"

He looked down at me, his eyebrows drawn together. I think now the question must have seemed too blunt. And I suppose from a parent's point of view it was. But I wasn't a parent. What had happened to David's family seemed fathomless to me, and what I felt, more than anything else, was curiosity.

"The casket was closed," he said.

We walked another block, neither of us speaking. My father's breath came out as white smoke.

"I think," he said, "that David is with God."

I slipped, one of my feet shooting forward and the rest of my body following. My father put out his arm and caught me. This was the first time I could remember him ever saying God's name out loud.

We went to mass every Sunday. But my mother was the one who seemed to care about it. She was the one who woke us on Sunday morning, who made sure we were ready, who paid attention to church seasons—we always had an advent wreath and during Lent she made certain we said special prayers.

"We better go back," my father said. We were about a half a mile from our house, at the corner where St. Augustine's was. I wanted to keep going, but he said he was cold. The tips of his ears were bright red. "Your mother will be wondering what became of us."

As we passed the Gordons' house on the way back all the lights downstairs were off. Two of the upstairs windows were lit—one at each end of the house.

"What do you think they're doing?" I asked him.

"I don't know, Janie," he said. "I can't imagine."

I couldn't either, though over the next several months I tried to. If I could understand what went on inside the Gordons' house, it seemed to me, I might understand, well, everything.

They were a clean family, David's family. Mrs. Gordon especially. In the mornings she would hose off their front porch and the driveway, even in the winter most days. I would see her when I walked to school. She wore black dresses and boots and these yellow rubber gloves. Before David died I'd hardly paid any attention to her. She seemed only a part of the neighborhood, like the new young trees that lined the street there. After David died I began to watch her more closely. I watched how slowly she worked. How sometimes in the mornings she'd be standing on the porch staring, her hose pointed upward and water coming out of it like a fountain.

Other than that time in the morning, and on Sundays and Wednesdays for church, Mrs. Gordon barely left the house. According to Mrs. Bianco, this had been true for some time. Mrs. Bianco was a widow who lived next door to the Gordons on the other side. She knew everything that happened in the neighborhood and liked to talk about it, sometimes stopping us on the church steps after mass on Sunday morning and telling us things. Shortly after we moved in, she stopped us one morning and told us that Mrs. Gordon had lupus—a bad illness which, though not cancer, got worse outside. She said if a strong sun touched Mrs. Gordon's skin it could poison her blood.

"She could wear a hat," my mother often said before David died. "She could wear sun tan lotion. She could walk outside long enough to come next door for a cup of coffee." She missed her friends from Kirkwood more, I think, than she'd expected she would.

But after David died she no longer said that. Instead, she began looking at the Gordons' house as if the house itself were the problem, and frightened her. Though my parents never mentioned it, and at the time had told Mark and me it was only vicious gossip, I had not forgotten one other thing Mrs. Bianco had told us—how she had walked home with us after mass one Sunday shortly after David died and told us Mrs. Gordon not only had lupus but she drank besides.

"I think," my mother began saying, "that sometimes you have to know when it's time to leave people alone."

Usually my father wouldn't answer her whenever she said this, but I can remember one afternoon toward the end of the winter when he did. She was standing at the bathroom window looking out at the Gordons' house. He came up behind her, lifting her hair and setting his hands on her shoulders. Since we'd moved to the new house, he was often touching her like that, as if, it seemed, he had discovered a new habit; as if he were constantly trying to make up with her.

"Maybe you could take her a coffee cake," he said. "Or those cookies you make with the raisins and coconut in them."

She stiffened but didn't pull away. "Cookies wouldn't do any good," she said.

He didn't answer her then. He only shrugged, all the time keeping his hands where he had set them, there on her shoulders.

The Gordons had a white poodle the size of a small horse which David had always walked after school. Its name was George. That winter, after it got dark, Tom Gordon would go by the house with George on a leash. George would be ahead, pulling. Sometimes after supper I would see my father standing at the window in the living room, turning off the lamp and pulling back the curtain, peering out. And it sticks in my mind now that it was then he got the idea.

One Sunday afternoon in the spring and without telling my mother, my father walked next door with me and knocked on the Gordons' front door. Tom answered. My father asked him if he would like to come over for a drink. Tom said he didn't drink, but that still he would like to come over. He was a small man—thin and bald with small features. When he spoke there was something formal and serious about him. It reminded me of David the day he'd come selling the light bulbs.

That afternoon Tom stayed out on the back deck with my father until suppertime. After that, the two of them were friends, all at once it seemed, and Tom began coming to our house on Sunday afternoons. If my mother asked my father what it was they did all that time, he told her they were bird watching.

My father would make a gin and tonic for himself, and a glass of ice water with a slice of lime in it for Tom. Then he would carry the two drinks and Tom would carry the encyclopedia of birds and the two of them would go out back. It occurs to me now that the bird watching was only a kind of excuse—women can sit talking for hours over coffee, but men, it seems, need to believe they are actually doing something. At the time I remember only how strange it seemed to me that they called it that. There were geese and a few ducks, and sometimes sparrows and wrens, and every now and then a cardinal, but there were no gorgeous or unusual birds. And if a bird, by some chance, did happen to settle on the railing of the deck, they hardly paid any attention to it.

Mostly they just looked out over the woods. When they talked they talked about baseball. My father loved the St. Louis Cardinals. He talked about the players as if they were his friends, men he worked with. In the spring the Cardinals played exhibition games in different cities in Florida. That spring it seemed they were winning nearly every game, and when my father spoke of them there was in his voice a suppressed excitement. Tom liked baseball too and knew statistics. My father could mention a stolen base or a great catch from ten years ago and Tom would remember it exactly.

I sat on the floor of the deck leaning against the house. I wasn't particularly interested in baseball, but I liked the sound their voices made—the rise and fall and the seriousness.

By the end of May the Cardinals were in second place. Sometimes my father would bring the newspaper out on the deck and read the sports page out loud. One afternoon when he had just finished reading the standings and was inside making a second drink, Tom rolled up the sleeves of his shirt, a white dress shirt like he always wore to our house on Sunday, and asked me if I had been saved.

"Saved?"

Though this was, in fact, what my mother had, in her way, warned me about, I realized I had no idea what the word meant.

"Saved," Tom repeated. He took a sip of his ice water. "Baptized."

It was a clear afternoon, warm, but not hot the way it would be later. A breeze was blowing. It smelled like the pond and the woods, and there was a bitter smell in it too from the geraniums.

"We go to St. Augustine's," I said, remembering and trying to imitate the tone of politeness my mother used at the front door when she said these same words. It had always worked for her, causing the young man or woman at the door to wish her a good day and leave quietly, but now Tom was looking at me hard.

"I was baptized when I was a baby," I said. "And I've made my first communion." Saying this last part, I felt not a little proud. I knew from my mother that Baptists didn't have communion.

"It's not the same."

My bubble of pride collapsed. "The same as what?"

"You let that water touch you," he said. "And it changes you."

I wanted to ask him what he meant. And what water? But the door opened then and my father walked out with his drink. "Janie. It's Sunday. You've got all week to read. Why aren't you out playing?"

"I'd rather read," I told him.

"Not the bird book again." He closed his eyes and made a big show of groaning. For the last month I'd been reading a book I'd checked out from the library on attracting birds. I'd been telling my father, daily, that we needed a bird feeder. I hadn't even mentioned the bird bath yet which was another one of their strong recommendations.

"We could get a hummingbird feeder," I said. "They're real small."

"Come here," my father said. He was sitting with his drink balanced on one knee. He patted his other knee. "Come here, Janie."

I walked over and sat down. He turned my head to the side, setting his eye up close to my temple. "Like I thought." Then he pulled away, touched my temple with his finger. "Do you see that, Tom?"

"See what?"

"The hole," my father said.

"The hole?" Tom leaned forward. He didn't know that my father was joking. It was an old joke, something my father used to do with me when I was much younger—six and seven. I had always liked it, because for it I had to sit in my father's lap, and because, even though it was exactly the same every time, it always took me a little off guard.

"I can see clear through," my father said. "To the woods on the other side."

Tom laughed then, a deep wonderful laugh which surprised us.

"What do you think?" my father asked, now laughing himself, pleased. "Should I get her the hummingbird feeder?"

"By all means," Tom said. He touched my temple. "I would get her the bird feeder."

I liked Tom. I guess you could say I had a crush on him of sorts. On Sundays after lunch I'd lie on my bed and wait for his knock at the back door. I'd be on my stomach, watching the clock, straining to hear his steps on the deck. Because I wanted him to come, I was always afraid that he wouldn't. Then I'd hear his knock. The door opening. My father welcoming him.

"Where's Barbara?" my father would ask. Barbara was Mrs. Gordon. He'd told Tom, after the first Sunday, that it might be nice some time if Barbara came too. "She couldn't make it," Tom would say. Sometimes he'd say her lupus was acting up, or that she was sleeping. They both acted as if she might come some time.

"Ellen?" That was my mother's name. Tom was asking her to join them.

"Thank you," she'd say. "I'd like that. But I'm busy. I have a million things to do in the house. I can't. Really." There would be a slight edge to her voice, and I'd notice a way she had when she was angry of opening and closing her hands into small fists. Sometimes she was busy. But she was just as likely to spend the afternoon looking at a magazine, or sitting in front of the television watching golf.

One day I finally got around to asking her—why she didn't like Tom. We were fixing strawberries for supper. I was rinsing and hulling them, and she was slicing them in her hand, drawing the paring knife towards her thumb. It's one of the few things I can ever remember her doing which seemed dangerous to me.

She picked up the last strawberry and held it between her thumb and forefinger. "I like Tom just fine," she said. Then, without pausing, she told me to get the canister of sugar and bring it over. When she didn't want to talk about something she would often find small chores for me to do.

I set the canister on the counter between us. There was another question I'd been waiting to ask her. I studied a spot on her forehead. "Can Catholics be saved?"

She sprinkled the sugar over the strawberries. "Catholics," she said, "don't talk about it that way."

"How then?"

She set the bowl of strawberries in the refrigerator and told me she had clothes to take out of the washer. I followed her down into the basement.

"Catholics," she said, "are generally quieter about it."

I knew what she meant—the hushed seriousness I'd come to associate with confession and communion both. And I started to tell her what Tom had said—how it wasn't the same. But before I could get past his name she touched my arm. Her hand was damp and cool from the wash. "I think your father has gone too far with this thing."

I didn't want to hear this. Out back Tom was offering us something totally new—something that could change everything—and here was my mother, stuck inside the house, talking the same old way she always had.

Too far. These were the same words she'd used one afternoon to my father when he'd come back late from one of his drives with Miss Gunther. He'd been gone two hours instead of the usual hour. My mother was standing at the dining room window. "I think," she said, "you're going too far with this."

He stopped in the doorway. He was alone, having as usual dropped Miss Gunther off at her apartment. "We just drove to Lone Elk," he said. Lone Elk Park was a forty-five minute drive one way, farther than we usually went. He walked over and stood behind her. "Just there and back."

"That's not what I meant," she said.

He set his hands on her shoulders. "The woman's had a hard life. She doesn't have any friends."

"I know that," my mother said.

"Come with us. Next Sunday. Please." His voice was gentle, but there was an urgency beneath it I couldn't remember hearing before this.

The next Sunday while my mother was washing dishes and I was putting them into the dishwasher, she told me she might go with them the next week after all. Maybe, she said, we could both go. I told her that would be great. It was what I'd wanted, but at the same time I couldn't imagine it.

At ten o'clock that night my father was still not home. We watched the news and then an old horror movie, but none of us could concentrate; we were sleepy and jittery both. After the movie the screen went blank. Mark got up to turn off the set. With the television off we could hear the rain—the sound it made against the sidewalk and rushing out of the drain pipe.

"They must have been in an accident," my mother said. "I should call the hospital. The police."

But she didn't get up. Instead, she stayed in the chair next to the window, leaning forward to look out whenever she heard a car, and then, when the headlights would go on past, swearing softly under her breath.

When my father's car finally did pull in the driveway she sent Mark and me upstairs. Mark stayed in my room, sitting on the end of the bed, while my mother spoke to my father in the low harsh tones more ominous to us than if she had screamed or even begun hitting him. Mark and I spoke of it just once that night. It had gotten quiet downstairs. He was standing at the door.

"I think they're going to get a divorce," he said.

Both of us believed that was the worst thing that could happen then, but we didn't see any way out of it either. I nodded. "I bet they will."

When I woke up later it was thundering. My room was dark, a cool spray of rain on my face. I lay very still. My mother was in Mark's room closing his window. She was always the one to get up and close the windows when it stormed. I heard her in the bathroom, the hall, before she opened my door and came around my bed. The first window closed easily, but the one next to my bed was giving her trouble. The windows were wooden, this particular one was warped, and on wet nights it must have swollen. As she pulled down on it, trying to close it, the window seemed as if it were some adversary, alive; I could feel myself straining with her, could feel it as if it were my own arms, and then her relief when it finally gave, and she closed the window and locked it and the upstairs was quiet.

There were times when I felt I was beginning to understand my parents. The differences between them. What I could hope for. One Sunday, not long after I'd asked my mother if Catholics could be saved, I told my father what we needed, more than we needed anything else, was a bird bath.

I didn't whine or plead. I never did when I was asking for something important. Instead I stepped back and stood next to the railing, my arms down at my sides, trying to take up the space I thought a bird bath would. As I spoke, I pictured cockatoos and flamingos and peacocks, all of them balanced on the edge of the bird bath, dipping their heads down to drink.

"Janie," he said. "You've been reading too much."

He had a hundred excuses. A bird bath was too heavy for the deck. It was too expensive. And besides, he said, we had a pond behind our house the size of a thousand bird baths that was free and, even more important, we were never going to have to clean it.

"That's it," I said. Since we'd moved into the new house I'd been trying without any success to get him to go down to the pond with me. "The three of us could go swimming."

He shook his head. "It's too early. The water will be like ice. We'd freeze."

Tom held his hand up, turning it back and forth. "The air seems warm enough."

The hummingbird feeder was hanging by a wire from the rail of the deck. I reached up and pushed it with my finger so that it swayed back and forth. We'd gotten that after all because Tom had approved.

My father set his hands on his thighs. He was wavering. But then, without warning, he stood up and headed toward the back door. "Your mother," he said. "I don't think she'd go for it." The screen door banged behind him.

I looked at Tom. "Thanks anyway."

"You're welcome."

"He'll come back," I said.

Tom nodded. The encyclopedia was open on his lap. He took his glasses out, polished them on the cuff of his shirt, and put them on. I started a game I sometimes played out on the deck when I was alone. I would see how many times I could walk back and forth, one foot in front of the other, along a single plank without touching any of the other planks and without holding on. With practice the game had gotten easy, too easy. I was hot and bored. We were never going to go swimming. My father was never going to get us a bird bath. Nothing new or beautiful was ever going to happen. After the fourteenth time back and forth, I stopped directly in front of Tom, close enough so he had to look up.

"Yes?" He was looking at me over his glasses.

"What," I asked him, "would a person do if they wanted to be baptized?"

Full minutes seemed to pass while he considered this. He

took off his glasses and set them on the encyclopedia. "They would have to want it," he said.

Instead of looking at Tom's face I looked down at the book. "How would they know?"

He lifted his hand, and for a second I was sure he was going to touch me, but then he seemed to change his mind. He dropped his hand next to his glasses. "They would feel it."

I nodded. I had a peculiar sensation, not unlike one I had sometimes when my mother combed out my hair—a tingling across my scalp. It was as if Tom were actually touching me, as if his hand were settled on the top of my head, resting there, the way I'd seen the bishop do this with the older kids at confirmation and the way it seemed to me the Holy Spirit might have hovered over the heads of the apostles at Pentecost. I looked up to find myself staring into Tom's face.

"Have you been saved?" I asked him.

I was feeling solemn—as solemn as I'd ever felt during consecration or walking back to the pew with the host in my mouth. When Tom started laughing I was mortified.

"What's so funny?" I asked him. My cheeks were burning.

"No, Jane, I'm not laughing at you. I was just remembering. I was thirteen. The last thing I thought I wanted or needed was Jesus Christ pushing his way into my life. But my mother wanted me to do it, and so I did." He shook his head. "There was a basin up at the front. It must have stood about as high as my chest. The preacher picked me up and dunked me into that water, clothes and all. When I came up for air I turned around and there in the second pew were two girls I knew from school. The only thing I felt right then was embarrassment."

This wasn't what I'd expected. I was trying to absorb it. "But it changed you? You weren't the same after that?"

I don't think he heard me. He got up and walked over to the edge of the deck and looked over at his house. A tall hedge separated the two yards, but from the deck you could see down onto the grass, a smooth deep green. "It's funny," he said. "One day you start needing it enough you don't feel embarrassed anymore."

I looked at the back of Tom's head—the place where his hair fell in a neat line against his neck. "David?"

David hadn't been mentioned in front of Tom that whole spring. The name seemed to hang there in the air between us. The question I was asking was whether it was after David died that he, Tom, had started needing it.

But Tom heard a different question. "I didn't want to push him," he said. "I only wanted him to know—what was available."

I held myself still, waiting. Was that what had happened? David had died because he had missed this?

Tom looked down at me. "What's that, Janie?"

"I didn't say anything—"

The screen door opened. I turned around. My father was standing in the doorway, holding a tray with three glasses of lemonade. "You two aren't still talking about that bird bath."

"No, Dad." I walked over and took my glass from him.

"This is important to you, Janie?"

I was thinking about Tom, what he'd just told me. "It's important."

"Okay then," he said. "We'll get the bird bath."

I stood up on tiptoe and kissed his cheek. "Thanks, Daddy."

He nodded. Then he crossed to the edge of the deck. Before he handed Tom his glass, he held the tray up high as if he were imitating a waiter in some fancy restaurant. It was the kind of thing he might have once done inside with Mark or me, or even with my mother, and we would have thought it was funny; standing next to Tom it made him seem young.

Tom drank his lemonade in two long swallows. "Thank you. That was very good. I better be going now." He sounded even more polite, more stiff, than usual. He shook my father's hand; then he went down the steps and across our yard. At the hedge between the two yards he turned around. "Thank you again," he called out. I waved. It was as if he were leaving for some faraway place and not just going next door.

Then my father waved. "It was a privilege."

In the evenings after Tom had gone, the house felt especially empty to me. I must have shown it in my face, because sometimes my father would tease me. "The bird watching really seems to tire Janie out."

Or another night, "Sometimes, Janie, I wonder if you don't like Tom better than you like me."

"No, Dad." I was fierce about this. That he understand I only liked Tom in a different way.

Then Mark would be in on it too. Maybe, he'd say, you need to find a boy who is closer to your own age. I'd try to hit him and he'd run. My mother would stand in the middle of the kitchen with her arms out at her sides to catch us. "Stop. Right now. Both of you."

Often on Sunday nights she would be quieter than usual. At supper my father would talk and talk, while she would pick at her food.

"I don't understand," she said one night finally, "why he has to stay the whole afternoon."

"You don't want him to come," my father said.

My mother got up and went to the stove. "I didn't say that." The gravy was smoking, but she didn't touch it. She stood with her back to us, opening and closing her hands. "I'm just not sure it's a good idea. For Janie."

"Janie loves Tom." My father touched the back of my hand. "Don't you?"

"She loves him to death," Mark said.

My mother came back and sat down. She'd hardly touched her food. Now she set her elbows on either side of her plate and folded her hands. "What about all the things you could be doing around the house on Sunday afternoons?"

My father looked up from his plate, genuinely puzzled. "What things?"

I don't think she could think of anything specific. She started rubbing her eyes, which she often did when she was about to lose her temper and was trying to calm herself. "There's just something wrong about this."

"Tell me."

"The way you're always so happy out there. The way you look forward to Sunday afternoons." She hesitated. "It's just like it was before."

If she'd said Miss Gunther's name it couldn't have been more clear what she meant. We were never going to be over it.

My father stood up and pushed his chair away from the table.

He looked older to me, more stooped in the shoulders; it is a way some people walk all the time, as if they are carrying the world, but I had never seen it in him before. At the back door he stopped, his hand on the knob. "I'm going for a drive." He opened the door. I wanted my mother to tell him to come back. Even after he was outside it seemed to me there was time. Time for him to turn around. I had this idea they could come together there in the kitchen, and kiss, the way it might have happened in a movie, but as I watched him walk across the deck and down the stairs I knew—as well as I'd ever known anything—no kiss was going to appear there out of thin air. After a minute we heard the car start like a small explosion, and then it was quiet.

The next Sunday it rained. I spent the afternoon lying across my bed waiting for Tom. At supper, when Tom still hadn't come, I asked my father what he thought had happened. He said it must be the weather. But something about the way neither he nor my mother would look me in the eye, I knew he had talked to Tom. After supper I went into the downstairs bathroom and locked the door and looked out the window at the Gordons' house until it was time to go to bed.

I woke to someone knocking. It was dark. I got out of bed and opened the window and pressed my face against the screen. The rain had stopped. The porch light was on and Tom was standing beneath it. I pulled my nightgown off over my head, put on shorts and a sweatshirt, and went downstairs.

My father was sitting at the kitchen table, still in his pajamas, tying his shoes. Tom was standing just inside the back door. The door was open, and moths were flying around the light over the kitchen table. Neither Tom nor my father seemed to notice me. I stayed back away from the light so they wouldn't.

Tom left first. Then my father. The kitchen light was on and the door standing open—the kind of thing my father wouldn't have let happen under normal circumstances. I waited a few seconds and then followed them.

It was warm outside and smelled the way it does sometimes in the late spring after a rain—grass and honeysuckle and another smell that seemed to come out of the earth itself. The sky had cleared. There were stars and a half moon and from the deck I could see the two men running, my father lagging a few steps behind. His pajamas were a pale blue and in that light they glowed a little.

When they got to the hedge, Tom parted the bushes with his hands and let my father through. There were prickers in those bushes. My father swore once. Then they were both gone. I ran down the steps and across the yard to catch up. The bushes were taller than I was and close together. I scratched both of my arms going through. Once on the other side, I stood completely still. It was the first time I'd been in the Gordons' yard. They were strict about children coming in their yard. If my brother and his friends were playing hotbox out in our back yard and the ball flew up and over their hedge, it was lost.

I turned around and looked back over the hedge at our house. All the lights upstairs were off. I'd forgotten about my mother, but now I was almost certain she was awake, standing at the window looking down. I brought my hand up in a kind of wave before I turned back to the Gordons' house.

My father and Tom had already disappeared inside. I checked the back door. It was unlocked. The next thing I knew I was in the Gordons' kitchen. There was a small light on over the sink. The kitchen was clean. The counters were white and bare and the sink was white and the floor was pure white linoleum without any pattern. In the middle of the kitchen table was a trivet made out of wooden clothespins. We had an identical one at home—something Mark had made years ago in Scouts. Around the trivet were three place mats and there were three chairs around the table, evenly spaced. Tom and Mrs. Gordon and David. There was a noise from farther back in the house. My father swearing again.

I followed his voice through the dining room to the living room. He was squatted on the floor in the middle of the room. Next to him Mrs. Gordon was lying on her back in a white bathrobe, her legs sticking out. My father had a handkerchief pressed to her forehead. There was blood on his hand, and some of the blood had worked its way down onto Mrs. Gordon's cheek, her chin, and there were a few spots on her bathrobe.

"What happened?" It came out before I'd meant to say anything.

My father looked up. If he was surprised to see me there, he gave no sign of it; in fact he seemed grateful. "Call 911," he said, pointing to the phone. "Give them this address." He wore an excited look I'd seen him have before in emergencies—once before with a grease fire on the stove.

Tom was standing next to Mrs. Gordon's feet. He seemed frozen there, his eyes fixed ahead. I had to squeeze between him and one of the armchairs to get to the phone.

"Tell them, Jane," my father said, "that she's unconscious but breathing."

I did. Then I gave them the address and her name. After I'd hung up I told my father how they'd said not to move her. He nodded. My one job finished, I went over and sat on the couch behind him. Once on the couch I had to pinch the inside of my leg. The light in the room had a bright unreal quality I associated with dreams.

Everything in the room was white. Maybe that was the reason for the glare. And then too, there was none of the clutter I was used to in our house or the houses of my friends. The room was bare, except for a couple of candles on the mantle, and an empty vase, and on the coffee table a stack of magazines layered the same way my mother did them when she was having company. But Mrs. Gordon wasn't expecting company. In fact I couldn't remember the last time I'd seen a car pull in their driveway that wasn't theirs. For a second I thought I could picture what her life might be like in this room.

One of the armchairs stood off by itself next to the window. She would, I was certain, be sitting there. Maybe it would be raining outside, or cold, or worse, it would be clear, a Sunday afternoon when up and down the street people would be out in their yards and Tom and my father would be out back with their drinks. In any case, the drapes would be drawn. Inside the light would be dim and cool, like winter, that long dead time of the afternoon when it seems as if clocks are standing still. The magazine would be open across her lap, but she wouldn't be reading it. I knew all this, even the look on her face—a look that was all inward; the kind of look where you could stand directly in front of her and she wouldn't see you. Sometimes I would walk into the living room on a Sunday afternoon and come up on my mother just like that.

"What happened?"

It was the question I had on my mind, and for a second I thought I'd spoken it again. But the voice was my father's.

Tom took a deep breath and then blew out hard. "She fell." His voice came out flat, like I'd never heard it. "She hit her head against the coffee table. She was drinking."

My father flinched. "That's not possible." The center of his birthmark was a dark purple. "She doesn't drink. Neither of you do."

We waited. Maybe now Tom would explain this to us.

"I think she's cold," Tom said.

A white afghan was hanging over the back of one of the chairs. He lifted it, and crouching down next to her, laid the blanket over her legs. It was hot in the room. I could feel the afghan as if it were lying there, rough and scratchy, against my own bare skin. Tom looked at my father. "She thinks it was her fault."

"David?"

Tom made a motion with his hand as if to take in the whole room, the house. "All of it."

Behind Tom's voice I could hear the siren, rising and fading and then rising again. My mother had told me once that whenever I heard a siren I should say a prayer; that whatever it was—a fire engine or a police car or an ambulance—it was likely headed toward somebody in pain. For the first time since she'd told me this I though I had a glimmer of what that could mean. The siren got louder and then stopped.

"I don't get it," my father said.

Tom shook his head. "This house. For a long time—"

The front door opened, interrupting him. "In here," my father called out. Then the two men from the ambulance were standing in the doorway with the stretcher.

They looked at first like gas station attendants. They wore orange coveralls with their names stitched over the pockets. But then I saw their faces—more serious than that. The older one, Ray, seemed to be in charge. As soon as they'd set down the stretcher, he squatted down next to Mrs. Gordon and set two fingers against her neck. "Pulse is strong," he said. He lifted my father's hand from her forehead. He shone a light in her eyes. "What happened?"

My father indicated Tom with a nod. "He's her husband. He was here."

Ray turned.

"My son died," Tom said.

"Where?" Ray's eyes flickered around the room, stopping at the staircase.

"Upstairs," Tom said. "In his bedroom. Six months ago."

"I'm sorry." Ray lowered his voice. "But tonight, Sir. What happened tonight? Here?"

Tom told him about the drinking and the fall and then about her lupus. As he spoke, Ray wrote everything down in a small notebook. Then the two men lifted Mrs. Gordon up onto the stretcher. They were gentle. When Tom asked if the blanket could go along with her, Ray told him that would be fine. Then he asked Tom if he wanted to ride with her in the back. Tom nodded. My father touched Tom on the shoulder. Then they were gone.

My father was standing in the hallway looking out the front door. I got up off the couch and went and stood behind him. "Do you think they'll be all right?"

He turned around. "I don't know, Janie." He looked past me, back into the living room. "I think there's been sadness here for a long time now."

I nodded. "Tom told me."

This was only partly true. Because he hadn't really. Not in so many words. He hadn't told me about Mrs. Gordon, or why David had killed himself, and now I'd been inside their house and still I didn't understand—not any of it. But for reasons I couldn't have articulated, it was important to me that my father believe that I understood.

"Tom told me," I said, "that if you needed it bad enough you wouldn't be embarrassed anymore."

"Needed what, Janie?"

I stammered. "Well—" Now that he'd asked, I couldn't think of any word that could contain what I wanted to say.

"That's okay." He put his hand on the back of my neck. "It's late. We need to be getting home."

He locked the front door. Then, with his hand still resting on my neck, he steered me back through the house. In the living room he turned out the lights, but he left the kitchen light on over the sink. "For when they get back," he said.

I nodded.

Outside it was quiet, hot. There wasn't any breeze, but if I strained I believed I could smell the pond—the coolness of it. We crossed the yard and then made our way through the hedge, my father first. Our house was a huge shape ahead in the dark.

"It might be better," my father said, "if you didn't tell your mother about this."

I looked up at her window. He thought she was asleep, had missed this. But I was certain now she was up there, watching. That she knew already what had happened—knew how things could turn out. I was equally certain she would never talk about it.

"I won't tell her," I promised. "But, Dad—"

"What, Janie?"

I hesitated. I was trying to think of the right way to say this. If I said it wrong I could ruin everything. I cleared my throat. "I think, Dad, that maybe we should go down to the pond swimming."

"Now?"

"Tonight."

"But it's late. Your mother—"

"She won't mind. I think we should." I wasn't pleading. I was only telling him what I knew now to be true—that we needed this. Not just the coolness of the water, but something else too. We needed something bigger than ourselves, outside us. We needed to be saved.

"This is important, Janie?"

I nodded.

He looked back up at the window again. "Okay then," he said.

We started down. As we got closer to the pond the air changed. It was heavier, and the smell of moss was in it, dark and green and cool. When we came out of the trees into the clearing the water was an unbroken sheen.

"Where do you think the ducks go at night?" I asked him.

"I don't know, Janie."

That was one of the things I always appreciated about my father. He never pretended to know when he didn't.

He crouched down and untied his tennis shoes. He was standing there in his pajamas and his bare feet.

"Go on," I said.

"Are you coming?"

I nodded. "After."

And then he waded in. That was the amazing thing. I'm certain he didn't believe in the power of the water, at least not the way I did that night. He was doing it because I asked him. The kind of thing a parent can do—let you bless them like that—and you won't ever forget it.

Looking for Frank

BY DIANE SHERRY CASE

I never could understand why Mom used to sleep so much in those days. She was the one who wanted to find someone richer I think. That's why she kicked Dad out. So I don't know why she slept all day instead. Or why she saw that cop. Maybe it was the dreams.

I'd get home from school and she'd be asleep and I'd be hungry. There was never anything to eat so I'd fix a bowl of Frosted Flakes or something and then realize the milk was sour. Then she'd wake up.

"What time is it?" she asked and poured herself a glass of tonic while she heated up the coffee at the same time.

"I dunno, 'bout four," I guessed. The clock above the sink had been broken since way before Dad moved out and I don't think the one on the stove was ever meant to work at all. And all the numbers were scrubbed off the temperature knob so you never knew how hot the oven was.

"Oh crap, I forgot to defrost anything." Mom went into the other room and sloshed some Vodka in her tonic. "Alex didn't call?"

"Nobody's called since I've been home. Except Dad."

"What did he want?" I got the Oreos and went for the milk but changed my mind when I smelled it. "What did your father want?"

"Oh, he wanted to know if I was going to see him Sunday."

"Is that all he said, are you going to see me on Sunday?" I watched as she poured herself some coffee, added sour milk,

288

and took a sip. "Oh shit." She slammed the cup down. "Why didn't anybody throw this out?" She screamed real loud. "Anybody" meant me, so I emptied the milk. Then I turned on the TV. She glared at me and I pretended not to notice.

We did that for a while and then Mom sat down, stared at the TV and started pulling at her hair, picking one strand at a time from her cowlick place like she always told me not to do. The news was on but I wasn't paying attention. I'd found a quiz in last month's *Cosmo*. Mom stared at the TV and picked at her hair for twenty minutes. Then she suddenly said, "Would you change that, it's so irritating." She hated the news.

I had just answered the last question in the "How sensual are you?" quiz when the phone rang. It was right beside me, but Mom dashed for it quicker than I could. I knew it was going to be Alex by the sweetie-pie voice she used when she said hello. "Oh great, what time?" She had this little girl smile on her face and she was playing with her toes.

When she got off the phone she started scurrying around, picking up newspapers and emptying ashtrays and old Kleenex in them. "Honey, will you do me a big favor?" She handed me ten bucks. "One of those barbecued chickens and some lettuce and, um, tomatoes. And cigarettes."

"Dad wanted to know if I was going to Grandma's with him," I told her. He hadn't really asked me but I figured he would.

"When's he going?"

"August."

"What about summer school?" She was trying to haul the big fan out of the hall closet when she rammed herself in the shin with it. "Shit. Can we talk about this later?"

I waited until I was almost out the door before I said, "He's bringing his girlfriend to the farm with us." That was mean, I know it. Even though the divorce was her idea, she still didn't like the thought of Dad with another woman. But I said it anyway.

The truth was Dad didn't really have a girlfriend. I'd been telling her that for weeks, but it wasn't true. I told her that she was sweet and blond and cooked wonderful French food and flew airplanes by herself. And when Mom would ask, "Is she

pretty?" I'd sort of casually say, "Yeah, she's pretty." And she'd
say, "What's she look like?" And I'd tell her that she had long
blond, wavy hair that was parted on the side and fell over one
eye. And when she'd ask me if she had big tits I wouldn't
answer. Then she'd say, "Well, is she pretty?" And I'd tell her
again. "Yeah, she's pretty." I named her Anna. With a soft A.
     Like I would know anyway. I saw him every other Sunday
morning. He'd pick me up and say, "What do you want to do?"
and I'd say, "I dunno. Eat?" And we'd go eat and talk about
pancakes and how many different kinds of syrup there are and
how finicky people are about their eggs and then he'd take me
home. There was nothing else to do.

     Mom was in a great mood when I got back from the market.
We set the table with bright yellow place mats and joked about
how hot it was, trying to top each other with "It's hotter
than . . ." "It's hotter than a blistered pussy in a pepper patch,"
she said and we both laughed so hard we almost wet our pants.
Then Alex arrived and she told me I was too young to wear
lipstick and that I should go put on a bra.
     Alex was looking very grim and he had sweat on his hairy
neck. Mom gave him a big hug and he grabbed her ass and lifted
her so her bare feet were barely touching the carpet. He didn't
look quite so grim when they'd finished. Then he finally said
hello to me. We never really talked much. He hadn't been
around long, just a few weeks, and most of that time he was
busy doing it with Mom. I don't think they ever talked much
either.
     I never knew why she liked him, he wasn't very cute or good-
looking or anything. He had hair every place but where it was
most important and his lips were huge and nasty looking. She
did like him though, and they couldn't keep their hands off
each other.
     So that night they went more or less straight to the bedroom.
Only instead of the usual bedsprings, I could hear them talking.
I went ahead and ate by myself. Then I got on the phone and
called everyone I could think of that might give me a ride to the
library or somewhere. I wanted to go out.
     Mindy said her brother might take us one at a time on his

motorcycle. He was four years older than us, almost eighteen, and he was on probation. They said he'd stolen some stuff, diving equipment I think. But I never believed that. Frank was smart even though he wasn't good in school. That's what Mindy'd always said. She was real proud of him because he was dark and casual-looking and played guitar.

I waited for her to call and got antsy and didn't know what to do with myself. Pretty soon the bed noises started happening and I knew I had time to sneak some vodka. It tasted awful even in orange juice.

The cop stayed until after midnight, as usual. I was in my room trying to draw a picture of Frank on his motorcycle, and I heard them talking seriously again. "Just give me time," he said. When the door closed I turned off my light real quick so Mom wouldn't come in and start blabbing at me.

Whenever I'd think about Frank my soul would get all tingly. That night, and every other night in those days, I lay there under too many covers for how warm it was and made up stories about us. He'd come up to me and touch my neck and say, God, you're pretty, prettiest girl I've ever known. And then he'd ask me if I wanted to go for a ride on his motorcycle. I'd say sure and wrap my legs around his hips and my arms around his waist and press my breasts against his back and off we'd go, fast and free. I'd ride for days behind him close, and nights we'd laugh and kiss. We'd end up at the ocean and finally make love and be carried out to sea. I'd never made love, but I knew just what it would be like. Like floating in the ocean with colored fish all around.

Now that Mom was in love, she decided to stop sleeping all the time and fix the house up. Her first move was to try to paint. It was about time too. The white walls had been almost brown for as long as I could remember. Before she got divorced she had started having ideas, cutting pictures out of *House Beautiful* and *Better Homes and Gardens*. But she never actually did much. She'd made Dad buy her lots of posters, pictures of places she wanted to go, cafés on the Left Bank and some Greek Island with broken statues. Dad moaned at the money it cost to have them all framed but she insisted. Then she never hung them. They leaned against the wall in the hall for over a year. Which meant she didn't have to take them down when we started to paint.

She had also decided that I was going to help her, in the one week I had between school and summer school. I was pissed. It was hot again and I wanted to hang out at the beach, but we made a deal. If I helped her for three days, I could ride with whoever I wanted to the beach.

We went to Builder's Emporium and bought enough paint for every room in the house. She chose a disgusting pale green for the living room and a peachy color for her room. "Flesh tone makes your skin look nice." I saw the article she got that idea from. It was something Meryl Streep said. "So what's pale green gonna do?" I asked her. She looked at the swatch of color and thought about green skin in the living room and then asked me what color I thought we should get. "You're supposed to be the artsy one, you pick the color." So I stood there forever trying to decide and when I finally showed her the two colors I had come up with, she looked at them like she'd eaten something rotten. "You don't like either of them?" She shook her head no and bought white.

We got Japanese wallpaper with bonsai trees all over it for the bathroom. I stuffed a bunch of color swatches in my pocket and we loaded up the car. When we got home I set the fan up in the living room and another fan up in the hall. We moved furniture all over the place and set out ripping wallpaper off walls and painting. It was a huge mess.

By noon the second day Mom started calling real painters and I put on my cowboy boots and bathing suit and headed for the beach. It was too late to get a ride so I had to walk. By the time I got there it was overcast and everyone was hanging out in the parking lot, Mindy and her brother and a bunch of his friends, guys with cars painted in all sorts of bizarre colors.

I was talking to Mindy when her brother came up to tell her they were leaving. Frank's long black hair was wet and he looked like a Cherokee warrior. Mindy took off to get her stuff.

"Cool boots," Frank said. "New?"

"Yeah," I answered, really glad I'd worn them.

"They'll be good in a couple of years. You gotta rough 'em up a little."

I looked down at my boots and saw what he meant. "How?"

"Kick stuff. Wear 'em a lot. Don't be careful."

"Okay."

"Yeah." He nodded and kept looking at me. "Now you need a hat," he said.

"A hat?"

Frank nodded again. "You'll look like Debra Winger, y'know?" I smiled my prettiest smile as he turned to walk away.

I stood there alone for a minute, watching Frank, confused and wondering how I was going to get home. Frank threw his tank in the trunk of a Buick and yelled over his shoulder at me. "You coming?"

The car we rode in had a steering wheel shaped like a big white hand and the interior was done in red patent leather plastic. The guy that owned it checked us all out to make sure we were dry and had no sand or tar on us. Then he laid a blanket over the back seat and we all squeezed in, five guys and two girls. I'd been praying that I'd get to sit next to Frank, but it didn't happen. Frank sat in front and talked about diving and where he was going when his parole was up and I ended up in the backseat on Blackie Blancia's sweaty lap. Frank didn't say a word to me the whole way back. But he waved as I was getting out of the car.

When I got home Mom was looking out the window and Alex was sitting on the drop cloth that we'd put on the couch, staring at the TV. It was deadly silent. I went into the kitchen so I could eat something and still keep an ear open for what was going on. Nobody said anything for a long time and I fixed myself some peanut butter and celery.

"I wanted to watch that," Mom finally said in her bitch voice. I had to stop with the celery so I could hear. Alex kept changing the channels. "I said I wanted to watch that!"

"What the hell's the matter with you?" Alex said. "Jesus Christ. This is getting worse than home." He stomped toward the front door.

"I'm sorry, baby," Mom whined, following him.

"It's too hot for this shit," he shouted as he slammed out.

I was just about to head for my room when Mom came in to pour herself a drink. "How many times have I told you I don't want you riding with carloads of drunken surfers?"

"No one was drunk."

"How do you know?" I looked at her and tried to figure out what she wanted me to say. "How do you know, Miss Smartass?"

"You said I could ride with whoever I wanted," I said. And then I added something I shouldn't have. "They're not surfers."

"I don't like the way you're talking to me lately."

"How am I talking to you?" I said under my breath.

"You know what I'm talking about. Little bitch."

"No, I don't," I said and headed for my room.

"You little bitch!" she screamed and followed me until I slammed the bedroom door.

Whenever Mom was mad at Alex she'd dress herself all gorgeous and pick me up from my Saturday job so she could flirt with my boss. Jack was forty or fifty or something, and he had two grown sons. We'd met him when Mom was on her clothes buying binge after she kicked Dad out. We'd gone to every store within fifty miles until she finally had to tear up all the credit cards.

Mom thought Jack was good-looking but once men had bald spots I could never call them good-looking. He wore his shirt half unbuttoned which was surprising, given that he had good taste in clothes. Some of the hairs on his chest were gray and there was a scar up the middle like someone had opened him up to store ice.

Jumping Jax was the kind of store that old rock stars shopped in. Every kind of cowboy boots imaginable and lots of black clothes. Stretchy dresses that showed everything and things made of rubber lace. I liked being a salesgirl and I'd learned that money earned freedom. But as much as I thought about saving for the future, it wasn't really working out. The first time I'd gotten a paycheck I'd used the whole thing to buy bathing suits. And the second month I spent it on cowboy boots. Now I had to buy a hat.

I'd been working there at least two months before Mom
finally got Jack to ask her out. She'd meet him for drinks so he
wouldn't see our house. They'd go out once or twice and then
Alex would call and she wouldn't talk to Jack again until they
got into another fight. That made Jack like her even more and
he'd send her presents, clothes from the store and flowers and
stuff.

I used to think Jack liked me because he didn't have a
daughter. He gave me the job even though I was too young and
he spent lots of time showing me how to do stuff. He even gave
me rides home in his antique Mercedes, all the way to Venice
from Beverly Hills. "So, you like working for me?" I told him
yeah, I liked it, and he told me I was doing a good job. That felt
good. Yeah, I thought, people actually bought clothes and I
helped them and made money doing it. What an amazing
thing.

I didn't mind summer school at all because I knew that Frank
had to take summer school in order to graduate. Then he would
be gone. So it was my last chance.

The truth was that Frank had been on my mind for years and
years already, since before I was supposed to be thinking about
men. People don't know, but even eight-year-olds dream
amazing things. Frank would tie me naked to a cross and I'd get
all warm. And then he'd do things to me that shouldn't feel
good. But they did. There were many different kinds of dreams
in the years of Frank. My nights weren't always soothing
oceans.

I looked for him that whole first week. Finally, on Friday, I
wandered out onto the lawn when I was supposed to be in class.
And there he was, sitting under a tree, smoking a cigarette
backwards in his palm so no one could see.

"Aren't you going to class?" I asked.

"I dunno. Too nice a day."

I didn't think it was nice. It was hot. But once Frank said so
I realized he was right. "Yeah, it's summer all right."

"Assholes," he said. "They aren't going to let me graduate
unless I finish my detention. On top of fucking summer
school."

"Gee, that's shitty," I said.

"Sure is. I have to stay an extra hour every day for three weeks. If I want to graduate. Which maybe I don't."

"You might as well," I shrugged.

"Yeah, well I dunno. It's summer, man!" Frank threw his cigarette down and suddenly got up. "Let's get out of here," he said.

"Okay," I answered and shrugged like a jerk again.

"I got a stop to make. Take care of some business."

"Cool," I said, forcing my shoulders to stay down this time.

Two minutes later, I was on the back of Frank's bike with my arms around him. All I could do was smile.

Frank parked in front of a tattoo parlor and I followed him in. We looked at tons of drawings and he picked one that was big enough to cover the Ava on his arm. It was a picture of a big red koi fish.

"Who's Ava?" I asked.

"Can't tell you," he said and settled into the barber chair.

A huge Harley kind of guy smeared Frank's arm with alcohol. "Those boots'll get good in a year or two," Frank said to me as the guy stuck a needle in his arm.

"Yeah, they're still kinda new." I watched as drops of blood gathered around Ava. "But they hurt my feet."

"Too tight?" Frank asked, acting like nothing was bothering him.

"Just the left one. Just a little."

"Put water on it. When you wear 'em. They'll stretch."

"Soak 'em?" I asked.

Frank's lips tightened just a wee bit and he didn't answer for a second. "Spray 'em. They'll fit good. Water. Water's the way."

The tattoo took forever. It looked like it hurt a lot, but Frank pretended it was nothing. Finally the big guy put a bandage on it and we got up to leave.

"Okay, that's fifty bucks," the leather guy said. "They like those kois in Japan. Know why?"

"Why?" Frank asked, pulling out his wallet.

"Cause. They're the only kind of fish that doesn't flop

around when you go to cut its head off."

Frank gave him the money. "Yeah, right," he said like he already knew that.

The sun was getting red when Frank dropped me off. We pulled up a little ways from my house, so Mom wouldn't know about the bike.

"Next time we'll do something good. Beats school, anyway, huh?" he asked.

"Yeah, sure," I smiled and watched Frank pull away. I was glad about Ava being gone. Whoever she was.

When I got home, the furniture was still all over the place and the walls were still brown. I put my books on the kitchen table and was about to get some cereal when Mom came in. "Quit leaving your goddamned junk on the kitchen table." I took my stuff and the smile I had left from Frank and went to my room. I was still sitting on my bed remembering things when I heard her crying. I tried to ignore it for a while, but it seemed to get louder and crawl into my head.

She had her arms wrapped around a wet pillow with eye makeup all over it. I asked what the matter was. "I just can't stand it anymore," she said. "I just can't stand it." I stroked her head like she used to do when I was little. That seemed to make her cry more so I didn't know what to do. Finally she said, "Look at this, and showed me a picture in the local paper. "Just look at that." It was an awards ceremony for cops and Alex was there with his policewoman wife, looking perfectly happy and posing with the mayor. "Look at it," she said. "I feel like a goddamned fool." I wanted to tell her she was one, but I didn't.

I hated to see Mom cry, I really did. I brought her dinner in bed that night and she was really grateful. She just loved to have someone take care of her. "You're not mad at me anymore?" She reminded me of a silly sixth grader that used to have a crush on me. "No, I'm not mad," I told her.

"You know I'm not used to sleeping alone," Mom said, putting her head down on my lap. "Your father and I got married when I wasn't much older than you." I knew that and I also knew that she never got to go to her senior prom because

she was pregnant with me and had to drop out. And that Dad
had to walk forever to school in the snow and that I had it real
good. So I made her a drink and lay down with her till she fell
asleep.

Alex came over a few nights later and she wouldn't let him in.
"What do you want?" she said at the door.

He wasn't in uniform and he had a little stubble on his face.
"How come you're hanging up on me every time I call?"

"Because I'm through with us," she said. But she kept
standing there with the door wide open. I knew I should leave
the room but I didn't.

"I brought you this." He handed her a little box that was
wrapped in stupid pink paper with cupids all over it. She looked
at it suspiciously and asked what it was. "Open it," he told her
and when she finally took it from him, he sort of slid into the
living room. "Hi, Shawn. How are you?" He'd never asked me
anything like that before and I wasn't about to answer.

"Alex just asked you a question, Shawn." Mom was suddenly
on his side.

"Fine," I said. "I'm fine."

It wasn't even ten minutes before they'd already made up and
were kissing. When they closed the door to her room I knew it
was a good time for me to get out of there with no questions
asked. I changed into a T-shirt and shorts and the cowboy boots
that made me look like Debra Winger. Then I took five dollars
from Mom's purse and headed toward Washington Boulevard
looking for Frank. But I never found him.

Jack had been sending Mom tons of presents and she would
make me answer the phone and tell him she was out all the time.
"I thought you wanted someone rich," I'd tell her. "Love is
more important," she'd say and wait for Alex to call.

Jack used to question me about my mom's social life. She'd
told me not to tell him about Alex so I'd just say I didn't know.
I knew he was used to getting what he wanted and he was
getting pissed. Finally he stopped sending her presents and
started calling her a bitch. "How's that bitch you live with?"
he'd ask. "She's fine," I'd tell him.

One day, after all the other salesgirls had gone home, he called me up to his office. I didn't know if he was going to fire me or give me a raise or what. "Your hair is so pretty," he said and moved it behind my shoulders. "But you shouldn't let it cover those." He touched my nipple and then cupped his hand around my breast. "Don't pull away, I'm just admiring you." It didn't hurt, I mean, I couldn't think of any excuse not to let him.

He took the shoulders of the uniform tank top he insisted we all wear and pulled them down. "So pretty," he said and then he licked my nipple with his tongue.

"Look, I gotta go to my dad's." I was lying.

"Just let me for a minute. Just one minute. Please."

I didn't want to lose my job and he did keep it under a minute.

The next day in school I went to the bathroom about fifty times, hoping to run into Frank in the hall. When that didn't work, I started hanging out at my locker, pretending to put things in it. I figured if I just stayed in one place long enough, he was bound to pass. So I'd stand there for an hour, putting books in and taking them out again so I'd look busy when he finally did walk by. Every time I'd hear big-sounding footsteps, I'd get all nervous. I'd try to be cool and not look at the face right off, knowing I'd recognize him from the waist down. Probably even recognize one finger. But I never saw him that whole week. Once I even stayed out of class until right at the break. Hundreds of faces passed, but none of them was Frank.

I stayed home every night that week, thinking maybe Frank would call. I sprayed my cowboy boots with water every day. They were starting to feel better. Frank knew so much.

Finally two weeks had passed since I'd seen him and I couldn't stand it any more. I didn't know what had happened. I called his house a couple of times and Mindy answered but I couldn't really find out anything and didn't dare ask for him. If she ever knew she'd ruin it. So I made a plan and asked her if she wanted to come over.

When she got there Mom was packing to go to San Diego and Alex was waiting in the living room. I'd told Mom I was going to stay at Mindy's that weekend. I had to keep Mindy in my room so neither would know I'd lied.

"How's your brother?" I asked after we'd talked a reasonable amount of time.

"He's fine," she said and then she changed the subject. "He gave your Mom a ring?" she asked.

"Yep. They're getting married."

"What about his wife?"

"He's going to leave her. That's why they're going away. They're celebrating."

"Are you going to your dad's?" Mindy was so nosey.

"No. I'm staying here," I told her.

"Alone?" Mindy looked jealous. "God. Your mom's nuts."

"She is not. She just trusts me."

After Mom left and while Mindy was on her way home, I called Frank. I'd practiced talking slow and sexy but when he answered I just sort of spit it out. "Mom's out of town so you can come over tonight if you want." There was a strange pause and then he said, "Who is this?" But when he heard it was me, he said maybe he'd come.

Blood shot through me like liquid lightning. I cleaned the house and put flowers and candles everywhere. I made my bed for the first time in years and spent an hour trying to figure out what kind of music to play. And then I kept playing the same tape over and over so that the right music would be still playing when he got there.

I waited and waited. After a while I tried to eat a frozen dinner that I'd cooked and thought I wanted. I couldn't really sit still long enough to eat. I walked around in circles and as the minutes passed and he didn't show, the middle of me just got to feeling sicker and sicker. At midnight I was still alone.

I guess Mom and Alex never made it to San Diego. It was just getting light when Mom came into my room. "Did Jack call today?" She acted like it was the middle of the afternoon. It didn't even dawn on her that I was supposed to be at Mindy's.

"What's wrong?" I asked her.

"Nothing," she said. She was on the other side of tears. "Nothing for you to worry about."

"Didn't he tell her?" I asked.

"He's just an asshole. That's all. A complete ass. C'mon.
Come climb in my bed. We'll watch TV together."

I thought for a minute that we were going to get off easy on
this Alex thing, but as soon as I turned on the TV, she started
to flip out. It was one long night.

Mom pulled herself together real quick after the Alex disaster. She called Jack right away and he sent her two dozen roses
and then a crystal perfume sprayer. She bought a bunch of new
make-up and they made a date.

When Jack came to our door for the very first time, Mom was
mad that I wouldn't answer it. I never told her why I hated him.
I just wouldn't answer the door or say hello. "You little bitch,"
she said with her new orange lipstick on. When they left that day
I poured the perfume out of the bottle Jack had bought her and
replaced it with bug spray.

I finally saw Frank, on the last day of school. He was just
starting his bike and I ran up to catch him before he could pull
away. When I got there I couldn't think of what to say. I just
stood there in the bike noise.

"Want a piece of gum?" Frank yelled.

"No, thank you," I answered, although I did. I stared at the
ground for a while with my mouth closed tight. He turned off
the bike.

"You mad at me or something?" Frank asked.

"I don't know."

"I fell asleep that night," Frank said. "The night you called."

"Yeah, well, I thought maybe you were coming over."

"I never said for sure," Frank answered, cocky, like he was
talking to a grown-up. But it was true. He had said maybe.

Frank started up his bike again. I had to say something quick.
"Your tattoo looks great," I shouted. He was wearing a tank
top and his muscles glowed.

Frank turned to me and smiled. "Yeah, turned out all right,"
he said and then he stared at me a moment. "So you're fifteen.
Right? This week?" I couldn't believe he thought of it. "So
happy birthday, then."

"How'd you know?" I said, figuring Mindy must have told

him.

"How do you think?" Frank started to pull away. "You coming? Hop on."

We pulled into a shopping center and Frank made me wait with the bike. When he came out he was carrying a birthday cake. We drove up to Mulholland and ate it with our hands. "Check this out," he said, getting chocolate on his passport. "You should get one of these things. Never know when you might wanna go somewhere," he said and then he told me about all the places he was going to. Places with coral reefs and islands where people played music in the streets day and night. "Where I'm going there are stars in the sky and the water is as warm as the air." Listening to him took me away. "All I'm taking is my guitar, my scuba gear and two bathing suits. I'm not comin' back here for a long time."

"Why not?"

"Don't feel like it," Frank said and put his passport in his hip pocket.

"Too many other places to be. Lots more oceans to swim in."

"God," I said, dreaming. "Sure wish I could go with you."

"You'll get out of here, soon enough. The whole world's waiting." Frank threw his hair back over his shoulders and his face lifted up to the light and he laughed gently like the sky was all ours. I couldn't believe how beautiful life was.

"Thank you for the cake," I said as we pulled up to my corner. My hair was all blown free and my smile was close to bursting. "See you tomorrow?"

"I'm history," he said and my insides almost fell out.

"You're really leaving?" Frank nodded and grinned from ear to ear. "You mean, soon?"

"Late. Midnight flight."

"What about school?"

"Wish me luck," he said and kissed me on the forehead.

"Can I see you?"

"You're seeing me now. I'm here."

"But . . . "

Frank laughed. "Leaving for the airport at ten. You coming?"

The house was ridiculously clean when I got home. "Your father's coming over for birthday dinner," Mom informed me. I must have given her some kind of look, but I didn't say a word. "What's wrong with that? Your father and I happen to be old friends. I've known him longer than I've known anybody."

"Fine," was all I could think of to say.

Dad came and knocked on the door, which felt really weird. He'd lived there for six years and now he was knocking on the door like a stranger. "What's the matter with you, aren't you going to answer it?" Mom yelled. She was in the bathroom primping just like she did when Jack was expected. Putting bug spray behind her ears no doubt.

After I opened the door, Dad just stood there, awkward. He had flowers in one hand and a brown paper bag in the other. "Happy birthday." He handed me two jars of gooseberry jam that Grandma had sent back with him and a birthday present. I put the jam in the kitchen while Dad came in and stood around kind of out of place in the living room.

After a short time Mom breezed out of the bathroom like she was joining a mid-summer dance. She seemed a bit knocked off balance the second she saw him, though, and they both sort of stood there in shock for a moment. And then Dad handed her the flowers. "The place looks neater than it ever did," he said, meaning, I leave and you start cleaning house.

Mom got it. "Flowers for me?" she said. "That's a first." Dad cracked his knuckles.

"I'm going to Mindy's." I started toward the door.

"You're not going anywhere," Mom said.

"What's the matter with you?" Dad asked. Just like when we all lived together.

I tried to sit still for dinner. Dad talked about his work and how it was coming upon the busy season at the store and Mom talked about her new rich boyfriend and how we should all have Thanksgiving together. I didn't say a word until nine forty-five when I excused myself to go to the bathroom. I grabbed my hat, climbed out my bedroom window and ran all the way to Mindy's.

I got there just in time. Frank had already put his guitar in

Blackie's car. I rode in back and they joked around. There wasn't much to say on the way to the airport.

Frank checked his gear at the curb. "Bye kid," he said. "I'll send you a card."

I tried to hide so he wouldn't see but he put his hand on my head and turned my face toward his. "Cool hat," he said. "But you gotta rough it up a little."

"How?" I asked, though I could barely talk.

"I dunno. Run over it with a truck."

"I don't have a truck, Frank."

"Here. Let me have it." Frank grabbed my hat and threw it on the ground and stepped on it with his boot a few times. Then he brushed it off and put it back on my head. "There you go." I had to laugh. "See, isn't that better?" he said. Then he grabbed my face and kissed me deep, like I had always wanted. And then he was gone.

Jack sent Mom so many presents that she finally fell in love with him. They got married at the spur of the moment one afternoon on a boat he'd bought and named *Sara* but was in the process of changing to *Carol Ann*.

Of course I had to go to Carol Ann's wedding. Even though she knew I hated Jack. They pulled me out of school and drank champagne in the car all the way to the marina. Their friend with the mail order preacher's license drove and drank with them.

They said their *I do's* on the boat and then the preacher fell asleep and Mom and Jack made out while I watched the pelicans dive for fish. It was incredible how those ugly creatures became beautiful missiles and then dove into the water.

"What's with you today, Miss Sourface?" Mom asked after she was sick of necking. "When are you going to get rid of that stupid hat?"

"She's a case all right," Jack answered as he opened another bottle of champagne.

"Let's drink to our little family. C'mon, Shawn!" Mom giggled as champagne sprayed all over them and Jack licked it off her chest. They toasted each other and then Jack grabbed her ass and they collapsed onto the deck laughing and licking and I looked beyond the boat where the ocean went on and on and somewhere got warm.

For months I looked for Frank. Even though I knew he was a million miles away. I went places he might be and I watched faces everywhere. There are so many motorcycles in this world and every time I'd pass one my heart would race and I'd look to see if it was Frank.

I did get a postcard. Just like he'd promised. It said: "Dear Shawn, You won't believe all the colors of the fish here. Stay cool and you can look for me when you get out of there. I'll be somewhere near the ocean." He signed it "Love, Frank."

I wrote him, too. Dozen of letters. I didn't know where to send them. But I wrote him anyway. And I got passport photos taken. You never know when you might want to go somewhere.

Contributors

ANNE CALCAGNO, who was raised in Rome, has worked as a copy writer, editor, journalist and translator. Her stories have appeared in *The North American Review*, *Denver Quarterly*, *Epoch*, and other magazines. A finalist for both the Drue Heinz competition and the PEN/Nelson Algren Award, she has also been nominated for a Pushcart.

BARBARA ASCH CAMILLO is a painter and has traveled with the Carson and Barnes Circus. She received an MFA from Iowa, and currently lives in Iowa City with her husband, Victor Camillo, and their son, Seth. Her story "Weigh Station" is from a novel in progress.

DIANE SHERRY CASE was trained as an actress and has appeared in a number of films. She says that both writing and acting are ways of "getting to know imaginary strangers better than we know ourselves." Her story is part of a collection entitled *Things That Felt Like Love*. She lives in California with her husband, Peter. They are expecting their first child.

DAVID COLE grew up in New England and now lives in Seattle. This is his first published story.

MARVIN DIOGENES is an Assistant Director of Composition at the University of Arizona. His fiction has appeared in *Other Voices*, *Cimarron Review*, *Beloit Fiction Journal*, and *Oxford Magazine*, as well as two editions of *O Henry Festival Stories*.

HEATHER BAIRD DONOVAN is a current Stegner Fellow at Stanford, and is completing her Master's Degree at San Francisco State University. She lives in San Francisco with her husband, Dwight Donovan, and their daughter, Haley Fiorenza.

PERRY GLASSER is the author of two short fiction collections, *Suspicious Origins* (New Rivers Press) and *Singing on the Titanic* (University of Illinois Press). In addition to being a recipient of two PEN Fiction Awards, he has published reviews, articles, and stories in *The New York Times Book Review, The North American Review, Confrontation,* and *TriQuarterly.* He teaches at Bradford College in Haverhill, Massachusetts, where he lives with his wife, Debi, and their daughter, Jessica.

JOANN KOBIN makes her second appearance in *AF.* She has also had stories in *The Virginia Quarterly Review, Massachusetts Review, Ploughshares, The Boston Globe Magazine,* and many other magazines. She lives in Northampton, Massachusetts.

MARILYN K. KREUGER lives with her husband, five dogs and a cat on a cattle ranch in the Wallowa Mountains of Oregon. She has had fiction published in *Trout Creek Press* and *Northwest Publishers.*

JONATHAN MANEY graduated from the Iowa Writers' Workshop and holds a Ph.D. in English. His stories have appeared in *Neo* and other magazines, and he has worked as associate editor on two fiction anthologies, *The Best of the West* and *Sudden Fiction International.*

CLINT MCCOWN, this year's winner of *AF's* $1000 First Prize, teaches creative writing at Beloit College, where he also edits the *Beloit Fiction Journal.* His books of poems include *Sidetracks* and *Wind Over Water.* His stories and poems have appeared in *Gettysbury Review, Northwest Review, Kansas Quarterly,* and the *Southern Poetry Review.* He is married and the father of two daughters.

EMILY MEIER'S short fiction has appeared in numerous journals, including *The Threepenny Review* and *Passages North.* She has also had a novella published in *Sands,* and work forthcoming in *The House on Via Gombito,* a New Rivers Press anthology. She lives in Menomonie, Wisconsin.

DIANE STELZER MORROW makes her second appearance in *AF* in as many years. She worked as a family practice physician until 1988 when she left her position to pursue her MFA in creative writing at George Mason University. She lives in Gaithersburg, Maryland, with her husband, Charlie, and new daughter, Rebecca.

EDWIN MOSES received a Ph.D. from SUNY/Binghamton. The author of two novels, as well as numerous stories, essays, and reviews, he teaches at Bloomburg University and lives with his wife and two sons in Williamsport, Pennsylvania.

KAREN PETERSON has published fiction and poetry in *Other Voices, West Branch, Spoon River Quarterly* and other magazines. She was a winner of the 1989 *Quarterly West* novella competition and a past fellow of both Yaddo and Ragdale. She lives in Chicago.

ANNE WHITNEY PIERCE is a native of Cambridge, Massachusetts, where she lives with her three daughters, Natasha, Anna, and Sofia. Her short stories have appeared in *The Southern Review, The North American Review, Kansas Quarterly*, and many others. She has work forthcoming in *The Massachusetts Review*, and was a past Nelson Algren award winner in fiction.

ROGER SHEFFER teaches at Mankato State in Minnesota. He has published two collections of short fiction: *Lost River* (Night Tree Press, 1988), and *Borrowed Voices* (New Rivers, 1990).

JOY TREMEWAN lives in Memphis and has hosted a radio book review program called *Reading Aloud Here*. Her story "Games of Chance" won the $1000 *Memphis Magazine* Fiction Award in 1989. She is also working on a novel called *Where Energy Comes From*.

MARY TROY worked as a technical writer at the University of Hawaii and later received an MFA from Arkansas. She teaches creative writing at Webster University and has published stories in several literary journals. She is married to Pierre Davis and lives in St. Louis.

LEWIS TURCO was founding director of both the Cleveland State University Poetry Center and the Program in Writing Arts at SUNY/Oswego. He is the author of several books, including *The Book of Forms: A Handbook of Poetics* (Dutton, 1968); *Visions and Revisions of American Poetry* (Arkansas, 1986); and *Dialogue: A Socratic Dialogue on the Art of Writing Dialogue in Fiction* (Writer's Digest Books, 1989). His stories have appeared in *Ploughshares*, *The North American Review*, and the PEN/NEA Syndicated Fiction Project.

The Editors

LOUISE ERDRICH, this year's Guest Judge, has published three novels (*Love Medicine, The Beet Queen,* and *Tracks*) and two books of poetry (*Jacklight* and *Baptism of Desire*). Along with her husband, Michael Dorris, she is the author of the forthcoming *Crown of Columbus.*

MICHAEL C. WHITE, Editor, has had stories in *Redbook, Green Mountain Review, Folio, Permafrost,* and *Oxford Magazine,* and has work forthcoming in *New Letters, Mid-American Review, Four Quarters,* and *Redbook.* He teaches at Springfield College in Massachusetts.

ALAN R. DAVIS, Associate Editor, has had work in many magazines, including *The Quarterly, Kansas Quarterly, Denver Quarterly,* and *Greensboro Review.* In addition to being a finalist in both the Iowa Short Fiction and Drue Heinz contests, he is a recent recipient of a Minnesota Arts Grant and teaches creative writing at Moorhead State University.